THE INTR

Charles Beaumont was born Charles L·
dropped out of high school in the tent¹
of jobs before selling his first story to ⸻
his "Black Country" became the first work of short fiction to appear in
Playboy, and his classic tale "The Crooked Man" was featured in the
same magazine the following year. Beaumont published numerous other
short stories in the 1950s, both in mainstream periodicals like *Playboy*
and *Esquire* and in science fiction and fantasy magazines.

His first story collection, *The Hunger and Other Stories*, was published in 1957 to immediate acclaim and was followed by two further
collections, *Yonder* (1958) and *Night Ride and Other Journeys* (1960). He
also published two novels, *Run from the Hunter* (1957, pseudonymously,
with John E. Tomerlin), and *The Intruder* (1959).

Beaumont is perhaps best remembered for his work in television,
particularly his screenplays for *The Twilight Zone*, for which he wrote
several of the most famous episodes. His other screenwriting credits include the scripts for films such as *The Premature Burial* (1962), *Burn,
Witch, Burn* (1962), *The Haunted Palace* (1963), and *The Masque of the
Red Death* (1964).

When Beaumont was 34, he began to suffer from ill health and developed a baffling and still-unexplained condition that caused him to
age at a greatly increased rate, such that at the time of his death at age
38 in 1967, he had the physical appearance of a 95-year-old man. Beaumont was survived by his wife Helen, two daughters, and two sons, one
of whom, Christopher, is also a writer.

Beaumont's work was much respected by his colleagues, and he
counted Ray Bradbury, Harlan Ellison, Richard Matheson, Robert Bloch,
and Roger Corman among his friends and admirers. His work is in the
process of being rediscovered with collector's editions of several of his
works from Centipede Press, three reissues from Valancourt Books, and
a new collection from Penguin Classics.

Cover: The cover of this edition reproduces the original jacket art by
Ronald Clyne from the 1959 first edition. Clyne (1925-2006) was well
known for designing over 500 covers for Folkways Records and also
designed many book jackets, including those for Beaumont's *The Hunger
and Other Stories* (1957) and many books published by Arkham House.
The Publisher is grateful to Mrs. Hortense Clyne for permission to
reproduce his design.

THE INTRUDER

A NOVEL BY
CHARLES BEAUMONT

with a new introduction by
ROGER CORMAN

VALANCOURT BOOKS

First published by G. P. Putnam's Sons in 1959
First Valancourt Books edition 2015

Published by Valancourt Books, Richmond, Virginia
http://www.valancourtbooks.com

ISBN 978-1-941147-85-6
Also available as an electronic book.

All Valancourt Books publications are printed on acid free paper
that meets all ANSI standards for archival quality paper.

Set in Minion Pro 10/12.4

INTRODUCTION

Long before *The Intruder* I was aware of Charles Beaumont as
a unique writing talent. I had read with interest and delight his
short stories and profiles in *Playboy* magazine, and, soon after,
hired him to write several screenplays for me. The films were
based on classic works by Edgar Allan Poe and Chuck captured
the tone of each story beautifully. We developed an excellent
working relationship and I was pleased when he gave me a
copy of what he considered to be his first serious novel. I knew
that Chuck's interests covered a wide and varied spectrum; he
knew about art and music, he read voraciously, he raced cars
in his spare time. He always seemed to pack twice the amount
of living into his days as anyone I knew. And then he would sit
down and put it all into his stories, and especially into his characters.

When I read *The Intruder*, I saw that Chuck had done something remarkable. He had written a socially conscious, "political" story, but he had managed to write it in such a way that it
avoided the usual pitfalls that accompany these types of stories.
Many socially oriented novels slip easily out of "story" and into
"lecture;" that's usually when most readers surrender to a yawn
and close the cover, never to return. But Chuck had created
characters that pulled you in and compelled you to live the story
through them.

The integration of schools in the South was a new and very
dangerous idea back in the 1950s. There were so many tendrils of
hatred and prejudice that it was extremely difficult to find a way
into the subject that didn't put up a wall of controversy between
the reader and the story. But just as Harper Lee seduced an audi-
ence into a "political" story by creating Atticus Finch and letting
him lead the way, Chuck created Adam Cramer; bright, charming, deeply caring and dangerously seductive. Cramer was a pied
piper with a dark agenda hidden from view. He was a character

so complex, so rich, so interesting that I couldn't help but follow him wherever he went.

I was impressed enough that I told Chuck I wanted to purchase the rights and turn the novel into a film. The subject matter was such a "hot button" that I couldn't get financing from any of my usual sources, despite the success of my other films. So my brother and I mortgaged our houses and put up the money ourselves. I decided to shoot the film in Missouri, thinking it was far enough north to keep us safe. I was wrong. I learned that one didn't have to go all the way to Alabama or Mississippi to feel the simmering racism that existed in the country at that time. We had to "shoot and run"—filming our scenes quickly and then moving to a new location before the locals learned the subject matter of our story. The danger was real and I remember telling the cast (which included Chuck as the High School Principal) and the crew to pack up early on the last day of shooting. I wanted to be ready to go as soon as we got the last shot. The scene was of a Ku Klux Klan rally through the streets of a small town and the residents were asking some very uncomfortable questions. The moment I yelled "cut!" "print!!" on that last shot, everyone raced to their car and drove, nonstop, all the way back to St. Louis!

The movie turned out to be ahead of its time. It was a critical success—earning great reviews across the country—but not a commercial hit. We all learned how perilous it can be to hold a mirror up to the darker angels of our national character.

But, financial success or not, I remain extremely proud of the film. We stayed very close to the structure and the characters of the novel, and the film worked just as well as I thought it would.

It's sad that, in many ways, the "political" subject matter of *The Intruder* still has resonance today, more than fifty years later. While some progress has indeed been made, racism and prejudice are with us still. But it is this reality that makes it all the more important that *The Intruder* is now being reissued, giving a new generation of readers a chance to experience Adam Cramer and the complex motives he so charmingly presents.

I invite those readers to experience what I experienced all

those years ago: the thrill of discovering a novel well written, and a cast of characters that illuminate the hidden corners of the human spirit.

ROGER CORMAN
April 2015

ROGER CORMAN is one of the most influential filmmakers in cinematic history. Almost singlehandedly creating the low-budget and genre film, he has produced more than 400 films, the most famous of which are his Edgar Allan Poe cycle starring Vincent Price. In 2010 he received an Academy Award in honor of his filmmaking career.

This book is gratefully dedicated to
JOHN TOMERLIN

What is it that makes a man reject reason and turn his face against the tide of history, enslave himself to a lost and discredited cause, rationalize his way into a course that can only shame his nation and leave for his progeny a legacy of ridicule? . . . How do you talk men into challenging the courts, the federal government and all the power that lies behind them, when these men know that they cannot win, because they tried it almost a century ago, when the battle was at closer odds, and they could not win?

—Carl T. Rowan,
Go South to Sorrow

The Intruder

Adam Cramer, Adam Cramer,
A strong young man were he,
He come from California
To fight for Liberty!

FRAGMENT OF A FOLK BALLAD

1

He couldn't sleep on buses—he'd made up his mind about that long ago—but he was sleeping now and this annoyed him. There was something shameful in it (did Hannibal doze on the way to Saguntum?), something frightening, too. The movement of the bus, he told himself, was responsible. All this plunging and dipping, and the fact that he'd been awake for thirty hours or more. Still, it wasn't right.

The lids of his eyes came apart, snapped shut against the hot and burning light. He fought, sluggishly, but the heat pressed in and the giant black wheels kept turning beneath him and the seat kept rocking . . .

"Caxton next!"

He sat up, stiffly, in the seat and looked about. There were four other people with him. An old man in a stained gray suit, a woman of indeterminate age, a young boy, and the driver. The woman was smiling. She had been watching him. He returned the smile.

Outside, the rolling blue-green mountains swept by, and soon restaurants and gas stations began to dot the road. A sign loomed up and disappeared:

WELCOME TO CAXTON
A GREAT PLACE TO LIVE!

And then the bus crossed a small bridge, turned right off the highway, and slowed. At a restaurant, the big orange-and-white machine groaned wearily to a stop. Dust swirled around its wheels.

"Caxton."

He lifted his suitcase off the rack, said "Thank you" to the driver and stepped out into the blazing afternoon. The bus groaned again, pulled back to the street. Soon it was out of sight.

He stood in front of the restaurant for a moment, his eyes roving across the drab, unlovely town, across the gray rows of grocery stores and cafés and cleaning establishments and offices and churches, all so quiet now; across the slowly moving people, also gray, also quiet.

Then he transferred the cardboard suitcase to his other hand and began to walk.

He asked a large man in overalls where a good hotel was. The man told him, "Up George to the tracks. The Union. It's a nice place."

He thanked the man and walked to the rotting railroad-tan depot and paused. He brushed the lank strands of hair from his eyes and opened the glass door of the Union Hotel.

Three women sat on a red leather couch. They glanced up without interest and returned to the television program they'd been watching. The sound was turned high, but the loudspeaker was bad and it was difficult to understand what was being said. In a chair by the wall sat a middle-aged man in a blue sports shirt, dozing.

There was no one behind the desk. He set down his suitcase and peered into the long hall. It was empty.

A big clock hung silent on the wall, its hands lodged at ten-fifteen.

He cleared his throat loudly, but nothing happened, so he went to the couch. "Excuse me, ma'am," he said softly to one of the women, "I hate to interrupt you, but there doesn't seem to be a desk clerk around."

The woman looked up. "You want a room?" she asked.

"Yes, I do."

"Well," she said, nodding her head toward the sleeping man, "that's Billy there. Give him a push."

He hesitated.

"Never mind," the woman said, "it's the commercial, anyway." She strained to her feet, walked over to the desk and brought the flat of her hand down on a rusted call-bell. "Billy!" The man mumbled something. "Billy, now. Well, that's the way it is. You just hold on and I'll get Mrs. Pearl Lambert."

The woman went into the hall and knocked on one of the doors. It opened, and there was a muffled conversation; presently another woman came out.

She was extremely short, perhaps not quite five feet tall, and her face was parchmented and wrinkled, but there was a definite swing to her stride. She had on a thin kimono.

"I'm Mrs. Pearl Lambert," she said. "I was cooling off in my room, looking at the TV." She smiled at the first woman, who had resumed her station on the couch. "Thank you, Luce. Billy I think would sleep through a three-alarm fire. But he's a good boy, he helps me around the place a lot."

"I'm sure he does."

"Well, now. I suppose you're after a room." The little woman stepped behind the desk and opened a drawer. "Our singles run three and a half dollars a night, depending how long you plan to stay with us."

"I think I'll be here quite a while, Mrs. Lambert."

"Over a week?"

"Oh, I think longer than that. Probably several months."

The woman's eyes gleamed. "Then the charge is two-fifty. We always reduce it for our temporary permanent guests."

"That's very nice of you."

"It's just fair, that's all. We like to be fair in this town. Why should a temporary permanent guest have to pay as much as the people that just flit in and out?" She found a dusty registration card, pushed it forward.

He wrote: *Adam Cramer*; paused; listed the Union Hotel, Caxton, as his address.

"I'll put you in number twenty-five. That's upstairs." The woman thumped her fist on the call-bell six times. "Billy!"

The middle-aged man awoke with a start, looked around, got up. "Yes, Mrs. Lambert? I was just resting."

"I thought you'd taken root. Billy, this is Mr. Cramer. He's going to be with us for a while."

The middle-aged man blushed. "I'm proud to know you, Mr. Cramer."

"Go on up to twenty-five," the woman said, "and get it aired out. And see if Mabel dusted, too."

"Yes'm."

"That boy," the woman chuckled. She plucked a key from the pigeonhole. "It'll only take a minute; I wouldn't want you to step into a dusty room. Mabel's a good little old worker, but sometimes she gets forgetful. I have to keep after her. But then, I ought to have something to do around here."

The ladies on the couch laughed, suddenly, in unison. Through the blizzard of white specks on the television screen, a cowboy with a guitar bowed.

"You're welcome to come down here and watch the TV any time," Mrs. Pearl Lambert said.

"That would be nice." The heat had soaked into his clothes now, and perspiration dripped into his collar.

"I suppose you're a salesman."

"No. Do I look like a salesman?"

"Not exactly. But that and railroad men are about all we ever get in Caxton. And I know you ain't a railroad man."

The little woman cocked her head to one side. "It's not a solitary bit of my business," she said, "but what line are you in, anyway?"

"You might call me a social worker, Mrs. Lambert," he said.

The three women on the couch laughed again.

"I'm here to do what I can for the town. I read about your difficulties."

"What difficulties is that?"

"The integration issue, Mrs. Lambert."

"Oh?" The woman stared. "But that's all over, I mean, they got twelve nigras enrolled at the school already, it says in the paper. Starting up Monday."

"Do you think it's right?"

"Right? You mean right? No, I sure don't, and neither does nobody. But it's the law."

"Whose law?"

The little woman thought a while and shrugged. "I'm not too good on politics, y'see, but Mr. McDaniel says there's nothing we can do about it and that's that."

"Who is Mr. McDaniel?"

"He's the editor over to the *Messenger*. A fine man, too; his wife's mother and I were best friends until she died. He thinks letting the nigras in is the worst thing that could happen, and it was him and Mr. Shipman and Mr. Satterly, who's the Mayor, that

got Mr. Paton and the other people on the school board to complain to the Governor. I mean, he's against the whole thing, just
like everybody, but the law is the law, he says, and so there ain't
no more to it."

The man called Billy appeared.

"It's as clean as a whistle, ma'am," he said. "She dusted everywhere except behind the bed, and I dusted there myself, so it's all
right, I guess. He can go on up."

Mrs. Pearl Lambert began to walk quickly toward the stair-
case. "Just follow me, mister. You want Billy to tote your suitcase?"

"No, it isn't heavy. That's all right."

"Yes, sir."

They marched up the creaking stairs, up into an utterly airless
landing. There was a table, buried under magazines, and a large
pot with a fern growing out of it. The wallpaper was stained and
faded to a neutral gray.

"It ain't too fancy, but we keep our rooms clean and you can
open a window, if you like."

"It looks fine to me," he said.

They stopped in a black alcove; the little woman kept nodding as she fumbled for the doorknob. The door opened and they
went into a large room.

It was surprisingly light, with cream-colored walls and ceil-
ing, a green rug, and two lamps with white cloth shades. The bed
was huge and old; a thick, lumpy mattress on a foundation of
iron, covered by a much-laundered bright yellow spread. There
was a dresser and a steel closet that looked, somehow, like a filing
cabinet.

"This is your bath here. The shower doesn't work, I don't
know why—I've had Crawford fix it a dozen times; but the tub is
new calked and we have plenty of good hot water."

He started to put his suitcase on the bed, set it down on the
floor instead. "It's just fine, Mrs. Lambert," he said. "Really."

"I'll have Mabel put you in a radio tomorrow when that couple
moves out of twenty-one."

"Thank you. I'll take care of the room myself, though, if you
don't mind."

"Well, I don't see anything wrong about that, I guess. But what about your towels and sheets?"

"When I need new ones, I'll come downstairs and let you know."

"Mr. Cramer—" The woman looked at him closely. "I hope there ain't going to be any trouble or anything like that."

"Trouble?" He smiled. "Absolutely not. I just want some privacy, that's all."

"Well, don't think Mabel's gonna cry about it. You'll be her favorite guest!"

He took the old woman's hand in his and smiled. "I really do appreciate it, Mrs. Lambert," he said. "And if you're up tonight, maybe we can watch the mystery together."

"I'll be up. It's too blame hot to sleep, anyway."

"Fine."

The woman nodded, checked the room with her eyes, and went out.

He waited for the sound of the footsteps to disappear, then he turned the key in the lock, went to the window and pulled down the shades.

The heat was stifling; not really moist, yet it permeated the room, drawing moisture from every pore of his body. He whipped his coat off, widened the loop of the military-stripe tie and lifted it over his head; tore loose his sodden blue shirt and hurled it onto the bed; scattered his clothes as if they were contaminated.

The water pipes bucked loudly when he turned on the cold faucet, and for a while an orange fluid seeped out of the crusted metal; then the water flowed in a limp stream. He opened the cardboard suitcase and got out an electric shaver. He looked in the bathroom for a socket, but there was none; so he unplugged one of the lamps and connected the razor there.

Bathing quickly, he returned to the bedroom and put on the one wrinkled but clean shirt that remained. He shook the charcoal flannel trousers and put them on, too.

He surveyed himself in the mirror. The image thrown back was that of a fairly handsome, masculine young man, the sort you would be likely to encounter in some minor New England college. The hair, dark brown, almost black, was straight. The nose was somewhat bent, though not noticeably, and the lips were rather thick.

He added a last touch to his hair, smiled at his reflection, and began to unpack his suitcase.

It contained two pairs of shorts, one undershirt, three extra pairs of socks, a faded brown sports shirt, a plain green cotton tie (rolled neatly) and some handkerchiefs. These he removed and threw into the middle drawer of the dresser. The bag also contained several large brown envelopes, which he treated with greater care. He opened the top envelope and took out some white typing paper and placed the paper neatly on the rickety folding table by the wall.

There was one other item in the suitcase. A worn 32.20 Police positive pistol. He picked it up and thumbed the cylinder release. The breech fell loose. He reached into the side pocket of the suitcase, removed five copper bullets, slipped them into the pistol and snapped it together.

He returned to the table and sat down. For several minutes he stared at the paper. Then he uncapped a long blue ballpoint pen and wrote: *Dear Professor Blake—*

"No," he said, beneath his breath, and crumpled the paper.

Dear Max—

He wrote until the page was covered. Then he folded the letter into a business-size white envelope carefully, and printed the name Max Blake, printing also the many degrees after the name and the involved address.

Then he went to the window and pulled up the shade.

Below, a woman was wheeling a baby buggy across the street, walking heavily and with great effort.

Men were lounging against cars, smoking and moving their lips in silent conversation. Slow as the blue haze that drifted over the distant mountains, slow as the clouds, they moved, as if they were all waiting. And the air was hot and hushed.

A little gray town, the color of gunpowder.

2

Ella McDaniel glanced at the clock and sighed. She'd felt sure that an hour had passed since the last look, but it was only 4:10, which meant that seventeen small minutes had crept painfully by and no more. She wished that she could turn the clock around to face the wall, but, of course, that wouldn't do. Mr. Higgins wouldn't understand.

She picked up a sponge and, for the fifth time since the last person had come in, proceeded to wipe the black marble counter. She then polished the nozzles of the water dispensers carefully, and wandered over to the magazine rack. There wasn't anything new, and wouldn't be until Tuesday, and she'd read everything except the hot-rod journals and *Harper's*. She straightened the magazines, lined them all up in their proper places, switched them.

4:19 P.M.

She yawned. This was the hardest time of all. From one to three there were customers, and she was kept busy making malted milks and sodas and cokes; and around six-thirty the kids started dropping by and she had someone to talk to. But in between, it was bad. It made her realize just how dull her life really was.

She wished now that it was Sunday and that she and Hank had made up (somehow) and were down by the river, Hank barechested, in his faded blues, and she in the outfit that Daddy didn't like her to wear in public.

The wish became real and she stood there quietly, following it as if it were a film.

Ella was small and compact. Her flesh was firm. Its pigmentation was such that she seemed always to have a slight tan. Whereas the legs of the other schoolgirls were white, straight, with little bruise marks showing at the ankles, hers were almost golden, and the calves tapered downward to squared-off tendons. For this reason, she disliked wearing the regulation white socks;

but she had to, anyway. Even with grown women, it was considered brazen in Caxton to go about with naked ankles.

She hid her breasts, usually, in the loose-fitting white silk blouse that was part of the unofficial school uniform; and a plain dark skirt concealed, though with less success, the slender waist and sharp, curving hips. A sexy haircut was about the only allowable concession, and she worked on this continually.

Sixteen years exactly showed in her face; however, with some effort, and the application of make-up, she was occasionally able to look older.

She thought of herself as the Doris Day type, as opposed to the Marilyn Monroe type, and she guessed that it was this youthful quality that made Hank so shy around her. It was understandable, of course. Seventeen-year-old boys were almost always shy. Still, she was missing out on an awful lot; she knew that. Cora Dillaway, who wasn't nearly so pretty, had been practically raped by Jimmy Sorentino one night at the Star-Lite Drive-In, she knew, and Sally Monk was keeping very quiet about the date she had with Thad Denman.

A sudden anger filled her, as it had so often in the past week; and a certain small sadness. She could have put up with the whole thing, all right, because Hank was certainly the most popular boy at Caxton High. But when she learned that he'd taken Rhoda Simms to Rusty's and that they hadn't got back until one in the morning, that ruined everything. Rhoda was loud and the boys whistled at her, but her underwear wasn't always clean, and she had a habit of spitting pieces of cigarette tobacco out of her mouth. She had other habits, too.

Well, it only proved one thing. Hank might be big and handsome, but he was still a little boy. He was a little boy and Ella was a woman, and that was the trouble right there.

Vaguely she wondered if all women had to just stop and wait for boys to catch up with them.

She wiped the black marble and fell back into the wish. Hank had been talking to her, as he did whenever they were alone; then suddenly, he stopped. The rain had just turned everything silver, and a chill was in the air.

Hank looked over his shoulder. There was only the field,

the thick grasses, the softly singing river. And the two of them, together.

He moved toward her.

"Ella," he said, *"I want you to know something. I want you to know that you're a very beautiful and a very desirable girl."*

Then he gathered her in his arms and pulled her to him and pressed his lips, roughly, against hers . . .

She was lying next to him on the wet grass, telling him that she had never been kissed, *really* kissed, in a grown-up way, in her whole life, when the bell tinkled.

Ella blinked and looked up.

A young man in a dark suit stood in the doorway. He was tall, with straight black hair, and his eyes were on her.

He closed the door, and the bell tinkled again. "Hello," he said.

Ella smiled, tentatively. She said "Hi," but her accent turned the word into something that sounded like "Ha" and she felt embarrassed, because this was a stranger to town. Someone from the East, probably. You could see that.

He walked over to the counter, close to her, and returned the smile. "I wonder, miss," he said, "if you could give me some change. I need a whole lot of dimes."

"Just a second," Ella said, "and I'll see." She pressed the NO SALE button on the cash register. "All right," she said.

The stranger had climbed onto a stool. He gave her two one-dollar bills. "Can you spare twenty of them?"

"I guess so."

She dug out a handful of dimes, counted twenty, set them in a pile on the counter. She couldn't imagine what anyone would want with so many dimes, but she didn't feel it would be right to inquire. A long-distance call would require a lot of change, but you could use quarters in the coin box.

"Thanks."

It was suddenly very quiet: only the sound of the electric fan, turning lazily, and the tick of the clock, and her own breathing.

The stranger's eyes seemed to cover her, but they were warm and friendly. There was nothing to be afraid of, after all. Mr. Higgins would be back in a few minutes.

"Would you care for anything else?" she asked.

"Well," the young man said, "I think maybe I could use a cup of coffee." His voice was clear and solid, yet not in the least hard. It was a very nice voice.

Ella nodded and walked over to the glass coffeemaker. The white drugstore uniform was cinched tight around her waist, it clung to her hips and outlined her figure far better than street clothes ever did. She knew this and made a point of walking lightly, putting her weight on her toes.

She placed the coffee cup on the counter and asked if he wanted cream; almost no one ever used it in Caxton. He answered, "Please," and she returned with a small wax carton.

"I hope you're not going to ask me if I'm a salesman," the young man said, finally.

Ella said, "Huh?"

"I must look like one, because that's what everybody has asked since I got into town. 'You a salesman, fella?'"

"Well, we get quite a few of them in Caxton. They lay over here."

"How come?"

"I don't know. They just do."

The young man sipped his coffee. They were silent for another moment. Then he said, "You live here in town, don't you?"

"Uh-huh."

"Go to the high school?"

She hesitated a second, aware that she was doing exactly the thing her father had warned her about: talking to a strange man.

"Yes. I'm a junior. Or, I mean, I will be when school starts."

"Great," the young man said, and paused. "You know, I've heard a lot about Southern hospitality. I'm just wondering if it exists, actually. Does it?"

"I guess so; sure."

"No, I mean really. See, here's the way it is: I just moved here, I'm going to stay for quite a while, but I don't know a darn thing about the town—and I don't know a soul."

Ella's heart beat a little faster as the stranger continued. He was handsome, in a peculiar kind of way, she thought. And anyone could see that he was a gentleman.

"Look," he said, "let me ask you a few questions, would you?

You don't even have to answer them if you don't want to. Okay?"

She shrugged noncommittally.

"Now you're probably thinking that we ought to be introduced, though, aren't you? All right. My name is Adam Cramer. I'm twenty-six years old. I'm nice to dogs and cats and other animals and I help old people across streets. Who are you?"

Ella grinned, though she hadn't planned to. "I don't think I'd better—"

"Oh, come on, now. Southern hospitality. You don't want a Yankee to get a bad impression, do you? I might go home hating everybody in the South, just because of this. And I know you wouldn't want that to happen." His eyes, Ella thought, are certainly blue; and he has a wonderful smile.

"Well, no, I guess I wouldn't want that to happen."

"Fine!"

"But I don't see why you have to know my name."

"Because names are important. You've got one and I've got one, and that gives us something in common right off the bat."

"I'm—" She felt a delicious sense of danger. "I'm Ella McDaniel."

"Hi, Ella."

"Hello."

"See, we're getting along already!"

They both laughed, and Ella forgot about the clock, she forgot about the dullness and about Hank and about the wish.

"Next question," the young man said. "Do they ever let you out of this place? Or are you chained to the wall at night?"

"That's silly."

"It is not. Where I come from, they have little children working in coal mines. Some of them grow up without ever seeing the light of day."

"Where do you come from?" Ella heard herself asking.

"Northern Rhodesia," the stranger said, lowering his voice.

"Really?"

"Well—almost. Actually, it's Los Angeles."

Ella was rapidly becoming fascinated. At the mention of Los Angeles, a vision of motion picture stars and studios and mansions came into her head.

"Disappointed?"

"No. I mean, why should I be?"

"Then we're friends?"

"Well . . . what do you mean?"

"Friends—you know. Acquaintances. What I'm getting at is, I'd like a date with you. There we are, out in the open. I-would-like-a-date-with-you."

"I'm afraid—"

"Of course you are. Why shouldn't you be? After all, I'm a stranger. So look, let's do it this way. I'll let you say no, now. Absolutely not, you refuse to go out with me and that's all there is to it! Then I'll ask you again in three minutes. Having turned me down once already, you wouldn't have the heart to do it again."

Ella shook her head firmly. She said, "I don't know what you'd want a date with me for."

"For a lot of reasons," the young man said. "One, you're an attractive girl. Two, I'd like somebody to show me around the town. If I'm going to be living here, it'd be nice to get to see the place."

Ella was about to answer, but the bell sounded and a portly woman with a bandage over her eye came in.

The young stranger grinned. "See you later, Ella," he whispered. He turned and walked to the telephone booth and began to go through the directory. Ella watched and wondered, briefly, what he was doing. The excitement coursed through her.

"Is Mr. Higgins in?" the portly woman asked.

"No, Mrs. Dodge. But he ought to be back in a few minutes."

"Well, I don't see why he can't stay around more. It ain't right for you to be left alone in this place, now. I tell you that. It ain't right."

"Oh, I manage, Mrs. Dodge. There isn't ever much to do this time of day."

"That ain't what I'm talking about, Ella. Rolfe Higgins is making himself I don't know how much money, and the least it seems he could do is stay around and at least *count* it."

Ella said "Yes'm" and glanced in the direction of the phone booth.

"That stuff he give me made things worse. This old stuff." The woman took a bottle from her purse. "My eye is still hurting, and it's all pooched out, too, just like it was."

"I'm sorry."

"Well, I am too." She jerked her thumb. "Who's that in the booth?"

"I don't know," Ella said. "A customer."

"That's what I mean," the woman said. "He could rob the store and do the Lord can only say what else; a young girl like you all alone! I'll talk to Rolfe, now, I'll do that."

Her voice went on, droning, and Ella smiled and nodded courteously, but she heard very little.

Then a deeper voice said, "Mabel, are you here again?"

"You're doggone right I'm here again, Rolfe Higgins, and you can take this here ointment and throw it in the garbage. It don't do no good at all."

"Well," said Mr. Higgins, a surprisingly slight man to own so profound a bass, "I told you to have it lanced." He clicked his tongue. "Hello, Ella. Everything go all right?"

"Yes, sir."

"And a wonder, too," the woman said. "I think it's criminal for you to leave this little girl alone—"

The two began to argue, and Ella went back behind the counter and turned on the carbonated water dispenser so that she wouldn't have to listen. Mrs. Dodge was an old grouse, a nasty, crotchety old grouse.

"—what if one of them niggers off of Simon's Hill was to go by and see her, what would happen, do you suppose?"

"Not a thing, Mabel. We've got good nigras and you know it. Besides, they don't ever come into town, and you know that, too."

"Well, they'll be coming down soon enough. You just wait: the minute they let them into the school, they'll take over this place. You'll have them sitting right up at your counter, asking to be served!"

"I don't think so."

"You don't think so. I guess you never traveled much, then, that's all I can say."

"All right, Mabel. All right!"

They wrangled for almost ten minutes, then Mr. Higgins gave the woman a tube of zinc oxide and told her that it wouldn't make the swelling go down on her eye, but that it would at least keep the germs away.

Mrs. Dodge remarked that he was a poor excuse for a pharmacist, a poor excuse, and exited.

Mr. Higgins glared after her. "The weaker sex," he commented.

Ella nodded. "She certainly does get excited."

"Well, that's the way with ignorant people. She's got a sty on her eye. Doctor could have lanced it last week, and she'd be feeling fine now. Only she hasn't got the gumption to do what's right, because some time somebody told her never to let a doctor operate. So what happens? The sty gets bigger and hurts like the devil. She can't blame herself, of course. That wouldn't do. So she hates me because I can't cure her."

Mr. Higgins crushed his cigar in a tray.

"Well," he said, "I better get to work, I suppose. If you need anything, I'll be back in the back."

Ella felt sorry for her employer and wondered at the same time how he managed to retain his good humor. People were always complaining that his medicine didn't work. She watched him put on his white jacket, then she washed the coffee cup and saucer and dried them.

The stranger called Adam—she couldn't remember his last name—was still in the telephone booth, talking, hanging up, putting another dime in, talking. She thought of the way he'd gone about asking her for a date—a way that kept her from even realizing what was happening!—and she felt the quickening of her heart again.

She tried to forget about his presence in the store, but could not. Even as she fussed, aimlessly, joggling things out of order and setting them straight again, she knew that he was there.

He came out once and, after removing his jacket, asked for a Dr. Pepper. Perspiration had beaded his forehead. His shirt was stained dark below the armpits and around the waist, and for some reason this looked odd. It was odd to think that the stranger perspired the same way everybody else did ... But then he went back, closing the door after him. Nothing much had changed, except that his face bore a slightly different, slightly more cheerful expression.

Ella forced her thoughts to the coming first day of school; what she would wear and whether Daddy might be talked into giving her the money for a couple of new blouses. She had one in mind that was regulation white, but it had a tailored look to it that set it apart, and it cost $9.95. She considered the blouse in her mind, then went on to her new status as a junior and the possible hardships of the course. She wondered vaguely if one of the Negroes would be assigned to any of her classes. She hoped not, without hoping. Like almost everyone else in Caxton, she assumed that the proposed integration would not actually take place. Something would come up, some loophole or something. The subject dissolved and was replaced by further contemplation of the situation with Hank Kitchen. Perhaps when she became a junior, he'd stop treating her like such an awful child: perhaps he'd sort of suddenly discover she was a woman, the way it so often happened in the movies. He'd be helping her down from a wagon and have her in his arms and they'd be laughing; then, all at once, their eyes would meet and he'd stop laughing. And he'd pull her very close to him. It could happen while they were swimming, too, for that matter. Easily. Hank hadn't seen her in a bathing suit for quite a while . . .

But, of course, they weren't speaking now; and maybe they wouldn't ever, ever again. Certainly not until he apologized. And he was pretty strong-minded.

"Hi. How about another coffee?"

"Okay, but I don't know how you can drink hot coffee on a day like this."

"I don't, either. It's all in the way you were brought up, I guess."

Ella shook her head and served the young man. The peculiar thing about his eyes, she decided, was that they were old—much older than the rest of him. They didn't fit, exactly.

"You must have been brought up in a telephone booth," she said, laughing.

He laughed with her, but was obviously not inclined to explain the phone calls. He pulled his shirt away from his flesh. "Don't you get hot?" he asked.

"Sure."

"But I mean, how do you stay so fresh?"

Ella shrugged.

"No pores," the young man said. "That's it. Listen, you haven't answered my question—the one I asked an hour ago."

"I can't remember what it was," Ella said, glancing over to see if Mr. Higgins was watching. He wasn't.

"Now, now. I asked if you'd show me the town. How about tonight? When do you get off work?"

"At nine-thirty, but I'm afraid—well, see, my father, he always picks me up after work; and besides, you couldn't see very much of the town in the dark, could you?"

"You're right," the stranger said. "Absolutely and positively one-hundred-percent right. Leave it to a woman, I always say, to look after the practical side of things."

Gradually, throughout the conversation, a plan took form in Ella's mind. She didn't go out with boys very often, Hank knew that, and maybe that was why he acted the way he did. Maybe if he found out that she had a date with a perfect stranger—from Hollywood!—then he'd be a little nicer and not so big brother about things.

The young man said, "We could use a flashlight," and they both chuckled; then he said, "Seriously, are you doing anything tomorrow night?"

"Gee, I don't know. I've got—"

"Southern hospitality, remember."

"But I don't even know who you are or what you do or any-thing."

"I told you—I'm Adam Cramer, and I'm going to be working with an organization right here in town, here in Caxton. Why don't you give me your home address and I'll drop by and meet your folks. If they don't like me, I'll slink away, never to be seen. If they do, we'll go to a movie. Fair enough?"

Ella swallowed. Feeling quite sophisticated and adventurous, she said, "I live at 442 Lombard, up the hill on Bradley Street. You know where the post office is?"

"No, but I'll find it." The young man removed a small note-book from his pocket and wrote down the address. "Thanks, Ella," he said. "Now I don't feel so alone."

She found that she was unable to meet his eyes. "I didn't prom-ise anything," she said.

"Eight o'clock?"

She shrugged.

"Eight o'clock. See you then." He pulled his jacket on, smiled again, and walked out of the store.

3

As he pulled up in front of the drugstore, Tom McDaniel thought of the word he had been searching for and tried to find a pencil; but, of course, his pockets were empty.

"Schism," he said aloud, "schism," and walked to the glass door. "The organized Citizens' Councils are a dangerous schism—"

He knocked.

The door was opened by Rolfe Higgins, who wagged his finger. "Late again," he said.

"I know. I know." Tom smiled at Ella. "I got swamped. The second press is out again, and—"

"—you-just-let-the-time-slip-by." Higgins laughed and turned to Ella. "It's a wonder your father remembers to put his pants on in the morning!"

"Oh, come on," Tom said. "It isn't that bad."

"Pretty bad. You know, you haven't picked her up on time since she's been working here; and there was twice we waited forty minutes and I had to drive her home myself!"

"Well . . ." Tom grinned sheepishly, secretly wishing that Higgins would shut up. It was good-natured digging, but there was real accusation behind it, somewhere. "Ella understands," he said. "Don't you, kitten?"

Ella said, "Sure."

"Tom—" Higgins went behind the counter, poured a glassful of water, drank it. "Why don't you just forget about sending her to school this term? I'll raise her to a dollar and a half an hour, if you do."

"That's an idea," Tom said. The column was only half finished and there was page six to lay out and the letters had to be written, but he tried to keep his voice casual and amused. The truth was, he ought to be grateful for the break. He'd been working since morning and had taken off only for a sandwich at six. "How about it, kitten?"

Ella giggled.

"No fooling," Higgins said. "She's been a real little help to me. I hate like the very dickens to lose her."

"You cut that out. She's spoiled enough as it is!"

"You're wrong. She's a fine girl."

Higgins patted Ella on the back; then he wrote out a check and gave it to her.

"Next year?" he said.

Tom nodded. "Next year. If they haven't condemned the building."

He waited for Higgins to unlock the door, then he and Ella walked to the car and got in.

He asked his daughter if she'd had a hard day and she said that she hadn't, and he asked her if she was looking forward to school and she said that she was, and then he stopped talking and it was quiet in the car. He loved Ella, and knew that she loved him—at least in the sense that not to love him would entail effort; though he also knew, in an odd, vague, unstated way, that it wasn't (as he had heard her remark once to a friend) anything personal. Not that the two of them were uncomfortable together. It was just that Ella was a growing girl, with a thousand problems he could never hope to understand (perhaps because she did not bring them to him; or, it had occurred to him, perhaps because he'd never really tried to understand them), and he was, after all, quite busy these days. Of course, with a less demanding job, things would be different. He could then afford to take time off, talk to Ella, get to know her. He could find out what a fifteen-year-old *really* thought about. Be a friend.

I've got to do it, he told himself, as he had done a thousand times before. I've got to *make* the time. It isn't right, leaving everything for Ruth. A girl needs a father as well as a mother . . .

Hell!

He turned sharply into the driveway and inched into a narrow doorless garage.

"Sorry I was late," he said, again.

Ella shrugged and they got out of the car and walked toward the small red brick house. It was newly built, and looked it. The lawn was just beginning to form a green crust over the earth, and there was the inescapable (though not, to Tom, unpleasant) odor of manure in the air. Across the road stretched a forest of slender, white-gray trees, and sparse foliage. Someday it would be a neighborhood.

Inside the house there was still the after-smell of dinner pork chops, and the sound of percolating coffee. Tom threw his coat over the couch and walked through the living room. It was large and not yet "lived-in." There were a few pictures on the tan-painted walls, hundreds of books stacked about in cartons on the floor (Tom planned to build shelves, but he kept pushing the job out of his mind), a number of lamps and knickknacks. In a corner sat the television set, flickering as all television sets in the area did.

In front of it sat Gramp. He was watching a quiz program.

Tom went into the kitchen, where Ruth was doing the dishes. She looked young and fresh, much younger and fresher than Tom ever did.

"Hi."

She turned and flashed an automatic glance at the stove clock. "Honestly," she said, and unplugged the percolator. She poured a strong dark brew into three ready cups. "Why don't you just *live* at that office?"

"I do," he said, and kissed her. Then he noticed the expression on her face. It was a look of worry, the look he'd come to recognize.

"Oh-oh, what's wrong?"

Ruth smiled. "Well," she said, "nothing, actually."

"Come on, now."

"Well—" She turned to Ella. "Honey, why don't you look at TV with your coffee?"

"With Gramp?" Ella said. Her grandfather had a remarkable talent for selecting the worst programs on the air. And he always had his way—always.

"Then read a book or something, would you? I'd like to talk to your father."

Tom put up his hand. "You're forgetting something," he said, smiling. "Kitten's a junior now. She's grown up."

Ruth glanced at both of them. "All right. Not that it's anything, really. But—I got a funny kind of phone call today. Dad took it and he was talking a mile a minute, and I took over to see what was up, you know, and—well, it kind of made me upset."

"What was it? A salesman?"

"No. I don't know who it was. Sounded like a young fellow. But he's not the . . ."

Tom sighed and took a sip of his coffee. There was no way to hurry Ruth.

"Well," she went on, "I took the phone from Dad and asked who it was. 'Who are *you*?' they said. I told them. Then they, I mean, this fellow, whoever he was, said, 'I'm making sort of a survey,' and would I answer a few questions."

"Uh-huh."

"I told him I couldn't see anything wrong with that, even though I did get stuck with that vacuum cleaner that time. But he sounded like a nice fellow. So he asked me—Ella, now, I wish you'd go into the other room."

Ella said "Oh," pleadingly; she looked very interested.

"Go on," Tom said. "Ella's old enough to take part in what happens around here. What'd the guy ask you?"

"I'll—well, I'll give you his words, exactly. He said: 'Ma'am, I'd like to know if you have any children in high school.' I told him yes, I did. A girl. Then he said: 'I'd like to know what you think about your child going to the same school and maybe sitting in the same classroom with a bunch of niggers.' "

"I see," Tom said slowly. "Well, what'd you tell him?"

"I didn't exactly know what to say, but I told him the truth, that I didn't like the idea."

"Yes. And then what?"

"He asked me if I was willing to work to keep it from happening."

Tom set his coffee cup down on the saucer.

"I said of course, but what could a person do? He said, 'Plenty.' "

"Oh, he did?"

"Yes. He said he was the head of an organization that was perfectly legal and he knew he could get rid of this problem for us in a hurry . . . if we'd all pitch in and help. And he went on like that, and I told him he'd better talk to you, and he said of course and he'd phone you tomorrow or speak to you at the office. I told him who you were and where you worked."

Tom leaned back. "That's pretty interesting, all right," he said. "Did this fellow ask you for money?"

"No. At least we didn't discuss it."

"And he says he has a legal way to stop integration."

"That's what he said."

"Did he give his name?"

"He might have, but I forgot."

"Well, if he's on the level, I'll be glad to see him. It's probably some crackpot, you know, but I suppose it's possible that there's some loophole we didn't think of. I can't imagine what it would be." Tom poured some more coffee. "What's making you so nervous about it?"

"Dad," Ruth said, rubbing her hand on her apron nervously. "He got awful excited, you know, the way he gets sometimes."

"Oh."

"And you know what Doctor Meehan said about him staying absolutely quiet."

"*That's a lot of goddamn nonsense!*"

Tom winced. His father-in-law stood in the archway, skin dry and old, wrinkles deep. He'd had cancer of the throat some years back, which made it necessary for him to wear a silver tube in his thorax; a small gauze pad, on the outside, fluttered with his ragged breathing now. He made no attempt to disguise the affliction and was, indeed, quite proud of it, since it made him look grotesque and pitiable, yet did not disturb him in the least. Tom had long ago decided that the old man would never die. The Parkinsons were a hardy clan, with a record for extreme, almost absurd, longevity.

David Parkinson was exceptionally fit. Despite the warnings of various physicians, he made his regular weekly trip to town where he would catch a bus and go to Rusty's for however many beers he desired, usually five.

Tom would have to pick him up, of course, and the old man would invariably be drunk, but it never seemed to affect him. When reprimanded, he would begin to grumble or cry, claiming that it was his sole pleasure. Actually, he had many pleasures: life was full and rich for him. But he was spoiled. To Tom's mind he was nothing more than a stupid, willful child, insisting on his way no matter what the circumstances.

Gramp had come to live with Ruth and Tom in 1944, after they'd been married nine years. He had no particular reason for doing this, except that he was "lonely" and "terribly, terribly ill of cancer." Living alone in a room was all right enough for a well man, but when you can sink at any moment, sink so fast you can't even reach a telephone (if, Tom would think, he had ever learned how to use a telephone in the first place), then it was a goddamn sin. Then, too, his wife had passed on to her reward, and if his own daughter couldn't comfort him and take care of him, what in the name of hell kind of a world was it?

The truth was—or so Tom felt—that the old bastard simply wanted to cause trouble and have things done for him instead of doing them himself. He was, discounting the cancer, which had been halted, as healthy as a dray horse. And at eighty, if past experience meant anything, he had another ten solid years to go before weakening. Unlike his brother Llewellyn, who managed to get himself killed by an automobile at the age of seventy-four (*"Cut off in his prime!"*), Gramp would pass the ninety mark. There was no doubt of that.

He stood there, sternly. His fists were balled. "Nonsense," he repeated, and entered the kitchen.

"Program over, Gramp?" Tom asked, with some irritation.

"What? No. Them are all put-up deals anyway, them quiz shows. They think they're fooling everybody, but they ain't. Any fool son-of-a-bitch who'd get took in by that bullshit deserves it."

"Dad," Ruth said, although she knew, as they all did, that it would do no good. Her father's tongue would never be laundered.

"I guess you drunk the coffee up."

"No. I'll pour you—"

"Never mind. It's all right, I know I don't rate. Listen, Tom, now: I think maybe you're gonna have to get up off your dead ass and do something on that fool paper. We got a telephone call from—"

"I know all about it, Gramp," Tom said.

Gramp groaned slightly and sat down in one of the kitchen chairs. "I been wondering," he said, "how long you-all was gonna sit around and play with yourself in this here thing."

Tom's eyes flashed angrily. The old man was bearable most of the time because most of the time he sat in front of the television screen, mouth open, silent. Sometimes, though, Gramp got off on a talking spree—and this was clearly going to be one of them.

"Cut out that kind of language in front of Ella."

"You ain't gonna tell me how to talk, mister. Get that straight right here and now. I'll talk the way I damn please."

"Not in front of Ella."

"In front of anybody. Anybody!"

Tom slammed his hand down on the table. "That's enough," he said. "Either clean up your mouth or get out of the kitchen."

"Tom!" Ruth said.

Gramp trembled. Then his shoulders sagged. "All right," he said, "all right. It's your house, and I guess I ain't gonna forget that; no, I guess not."

Ruth McDaniel got up and began to wash the cups and saucers nervously.

There was a pause.

Then Gramp said, "Well, all this pussyfooting around you been doing is sure done a lot of good. I expect it don't matter none to you, though. I expect you don't care whether little Ella here marries a coon or not."

Ruth said, "Dad, for heaven's sake."

"You keep quiet! I seen the news tonight. Twelve black-ass niggers is going to the school. Young bucks, some of them. Big husky fellas."

"Gramp," Tom said, his voice on the edge of control, "I'm telling you to—"

"Go ahead!" cackled the old man gleefully. "Go ahead! Go

right on ahead and hit an eighty-year-old man—that's about all you're able to do, with your big college education! Huh! Listen, you just listen: We got us somebody in town with a little piss-and-vinegar now. We got somebody that knows it ain't right for black coons to mix with our white children, and that somebody's gonna stop it, you watch. He ain't gonna sit around, just sit around, writing little words on paper and all that bullshit."

"Be quiet, will you!"

Gramp stamped his foot. "You're for this thing, Tom McDaniel, that's what the hell what. Go on, why don't you admit it—ain't you?"

"No!" Tom said angrily. "You know as well as I do that I fought it right from the beginning. While you were boozing it up at Rusty's, I was in Farragut, talking—oh, what's the use?"

"Sure, that's right, what's the use? *Talking*. The fella on the phone, he said that the time for that was over and done. Words ain't gonna do no good now."

"Then what will?"

"Action!" the old man squawked.

His face took on an inner brightness.

"Action," he said again; and Tom knew that he was returning to other years. Whether they had existed, whether David Parkinson had ever been a young man with firm flesh, that was something else.

He was flickering over the past now, the mighty past, when he'd been a Dragon in the Klan, when he'd ridden black horses and set fires and issued orders in a loud voice.

The mighty past.

"Got to do something . . ."

Tom disliked being in the same room with Gramp—Gramp with his snuff, his chewing tobacco, his cheap cigars and vile language. Many times Tom wondered how Ruth had turned out to be so quiet, so ladylike, so *different*— But he supposed that the old man was not *all* bad. He would perform sudden acts of generosity, usually at the tag end of a tantrum, and these would always have a certain flair. Like the time he went out and spent his month's pension check on the coat at Bennett's that Ella had been admiring for such a long time. No—not all bad.

"All right," Tom said, after a full minute. "All right. Let's not argue."

"Who's arguing?"

"You are."

"Sure, always me, never you. Ruth, get my medicine—it's on the top shelf. Your goddamn husband is doing his best to give me a heart attact."

Ruth McDaniel sighed, hesitated, as if trying to find exactly the right set of words that would shut her father up; then she went out of the room and came back with a small bottle.

Gramp, disdaining a spoon, swigged directly from the bottle. He hawked loudly. "What about you, Ella? What do you think about having a bunch of niggers sitting in the same room with you?"

"Let me tell you something," Tom said sharply. "Let's see if you can get it straight for once. On January fourth, nineteen-fifty-six, Judge Silver ordered us to integrate the high school. He acted on orders from the Supreme Court of the United States. So now it's law; you understand? It's *law*. And whether you like it or not doesn't make a bit of difference."

"I ain't so sure of that," Gramp said, "and neither is that fella that called up. He talks sense."

Tom rose from the table. He sighed. "Well, if he's got any ideas, I'll be glad to listen to them."

"Will you?" Ruth asked.

"Of course!"

"I mean, Tom, actually—the idea of them going to school with Ella . . . well, it isn't a very nice thing to think about. If there's *anything* we can do, then I think we ought to try, don't you?"

"Certainly."

"Well, you don't need to sound like such a bear."

"I do not—oh, never mind."

Tom got up and walked into the living room. Viciously, he snapped off the TV set and found the novel he had been trying to read for months.

He made a great effort to concentrate, but could not avoid hearing Gramp's voice from the kitchen.

"What's he got his back up about?"

"Nothing," Ruth said. "Tom's just been working hard. He's tired."

"Is that what's the matter with him lately?"

"Yes, Dad. Yes. That's what's the matter with him lately. I'm sure of it."

4

It was exactly the same: No beginning, no explanation; just himself, materializing suddenly with the picture. He was in the lowest cabin of an ocean cruiser. The room was small and unfamiliar. Through the portholes, he could see the bright green water, rising in waves, thrashing endlessly beyond the horizon. He stood there, watching the water for several minutes; then he turned.

A girl lay on the bed, her body covered by a thin sheet. She was perhaps the most beautiful creature he had ever seen, but she was a stranger. He studied her rich black hair, which glistened against the spotless linen, and he studied her face, and he knew that he was in love with her. The moment he realized this, the girl's eyes opened and her arms lifted and she beckoned, calling his name silently.

He walked to the bed, sat on the soft edge, and carefully pulled down the sheet.

The girl began to tremble. He asked her not to do this, and he reached out his hand. His fingers touched her lips. She stopped trembling.

He gathered her into his arms and kissed her, gently, and stroked her hair. He held her close to him.

Then, someone laughed. He drew back, afraid, and forced himself to look at his hands. They clutched the lustrous hair. He touched the girl's shoulder: a ribbon of flesh stripped away.

He screamed; again the laugh came; and he watched, watched while the rich black tresses began to fall from the girl's head, while the soft white flesh melted and slid from the bones, until at last there was only a grotesque skeleton on the bed.

The laughter became hysterical now. He leaped up, walked

quickly over to the glass door and wrenched it open. It gave onto a closet. Within, men and women, hanging from hooks, were laughing at him.

He begged them to be quiet.

He struck them, again and again, and demanded that they be quiet.

But they would not be quiet . . .

When he awoke, his mouth was dry and his head ached: a steady, rhythmically throbbing ache, at the temples. The morning heat lay still as mold in the airless room, hot sunlight piercing through the shades and through the closed windows.

Adam Cramer shook the dream away, waited for the hysterical laughter to recede, and remained quiet, unmoving, for almost twenty minutes. Then he went into the bathroom and swallowed four Empirin tablets. Cold water revived him. The headache dulled away to the usual small, inner pain he'd managed to adjust to over the years.

It was eight-thirty.

Although he was hungry and in need of coffee, he sat down at the table and uncapped the ballpoint pen. In a way, he supposed, writing to Max would become a nervous reaction, like prayer, for these letters were taking the form of duty; still, it was certainly true that Max deserved to know what was happening.

The "Max" came, as usual, with effort. For uncounted months the two of them had been close, but "Professor Blake" had always seemed proper. It *was* proper, he thought, then. I was a student. I'm no longer a student.

Dear Max:

Probably I ought to number these notes because probably they'll arrive two or three at a time. Too much school has made me report conscious, or something. (Daddykins, rest his sweet moldering bones, always demanded reports. Never trusted me. Got so I couldn't take a trip to the crapper without listing the number of tissues used. Really!) Anyway, bear with me, Max, I know I'm making you my diary.

It's morning now. I am full of Empirin and confidence. Yesterday afternoon I overwhelmed a sample of the local fauna with my charm (!) Her name is Ella, she is around fifteen or sixteen, very pretty, very stacked in a way the girls never got back at the university (with their damn bony shoulders and long necks). Typical high school kid, you know, nothing in her head but movie magazines and brassieres. Doesn't even know what integration is, probably to do with sex. Anyway, she dug the handsome city slicker, and I do believe this is going to turn out to be the pipeline through to the high school set—very important.

The phone calls were enormously successful—to tell the truth, I didn't expect such a great general reaction. Everyone sounded alike— No, we sho don't like this yere sitchywashun; etc.—and there's no more doubt whatever in my mind. After breakfast I'll see the money boy I told you about (write you result tonight) and if he goes along with it, I think we'll be rolling.

More later—

ADAM

P.S.—You might start thinking about what you want to be in der new order. Minister? Director of Propaganda? Official Philosophizer? Don't laugh!

He folded the letter into an envelope and went downstairs. The television set was on, still flickering, and the three women were again seated on the red leather couch. Their heads swiveled, swiveled back.

"Good morning!" he said.

They mumbled a greeting.

He started outside but was halted by Mrs. Pearl Lambert, who had been sorting laundry behind the desk. "You right sure now you don't want Mabel to clean your room?" she said.

"It's all done," he said, smiling. "How are you this morning?"

"Can't complain too much, I guess," the little woman said. "I'm sorry if I spoiled the mystery last night for you. I mean, by telling you who did it."

"Not a bit. I enjoyed myself a lot."

"It was good to have company."

A man and a woman walked into the lobby. "'Morning, Mrs. Lambert!" The man was stocky, about fifteen pounds over-weight, and had a complacent, pleased expression. The woman was young, but not youthful. Her hair was black, and she wore it in a faintly old-fashioned style, heaped upon her head. Her dress was black, also, but it was stylish. With a set of caps over those teeth, Adam thought, she'd be all right. A pretty good body. Nice legs.

"'Morning," said Mrs. Lambert. "This here is our new perma-nent temporary guest that I was telling you about; he looked at the mystery with me last night. Mr. Cramer, I'd like you to meet Mr. and Mrs. Griffin."

The man stuck out his hand in a broad, unhesitating, sena-torial way. "How are things, Mr. Cramer?"

"I'm glad to meet you."

"The Griffins been staying here on-and-off for—how long is it, Sam?"

"Well," the man laughed, "I guess about four years."

"Four years," the little woman said.

Adam nodded. "That speaks well for your hotel, Mrs. Lam-bert," he said, "and for Mr. Griffin's taste."

"See?" Mrs. Lambert said, grinning mysteriously.

The Griffins grinned back. "Yeah," the man said. He turned to Adam. "Had chow yet?"

"No."

"Neither have we. We're just headed down to the Palace. If you care to join us, you're welcome. Isn't he, Vy?"

The woman in the black dress said yes without a great deal of enthusiasm.

Adam looked at her. There was a hardness of line about her eyes, a weariness, that contrasted sharply with her husband's open features. She was maybe thirty-three. But her eyes were older. "Well, I don't know, I hate to barge in—"

"Barge in? Listen!" Griffin gurgled with amusement. "Now you wouldn't want to disappoint my little girl, would you?" he asked.

Mrs. Griffin seemed to wince, automatically.

"Come on. Treat's on Sam Griffin!"

They walked by the three sitting ladies, out the glass doorway, into the town.

"A great day," Sam Griffin said, taking a mighty breath. "Ain't it, Vy?"

"Sure, Sam."

"Yes, sir. Mr. Cramer, you like this climate?"

"Oh, very much," Adam said, putting a little extra dash of softness into his voice. He had much to do today, but there was something here: he sensed it.

"We love it, the little girl and me. Listen, you sure did make a friend of Mrs. Pearl Lambert, mister—seeing the late movie with her. She's a wonderful woman. Really wonderful, you know what I mean? We first come here in—when was it?"

"Nineteen fifty-two."

"Nineteen fifty-two. Just passing through, on the way to Farragut. But we been traveling for hours, you know the way a person does, and were we bushed! I mean. Well, she gave us a room and said, 'You all look like you been working too hard. Why don't you take a little vacation, stay a while?' Remember, Vy?"

"Yeah," the woman said, "I remember."

Adam smiled and turned his attention to Mrs. Griffin. She had a very nice sway to her hips as she walked, and a sensuousness that neither the hair-do nor the plain black dress could conceal. She's trying to be unattractive, he thought. Why?

"Where do you hail from?" Griffin asked.

"Los Angeles."

"Los Angeles! Say! Do you know the Fairgrounds at Pomona?"

Adam said he did.

"Vy and me worked the Fairgrounds twice, and it was good, too. Real good. We was pushing something called the Air-Flow-Master." He chuckled. "Made close to six hundred a day on that gadget. I mean, it was perfect for a pitch: see, what it did—"

"Sam, *please.*"

"What do you mean?"

"I—" Vy Griffin shrugged. "Nothing, honey. I didn't mean to interrupt."

"Heck, that's okay, I don't mind. I talk a-mile-a-minute, anyway—you probably noticed, huh? Old blabbermouth Sam.

But when you're spieling all day, almost every day, it gets to be a habit."

"I don't see anything odd, the way you speak," Adam said, glancing at the woman.

"Vy does. My little girl is a real lady, you can tell that a block away, and sometimes I get on her nerves. But—well, this gimmick, what it did, it broke up the flow of gasoline to the carburetors of your car; and that makes for smoother feeding, better mileage, faster acceleration, and everything. That's what we said, anyway. It should have worked, too—I mean, it made perfect sense. Only it didn't work. What'd they cost us, baby?"

"Thirty-five cents."

"Yeah, that's right, thirty-five cents. And we sold them for three dollars . . ."

Griffin elaborated on the methods he and his wife had used to push the Air-Flow-Master, what he thought of the California climate, how he handled hecklers, and Adam listened and watched Vy Griffin as he listened.

". . . of course, I say we. The little girl hates doing that kind of work, and I don't blame her, in a way, so she always stays home. Old Sam don't mind . . ."

At a restaurant called the Palace, Griffin stopped talking.

They went inside—it was a big room; deserted—and took a booth in the center.

"Food ain't really too good here," Griffin whispered, "but it's better than anywhere else this time of day. Get your eggs scrambled."

A woman with a bleached and naked face appeared; in her weariness, in the lackluster eyes, she provided a perfect contrast to Sam Griffin's flashing red vitality.

"Watch this," Sam whispered; then he said, "We want three orders of framistan covered in fortis oil with a little sumis on the side."

"Beg pardon?" the woman said, not smiling.

Griffin roared, thumping the table. "Scrambled eggs and coffee. Three orders."

"Yes, sir."

"Holy cow! Every morning, that's what I say; and she still

don't get it. 'Beg pardon?' Oh my. Well, anyway, Mr. Cramer, you're staying a while in Caxton? You'll like it." His voice rang even more loudly than before. "You'll like it: it's a fine place. The people got brains—except for that waitress. They work at their clubs, you know? Lions, Elks, Rotary; all like that. Very community-minded, I mean. And they're honest. When Vy and me settle down and get through with all this running around, I don't know but what we won't pitch tent right here. What about that, baby?"

Vy Griffin said, "Sure, why not?"

"Great little girl. She always says yes, but I guess you know who wears the pants in this family, huh, Mr. Cramer? I mean trousers. *Trousers!*" Sam Griffin threw his hands up to guard against an imaginary attack, and laughed. "Got to watch my mouth."

Breakfast arrived and the stocky man suddenly fell silent, directing his energies to the task of eating. It seemed to take most of his concentration.

Adam waited for the proper moment, then let his eyes travel openly over Vy Griffin's face, over her breasts, up again to her face.

She looked away quickly, touched her lips with the napkin and rose. "Excuse me," she said.

"I guess we might do that."

She turned and walked to the back of the restaurant.

"Really something, huh?" Sam Griffin said. He clucked his tongue and shook his head. "Boy. And crazy over old Sam, can you beat that! I mean, how lucky can a fellow get?" He removed a cigar from his shirt pocket. "Boy."

Adam suppressed a smile and finished off his coffee.

"I see you're a single man, Mr. Cramer."

"Afraid so."

"Well, don't give up the ghost. I thought I wasn't ever going to find a woman, a real woman, you know? I mean, let's face it—I'm kind of a slob. I make my living off gullible people. I talk loud. And I know there are maybe a couple of handsomer men around in the woods. But, the good Lord didn't forget Sam. So keep looking, you hear me?"

"I will."

Vy Griffin returned to the table. Her walk was graceful, the sway of her hips an entirely natural, unconscious thing.

"I was just telling Mr. Cramer here that he shouldn't give up trying to find a woman."

"Oh? Have you had trouble in that direction, Mr. Cramer?"

Adam smiled at her. "Well," he said, "let's say I haven't been as fortunate as Mr. Griffin."

"Sam! Sam! I hate all this 'Mister' stuff."

The waitress came over and refilled the coffee cups. Adam watched Vy move closer to her husband, watched her light the cigarette, nervously.

"I'm afraid I'm going to have to get to work," Adam said. "It's been very pleasant."

"Yeah. Lousy food, but it fills the gut. If I didn't have a type philosophy like that, we'd starve, in some of the places we been; ain't that right, Vy?"

"That's right, honey."

They got up to leave. Adam reached for his pocket with deliberate awkwardness, put up a weak struggle for the check, gave in at last.

"Heck, we got plenty of money," Griffin said. "Pushing a real nice line now; really raking it in. Keep this to yourself, but we been averaging four hundred a day in the dime store at Farragut!"

They went out of the restaurant. Adam wondered how he could break away discreetly, for the man showed no signs of letting up.

"Farragut's only twenty miles," Griffin boomed. "You ought to come over and hear my pitch. I'm pushing a ballpoint pen, no better and no worse than any other. But here's the secret, here's how come we get two bucks for them. We took out a trade name R. Rand—patented it—and it's printed on the pens. Get it?"

"Not quite."

"Easy. People see it, what do they think? R. Rand. Why, that must be Remington Rand! And everybody knows Remington Rand's a fine old company, so they figure they're getting more than their two dollars' worth. It's the old principle. 'Something for nothing.' See, there's a little tiny bit of larceny in everybody's heart. I make them think I'm kind of dumb, so they believe they're taking advantage of me. Something for nothing; you know? You can sell people all kinds of things they don't need, easy, you can make them do things they never would think of doing, just as long as they believe they're special, important, getting in on the ground floor—you know? Boy."

"That's a very interesting theory," Adam said.

"It ain't a theory; it's a fact. I been living on it for most of my life, I ought to know!" Sam Griffin laughed. "It's a funny way to work, I guess—I mean, I admit it, I'm what you might call a con man—but, I ask you, is it much different from any other business? Advertising, politics—just great big pitches, that's all. Selling the public something they don't need, making them like it. Boy, what church you go to?"

Adam passed a hand through his hair. "I'm—a Baptist," he said.

"That so? Well, you won't find no trouble in Caxton. They got practically nothing but Baptists here, Baptists and Methodists—but not too many of them. Vy and me ain't anything in particular, really; we believe in the good Lord's word and what the Bible says, but when you're all the time making jumps, you don't get a chance to worship much formal. But you know"—Griffin paused for a moment, as though assembling the important parts of the story to follow—"I come within an ace of being a preacher myself, a couple years ago! Yeah, I did. Vy and—"

Vy Griffin nudged her husband and laughed. "Come on, Sam," she said, "stop bending Mr. Cramer's ear. He hasn't got time for that story. I clocked you at forty-five minutes when you told it to that DeSoto dealer."

Griffin shrugged. "Well, doggone it, it's a good one. We'll get together some night, Adam, and I'll tell it to you. How about that?"

"That'll be swell."

They entered the Union Hotel. The three ladies on the couch had not stirred. The TV still flickered.

"I'd like to thank both of you," Adam said, shaking Griffin's hand.

"What for?"

"Breakfast."

"You mean that scrambled framistan with fortis oil!" The stocky man chuckled again. "Yeah!"

"I'm going to the room," his wife said. She turned and walked away.

Sam Griffin lowered his voice. "Adam," he said, "I wonder if I could ask *you* a little favor. I know we're strangers, but I like you—I mean, I'm a pretty good judge of character; you have to be, in this business—and, well, would you mind?"

"I'd be glad to do you a favor, Sam, if I can."

"I knew it. It ain't nothing, much—but, you see, I'm going to be hitting for Farragut right away. The first few days are kind of rough, so I'll be staying overnight, most likely. I'd just appreciate it if you'd maybe look in on Vy once in a while. She gets bored, and the women here are all too old for her; you know. I mean, if you get a chance. Maybe take her to a movie. Or play cards with her; she likes cards."

Adam studied the man carefully, decided that it was not a joke.

"She don't really go for this kind of life," Griffin said. "Not really. We're saving up our dough and in a couple years we'll be able to buy a motel, or something, and take it easy; that's what she wants. She's a wonderful little girl, and old Sam hates to see her unhappy."

"I'll do my best," Adam said.

"Good!"

Adam walked carefully around Billy Matthews' outstretched legs, climbed the stairs and went into his room. From the dresser he took three thick white envelopes and shoved them into the breast pocket of his coat; then he went back to the lobby and picked up a telephone directory.

Shipman, Verne J., he found, lived at 22 Myrtlewood Lane . . .

He approached the three figures on the couch. To the first lady, a wax carving in a faded organdy dress, he said: "Excuse me, ma'am, but I wonder if you could tell me how to get to Myrtlewood Lane?"

She did not answer or move.

"Thanks anyway," he said and went out the doorway, trying to erase Vy Griffin from his mind. There would be time for that later, perhaps.

Yes, he decided. Definitely. There would be time.

5

He sat at the heavy oak table, chewing resolutely at a final fibrous shred of breakfast steak, wondering what to do with the day. The dogs could be heard faintly, and that reminded him that the tournament would be coming up soon; but there was nothing he could do now, except practice. And that was pretty stupid, when you got right down to it. He had the best dogs in the state: no other animal had come close to matching Rupert's stance, and Prince was just sloppy enough to make his retrieves popular. He would win the tournament, there was no doubt of that. So why should he even bother to enter?

The question was vague and unspoken, just as all other questions were, these days.

He yawned and pushed the table forward. His dark silk dressing gown was stained where he had spilled coffee onto it, and his face seemed stained, too: it was square and thick, covered by a three-day growth of beard. Two hundred and thirty pounds of meat stuck loosely to his bones; it bunched around the chest and stomach, even around the fingers of his hands. In the immaculate room with its white lace curtains and white walls and oriental rugs, with all its polished silver plates and candelabra, Verne Shipman looked grotesquely out of place.

He was quite aware of this fact, and felt it, also. His was a completely untenable position: having the instincts of an adventurer, wanting to start with nothing, as his father, Parke Shipman, had done, and work up a personal fortune of his own, he'd had to yield to his common sense and take the luck built-in. You can't disregard two million dollars. Yet, having it, what was there left for a man to do?

He hated his father, and venerated him. Old Parke had been one of those electric young men with bright lights shining deep behind their eyes. At the age of twenty-two he'd gone to California and bought a small lemon grove. The grove had been producing but losing money because of poor management; also, there was no way to fight the frosts then. Parke figured out a way, and soon had himself a thriving business; but it was not satisfying to him. There was nothing for him to do, once the initial rhythm had been set up. So he sold the grove and began to look around for something else to do. At that time, the most popular machine in America was the Model T Ford. The "T" was a stark, unlovely, uncomfortable, graceless conveyance; it had to be. Department stores therefore began to offer accessories, and the idea caught on. People started to "improve" their machines—adding special gimmicks to step up the power output, to give a softer ride.

Parke Shipman decided to climb onto the bandwagon in a hurry. What could he produce that was new, not yet thought of by the department stores?

He went into partnership with a man named Rogers, and together they dreamed up a series of luxury accessories for the interior of the car. Everyone else at that time was offering mechanical gadgets, considerations of comfort and beauty being largely neglected. So a vast field was open for such an enterprise.

Parke and Rogers decided to set up their shop in Caxton, both because it was Parke's home and because Negro labor would be cheap. They began to produce arm rests, cloth steering-wheel covers, and several other items. A Farragut bank financed them during this period. Then they began a heavy advertising campaign, and soon the business was flourishing.

As it flourished, the shop grew and, shortly before the decline of the Model T, Parke bought out his partner and built the fabric mill.

There was a trying period of readjustment to the new economy, but whenever his items became obsolete, Parke would invent others.

He spent small fortunes, but invariably made them back; and, at seventy-eight, he signed a long-term contract with one of the nation's largest automotive corporations, to supply accessories for all the cars to come out of their state factory.

They converted to plastics and, in 1949, the Shipman Mill added a second story.

Then Parke Shipman died, of a fistula, and his son was left to carry on.

Only, of course, there was nothing to "carry on." The contract was a long one, the orders were filled on time with great ease, the profits were sufficiently large so that an increase would only compound the tax problem. Had he the financier's interest in money for its own sake, Verne might have enlarged facilities, lobbied for new contracts, built the business into a colossal enterprise; but he knew that this involved tremendous work, work that was meaningless without the passion for business and the business world to carry it along.

Coming up from nothing, that was different; but adding frosting to an already over-rich cake—no. Two million in escrow and a regular $100,000 per year was enough.

It had occurred to Verne, when he was young, to change his name and strike out alone for Alaska or similarly virgin territory, to remain silent for a few years and then return with a fortune to match his father's—he'd dream this dream every night—but somehow he never got around to doing it. At the age of twenty-two he went to Europe and stayed there for a while, long enough to fall in love with an English girl and marry her; but it scared him, and, when they were home again, the girl scared him, too. The marriage lasted six months, then the girl said she wanted a divorce and would settle for two hundred thousand.

Parke paid it, gave Verne a feeble lecture, and returned to the mill. After the death of the old man's wife, he seldom ventured from the office, and took even less interest than usual in his son.

At forty-six Verne Shipman felt, without actually feeling it, that his life was over; that, in fact, it had never begun. Robbed of the chance to prove himself, cheated of all the adventure and force that had once sung in his blood, he could do no more than uphold the family name. And that was a poor job at best.

He picked up the Irish linen napkin, swabbed his lips; then, yawning, went upstairs and put on a sports shirt and a pair of light denim trousers.

Immediately upon leaving the house, he began to perspire.

He walked across the barbered green lawn, toward the kennels. The dogs were pacing, a few of them letting out futile cries behind the wire mesh.

Verne opened the first cage. A fine setter sprang out eagerly. "How is it, Rupert? You okay, boy? Everything okay?"

The dog pranced.

"Good. Good, fella." He ran his hand over the smooth back of the setter, and decided that they might as well go out and practice anyway. Practice never hurt.

He was about to call Lucas, the trainer, who lived in the reconverted stable at the end of the plot, when he saw Mrs. Mennen coming toward him. He frowned, for no good reason. Mrs. Mennen was an excellent housekeeper, and she cooked marvelously well, but somehow he felt that she begrudged him his position. She was continually comparing him with his father— and what did she expect, for God's sake? What was he supposed to do?

"There's someone to see you," the old woman said crisply. "He says he isn't a salesman and he's staying with Mrs. Pearl Lambert."

"What does he want?"

"I don't know. He won't tell me."

Shipman deepened his frown. "When they say they're not salesmen, you can be pretty sure that's what they are."

"I'm only repeating what he said."

"I know that. Mrs. Mennen"—he could never manage to call her Edna, as Parke had done—"I'm trying to get the dogs ready for some practice here, for the tournament. I'm very busy."

The woman's lips curled upward, almost imperceptibly.

"They've got to be made ready if we're going to win this thing, you know that."

"Do you want me to send him away?"

"Well . . . who is he, anyway? You ever seen him before?"

"No. A young fellow. He's staying at the Union."

In other words, Verne thought, since he's staying with your friend Mrs. Lambert you'd like me to see him.

"All right, all right. Send him out here. But tell him I can't give him much time; there's a lot to do."

Mrs. Mennen's eyes flickered—the look that Shipman could remember from childhood; the look that said, That's the whole trouble, there isn't anything for you to do, and you don't fool me for a minute—then she nodded, and went off.

He longed for the courage to fire her, but he knew he could never do this; and not merely because she was a fixture, either.

But why? Why couldn't he?

Rupert jumped up suddenly, planting forepaws on his master's chest. Shipman knocked the dog away gently and began thinking about which rifle he ought to take, what clothes he ought to wear, for the tournament. There was nothing else in his mind; not even the worry about the long empty weeks after the games. . . .

"Mr. Shipman?"

He turned. A young man stood near him, smiling.

"Go on, Rupert," he said gruffly. He always used a gruff tone around strangers. The dog frisked a moment, paused, leaped upon the visitor.

"Down, goddamnit!"

"No, wait, it's okay," the young man said. He rubbed the dog's ears, patted him, then watched as Rupert retreated to the cage.

"Did he get your suit dirty?"

"No, it's fine. I like dogs. You *are* Mr. Shipman?"

"That's right."

"My name is Adam Cramer." The stranger had a firm grip; and he looked at your face when he spoke. Shipman locked the kennel, muttered something, fumbled for his pipe.

"I know you must think it's a little odd for me to come bursting in on you like this, and I'm sorry if I'm interrupting."

"What's on your mind?"

"Well," the young man grinned, "quite a bit, sir. I think you'll be interested in hearing about it."

Shipman tamped some tobacco down in his pipe and applied a match. "I guess I've heard that somewhere before," he said.

"This is a little different, sir. You see, I'm not trying to sell you anything."

"Uh-huh."

The stranger stopped smiling. "Mr. Shipman, I've come down from Washington, D.C., as a representative of the Society of National American Patriots. Have you heard of the organization?"

"No, I can't say that I have."

"We're a group dedicated to helping the people of America understand the meaning of the Constitution. When we heard about the court's decision to integrate Negroes with whites in the high school here in Caxton, we decided to carry out an investigation—an investigation on how the people of Caxton feel about it. That's why I'm here."

"Well," Shipman said, "what do you want from me?"

"You're considered one of the most important civic figures of Caxton, sir," the young man went on, "so I simply would like to get *your* opinion."

"On what?"

"The integration issue."

"Oh." Shipman scratched his leg. He studied his visitor carefully, decided finally that if he was a salesman, he was a clever one, and it would be more entertaining to listen to a clever salesman than to practice with the dogs. "I can't spend a lot of time," he said.

"I realize that you're busy; but I promise it won't take long."

"All right. Let's go on back to the house, though. It's hotter than hell out here."

They started back across the lawn, which had been freshly watered by Lucas. It put out a clean, washed smell.

"You have a beautiful house, Mr. Shipman."

Verne grunted. The house had been planned as a Colonial mansion, complete with porch and hammock and pillars; but the wood hadn't lasted, and he'd been obliged to rebuild. He *tried* to keep it traditional, but small things went wrong. It somehow lacked the dignity of the old place. It was a facsimile. Maybe I'm a facsimile, too, he'd thought, once. All of us, everything. Stinking little imitations. Except for Mrs. Mennen . . .

"It has a real sort of quietness to it."

"In here."

Shipman went in first, striding with almost deliberate clumsiness through the cream-colored living room, past the grand piano, to the library.

He closed the door, motioned Adam Cramer to the large leather couch, and took his accustomed place behind the desk.

"Okay," he said, "what is it you want to know?"

"Well, sir, primarily this: how you stand—whether you're for integration or against it."

"Mister," Shipman said, "I'm a Southerner. I was born and raised in this country, and so were my folks. I don't mind telling you that I go right along with everybody else. I didn't like it when it first come up, and I don't like it now." He was a bit surprised at the firmness of his voice. The truth was, he hadn't thought about the question at all for several months. He'd never felt particularly concerned.

"Our organization agrees with you. We believe that the ruling is one of the greatest wrongs this government has ever perpetrated."

Shipman could see that it wouldn't do to display his indifference to a Northern outsider. Might be a newspaperman, or something. "It's a damn shame, all right."

"More than that, Mr. Shipman. We feel that it is the first big step toward the mongrelization of the entire white race in America."

Such a thing had never occurred to Shipman. He nodded noncommittally, and said "Yeah." It was odd to hear this sort of talk from so young a kid. When he was Adam Cramer's age, he was concerned with girls, mostly, and independence—for himself. Political issues then, as now, fell into the same category as mathematics and philosophy and the like. Certainly he had never had such a serious expression!

"That's why it's so important," the visitor said.

"Uh-huh. Well, I own the newspaper in town—I guess you know that—and we fought the thing right straight down the line. Then we got a delegation together and put in appeals and did, well, everything under the sun, but we might just as well have kept our mouths shut for all the good it accomplished." It was beginning to come back now. For a while he *had* been a little steamed up, a little annoyed; but the battle was hopeless, it always had been. "The way I figure, though, is like this. There's close to four thousand people in Caxton, and out of that four thousand, there's maybe three hundred and fifty nigras. See, they don't move in here any more because we don't use them at the mill any more, except as janitors, and what else is there for them to do? I mean, you know people don't have domestics like they used to. Can't afford it. So what'll happen? The same thing that's been happening—they'll drift off to Oakville. That's government operated, I suppose you know that; and they can get work there. But that'll be the end of it."

The young man shook his head. The gesture made Verne Shipman glad of his desk, suddenly. "If you don't mind my saying it, sir, there's a lot more to the problem than that. Don't you see? The government is using Caxton as a sort of test-tube case. If integration works here, then they'll order it everywhere in the South."

Shipman removed his pipe. "I don't—"

"If it works here, that will be the beginning of the end, believe me. We've studied the question and talked to people in Washington, and that's the way they're thinking. You say it will stop with the high school? You're wrong. Next will come the grade school. Pretty soon separate facilities will start disappearing everywhere. You know niggers as well as I do, better, even, and you know what happens when you give them an inch. Look at Alabama, and that bus business. Or just look at the whole picture in the North. Is it pretty?"

"Well, now, that's a good deal different."

"Certainly it is. Why? Because of all the niggers in America, only fifteen per cent of them are in the North. I don't imagine I have to tell you what trouble that fifteen per cent has caused . . ." The young man's voice was level and calm, but something was happening to his words. Shipman couldn't tell what it was. But he felt it.

He started to remark that he was quite familiar with the consequences of the situation, but again he was interrupted.

"Just add it up, Mr. Shipman. The vote will get easier for them, won't it, with desegregation? Washington is working on that. And remember, there might be only three hundred niggers here, but there are *fifteen million* of them in the United States. Did you know that?"

"I knew the figure was something close to that, yes."

"All right now, here's something perhaps you don't know. By actual statistics, Negroes represent only nine point nine per cent of the total U. S. population. The *total* population, see. But what per cent do you think they represent in the South? In Arkansas, Alabama, Florida, Louisiana, Tennessee?"

"I'm not sure."

"Well, let's put it this way. Out of the fifteen million in America, over seventy-five per cent of them are right here in the South. Over seventy-five per cent." The young man rose. "With desegregation, the next thing you know, they'll *all* be here. And the vote will be right in their back pocket! And then we are really going to see some changes...."

A hot redness was creeping into Shipman's face; a long-forgotten tension growing slowly inside him. "I never thought about it exactly that way," he admitted.

"I know," the young man said, "most folks don't. They don't realize. That's the trouble with the South—the people are too open and honest and trusting. They just can't believe that the government would betray them. But that's what's happening."

"Well," Shipman said angrily, "we *tried* to stop it. We did everything we could. It's a damn law now."

"Is it?" the visitor asked.

"What do you mean, 'is it'? Of course it is. Hell, the Attorney-General—"

"I thought this was a Democracy," Adam Cramer said softly, almost innocently. "And I thought a Democracy was a government based on the collective will of the people."

"Of course, of course."

"And is it the collective will of the people of Caxton that niggers are to be allowed to mix with whites right under the same roof? Study with them, eat with them, maybe even sleep with them? No. Mr. Shipman, laws can be changed; decisions can be altered—it's happened in the past. Labor unions have shown us that."

Shipman knocked the dottle out of his pipe. "You're gonna have a hard time selling me on labor unions, fella. I'll tell you that."

"I was only using them as an example," the young man said quickly. "I mean that group action, group *will,* can have a positive effect. It created the law in the first place, didn't it?"

"I don't follow you."

"Well, what do you think, that those nine old men on the bench just happened to sort of get the idea of integrating schools? They didn't. The Jew politicians behind the NAACP started it, Mr. Shipman, and they put the pressure on. But they were a group, you understand? They were organized. I figure that if a bunch of Communists—whose aim, I don't have to tell you, is to mongrel- ize and destroy the United States—if they can create a law, then I figure a bunch of white Americans can get it changed!"

There was a knock at the door. Shipman stared for a moment, then swiveled his head. "Yes? What is it?"

Edna Mennen came into the room. She did not look at Adam Cramer. "I thought I ought to remind you that you're supposed to be practicing with the dogs," she said. "I got Lucas to interrupt his work. He's waiting."

"Tell him to stop waiting," Shipman said, after a momentary pause. "Or, here—tell him to work the dogs himself. He knows more about it than I do, anyway."

"All right."

"And, Mrs. Mennen—I don't want to be disturbed for a while. No phone calls."

The old woman took a breath. "All right," she said, and looked at Adam Cramer and went out.

"Close the door!" Shipman waited for the footsteps to recede. "Okay," he said, "what you say may make some sense—in theory, anyway—but what can we do?"

The young man smiled. "A great deal," he said. "If you're seri- ous about wanting to stop integration—"

"But it's going to start tomorrow," Shipman said, remembering.

"I know. It can start; let it. That's even better. But, as I say, if you're serious—then you'll listen to what I have to tell you. Be- cause there is a way."

"Yes?"

The young man walked over to the window and stood quietly for a time. "Mr. Shipman," he said, "I don't want you to think that I'm encouraging you on something you don't really feel. Are you *seriously* concerned?"

"Of course I am. Always have been. But you haven't said any- thing yet. When you say something, I'll listen."

"All right, that's fair enough. I spoke of SNAP—"

"What?"

"The Society of National American Patriots."

"Oh, yes."

"Well, we have no state charter here; we've operated on a non-profit basis since the beginning, doing what we could. Now here's the thing. If we're able to get a charter, and funds for promotion, we can organize the people of Caxton into a fighting force. We can weld the strength of the town together into one strong unit, and—in different ways; in ways I'll explain—we can show the Supreme Court that desegregation is never going to work in the South."

Some of the tension faded from Shipman. He smiled, a cold, cynical smile. "I see," he said. "In other words, you want money."

"As a matter of fact," the young man said, "no. We'll need your acknowledged support now, and your financial support eventually—because this sort of work can't be done without capital. But I certainly don't expect you to take what I've said on faith. I don't want a penny from you now."

"Then what do you want?"

"Just this. Mr. Shipman, I'm going to go to the people of Caxton, from house to house. I'm going to introduce myself and tell them about SNAP; and then I'm going to ask them if they want to join the organization. If they do, it will cost them ten dollars membership fee. That's all. When I get fifteen hundred dollars, then I'll come back here and ask you to triple that amount. But—this could be a cagey little move, too, couldn't it? That is, you're thinking I could already have the fifteen hundred and just wait a while and come back with my song-and-dance. Maybe you'd believe I actually did raise the money, maybe you'd trust me and go along with the idea; then maybe I'd sort of disappear. Isn't that what you're thinking?"

"Maybe."

"So we'll work it another way. When I raise my part of it, I'll turn it in to you. And you'll know exactly where I got it and from whom. You'll hold the money in your bank and simply guarantee SNAP the rest, as it's needed."

"That would make me treasurer," Shipman said.

The young man grinned. "That's right," he said. "It would."

"I . . . don't know; I'll have to think a good deal more about it.

We've had the best lawyers in the state on our side, you know, and they couldn't do anything."

"That's no surprise, believe me. Lawyers are mostly fools: they work on entirely the wrong principle. Who do they talk to? Politicians. Officials. Bureaucrats. Judges. If you wanted to make your way through a jungle, Mr. Shipman, what would you do—try to talk the bushes into going somewhere else, or hire yourself some people to go out and cut those bushes away? I mean, did your lawyers ever once go to the *people* and enlist *their* aid?"

"I don't think that's the point."

"Of course it's the point. It's why they failed. We don't work that way; we know a lot better than to try to buck the red tape thrown around by all those government Jews. They're a minority race themselves, don't you see, that's one of the reasons they're so damned anxious to desegregate the South!"

Verne Shipman walked to the door, feeling, knowing, that a decision of considerable importance had suddenly been thrust upon him. He wasn't used to making decisions.

"We're going to show Caxton what's happened in the North, what's going to happen here, too. Like this—" The young man reached into his breast pocket, extracted a large newspaper photograph from one of the envelopes.

He put it down on the desk. "Look at it, Mr. Shipman. See how it makes you feel—even if you don't have children."

Verne moved to the desk and picked up the clipping. It showed a Negro soldier in the act of kissing a white girl. He stared at the photograph, then threw it back onto the desk.

"That's what's coming," the visitor said, "if we don't put a stop to it now. That, and a lot more."

"Do you have a working list?" he asked in a businesslike voice, after a long pause.

"Not yet," the young man said.

"Go to the Farragut County Federation for Constitutional Government, upstairs, next to the Reo Theatre. Find Bart Carey and tell him to phone me."

"I'll do that."

"I'm not promising a goddamn thing, mister. So far you've made noise; good noise, but not much else. I don't think you'll get a penny out of this town for any organization of any kind, frankly. Unions aren't popular in Caxton. But Bart Carey has a list of parents with school kids. If you can get them to go along with you, even for five hundred, I'll—be willing to lend a hand."

"That's all I ask."

"Okay. Now when do you think you're going to have this thing rolling?"

The young man smiled. "The money will be pledged before midnight tomorrow, Mr. Shipman. And at least a hundred and fifty new members of SNAP."

"That's ridiculous."

"Is it? I tell you what—you drop by the courthouse at seven-thirty tomorrow night. Just take a little drive into town, and drop by. I understand there's going to be some kind of a meeting."

The visitor took another sheet of paper from his pocket.

"Meanwhile," he said, "you might look this over."

Shipman took the paper, walked with the young man to the door, shook hands.

Then he went back into the library and sat down. He unfolded the paper, saw the large heading: INTEGRATION OF NEGROES WITH WHITES UNCONSTITUTIONAL!! and read the smaller print carefully.

He read it three times.

And each time he read it, his heart beat a little faster.

6

Ella was sexing up her hair, giving it that loose, wind-whipped look, when the doorbell rang. In a way, she had not actually expected to hear from Adam Cramer again—he was too unreal; too much a figure out of a movie, for belief—but she'd put on her best dress, just in case. Now she was glad. And, a little frightened. She'd told her father that a stranger might be by and that she might go out with this stranger, provided Tom agreed; still there was that feeling of an improbable fancy coming true. For there could be no doubt that it was Adam Cramer.

She waited a decent feminine interval, then came out. He

stood in the living room, looking exactly as he had yesterday; perhaps a bit more relaxed. He was talking with Tom.

"...hadn't realized Ella's father was the editor of the *Messenger*. I was planning to call on you this week."

Gramp hadn't looked up; he was deeply engrossed in an old Western movie on the TV set. Occasionally he grunted his annoyance at all the ruckus.

Adam saw Ella and smiled. "Hi."

"Hi," Ella said, with great uncertainty.

"Why didn't you tell me that your dad was a celebrity?"

"Huh? Oh—I don't know. I guess you two have met?"

"Yes, indeed," Adam said. "At least we've introduced ourselves."

"Well, wait a second; I'll get my wife," Tom said.

Ruth came in from the kitchen, drying her hands on her apron.

"This is Mr. Adam Cramer," Tom said slowly. "He wants to take Ella to a motion picture."

Ruth blinked. "How do you do," she said. "You're—the young fellow that called us yesterday, aren't you?"

Adam looked up. "Did I? Gosh, I don't know. I made quite a few calls. Trying to get things rolling." He turned to Tom. "I'm sorry I didn't have a chance to drop by in person today; there are so many houses to canvas. But we can have our talk tomorrow. I'll stop by your office—that is, if it's all right."

Tom rubbed his chin. "What exactly about, Mr. Cramer? You apparently didn't make yourself any too clear to my wife."

"About the situation at the school, primarily. You see, I'm the executive secretary of an organization in Washington, and we believe we can help Caxton, help the people fight this ruling. That's it, mainly."

"I see."

Ella wondered if this was another joke, decided it wasn't. "Come on, now, let's not talk politics and stuff when I'm supposed to be going out on a date. Or am I?"

"I'm not sure," Tom said. He turned again to Adam. "Mr. Cramer, it's pretty unusual, you just dropping into town and setting up my daughter for a date. Is there any good reason why I shouldn't refuse? She's only sixteen, you realize."

The young man smiled, winningly. "That's a good attitude, Mr. McDaniel. Where I come from—"

"Where is that, by the way?"

"Los Angeles. There, I mean, the parents usually don't give a darn where their children go. Or what they do. I admire that quality in you, and after I talked with Ella, with Miss McDaniel, I sensed it. That's why I insisted on coming over so you could get a look at me."

"We still don't know anything about you," Tom said.

"Well," Adam laughed, "I'm twenty-six, which I guess is old compared to Ella; but it's fairly young to most people. I'm a white American, Norwegian stock. And like I said, I'm in, you might say, social work. I'll be living in Caxton for quite a while, so I thought it would be nice to make a few friends. Frankly, sir, I'd hoped your daughter could tell me a little about the town, maybe show me some of it."

"In the dark?" Tom asked.

"Sure," Ella said, winking. "We're going to use a flashlight."

Ruth McDaniel's face assumed an expression of composure; at any rate, the apprehension was gone. "Would you care for a cup of coffee, Mr. Cramer?" she said.

"I'd love one."

Tom glanced at Ella. "Kitten, why don't you go and wash your face or press your dress or something. Mr. Cramer and I are going to chat a little."

Ella said, "Okay. But the movie starts at 8:17."

The visitor's relaxed manner seemed to reassure Tom. He motioned him to the couch.

"Let's be honest with one another, young man. Why are you calling people up, going through all this funny routine?"

"That's simple enough to answer, sir. We're on limited funds, and I felt—the organization felt—that it would be better to get a sort of cross-section of opinion before attempting any work."

"How many calls did you make?"

"About twenty."

"And what did you find out?"

"That the people are against integration, Mr. McDaniel. Dead-set against it."

"Goddamn right!" Gramp rose from his chair nimbly and walked over.

"This is my father-in-law, Mr. Parkinson," Tom said. "Gramp, Adam Cramer."

"I talked with you yesterday, boy. Didn't think you was so young."

"Well—"

"But I liked what you said, now, I'll tell you that. It don't take no campaign to find out what the people think in Caxton, though. They hate the idea. But they're too goddamn wishy-washy to do anything about it."

"Gramp."

"It's a fact, Tom, and you know it. Tom here isn't no different either."

"I'm sure you must be wrong, sir. Mr. McDaniel, I understand, carried out quite an extensive campaign in his paper."

Gramp laughed wetly. "Shit," he said. "A bunch of words. Take it easy, he says, don't rush, and all that kind of horse-hockey."

"Perhaps the trouble is simply that there's been no organized effort made. Wouldn't you say that, Mr. McDaniel?"

Tom shook his head. "No. We pulled every string there was, but it didn't work out. Those Negroes are going to school, starting tomorrow, and we might as well get used to it."

"I can't agree, sir," Adam Cramer said. "The Society of National American Patriots has, if you don't mind my saying it, a little clearer picture of things; after all, we're not right in the middle of it, if you know what I mean. And we've devised a number of methods which only involve the co-operation of the people. You're not licked yet, Mr. McDaniel."

Gramp's eyes shone brightly. "You probably mean good, sonny, but it's gonna be like coaxing a bear out of hibernation."

"I think I understand, sir. Still, you mustn't underestimate folks. Almost everyone on earth would sleep till noon if somebody didn't wake them up."

"And that's what you're going to do?" Tom asked quietly. "Wake us up?"

"We hope to be able to present the issues as they really are and show how they can be beaten."

"Mr. Cramer," Tom said, "you probably know that school starts tomorrow. By all rights, Ella should stay home and get some rest."

Ruth looked at Tom meaningfully.

"Dear," she said, "you must remember, Ella's no child any more. I honestly do think she deserves to go out; after all, she's been working in that drugstore every night, or practically every night, for months."

Tom glanced from the young man to Gramp to Ruth, finally to Ella. Coldly he said, "Very well. But, Mr. Cramer, I want her back by ten thirty, do you understand that?"

Tom and Ruth watched them get into the four-year-old rental Chevrolet sedan, watched until the car had backed out of the driveway and was out of sight.

Then Ruth said, "Why don't you like him, Tom?"

"I think he's too old for Ella. She's just a kid."

"You call twenty-six old?"

"Yes, I do."

Tom sighed and started for the easy chair in the corner. Gramp stopped him. "That fella's got some piss and vinegar in his blood, Tom McDaniel, you know that? That's why you don't like him."

"Not necessarily," Tom said.

" *Not necessarily*,'" the old man mimicked. "You don't fool nobody, Tom. *Nobody*. You're just worried now he might show Ella what a spineless fool her father really is!"

Ruth stamped her foot. "Dad, for heaven's sake, will you stop talking that way! *Please*."

"This is America," the old man said defiantly. "A body has a right to speak his mind."

"What mind?" Tom slumped into the easy chair and picked up a copy of the Farragut *Courier*.

Ruth stood still for a while, then asked: "Dear, please, tell me, why are you so upset? Don't you trust the boy with Ella?"

Tom did not answer.

"Well, what is it then, for heaven's sake?"

He folded the newspaper and removed his glasses. "Mr. Cramer," he said, "has been going from house to house today, asking people to join his organization. He's charging ten dollars membership. He got at least thirty-five families to go along with it so far."

"Well?" Ruth asked. "So what? I mean, he told you that himself, didn't he?"

"Not that part, no. I found it out from Ocie Collins, who *didn't* join. He gave me something to read, too. Some of the organizational literature the boy is handing out. Would you care to hear it?"

He got the paper out of his right pocket, straightened it and began to read, in a loud voice, over the blaring of the Western movie.

"*'Integration of Negroes with Whites declared unconstitutional!'*" he began. "'Don't be duped by the politicians in Washington. They want to cram desegregation down *your* throat, and they won't stop at anything until they do it. *Unless you fight back!* Yes! There is a way to fight. The Negroes can be removed from Caxton high school! *Your* daughters can be safe from contamination! For further details, come to ——'" Tom looked up. "He's penciled in 'The courthouse at seven o'clock Monday night, August 27.' It's signed Adam Cramer, Executive Secretary, Society of National American Patriots, Washington, D.C."

Ruth looked temporarily confused. "Well," she said, "maybe he does have some ideas, Tom. You couldn't be against him for that, could you?"

"Of course not, not for that alone. But, damn it, if he *has* ideas, why doesn't he go to some responsible members of the community and present them above board—"

"—and have them shoved down in a drawer, somewhere," Gramp snorted. "I'll tell you why, because he has brains, that's why. *You* tried that, and see what it got. Nothing, that's what."

"Besides," Ruth said, "holding a meeting is pretty open and above board, wouldn't you say?"

Tom let out a long breath. "I don't know. I just think that he's going about it in the wrong way."

"Ha!" said Gramp.

"He's going to see you tomorrow, dear," Ruth said, "didn't he say that?"

"Uh-huh."

"Well then? He seems like an awfully nice and intelligent boy. Doesn't he?"

"Yes. Yes."

Ruth stared at her husband for a time. Then she went into the kitchen.

Cautiously, Adam Cramer said: "Do you really want to go to a movie?"

Ella nodded her head.

"They're not actually moving, you know," he said. "It's all an illusion. What you're looking at is a million photographs, that's all, and they lie to you and tell you they're moving. I know. I once worked for a studio."

"You did not."

"I did. And I found out their dirty secrets. You say you want to see Gregory Peck. Well, what if I told you that I happen to know that Gregory Peck is actually a woman in disguise?"

"Now, listen—"

"Scout's honor. You have no idea the miracles those make-up men can achieve. They needed a leading man for a picture and one of the producers just happened to see this six-foot woman selling pencils outside the studio. Her name was Hortense. I had bought at least ten dozen Ticonderogas from her, and loved the old witch dearly, despite her odor. Then one day she wasn't at her usual corner any more. 'What has happened to dear old Hortense?' I asked passers-by, but they only shrugged. Then, some months later, I saw a picture called *Keys of the Kingdom* and there, playing the part of the missionary—you remember?—was my old friend, the pencil seller. Except now they called her Gregory Peck."

"Well, I don't know," Ella said, "I think we'd better go to the movie anyway."

"Why? You've seen it eight times already."

"I have not."

"Well, I have. Look—why don't we go somewhere for a coke, or something, and just talk? I'm kind of nervous; I couldn't stand all that shooting."

"There isn't any shooting in the picture. It's a comedy."

"Well, then, the laughing would bother me. Really, Ella, I

mean—can't we go somewhere? You know the town, I don't; so I couldn't very well be spiriting you away."

Ella was silent for a time: then she said, "We could go to Rusty's for a while, maybe."

"Rusty's? What's that?"

"It's kind of a place, you know. Over the bridge. Some of the kids go there at night—"

"That sounds great. I'd like very much to meet some of the high school students."

"Why?"

"For the work I'm doing."

Ella opened the window a few inches, letting in the soft rush of night air.

"But I've done a lot of work already today. So I'll promise not to ask any questions or anything like that tonight. You just introduce me around, okay? And we'll sit in a corner and slurp sodas or dance or whatever the kids do around here. And I'll get you home on time. Is it a deal?"

"Well . . ."

"Please?"

"Make a circle here and go back to Broad Street. Get on 25 W and go over the bridge. Then I'll tell you from there."

The car slowed, made a U-turn, and stopped. There were no streetlights in this area; only the dark houses, and the full dark trees. "You don't really think I'm crazy, do you?" Adam Cramer asked, in a soft voice.

"I guess not."

The car's wheels spun on the loose gravel and headed down the black hill . . .

"This is it, here."

They pulled into the crowded parking lot, and got out of the car.

Rusty's was a big log cabin. A sign in the window advertised Draught Beer—10¢. Ella led the way to the door.

Inside, the place was crowded with teen-agers. Many of them had cigarettes—which they handled awkwardly and self-consciously—and a few nursed glasses of beer. A juke box in the corner blared a rock-'n'-roll tune.

Some of the youngsters waved at Ella when she came in. She looked for a sign of Hank Kitchen, but he wasn't there. It was pretty early, though.

They took chairs at a large table occupied by two boys and a girl, none of whom bothered to stand.

"Hi," the girl said. She glanced coyly at Adam, then, with a certain admiration, at Ella.

"This," Ella said, "is Mr. Adam Cramer. Adam, Lucy Egan, Danny and George Humboldt."

A large man in a white apron appeared almost at once. "Two cokes," Adam said. "I never could stand the taste of beer. Used to try to pretend I liked it, but it just didn't work."

Danny and George Humboldt grinned. "Same with me," George said. He was a moon-faced, rather fat young man, with a very thick accent. "But I figured I'd mature to it, you know?"

"Maybe I will, too," Adam said, "but right now—*ugh*!"

"Yeah, man," George said, winking at Ella. "*Ugh.*"

"What's old Hank doing these days?" Danny Humboldt asked.

Ella shrugged. "I wouldn't know," she said. "I just plain wouldn't know about him." She paused. "Adam, here, comes from Hollywood."

"That a fact?" George said. "What the hell's somebody from Hollywood doing in this jerkwater town, that's what I'd like to know."

Danny lit a fresh cigarette from his previous one. "I bet I could give a pretty good guess." Then the music stopped, there was an electric hesitation, and another record came on. George Humboldt pounded the tabletop for a few moments, then said: "Hey, Ella, let's show 'em."

Ella shook her head. "Not right now, George."

"Come on, come on, it ain't gonna kill you. Tomorrow we die, you know what I mean; tonight we live. Come on."

The fat boy got up, pulled back Ella's chair.

"Go on," Adam said affably. "I'm not much of a dancer, anyway."

Ella and George began to move to the music, which was a fast fox-trot.

Danny continued to stare at Adam, who was now focusing his

attention on the girl. "You're down here on this integration business, aren't you?" he asked, finally.

"That's right."

"You figure there's anything you can do?"

"Yeah, I figure."

"What?"

"Well, if you want to know, why don't you stop by the courthouse tomorrow night about seven?"

"How come?"

"You'd like to see this thing stopped, wouldn't you?"

Danny Humboldt said nothing for a while. Impassively he took a drag on his cigarette. Then, in a quiet tone, he said, "You damn right."

"I thought so. Well, Danny, look: I promised Ella I wouldn't do any work tonight. So would you—you and Lucy here—do me a favor?"

"What's that?"

"Let all the kids know about the meeting. Get them to come."

Danny said, "I guess I can do that."

"It would mean a lot."

"Okay," Danny said, still staring.

The girl said that she would tell as many people as she could.

"I appreciate it. But I don't want you-all working for nothing. Would either of you get sore if I paid you ten dollars? It's from the Organization."

Danny looked at the five-dollar bill for a moment. "Why not?" he said, pocketing the bill.

"Good. Now you're on the team. Oh-oh, here comes Ella. No more business."

"How about you and her, anyway?" Danny asked. "How come you—"

Lucy said, "Oh, you be quiet."

"It's simple, Danny. I'm working with her father on this thing."

"With Tom McDaniel?"

Breathing hard, Ella fell heavily into the chair. George Humboldt was grinning all over his face. "Did we show 'em?" he said, "or did we show 'em, you know what I mean? Wow! You know?"

For the next two and a half hours Adam Cramer spoke of Hollywood, of the studios, of stars he had met; particularly of his five years of university training. Four years at UCLA and a year in Switzerland, studying philosophy, criminal medicine—he didn't go into it deeply, only skimming over the interesting parts.

He spoke of the sunny, white-glazed slopes, so ideal for skiing, of Fastnacht, and of the complaisance of the Swiss females.

"I was doggone glad to get back to America, I can tell you that," he said, at the conclusion of his rambling story. "Foreigners are the same all over. Except that there weren't many Jews in Switzerland, that was one thing, anyway . . ."

Then, suddenly, the clock showed 10:00, and he turned to Ella. "I'm afraid it's that time. If I'm going to get any co-operation from your father, I'd better scoot you home."

"See you on the battleground tomorrow," George said, managing somehow to keep the cigarette between his lips as he spoke.

His brother said: "If I see Hank later on, I'll give him your regards."

Ella took a swipe at the young man with her purse. "You just mind your own business, hear?"

"Sure, sure."

"I mean it."

Adam said that he was happy to have met the group, looked intently for a moment at Danny, and walked out with Ella. Her arm looped with his.

They drove back down the road, swung off onto the highway. By a fairly deserted section, in the general neighborhood of Ella's home, Adam stopped the car.

"I think the wheels dropped off," he said, grinning.

"Well, then, you just pick this little old car up and run with it," Ella said, pleased with the crack, with Adam, with the whole wonderful evening. He had made a tremendous impression; she knew that. On everyone.

"Okay," he said. "But first I'd like to tell you something. Do you mind if I tell you something?"

Ella was silent. He moved a little closer to her.

"I think you're a very lovely girl, and I want to thank you for tonight."

"I didn't do anything."

"No, you did, really. I don't feel like such a stranger now. I know I have a friend. I *do* have a friend, don't I?"

Ella nodded, slowly. She had nothing to fear, she was certain of that now, but her heart began its ridiculous beating and she couldn't tell why. Part of her wished that he would start the car again, another, stronger part wished otherwise.

Adam Cramer looked into her eyes, then gently took her by the shoulders and pressed his lips to hers. Nothing could have been softer.

"Thanks very much," he said, moving back to his position behind the wheel, quickly.

The car started with unexpected noise, and within minutes Ella was saying good night.

"Again?"

She felt the pressure on her hand and returned it. "I shouldn't go out on a school night, but—"

"Next week?"

She said, "Maybe," and went inside and tried to sleep.

7

The town of Caxton lies in a small, circular valley surrounded by the humped Carmichael Mountains. These mountains blaze fierce green throughout the years, for clouds come infrequently, and there is always the sun to pick up the million glintings of light. There is a smoothness to the mountains, also, as if they had all been carefully trimmed and groomed: a placid, cared-for smoothness to them, and to the town itself. Seen from above, Caxton appears as a clutch of brown and white leaves left at the bottom of an emerald teacup.

But the beauty vanishes when you walk onto the main street. The stores and offices have a sterile, crabbed look about them. The courthouse, a wooden, churchlike structure, is the hub of the municipality. It sits, a sullen hulk, atop a glassy rise of lawn, failing to look either proud or dignified. Its wooden planking is old, brittle, stained orange where the nails have bled; the whitewash is a delight to children, who sneak up at night and run their fingers along the wood and feel the paint flake away and fall, silent as snow, to the ground. The courthouse is, in fact, the ugliest building in Caxton: but it is the hub. The center. From its squat steeple a rusted bell tolls out the hours, reminding the people, in unsonorous tones, that they are a little closer to night, a little closer to morning, a little closer to death.

The main street, George Street, is curiously devoid of trees and grass. Like an approach to any city subsection, the places of business join one another endlessly: grocery store to tailor shop to children's wear to cleaner's to drugstore to dress shop; no inch of space is wasted. And this solemn gray front seems to lack the conviviality common to small Southern towns, but it is a wrong impression. The tradesmen within smile often.

The Caxton Theatre, once a popular and thriving motion picture auditorium, sits empty and silent in the middle of the town, like an abandoned circus. If there ever was gaiety inside, or laughter, or tears, you could not guess it from the façade. Rotted boards cover it. Black sockets stare blindly from the foyer. And dirt has caked into its open veins.

But this is not all of Caxton. At the bottom of George Street, if you turn right, you will see the green of growing things again, and the bright new bricks of the library and post office. Both are handsome buildings, clean and fresh, blending with the summer smell of oaks and shrubs. Dappled shade gives them a picture-book appearance. Beyond, if you keep walking, you will find the elementary school, an old, dark structure, and the high school.

The high school is centered in the middle of a lawn, and though there is no cement walkway to the front doors, the lawn has the smooth, soft quality of an expensive rug. The school, like the post office and library, is a study in red and white. New bricks flank the main office. Over to the right stands a gymnasium, not yet completed, also in red brick, trimmed with white.

These grounds possess a tranquillity, a quiescence, which is oddly missing in the downtown area. Tradition is here, for all the bright newness. And age. It is all like the campus of a small New England college.

But there is still more of Caxton.

Make a right turn at Shepherd Avenue, and you are confronted by a residential district. The houses are large and gray, all in their separate tree-shaded squares. They do not suggest prosperity, but neither do they bear any hint of poverty. Everything is neat and clean and orderly. Three- or four-year-old automobiles sit parked in the driveways, and these are mostly black; seldom do you encounter a gaudy new model.

It is very quiet, at any time of day or night, here. You will hear the hum of a television set perhaps, or the sound of a vacuum cleaner, but it is never so noisy that you cannot hear distinctly the crickets in the grass.

You continue past these houses, and suddenly the houses stop, and you face a steep hill. It seems to mark the end of civilization. The paving ceases to be; it is replaced by a rutted, chuckholed path of gravel and dirt. The forest and the fields close in. But you go on anyway, up the hill.

An incredible change occurs. You begin to see homes, but they are hardly worth the name. You look over your shoulder and see the green new cup of the town, then you look at the dark shacks that begin to surround you: the ancient, rusted haymows, useless for decades; the piled cordwood; the numerous automobile shells, turned over on their sides or simply sitting, like mechanical cadavers, waiting for the final rot; the square, toothless cages and the serene chickens, searching; and the shacks, the shacks, built of cast-off boards and cast-off nails, all appearing to teeter on the brink of collapse, of certain self-demolition.

You expect to see bowed Negro women in faded dresses, naked Negro children running in happy ignorance, brain-fogged Negro grandfathers sitting statue-still on the decaying porches.

But there are no Negroes here.

The people are white. They are the Poor Whites, the landless, jobless people, who live because they do not die.

Over the hill and down another lane and up another rise is Simon's Hill, marked by the big, square Baptist church which occupies the promontory above the country ground. This is Reverend Finley Mead's church, built by himself and his congregation early in 1932, maintained with solemn purpose ever since. Like the courthouse, this church has a bell; but it is a quieter bell. It disturbs no one.

Simon's Hill is a small section; a group of houses and apartments dotting the rocky landscape, hanging from the steep hillocks. It is almost, but not quite, a community. There is a restaurant—The Huddle—and a tailor shop and several groceries, a barbershop, and a sort of department and general store.

The apartments are new, made of plaster and chicken wire, all owned by Verne Shipman and F. G. Bennett of Caxton, and Carter Royal and other parties in Farragut. They are poorly built units, but the rent is low, and no one of the tenants would think of being late with a payment.

Simon's Hill is Caxton's Niggertown, and it is a world within itself. You never see a Negro in Caxton's center, and you never see a white in Simon's Hill.

That is the way it has been for forty years.

8

He lay on the patched green velvet couch, his hands behind his head, his body perfectly still, still as it had been for almost an hour. Albert was in a corner, reading a comic book. Billy was asleep. He wanted to sleep, too, but he had never felt so awake.

"Joey," his mother said, "Joey, you want some coffee?"

"No, Ma," he said.

"How about some warm milk? It'll do you good, it'll relax you."

"No."

He thought of the short night and of the long day ahead, of all the forces that had put him here, where he was, and he wanted to yell. But he couldn't do this. He could only lie still and wait.

Charlotte Green looked at her son, almost furtively.

"Joey," she said, "it's eight thirty. You been working hard. Why don't you slip off your shoes?"

"Ma, please. Can't I just lay here for a while?"

"Of course you can."

Joey leaped from the couch and strode to the main window. Uncle Rowan was sitting there, staring. "Ma, now, I said I'd do it. I'm going to do what you want!"

"All right, Joey."

He forced back the rage that had bubbled up hot in his throat, and smiled. "I'm just bushed," he said. "Getting everything cleaned up at the garage and all, you know." He stood there, a tall, powerful figure in the dim light. "I'm okay."

Uncle Rowan frowned. He sat in the chair and frowned, an ancient, time-wrinkled elf of a man. No one knew exactly how old he was, not even his niece, but he was past eighty—that much was certain. He seldom spoke. And he never smiled.

Joey walked back across the room and put a hand on his mother's shoulder. He knew that she was wrong, and that the whole thing would end badly—he knew it—but he knew, also, that he could never say this.

He remembered the long years of work that she had put in—for him; for Albert and Billy—and the knot in his chest tightened.

She actually believes it's going to be all right, he thought. She thinks the problem is over. Just open up the schools, and that's that.

Billy cried out in his sleep, turned over again. Albert put down his comic book. "I want some bread," he said.

"In the kitchen," said Charlotte Green.

Albert scratched his side. He was going to look a lot like Joey. He had the same wiry set of muscles, the same lean build. And his face was already growing handsome. "Hey," he said, "is he really going to the white school tomorrow?"

Charlotte nodded.

"I sure hate to miss that." Albert laughed. He was thirteen years old; he said what he felt like saying. "That ought to be a real lot of fun."

Joey said, "Yeah."

Albert looked first at his mother, then at his elder brother, shrugged and went toward the kitchen. "You think there going to be any fights?" he asked.

"No," Charlotte said, "there won't be any fights, Albert. You get your pajamas on. It's time for bed."

"Eight thirty?"

"Get them on."

"I want some bread first."

"All right, all right," Joey heard himself shouting, "you go get that goddamn bread, will you, and shut up!" He felt the blood pounding in his throat.

"Well," Albert said, "I guess there going to be some fights, okay," and he disappeared into the kitchen.

Uncle Rowan frowned.

There was a silence. Charlotte said softly, "Joey, I think maybe we ought to talk. Do you want to?"

Joey didn't want to talk; he was afraid of what he would say. But he nodded. "Sure, Ma."

"We've been through it before, but you're troubled, I see that, and it won't do any harm to speak." She paused, groping for words. She was slender, more youthful in appearance than her forty-nine years would suggest; but she moved slowly, and spoke slowly. "Your daddy ought to be here, but he won't be home until eleven, and I'm just afraid you aren't going to last that long," she said.

"I told you, I'm all right," Joey said.

"No," his mother said, "you're not. You're worried."

"Worried?" Joey tried with all his strength to keep calm, but the air had gone from the room, and there was only the still heat, filling him. He had tried in every way to keep his opinions away from his parents, to make them think he believed as they did, but now, tonight, it was more than he could do.

"Worried? For God's sake—"

The words came up; he felt them coming, sour and acid, and they told all that he felt; and he fought them. But why? She was going to get hurt anyway. Why not hurt her a little now?

"Ma—"

There was a knock at the door. A brisk, businesslike knock.

He let the breath out of his lungs, turned, opened the door.

"Hello, Joey."

A tall, husky man in a black suit stood at the threshold. In an odd sort of way, he resembled pictures of the great fighter, Jack Johnson; but there was nothing rugged about his features.

"Hello, Reverend."

Joey stepped back and motioned the man inside.

"No," the man said. He tipped his hat in the direction of Charlotte Green. "Charlotte, I wonder if you'd mind if Joey and I took a little walk?"

"You're welcome here."

"I know that. But it's a hot night, and I have something kind of private to discuss. Do *you* mind, Joey?"

Joey shook his head.

"Just be back in time to get some sleep," his mother said.

He walked down the steps with the man in the black suit, out onto the dusty road. The darkness was full; The Huddle had closed for the evening.

They walked for several minutes, then the husky man said, "Joey, I think you have a lot on your mind. A lot trying to get out. Maybe I can help."

Joey found it difficult to lie. He had known Finley Mead ever since childhood, had listened to the man's sermons—sometimes glowing and peaceful and full of poetry; sometimes thundering—and he respected him. More than that: he felt a kinship with him. Finley Mead was one of the few colored people in Simon's Hill with whom Joey could talk, without talking down. He was a preacher, maybe: but he was sharp.

"You know, Reverend," he said. "Don't you?"

"I think so," the man said. "See if I'm right. You don't want to go to the white school tomorrow. You don't think this integration idea is going to work. And you're afraid to say what you think out loud."

Joey sighed. Just getting it unbottled a little, just that much helped.

"It's tough on you," the minister continued. "Especially tough. You're twenty years old. You had to miss a lot of school to pitch in for the family. Now things are almost, you might say, wound up for you. One more year at that Farragut school and you can graduate and go on to college. In the East."

"Yes, sir."

"I understand, Joey. And it don't seem right to you, pulling you out of a good thing and putting you right back here in a nest of trouble."

Joey fumbled for a cigarette, dropped his hands quickly. "If I thought it would work," he said, "that would be different. But it won't."

"How do you know it won't?"

"You read as much as I do. Just look at things. Things as they are, I mean as they really are, not the way Ma wants them to be."

"You think you're going to make them better by running away?"

"I don't think it'll make any difference," Joey said. "Not now. People are people."

Again, silence. The night thrummed with insect noises, but there was no other sound. The streets of Simon's Hill were empty. Its houses were quiet.

"Joey," the minister said, "we've always gotten along pretty good, you and me. Isn't that right?"

"Sure," Joey said.

"You think of me as a friend?"

"Sure."

The heavy man put his hands in his pockets. He was a giant dark shadow standing over Joey; old, but strong. Very strong.

"You're not a baby any more; you're grown, almost," he said. "So I'm going to talk to you that way."

Joey sat down on a ledge of dirt.

"First off, I want to tell you that I know how you feel, and why. When this first came up, I felt pretty much the same way. Scared, kind of. Worried. Everything was going smooth, nobody had troubles, I thought—why stir things up? In fact, I'll tell you something secret: I asked your mama to quit. I did." He smiled. "Why don't you have a smoke? I think the Lord'll forgive it this once."

Joey nodded gratefully, lit a cigarette, pulled the smoke into his lungs.

"Well," the preacher went on, "she said she wasn't about to quit, and she told me why. I don't think I'm ever going to forget that night: Charlotte talked for two hours, I believe. She told me her reasons. And, Joey—I couldn't argue. I couldn't argue with those reasons. Because they were good, they were right: your mama was talking sense. She's a smart woman."

"I know that, Reverend."

"I know you do. But being smart isn't enough. She's got something else; she's got guts, Joey. And that, now, is quite a combination. See, I was comfortable then. Comfortable—just like everybody else. A long time ago, I'd said the same thing you just said—'People are people, you can't change people'—and I gave up. It was way too big to fight, I thought—so I shut it out. Shut it right out. And forgot about it. But just because you patch a hole and forget about it, that doesn't mean the hole is gone. It's there; it's there; and your mama, she showed me the patch. And that's all I can see now.... That's the way it is with the truth. Once it's out, there's no undoing it. A man can think he's white all his life —until he looks in a mirror and sees that he's black." Finley Mead paused. "But I'm preaching at you, Joey, and I don't mean to do that."

Joey knocked some ash off the cigarette. "I don't mind," he said. "But—well, sir, I looked into that mirror quite a while back, and I know what color I am."

"You never have been what I said, comfortable—have you, Joey?"

"No, sir."

"Then you're lucky."

"Lucky? Reverend, lucky? Listen, this 'truth'—what's so good about it? The people on the hill are happy, now. They're Negroes, and they can't go to the movie in town, and they can't go to the restaurants in town, and they can't get jobs in town. They're ignorant and dumb and poor—but, Reverend, listen, they're happy. Isn't that something? I only wish to God I could be that way. Look at my own brothers! You think it bothers them they've got to live in this filthy neighborhood? You think it bothers Albert?"

"Get it out, Joey."

"Albert's the happiest kid I know. He has a ball all day long." Joey flipped the cigarette away. "Well," he said, "isn't that what it's all about? I mean, so, all right, so we show Albert the 'truth.' We tell him he's got all the rights the white people do. He's just as good. 'Course, he doesn't believe it, at first—because, don't kid yourself, he's prejudiced—the most prejudiced people I know live all around me. They know they're coons and they know coons are inferior. That's the way it is. So what? All right; so we get Albert all hipped with the truth, and then, finally, maybe he believes it. Maybe he gets to thinking he *is* as good as anyone else. Then he goes into town and tries to order a milk shake at the drugstore. What happens then, Reverend?"

The preacher was silent.

"Can't you see?" Joey said, letting it all spill out now, all the things he'd felt and thought. "Albert's going to get mad when they pull him down off of that stool and kick his behind. He's going to get mad. I mean—oh, lookit, they're *happy.* The truth isn't going to do anything but make them miserable for the rest of their lives!"

Reverend Finley Mead removed a large handkerchief and blew his nose. He was quiet for a while, making a small sound in his throat that sounded like "Um-hmm, um-hmm." A worried, nervous sound. "I don't think you ever heard me say that the truth was easy," he said, very slowly. "Maybe it's the hardest thing in the world, I don't know. But where do you suppose we'd be without it?"

Joey smiled, without amusement. "Well, where *are* we, Reverend?" he said.

"Who do you mean by 'we'? You and me? I'm talking about the world."

"*This* is the world!" Joey said, sweeping his hand toward the dirt road and the wooden shacks and the crumbling apartments.

"You don't really believe that."

"They do. Ask Mr. Yates over there. Ask Jimmy Budlong."

"No. I'll ask you. Is it?"

Joey was silent.

"I wonder, Joey—do you still believe in God?"

He looked up at the big man, startled by the question.

"I don't mean the Baptist God, now, in particular. Just God."

"Sure," Joey said, after some consideration. "I do."

"Then you believe in conscience, in right and wrong?"

"I guess so."

"If you want to steal something at a store and stop because your conscience says no, you don't feel happy, do you?"

"No."

"To get right down to it, if it wasn't for the fact that you *know* there's a right and wrong, you'd probably have a lot more fun, now wouldn't you? Things would be easier. Well—there are people like that; all over. People who don't see the rules. If they want to steal something, they steal it, go right ahead—so what? They don't know any of God's restrictions . . . but they don't know any of His blessings, either. Do you envy them?"

Joey got up, wiped his hands along his trousers, tried to pull the warm night air into him.

"It's the same thing, isn't it?" the preacher went on. "Don't ever envy someone who doesn't see the truth, Joey, no matter how happy he seems to be. Because it's not real happiness. It's not a human being's happiness. And that's what you are: a human being. That's why I say you're lucky."

"If I thought it would work, Reverend—if I thought it really had a chance—"

"Joey, now, listen to me. I said I knew how you felt because I felt that way, too; and I didn't lie. But none of that makes any difference now. Because the tiger's loose, boy, and it's running. Everybody's going to get a good look at it. Everybody. We don't have any little dark secret to keep to ourselves, not any more. You understand? That's all past. That's why it's *got* to work!"

Joey picked up a fistful of soft dirt and squeezed it.

The preacher's voice got lower. "That's why I'm talking to you," he said. "Because whether it does work or not is going to depend an awful lot on you, Joey."

"On me?"

"That's right. Someone's got to hang onto that tiger—someone who's been around it for a long time. Otherwise, Albert *will* get mad; and that'll be the end. Because we can't go back. After tomorrow, nobody on Simon's Hill will ever be able to go back."

Joey wanted to look away, but he couldn't.

"You're a leader," the preacher said. "You're smart and the kids know it. They'll follow you. They'll do what you do. So what it comes to, pretty much, is this: if it works with you, Joey, it will work with the others. And everybody in the country is going to be watching; every principal in every school in every small town in the South; watching, waiting to see what will happen. So what you believe just doesn't matter any more. Do you understand what I'm saying?"

Joey felt tears stinging into his eyes.

"That's the way it is, sometimes," the preacher said, "sometimes a person just finds himself with a job that nobody else can do." He smiled. "It's going to be tough—tougher than you could imagine, I guess. You'll get fire in your blood and you'll want to fight, or quit, or let somebody else do it. You'll have the hate and the bitterness roaring in your ears all day and all night, Joey. And you'll curse me and your mother and God Himself; yes. I'm telling you in advance."

Joey listened to the wind. He thought of his parents and of his plans—his plans. And he felt that a steel cage was being lowered onto him, and that he'd never get out.

"Do you think you can do it?" the preacher asked.

"I don't know," Joey said.

"Will you try?"

Joey hesitated. The cage was over him. But the door was still open.

"Will you?"

Much later, long after the lights were out and he had made his answer, Joey heard his Uncle Rowan muttering:

"Some of these Negroes is gonna get a lot of us niggers killed."

9

They came down the hill together, in a group, moving slowly, treading softly, speaking hardly at all. A tall, lithe young man was at the front. He wore a white shirt and dark trousers and a lightweight jacket; he walked on the balls of his feet like an athlete, and swung his arms, but there was nothing cocky about his manner. Directly behind him were three young girls, two of them very dark, with kinky hair, the third a light tan color. Behind the girls were eight boys.

"Jesus," a man said to himself.

Phil Dongen turned his head away from the Negroes and

looked at the man, who was short, with the kind of hard, wrinkled skin one sees in those areas where men must work outside; the wrinkles ran like vast dirt-filled cracks along the neck and down the cheeks. He was staring openmouthed.

"Well," said Dongen in a whisper, "it's started."

The man nodded. "By Christ, look at 'em."

The Negroes were moving like a dark clot among the rushing stream of white children. The town was quiet. People lined the streets, eyes were focused like telescopes, but it was quiet; only a soft murmuring disturbed the morning air.

Lorenzo Niesen shook his head. A tiny core of awareness began to throb inside him: it was seldom that he summoned a thought or an emotion, his mind had fallen to rust, to decay over the long years, but now an awareness throbbed. Niggers were in town. Nigger children were on their way to the school. He was seeing it. And he wondered, how did it happen? Why didn't somebody tell me?

"Looka there."

Lorenzo Niesen shifted the wad of Beech Nut chewing tobacco in his mouth. He was a "jumpin' preacher" and insisted on a Reverend before his name, and, as with so many of the poor whites, he had once traveled a circuit, trying to preach. But he lacked the gift of language. He'd never been able to stir people's hearts, because he was never truly stirred himself; now, and for a decade, he existed on the meager handouts that came from an occasional Meeting—when hunger would throw his memory back to the nights he had spent aping the words of the Holy Bible. He lived alone, in a hillside shack that he'd constructed himself with the help of friends. He did have friends, all as poor as himself. And a few of them liked him. He needed little else. Only once in a while would come the urge for expression; but he did not recognize the urge. He called it "feelin' the devil" and cured it with the whiskey he bought, or begged, from Len Backus's still.

Life had cheated Lorenzo Niesen. He had a hot furnace somewhere inside him, a holy fire waiting to burn out sin—yet he lived in a placid, sinless town. He could rail against Sex, or thunder cautions on crimes uncommitted, but he did not have the ability to see sin where it was not. Long ago he had planned, vaguely, to go to the city, where godless practices flourished in every dark alley; but now he knew that he would remain forever in Caxton. He was sixty-two. He was an aging knight with a sword in his hand, and he would willingly do battle with any dragon that might wander into his country, but—there was no point in going out of one's way to look for enemies.

He lacked only one thing, and this galled him.

He lacked respect.

"By God," he said.

Phil Dongen nodded. He was a large man with round, rimless spectacles. He, too, had a weathered look; as if his skin were many layers thicker than ordinary skin, tougher and harder. He had straight dark hair that was gray about the temples. "It makes you sick to the stomach," he said, "don't it?"

Dongen had lived in Caxton for sixteen years; for sixteen years he had operated the Ace Hardware Store, on Broad Street, averaging sixty dollars a week. It was more than enough for him. He had helped Bart Carey on the F.C.G. and was violently opposed to integration: It gave him something to be against; something to occupy thoughts that would otherwise be diffuse, scattering cloudlike over the daily business of living. His wife Frieda shared his views, conversationally; but they meant nothing to her.

"That's the Green kid," Niesen said, "up there leadin' them."

"Yeah. Well, that's about what you'd expect."

"Yeah. By God."

The two men stood quietly, staring; then, when the little parade had passed, they fell in behind, walking in cadence, not knowing why they were following.

"You gonna be at the courthouse tonight?" Dongen asked.

"What for?"

"Got a man in town says he's gonna stop all this shit."

"Who?"

"I don't know. He's giving a speech."

"Part of the thing you fellas have, you and Bart?"

"No."

They walked. . . .

It was creepy, in a way, Ella thought: odd. She had never seen so many Negroes in the street before. Maybe some of them would occupy the same room—which she didn't want, in a sense, and, in another, craved. It was exciting; that was certainly true. She was dressed in the white blouse and dark skirt she'd ironed the night before, and her face was scrupulously prepared—just a touch, an invisible touch, of make-up.

She walked with Lucy, but they didn't talk. Once in a while, Lucy would look back and giggle, but they didn't talk.

They soon outdistanced the little troupe, crossed the wide lawn, mingled with the crowd of students, and forgot about the news.

Somebody said, "Hi, kid." Ella turned and saw Hank Kitchen. Her heart jumped a couple of times, settled.

"Hi," she said, dispassionately.

They looked at one another for a while. It wasn't possible, but Hank seemed bigger, huskier than before. He had a scrubbed and youthful look about him. His clothes were perfect. The flannels pressed and creased, the white shirt crackling, shoes shined to brilliance, hair exactly three-quarters of an inch high, squared off as though with a ruler.

"See you," he said, and vaulted up the stairs.

Lucy giggled again. "You going to go with him this semester?"

"I don't know," Ella said. "The way he's been acting; you know."

"Sure," Lucy said, "I know. And this new fellow, too."

They both took one more look over their shoulders, saw the band of Negroes moving toward the grass, and went up the stairs and into the dim and echoing hall of the school.

Harley Paton watched quietly. There was no emotion on his face, though laughter-lines webbing out from his eyes managed to give him a perpetually pleasant look. However, the feeling in his heart was not pleasant.

He glanced at the English teacher, Agnes Angoff, who was watching also, and said: "What do you think?"

Miss Angoff smiled. "I think I'm happy," she said. "I think that things are going to go fine."

"Why?"

"I don't know, I'm not sure. But—I have this kind of feeling. I think I told you, I checked into their scholastic records. The MacDowell girl is close to straight A."

"Good."

"And Joseph Green has received excellent marks."

"Well," Paton said, "you've got to remember though, Miss Angoff, that's at Lincoln."

"I know. But it's a good sign anyway."

"What about the others?"

"About the same as with any group of kids," the woman said. "A few laggards—the Vaughan and Read boys, for instance. But there's nothing unusual. No record of any troublemakers; that's the main thing."

"Yes, I suppose that's the main thing," Paton said, thinking that it would be even better if there were no troublemakers among Caxton's white students. But there were. Out of eight hundred or so kids, he thought, you'll always find a good number of wise ones.

Fortunately, he knew who they were. And he planned to give each of them a stern talk, tomorrow.

Miss Angoff was still smiling. The other teachers—Mr. Lowell, math; Mrs. Gargan, home economics; Mrs. Meekins, world government—wore noncommittal expressions.

Paton said, "I've always been a little afraid of this moment. After the vacation and all the relaxation, then the onslaught all over again. They're advancing on us like soldiers."

"But orderly soldiers," Miss Angoff said.

Paton shrugged. He watched the dotted, moving lawn, and sighed. His father was principal of the Carlson high school, twenty-eight miles away; his grandfather had taught at the University; he no longer wondered how it was that he had become a principal. It was inevitable. The fact that he didn't enjoy the job— except for the children, and the problems they brought to him —made little difference. The world went that way.

He watched the Negroes stepping onto the lawn, watched the townspeople—about seventy-five of them—following, watched the awkwardly loping white students, and felt that it was altogether too good to be true, too fine to last. In his university days he had dreamt of such a moment, but never with any degree of seriousness. Now it was happening; and he couldn't accept it.

"Do you think there will be trouble?" Mrs. Gargan asked suddenly.

Paton was about to answer, when Mr. Lowell broke in. "Of course there'll be trouble. These kids are their parents' children. But maybe it won't be too bad; maybe we'll be able to control it."

"Of course we will," snapped Miss Angoff. She was a stout but still attractive woman in her middle thirties. There was a quiet strength about her, but also an almost adolescent enthusiasm which sometimes rankled her colleagues. Nothing pained Agnes Angoff so much as to give a student a failing grade; however, she did not allow this tendency to show. On the outside—to the pupils—she was capable of being stern and cold and businesslike. They respected her, but they did not fear her.

"I hope so," Mrs. Gargan said wistfully. "I certainly do hope so. This is a nice school."

Paton felt a happily resistible desire to kick Mrs. Gargan in the fanny. He had experienced the urge many times before. For Mrs. Gargan was that paradox: a woman of intelligence—at least, a woman with an accumulation of knowledge—who nonetheless shared all the common prejudices, hates, likes, of the public. She never saw the dark, mysterious side of youth. She liked things to go well. As long as things went well, Mrs. Gargan was happy.

The Principal of Caxton High School came close, occasionally, to admitting that he had little respect for any member of his faculty, with the exception of Miss Angoff.

"Well," Mr. Lowell said gruffly, "I guess we better get ready."

"Yes," Paton said.

Tom McDaniel lit a cigarette and wondered why things had gone so smoothly: it violated all his fears, and many of his expectations. He was not actually disappointed, except in himself. He had been positive that there would be demonstrations: demonstrations would justify his apprehensions, the remarks he had made in his column, and the long fight he had waged. But the simple fact was, nothing whatever had happened. The Negro children had come down off the hill, they'd walked through the town, and now they were going across the lawn to the school.

Tom was about to leave, when he heard the first shout. It was a tentative, nervous little yell; but it carried.

"Hey-a, niggers!"

He jerked himself back to reality and began to search the ranks of the people. He saw one man, one red-faced man, and he knew at once who had yelled. Abner West. Employed at the Towne Dry Cleaners as a delivery man; a cipher. But a member of the Farragut County Federation for Constitutional Government . . .

"Git on home. We don't want you!"

The band of Negroes stopped, as though suddenly reined in. Joey Green swiveled, hands balled into fists.

Someone else in the crowd cried: "We don't want you, black niggers!"

Who was it?

Lorenzo Niesen—the Jumpin' Preacher; straining like a bantam cock, face all flushed, eyes excited.

Another voice: "This here's a white school!"

But no one moved. The voices rose and fell, like sporadic gunfire.

Then Tom saw other people walking—marching—toward the lawn. They were carrying placards, some pierced by sticks, others more hastily thrown together. He got out his notebook, flipped back the cover, readied a pencil, and tried to read the signs.

Most were marked: GO HOME NIGGERS!!!

Others were slightly more elaborate: THIS IS A SCHOOL FOR WHITE PEOPLE WE DON'T WANT NIGRAS!!!

Fifteen people, in all, with placards: some of them recognizable to Tom, others not. Six were women. He could pick out Mabel Dodge and Edna Callendar. They brandished their signs with a determination which was obviously necessary to cover their embarrassment. They were sure of their cause, but not of their strength.

Some of the sign holders were youngsters, high school freshmen. They all grinned self-consciously, as though they were not quite aware of what they were doing or why.

Tom wrote, hurriedly: . . . picket line formed. Orderly. Taunts from crowd led by Abner West.

"They don't look so goddamn uppity now," someone said to Tom. He turned to face Gilly Davenport, the town barber. Gilly was smiling happily. "Bet they're kinda pale underneath that tan," he said.

Tom walked away. He wondered where the signs had come from: the lettering was identical on each—a crude scrawl, but in dark ink, probably India ink. Only one store in Caxton sold India ink.

He made another note.

The Negroes were standing still as dark statues; then, Joey Green moved his head, turned, and started to walk toward the school again. The people moved in closer, but allowed room for passage.

The spell was broken; the white students who had not filed inside sprang again into motion; they went up the steps.

When Harley Paton appeared at the door, the placard carriers stopped.

The crowd quieted.

They saw the look in the principal's eyes—which was neither condemnatory nor angry but was clearly disapproving—and paused, also.

Joey Green led the eleven other children up the stairs and into the hall. Principal Paton stood quietly until all the students were in, then he went inside and closed the door.

In measured tones he said: "My name is Harley Paton; you've spoken with me before, I believe. I am the principal of this high school." He did not put out his hand. "Things are going to be a little hectic today, so you'll have to be patient. You'll all be assigned to your classes as soon as we can get around to it."

Joey felt some of the tension draining away. The gauntlet had been run, and it hadn't been as bad as he'd expected; still, he could see the signs and the looks on the faces of the people. . . .

He threw a glance of confidence to the children clustered loosely around him, and they lined up at the principal's office.

There was a lot of waiting, a lot of squinting of the eyes to ignore the bold stares and foolish grins of the white students, who were also in line; but eventually the business was over, they were all assigned to their classes, assigned to their seats, given their lists.

After what seemed like hours, Joey, Joseph Dupuy, and Archie Vaughan were seated in a large, green room. It smelled of dust and chalk, very much the way the room at Lincoln High had smelled. At the front was the teacher's desk, and behind it, the large blackboard—now hopelessly gray. Battered erasers lay on their five felt spines, along with new chalk. There was a bowl of flowers on a table by the window, which was open.

The teacher rose and smiled at the group. Joey tried not to think of the others, of the white children, or even of his situation; he looked ahead, trying to force everything but the first day at school from his head. He sat at attention.

"I am Miss Angoff," the teacher said, in a rather high-pitched voice. "You will learn English in this room, which will also serve as your base of operations, so to speak. Will those of you who have been with me previously please raise your hands?"

There was a showing of hands.

"Those who are new? Your hands, please?"

Joey raised his; Archie and Joseph followed suit. There were seven others.

"Now may I have your names? Beginning with the first row, left."

The new students spoke their names: Edward Haycraft, Julius Matthews, Neil Jay Hummert, Lucy Egan, George Lee Robinson, Ina Peters, Archibald Vaughan, Daniel Humboldt, Joseph Dupuy ("Doo-pwee," he said, carefully; and there was a ripple of laughter), Joseph Green.

"I am very glad to meet you," Miss Angoff said. "I hope you'll be glad to have met me." She took great care not to gaze at any student in particular. "I think we have a mutual obligation, class —and those of you who have heard this little speech will, I hope, bear with me. I mean to say, you all expect certain things of me. You expect me to be a good teacher, to know my subject, to express myself in such a way that you will all learn. On the other hand, I expect you to be good students. You're young, as I once was, and attention tends to wander, I know; therefore, I don't require you to concentrate solely on your lessons. That would be asking too much."

Another ripple of laughter—nervous, dutiful.

"However," the teacher went on, "I do think I have a right to expect the very best you're capable of. Whatever you may have thought about English up to now, however deadly dull you may have considered it, I think you're going to change your minds. For I happen to believe that English is not only one of the most important subjects in the world, but also—"

"Niggers get the hell out!"

The voice filtered in sharply through the open window. Miss Angoff stiffened, but went on. Joey watched her.

"Sentence construction will be abandoned in this course, and we will instead concentrate on—"

"Harley Paton's a no-good nigger-lovin son of a bitch!"

Miss Angoff paused; then, calmly, she walked to the window, closed it, and returned to her place by the desk.

Her voice was a bit strained now, and forced. "We will concentrate instead on usage. Correct usage."

Joey gripped the edge of the desk and said nothing. His blood was on fire, but he said nothing.

If this woman could control herself, so could he.

For a while, anyway. . . .

Tom McDaniel returned to the *Messenger* office in a hurry. He opened the door and walked over to the old man who'd worked in the building as long as there had been a building.

"Jack."

The room looked more like a stationery store than a news-paper office. There were two glass display cases, each containing pen and pencil sets, erasers, maps of the town, rulers, typewrit-ers. Tom's den was in a small room to the right. The secretaries worked behind the store.

"You have a customer this morning?" Tom asked.

Jack Allardyce looked up. "What?"

"Did you have a customer today?"

"Yeah. Young fella. He was waiting when I opened."

"Young fella. With dark hair, a dark suit on?"

"Uh huh."

"What'd he buy?"

"Why—some poster paper, I think. Yes. And some ink. What's wrong?"

"Nothing," Tom said. He wheeled and walked quickly into his den.

He moved the mountainous debris on his desk aside, inserted a yellow sheet of paper into the typewriter, and thought for a moment. Then he typed: THE WAY WE LOOK AT IT. And paused again.

He ripped the paper out, spinning the platen, and crushed it into a yellow ball in his hands.

He lit a cigarette.

Calm down, he told himself. What are you getting so excited about? You expected a display, didn't you? A bigger one than this. It was perfectly orderly, wasn't it?

Calm down.

Just a little reaction, nothing else to it. Never write when you're mad. Think things out. Then write.

Everything's fine....

In a short while he was breathing regularly again. Then Jack Allardyce poked his thatched head in. "How'd it go?" he asked.

"What? Oh. A little shouting, that's all. It went all right."

"It did, huh? I'll be damned."

The old man stood poised between rooms. "You gonna want to send me to that meeting tonight?" he said. "Or what?"

"Meeting?"

"Yeah, you know, that fella—he's holding some kind of a thing in front of the courthouse, seven o'clock. Don't know what it's about."

Tom reached for his cigarette. He stubbed it out against the side of the metal wastebasket, took a breath.

"Well," he said, slowly, "it probably won't amount to a damn thing. But I don't have much to do tonight. I'll cover it myself."

10

When the bell in the steeple rang to mark the half hour that had passed since six P.M., Caxton wore the same tired face that it always wore in the summer. The heat of the afternoon throbbed on. Cars moved up and down George Street like painted turtles, and the people moved slowly, too: all afraid of the motion that would send the perspiration coursing, the heart flying.

Adam Cramer sat in the far booth at Joan's Cafe, feeling grateful for the heat, trying to eat the soggy ham sandwich he had ordered. He knew the effect of heat on the emotions of people: Summer had a magic to it, a magic way of frying the nerve ends, boiling the blood, drying the brain. Perhaps it made no sense logically but it was true, nonetheless. Crimes of violence occurred with far greater frequency in hot climates than in cold. You would find more murders, more robberies, more kidnapings, more unrest in the summer than at any other time.

It was the season of mischief, the season of slow movements and sudden explosions, the season of violence.

Adam looked out at the street, then at the thermometer that hung behind the cash register. He could see the line of red reaching almost to the top.

How would The Man on Horseback have fared, he wondered, if it had been twenty below zero?

How would Gerald L. K. go over in Alaska?

He pulled his sweat-stained shirt away from his body and smiled. Even the weather was helping him!

He forced the last of the sandwich down, slid a quarter beneath the plate, and paid for his meal; then he went outside.

It was a furnace.

A dark, quiet furnace.

He started for the courthouse, regretting only that Max Blake could not be here. Seeing his old teacher in the crowd, those dark eyes snapping with angry pleasure, that cynical mouth twitching at the edges—damn!

Well, I'll write you about it, he thought. That'll be almost as good.

The picture of the man who had set his mind free blurred and vanished and Adam walked faster.

The Reverend Lorenzo Niesen was the first to arrive. His felt hat was sodden, the inner band caked with filth; his suspenders hung loosely over his two-dollar striped shirt; his trousers were shapeless—yet he was proud of his appearance, and it was a vicious, thrusting pride. Were someone to hand him a check for five thousand dollars, he would not alter any part of his attire. It was country-honest, as he himself was. Whoever despised dirt despised likewise the common people, God's favorites.

Was there soap in Bethlehem?

Did the Apostles have nail files and lotions?

He sat down on the grass, glared at the bright lights of the Reo motion picture theatre across the street, and began to fan himself with his hat. Little strands of silver hair lifted and fell, lifted and fell, as he fanned.

At six thirty-five, Bart Carey and Phillip Dongen appeared. They nodded at Lorenzo and sat down near him.

"Well, it's hot."

Others drifted into the area, some singly, some in groups.

"Hot!"

By six forty, over one hundred and fifty residents of Caxton were standing on the cement walk or sitting on the grass, waiting.

"You see 'em this morning?"

Fifty more showed up in the next ten minutes.

"Christ, yes."

At seven a bell was struck and a number of cars screeched, halted, discharging teen-age children. They crowded at the steps of the courthouse.

It was quiet.

Ten minutes passed. Then, a young man in a dark suit walked across the empty street. He nodded at the people, made his way through the aisle that parted for him, and climbed to the top step. He stood there with his back to the courthouse door.

"That him?" Phil Dongen whispered.

Bart Carey said, "Yeah."

Lorenzo Niesen was silent. He studied the young man, trying to decide whether or not he approved. Awful green, he thought. Too good of a clothes on him. Like as not a Northerner.

I don't know.

The crowd's voice rose to a murmuring, then fell again as the young man in the dark suit lifted his hands in the air.

"Folks," he said, in a soft, almost gentle voice, "my name is Adam Cramer. Some of you know me by now and you know what I'm here for. To those I haven't had a chance to talk with yet, let me say this: I'm from Washington, D.C., the Capital, and I'm in Caxton to help the people fight the trouble that's come up."

He smiled suddenly and took off his coat. "I only wish one thing, though," he said. "I wish school started in January. I mean, it is *hot*. Aren't you hot?"

Hesitant, cautious laughter followed.

"Well," Adam Cramer said, dropping his smile, "it's going to get hotter, for a whole lot of people. I'll promise you that. This here little town is going to burn, what I mean; it's going to burn the conscience of the country, now, and put out a light that everyone and everybody will see and feel. This town, I'm talking about. Caxton!" He paused. "People, something happened today. You've all heard about it by now. Some of you saw it with your own eyes. What happened was: Twelve Negroes went to the Caxton high school and sat with the white children there. Nobody stopped them, nobody turned them out. And, friends, listen; that makes today the most important day in the history of the South. Why? Because it marks the *real* beginning of integration. That's right. It's been tried other places, but you know what they're saying? They're saying, Well, if it works in Caxton, it'll work all over, *because Caxton is a typical Southern town*. If the people don't want integration, they'll do something about it! If they don't do something about it, that means they want it! Two plus two equals four!

"Except there's one thing wrong. They're saying you all don't give a darn whether the whites mix with the blacks because you haven't really got down to fighting; but I ask you, how can somebody fight what he doesn't see? They've kept the facts away from you; they've cheated and deceived every one of you, and filled your heads with filthy lies. It has all been a calculated campaign to keep you in the dark, so that when you finally do wake up, Why, we're sorry, it's just too late!

"All right; I'm associated with the Society of National American Patriots, which is an organization dedicated to giving the people the truth about desegregation. We've been studying this situation here ever since January, when Judge Silver made his decision, and I'm going to give that situation to you. Of course, many present now are fully aware of it. Many have done what they consider their best to prevent it from happening. But there are quite a few who simply do not know the facts; who don't know either what led up to that black little parade into the school today, or what real significance it has for everyone in the country.

"I ask you to bear with me, folks, but I give you fair warning now. When you do know the truth, you're going to be faced with a decision. You don't think you've got one now, but you do, all right, and you'll see it. And it'll get inside your blood and make it boil and you won't be able to run away from it! Because I'm going to show you that the way this country is going to go depends entirely and wholly and completely on *you!*"

Tom McDaniel put away his note-pad and walked over to his friend, the lawyer James Wolfe. Wolfe, he noticed, was staring, strained and curious and expectant, like all the others. And, for some reason, this annoyed him. "Sound familiar?" he said.

Wolfe started. "Oh—Tom. Yes, he seems to be a pretty smart kid."

"But a phony," Tom said.

"Oh?"

"Absolutely. The accent's fake; I talked with him earlier. He thinks it's going to work!"

"What?"

"The plain-folks routine."

"And you don't?" Wolfe nodded toward the crowd. "I can't say I entirely agree."

"Do you think it's trouble, Jim?"

"No," Wolfe said, glancing away from Tom. "The time for trouble's over."

"Everything," Adam Cramer was saying, "has got to have a beginning. And the beginning to what you saw today was almost
seventeen years ago. In 1940, a Negro woman named Charlotte
Green, and her husband, let it be known that they didn't care
much for the equal facilities that were being offered to their
children. No sooner were the words out of their mouths but the
NAACP swooped down. You all know about this organization,
I imagine. The so-called National Association for the Advance-
ment of Colored People is now and has always been nothing but
a Communist front, headed by a Jew who hates America and
doesn't make any bones about it, either. They've always operated on the 'martyr' system, which is: They pick out trouble spots
or create them where they never existed, and start putting out
publicity. Like take the Emmet Till case. A nigger tries to rape
a white woman and tells her husband he'll keep on trying and
nobody is going to stop him. The husband can't go to the police
with just a threat, so he makes sure, like any of us would, that
no nigger is going to rape his wife. Now those are the facts. But
what happens? The NAACP moves in and says that the white
man is a murderer! Yeah, for protecting his own wife! And you
know the bitter tears was shed over that poor, mistreated little
colored boy, poor little Emmet Till whose only crime was being
dark! Any of you read about it?" Adam Cramer shook his head
in mock consternation. "The coon was made into a martyr, what
they call, and things were rolling along real good, until somebody with some brains showed how Emmet Till's Hero Daddy
—you remember how they said that's what he was, and he died
in line of duty overseas?—was *hanged* and given a dishonorable
discharge for, see if you can guess it: rape! Uh-huh! Of course, the
jury wasn't hoodwinked and declared those men who taught the
nigger boy a lesson (and it wasn't ever even proved they'd done
anything more!) innocent. But the old N-double-A-C-P almost
had it knocked.

"Anyway, that's how those guys work. For all I know, they
hired this Green woman (she lives on Simon's Hill) to stir things
up in the first place. They put the pressure on between 1940 and
1949, pretending that all they wanted, you see, was really equal
separate facilities. Farragut County said all right and helped the

Negroes send their kids to an accredited school, Lincoln High, in Farragut. I visited this school, friends, and there isn't a thing wrong with it. It's a whole sight cleaner and neater than any place these nigger kids ever saw before, like as not; and that's for sure! But the Commie group tipped its hand right then and showed, for all to see, that it was after something different. Does September 1950 mean anything to you people? Well, it was the second big step toward today. In September 1950 a bunch of Negro boys tried to enroll in Caxton High! Remember?"

There was a murmuring from the crowd.

"Why?" Adam Cramer asked, modulating his voice to its original softness. "Do you think it was something they thought up by themselves? Would any Southern Negro have that much gall? No, sir. No. The NAACP engineered the whole operation, knowing in advance what would happen! The students were turned away; the county board of education refused to let them in—putting it on the line—and the usual arrangements were made for the Negroes to attend Lincoln. Then, three full months later, five of these kids—*with the full backing of the NAACP*—filed suit against the Farragut County School Board. And that's when the ball really got rolling. The Plaintiffs, these Negroes, claimed that the out-of-county arrangements didn't meet the county's obligation to furnish equal facilities. The District Court said they were crazy and ruled accordingly. All during 1952 and 1954 the case, which had been appealed, was held in abeyance, pending the United States Supreme Court's action in five school segregation cases under consideration at the same time.

"Well, the Commies didn't waste a second. They had most of the world, but America was a pocket of resistance to them. They couldn't attack from outside, so, they were attacking from inside. They knew only too well, friends, that the quickest way to cripple a country is to mongrelize it. So they poured all the millions of dollars the Jews could get for them into this one thing: desegregation.

"In August of 1955, the NAACP demanded a final judgment. Judge Silver, who is a Jew and is known to have leftist leanings—"

"Who says so?" a voice cried.

"The record says so," Adam Cramer said tightly. "Look it

up. Abraham Silver belongs, for one thing, to the Quill and Pen Society, which receives its funds indirectly from Moscow."

Tom McDaniel grinned. He said to Wolfe, "He'll hang himself!"

"You think so?"

"Oh, hell, Jim—people love the judge around here. He's a public idol, and you know it. Everybody knows it wasn't his fault about the ruling!"

"I'm not so sure."

"Well, anyway; the Quill and Pen—that's really stretching it."

"I'm not so sure of that, either," James Wolfe said, in a rather grim voice. "Don't forget, Tom: 'You can fool some of the people all of the time . . .'"

". . . so what did the judge do? He instructed the county school board to proceed with reasonable expedition to comply with the rule to desegregate. In spite of the complete disapproval of the PTA, in spite of the protests of the Farragut County Society for Constitutional Government, in spite of petitions presented by Verne Shipman, one of Caxton's leading citizens, and Thomas McDaniel, the editor of the Caxton *Messenger*—Jedge Abe Silver went right ahead and *ordered* integration for Caxton High School, at a date no later than fall, 1956.

"Mayor Harry Satterly could have stopped it, but he didn't have the guts to, because he knew the powers that were and are behind Silver. He knew how much his skin was worth.

"The Governor could have stopped it in a *second*, but I don't have to tell you about him; I hope I don't, anyway.

"And the principal of the high school, Harley Paton—*he* could have brought the whole mess to a screaming halt. But he's too lily-livered to do the right thing."

"That's a dirty lie!" A young man in a T-shirt and blue jeans walked up to the lower step and glared at Adam Cramer. "The principal done everything he could!"

"Did he? Did he close down the school and refuse to open it until the rights of the town were restored?"

"No, he didn't do that. But—"

"Did he bring the students together and tell them to stay away?"

"Hell, he *couldn't* do that."

"No," Adam Cramer said, smiling condescendingly. "No; he couldn't do that. It would take courage. It would mean risking his fine job and that fat pay-check!"

The young man bunched his fists, reddened, and when someone shouted, "Git on away, let 'im speak his piece, kid!" walked back into the crowd.

"Just a moment," Adam Cramer said. "I know that Harley Paton has a lot of friends. And if I were here for any other purpose than to bring the truth, I'd be smart enough to leave him alone. Wouldn't I? Now I don't say that the principal of Caxton High is necessarily a dishonest man. I merely say, and the facts bring this out, that he is a weak man. And weakness is no more to be tolerated than dishonesty—not when we have our children's future at stake, leastwise! I warned you that the truth would be bitter. It always is. But I ain't going to quit just because I've touched a sore point. No, sir. There's a whole lot of sore points that are going to be touched before I'm through!"

"Keep talking," Lorenzo Niesen called. "We're listening."

"All right. Now, you may think that the problem is simply whether or not we're going to allow twelve Negroes to go to our school; but that's only a small, small part of it. I'm in a position to know because I've been with an organization that's studied the *whole thing*. You don't see the forest for the trees, my friends; believe me. The real problem, whether you like it or not, is whether you're going to sit back and let desegregation spread throughout *the entire South...*"

Verne Shipman stood on the sidewalk, hidden behind the rusted lawn cannon, and listened to Adam Cramer. He listened to the same speech he'd heard earlier, the same statistics, and he observed that the people who comprised the crowd were listening also. Intently. Which, of course, they ought to do, for the words made sense.

However, there was yet no mention of money. No word about

the joining of this organization and the parting with hard-earned funds.

I will listen, he thought, but that will be the test.

"... and it's an indisputable fact," Adam Cramer spoke on, "that there could be no other result. The Negroes will literally, and I do mean *literally,* control the South. The vote will be theirs. You'll have black mayors and black policemen (like they do in New York and Chicago already!) and like as not, a black governor; and black doctors to deliver your babies—if they find the time, that is—and that's the way it'll be. Did you even stop to think about that when you let those twelve enter your white school? Did you?"

The minuscule festive note that had marked the beginning of the meeting was now instantly dissolved. Bart Carey and Phil Dongen wore deep frowns, and Rev. Lorenzo Niesen was shaking his head up and down, up and down, signifying rage.

"Some of us did!" Carey said, in a husky, thickly accented voice.

"I know," Adam Cramer granted. "The Farragut County Federation for Constitutional Government was a step in the right direction. But it didn't accomplish much because the liars have done their jobs well. They've made you think your hands are tied. You couldn't afford fancy lawyers, so you failed. But, Mr. Carey, I'm not talking specifically to you or to those like yourself who have worked to fight this thing. I'm talking to the people who are still confused, in the dark, who haven't fully realized or understood or grasped the meaning of this here ruling. To those, Mr. Carey, who have been soft and who have trusted the government to do right by them. It's a natural thing, you understand. We all love our country, and it's natural to believe that the people who run it are a hundred per cent square. But our great senator from Wisconsin showed us, I think, how wrong that view happens to be. He proved beyond a shadow of a doubt that there are skunks and rats and vermin in the government! Didn't he?"

"That's right!" shouted Lorenzo Niesen. "That's right. God bless the senator!"

"Yes," Adam Cramer said. "Amen to that, sir. We know now

that there are men with fine titles and with great power, wonderful power, who are doing their level best to sell our country out to the Communists. And it's these men, folks, and nobody else, who're cramming integration down your throats. There isn't any question in the world about that."

Slowly Adam Cramer's voice was rising in pitch. Perspiration was running down his face, staining his collar, but he did not make any effort to wipe it away.

"Here's something," he said, "I'll bet you all don't know. In interpreting the school decisions of May 17, 1954 and May 31, 1955, by the United States Supreme Court, Judge John J. Parker of the Fourth Circuit Court of the United States, speaking in the case—" he removed a note from his breast pocket—"of Briggs *versus* Elliot, said: '. . . it is important that we point out exactly what the Supreme Court *has* decided and what it *has not* decided in this case. It has not decided that the Federal Courts are to take over and regulate the public schools of the states. It has not decided that the states *must* mix persons of different races in the schools *or must* require them to attend schools *or must deprive them of the right of choosing the schools they attend.* What it has decided, and all it has decided, is that a *state* may not deny to any person *on account of race* the right to attend any school *that it maintains.* This, under the decision of the Supreme Court, the *state* may not do directly or indirectly; *but if the schools which it maintains are open to children of all races, no violation of the Constitution is involved even though the children of different races voluntarily attend different schools, as they attend different churches.* Nothing in the Constitution or in the decision of the Supreme Court takes away from the *people freedom to choose the schools they attend. The Constitution, in other words, does not require integration. . . .'*

"You get that, people? *'The Constitution does not require integration!'* That's an accurate record of a legal statement. A judge with a sense of justice and fairness said it. But I'm just a-wondering if Abraham Silver mentioned those little teeny things to you. Did he?

"We've got to follow the big law, the ruling and all that; except, I'll say it again, loud and clear, and you listen, every one of you listen: The Constitution don't require integration!"

Adam Cramer stopped talking. His voice had risen sharply on the last five words; now angry silence filled the air above the courthouse lawn.

He continued, almost in a whisper: "Now I'll tell you what this whole long thing is about. It isn't about integration at all—in spite of what that would mean, and I've showed you, I hope, what it would mean. It isn't about the Negroes or having anything against them, either. I don't, any more than you people do. No: the real issue at stake here, friends, is the issue of States' rights. That's what it comes to. According to the Constitution, each state in the union is supposed to have local control of itself, isn't that so? That's supposed to be the *point* of a democratic government. Look at Article One, Section Eight, Paragraph Five, of the U. S. Constitution. Read over your government books in the library. States' rights is the whole meaning behind America—local control of purchasing power, local control of state and county politics, local control of schools. Okay! Now, you let the Federal Government step in and start to give orders—like they're doing now—and you may think it's just a step toward socialism, but that ain't so. It's a step toward communism! The Soviet Union—Russia!—works just that way. A couple of the big boys decide that so much tax is to be levied in every town, or they decide the Siberians are going to share the schools with the whites—or whatever—and nobody can open their mouth. Why? Because in Communist Russia, no one single county *has* any rights of its own. It can't veto any judgments or stop any orders. It can't do anything but sit there and take it.

"You may think I'm getting off the point, or being a little far-fetched, but you're wrong! Friends, the eyes of the world are on Caxton. I've been in Washington, D.C., and I know that to be true. You all are the country's test tube, the guinea pig! That's why I say you've got the future, not only of Caxton, but of *America* in your hands!"

Lucy Egan nudged Ella secretively and smiled. "Boy," she said, "he is really some talker. I mean, he honestly is."

Ella had been listening with a peculiar mixture of pride and uneasiness, and the truth was, she did not know whether to be pleased or displeased. Tom had not seen her yet, for which she was, oddly, grateful (there being no reason to be grateful); he and Mr. Wolfe and some of the others, a few, did not appear to be very happy with the speech Adam Cramer was making, though most of the people were. You could see that.

"Sort of, if you squint, like Marlon Brando," Lucy Egan said, squinting. "Like, mean. A little."

It made no particular sense to Ella, the speech. This dry type of thing that her father and Gramp were always talking about, that was always in the newspapers these days, mostly bored her, and she would have gone back home (where, she supposed, she ought to be, anyway) except that the speaker was Adam Cramer. And she knew, sensed, that she would be seeing him again soon.

"He's really getting them worked up," Lucy Egan said. "There hasn't been anything like this in Caxton in I don't know how long. Don't you think he looks a little like Brando?"

"Kind of," Ella said.

"Did he kiss you good night?" Lucy Egan asked suddenly.

Ella hesitated, noting the anxiousness in her friend's eyes. Then she said: "Sure."

"Boy. I don't guess there was anything else, like."

"Oh, Lucy, come on."

"There *was*?"

"No, no."

"A lot of what you say makes sense," James Wolfe said, stepping forward during a dramatic pause. "And certainly we all agree with you that this ruling was ill-considered. But it is a ruling, and can't be abrogated. I assure you we've tried everything."

"Who are you, sir?" Adam Cramer asked.

"My name is Wolfe, James Wolfe. I'm a lawyer. I spoke personally, you may be interested to know, with Judge Silver, and I'd like to correct you on at least one point. You're giving the impression that a district judge has authority to overrule a federal ruling. That's entirely wrong." James Wolfe turned toward the crowd. "The judge had absolutely no choice in the matter. As a matter off the record, he doesn't think any more of the decision than we do."

"Abraham Silver is a clever man, Mr. Wolfe. You'd have to

have studied the situation and all of its ramifications to understand that, as we do. We—"

"Just a moment. Just a moment. As it happens, Mr. Cramer, I and a group of other qualified men *have* studied the situation. It's all very clear-cut. The Judge Parker quote that you take such stock in is ridiculous as applied to conditions in Caxton. Unless you propose to subrogate legal action with illegal action, I can't see that you've presented anything in the form of a positive idea."

Adam Cramer smiled tolerantly.

"As it happens, Mr. Wolfe," he said, "I do have ideas. And they're absolutely legal. They take courage and daring, now, I'll tell you all that right off the bat. But they're legitimate."

"All right, then, let's have them."

"First, I want to get one thing clear." Adam Cramer spoke distinctly, addressing himself to the entire assemblage. "Do you people want nigras in your school? Answer yes or no!"

There was a roar from the crowd. "No!"

"No," Adam Cramer said, and smiled. "Fine. Now, are you willing to fight this thing down to the last ditch and keep fighting until it's conquered?"

Another roar, like a giant wave: "Yes!"

"Yes. Fine!" Adam Cramer raised his hands, and the people were quiet. "Well, I'm willing to work with you. Maybe you want to know why. After all, I'm not a Southerner. I wasn't born in Caxton. But I *am* an American, friends, and I love my country— and I am ready to give up my life, if that be necessary, to see that my country stays free, white and American!"

Phillip Dongen, who had seldom been moved to such emotional heights, led off the applause. It was a frantic drum roll.

"Friends, listen to me for a minute." The young man's voice was soft again. It rose and fell, the words were soothing, or sharp as gunfire. "Please. Mr. Wolfe, over there, has mentioned something about keeping the attack legal. As far as I'm concerned, something is legal or illegal depending on whether it's right or wrong. If nine old crows in black robes tell me that breathing is against the law, I'm not going to feel like a criminal every time I take a breath. The way I see it, the *people* make the laws, hear? *The people!*"

The car, bearing an out-of-county license plate, swung slowly onto George Street from the highway. It was a 1939 Ford, caked with dust and rusty, loud with the groans of dry metal. It had come a long way. The five people within were limp with the heat, silent and incurious. Only a small part of their minds, like icebergs, were above the conscious level of thought.

Ginger Beauchamp did not move the gear lever from high as they commenced the hill, nor was he concerned with the misfires and rattles that followed. His foot was numb on the accelerator pedal. He could think only of getting through the seventy miles that remained, of falling, exhausted, onto the cot. There was no damn sense to visiting his mother. She didn't appreciate it. If she was so anxious to see him, why didn't she ever try to be a little nice? he thought.

Well, she's old.

I say I ain't going to make this drive no more, but I am. And Harriet will want to come along and bring Willie and Shirley and Pete.

Now, damn. If I could just go myself, then maybe it wouldn't be so damn bad. But I can't. She don't just want to see me, she wants to see the kids. And—

Ginger Beauchamp saw the people gathered on the lawn in front of the courthouse and slowed down.

"What is it?" Harriet said. She opened her eyes, but did not move.

"Nothin'. Go back to sleep, get you plenty of sleep."

He glared at his wife and swore that next week he would make her learn to drive. That would take some of the strain off. Then he could sleep a little, too.

"What is it, Ginger?"

"Nothin', I said."

The car moved slowly, still coughing and gasping with its heavy load. The overhead traffic light turned red. Ginger pumped the brakes three times and put the gear lever in neutral.

Sure a lot of people.

He started to close his eyes, briefly, when out of the engine noise and murmur of the crowd, he heard a sharp, high voice.

"Hey-a, look!"

Then another voice, also high-pitched: "Git 'em, now. Come on!"

Ginger looked around and saw a group of young boys sprinting across the street toward his car. They were white boys.

What the hell, now, he thought.

"Ginger, it's green, Ginger."

He hesitated only a moment; then, when he saw the running people and heard what they were yelling, he put his foot down, hard, on the accelerator.

But he had forgotten to take the car out of gear. The engine roared, ineffectively.

"You niggers, hey. Wait a second, don't you run off, don't you do that!"

Suddenly, the street in front of him was blocked with people. They surrounded the car in a cautious circle, only the young ones coming close.

"What's the trouble?" Ginger asked.

"No trouble," a boy in T-shirt and levis answered. "You looking for trouble?"

"No, I ain't looking for no trouble," Ginger said. The exhaustion had left him. Harriet was staring, getting ready to cry. The children were asleep. "We just goin' on to Hollister."

"Oh, you jes' a-goin' on to Hollister? How do we know that?"

One of the boys put his hands on the window frame and began rocking the car.

"Don't do that now," Ginger said. He was a thin man; his bones poked into his dark black skin like tentpoles. But the muscles in his arms were hard; years of lifting heavy boxes had made them that way.

"Sweet Jesus," Harriet Beauchamp said. She had begun to tremble.

"Hush," Ginger said.

Another boy leaped on the opposite running board, and the rocking got worse.

"Cut it out, now, come on, you kids," Ginger said. "I don't want to spoil nobody's fun, but we got to get home."

"Who says you got to?"

The circle of people moved in, watching. Some of the men

peeled away and approached the car. Their throats were knotted. Their hands were clenched into fists.

A small white man with a crushed felt hat said, "Nobody gave you no permission to drive through Caxton, niggers. They's a highway to Hollister."

"Well, sure," Ginger said, "I know that. But—"

"But nothin'. How come you in our street, gettin' it all messed up?"

The two boys were rocking the car violently now. Pete Beauchamp, aged seven, woke up and began to cry.

Ginger looked at the small man in the crushed hat. "What's the matter with you folks?" he said. "We ain't done nothin'. We ain't done a thing."

"You got our street all dirty," the small man said.

Ginger felt his heart beating faster. Harriet was staring with wide eyes, shuddering.

"Awright," Ginger said. "We sorry. We won't come this way no more."

"That's what you say," another man said. "I figure you lying."

"I don't tell nobody lies, mister," Ginger said. He was trying very hard to hold the anger that was clawing up from his stomach. Dimly he heard a voice calling, *"Stop it. Stop all this, leave them alone!"* but it seemed distant and unreal. "You all just please get out the way, now, and we'll be gone."

"You *tellin'* us?" a boy shouted. "Hey, the coon's tellin' us what to do."

Two more young whites leaped onto the running boards. The Ford rocked violently, back and forth.

"State your business here," the small man said.

"I did," Ginger said. "I told you, we trying to get home."

"That's a crock of plain shit!"

Ginger Beauchamp felt it all explode inside him. He clashed the gear lever into first and said, "You all drunk or crazy, one. I'm driving through here. If you don't want to get yourself run over, move out the way!"

The boy in levis and T-shirt reached in suddenly and pulled the key out of the ignition. Ginger grabbed him, but a fist shot into his neck. He gagged.

Young men with knives began to stab the tires of the Ford, then.

Others threw pebbles into the window. The sharp, hard little stones struck Ginger's face and Harriet's, and the children in the back seat were all awake now, shrilling.

"You crazy!" Ginger shouted. "Gimme back my key!"

"Come and get it, black man!"

"Sure, come on out and get it!"

A stone glanced off Ginger's forehead. He felt a small trickle of warm blood. Now the circle had engulfed the car, and the people were all shouting and yelling, and the Ford was lifted off its wheels.

"Maybe you learn now, maybe you learn we don't want you here!"

"Look at him, chicken!"

"Yah, chicken!"

Ginger forced the door open. The grinning boys jumped back, stared, waiting.

"Honey, don't, please don't!"

Ginger stood there, and a quiet came over the people. They stared at him, and he saw something in their faces that he had never seen before. He was thirty-eight years old, and he'd lived in the South all his life, and his mother had told him stories, but he had never seen anything like this or dreamed that it could happen.

It occurred, suddenly, to Ginger that he was going to die.

And standing there in the middle of the crowd of white people, he wondered why.

The word came out. "Why?"

The small man hawked and spat on the ground. "You ought t' know, nigger," he said.

There was no air. Only the heat and the smell of sweat and heavy breath.

The silence lasted another instant. Then the young men laughed, and ambled loosely over to the car. One of them supported himself on two others, lifted his feet and kicked the rear window. Glass exploded inward.

Ginger Beauchamp sprang, blind with fury. He pushed the

two boys away and confronted the one who had kicked the glass. He was a gangling youth of no more than sixteen. His face was covered with blackheads and his hair hung matted over his forehead like strips of seaweed. He saw Ginger's rage and grinned widely.

"Don't you do it," Harriet cried. "Ginger, don't!"

The thin Negro knew what it would mean to strike a white man; but he also knew what it would mean if he did not fight to protect his family. All of this passed through his mind in a flash. As quickly, he decided.

He was about to smash his fist into the boy's face, when a voice cried, "Awright, now, break it up! Break it up!" and the people began to move.

"Nigger here come a-lookin' for trouble, Sheriff!"

"Which?"

"This one."

"Awright, Freddy, you go on home now. We'll take care of it."

"He like to run over me!"

"Go on home."

The circle of people gradually broke off, moved away, some standing and watching from the corner, others disappearing into the night.

Ginger Beauchamp stood next to his automobile, his hands still bunched solidly into fists, the cords tight in his neck and in his arms.

A large man in a gray suit said, "You better get along."

Ginger could see only the red faces and the angry eyes, and hear the words that had fallen on him like whiplashes.

"I think he's hurt, Sheriff."

"Naw, he ain't hurt. Are you, fella?"

Ginger couldn't answer. Someone was talking to him, the kids were crying, Harriet was looking at him—but he couldn't answer.

The large man in the gray suit nodded to a uniformed policeman. "Tony," he said, "get 'em out of here quick. Send one car along."

"Yes, sir."

"Don't waste any time."

The policeman walked over to Ginger Beauchamp and said, "Let's go."

Ginger nodded.

Suddenly he was very tired again.

"Tom, I know how you feel," the sheriff said, "but we don't want to go flying off the handle."

"Why not?" Tom McDaniel's heart was still hammering inside his chest, and the fury at what he had seen filled him. "Those people might have been killed if I hadn't dragged you out when I did."

"What people?"

"The Negroes in the car!"

Sheriff Parkhouse gave Tom a sidelong glance. He began to fill his pipe with tobacco, slowly, rocking in the cane-bottomed chair. "I been living here for thirty years," he said, "and in all that time, I ain't never seen a nigger get hurt. Have you?"

Tom found himself actively disliking the large man. He particularly disliked the easy, slow movements, the unruffled calm. A little tobacco, up and down, gently, with the silver tool, a little more tobacco ... "That hasn't got anything to do with it," he said.

"Maybe not, maybe not. But answer the question, Tom. Have you ever seen a nigger get hurt in Caxton?"

"Yes," Tom said. "Tonight."

The sheriff sighed. His leathery, country flesh had begun to sag from the high cheekbones, and there was something incongruous about the crewcut that kept his white hair short and flat on his head. Here, Tom thought, in this jail, he's king. People fear him. People actually fear this ignorant man.

Parkhouse sucked fire into the scarred bowl of the pipe, released a cloud of thick, aromatic smoke. "Well," he said, smiling, "what you got in your mind for me to do?"

"Take action," Tom said. "Keep the peace. That's what you're getting paid for."

Parkhouse stopped smiling.

"That's right," Tom said angrily. "You're mighty quick to pick a drunk off the streets, Rudy, some poor fella that doesn't care any what happens to him. But when it comes to real trouble, you just can't bring yourself to move off that seat."

The chair came forward with a crack. Parkhouse stared for a moment, and his eyes were hard and small. "That," he said slowly, "ain't very polite."

"Polite!" Tom walked to the window and turned. "Let me get this straight. A family was attacked in this town tonight. You know who did the attacking and so do I. Property was destroyed and people were injured. There was blood. And you don't intend to do a thing about it. Not a single goddamn thing. Is that correct?"

"Yeah, that's correct! Now listen, it's real easy for you to sit back and say 'Take action.' Yeah. But you don't even know what you're talking about. What *kind* of action?" The sheriff began to jab the air with his pipestem. "There was at least fifty people around that car. You want me to arrest all of them?"

Tom opened his mouth to answer.

"Okay, let's say we do that. I arrest all of them fifty people. Charge 'em with disorderly conduct. Then what? This jail here was built in 1888, Tom. The doors are steel, but the walls are partly adobe: a thirteen-year-old could bust out in twenty minutes if he put his mind to it. Okay, fifty people. And they're hoppin' mad, too, don't think they ain't. I'd be. Now we got nine 18 by 18 cells and two runarounds, mostly filled as it is. You begin to get the drift?"

The sheriff brought his pipe to life again. "I like to see a real civic-minded citizen, Tom, I do. Somebody all the time thinking about the community. Shows real fine spirit. I just wish that you and your paper had of seen to it that we got us a decent jail before you come in here bellering for me to arrest half the town . . ."

Tom ran a hand through his hair. The sheriff's words stung, for it was all true. He hadn't ever taken much interest in the condition of the jail. The man had a point, anyway.

"But let me tell you something else," Parkhouse went on dryly. The way he looked, sitting there, made it suddenly easy to understand why certain people feared him. "Even if we had a calaboose the size of San Quentin, I still wouldn't go out and start hauling everybody in. Tom, you don't seem to see. Half of those people were kids. School kids. Throwing them in jail would be like giving them a Christmas present."

"What do you mean?"

"I mean, every kid wants to get put in a cell for a night or so. It's a lark. Hell, they'd have so much fun they'd probably tear this old place down to the ground!"

"Maybe so, but—"

"And here's something else that I guess you ain't thought about. Who, exactly, do we arrest? The ones who was actually touching the car? The ones in the street, whether they did anything or not? Or, just to be on the safe side, should we arrest everybody who attended the meeting?" Parkhouse chuckled. "That'd include you and your daughter. She was there, I heard."

"Who told you that?"

"Jimmy, or somebody. What's the difference? I'm just trying to show you why I can't 'take action.' And I wouldn't waste my time this way, either, if I didn't know you was a man with some sense."

Somewhere in the jail, somewhere upstairs, a voice was raised in song. It was not a particularly mournful or moving sound.

"But one thing still remains. A crime was committed and nobody's been punished. They got away with it, clean. So what's to stop them from doing the same thing tomorrow night?"

The sheriff took a bottle of pop from the refrigerator behind his desk and removed the cap.

"The people in this town are good," he said. "I ought to know that better than anyone else, ain't that so? They're good. But it's hot, and somebody just got them riled, that's all. Now it's out of their system. We—"

"That's right," Tom snapped. "Somebody got them riled. You might even say, somebody talked them into doing what they did."

Parkhouse nodded.

"You know what that's called, Rudy?"

"I don't get you."

"That's called 'inciting to riot.' It's a crime. If you don't believe me, look it up."

"I know what's a crime and what isn't," the sheriff said. "I don't have to look nothing up."

"Then why don't you throw Adam Cramer into jail?"

"Who?"

"Oh, for Christ's sake!" Tom slammed his palm down on the desk. "The kid who gave the speech! The kid who started the whole thing in the first place, who got the people all inflamed. Adam Cramer!"

"Oh." The sheriff emptied half of the bottle of Dr. Pepper down his throat and leaned back in his chair. "Well," he said, "I can't very well do that, either, Tom."

"You can't very well do that, either—*why not?*"

"Just take it easy, now, and I'll explain—just like I explained the other things. I can't arrest Cramer because he wasn't even around when the niggers drove up. To get him for sedition and inciting to riot, we'd have to catch him right there at the front of the mob, leading 'em on. As it was, he was in Joan's Cafe, having a cup of coffee with Verne Shipman, when it happened."

"With Verne?" The anger in Tom gave way suddenly to confusion, and fear.

"That's right," the sheriff said. "And you know, Tom, you can't put a man in jail for speaking his mind. If you don't believe me, look it up." He smiled. "Maybe you and me don't go along with that, now, but it's in the Constitution. If a man wants to, he can get out on a street corner and call the President of the United States a son of a bitch—and nobody can stop him. He can say America is no good and we ought to all be Communists—hell, he can say *anything*—and nobody's allowed to touch him. It's what's called Freedom of Speech. Besides, the way I heard it, this fella didn't say one solitary thing that everybody in town ain't been saying right along. What have you got against him, anyway?"

"Adam Cramer is a rabble-rouser," Tom said, in a hopeless voice.

"Well, hell, maybe we need a little rabble-rousing here!" The sheriff laughed good-naturedly. "But it could be I didn't get my facts straight. You were there. Did he tell those folks to stop the niggers in the car?"

"No."

"Did he tell them to do anything except maybe join this organization of his?"

"I—no. No, that's all he told them."

"Well, see, that ain't hardly grounds for arrest. Just good old Freedom of Speech in action, Tom!"

"Yes," Tom said.

"That's Democracy."

"Yes."

The sheriff slapped Tom's shoulder affably. "Don't get me wrong," he said. "I hate to see anybody get hurt in my town, I don't care whether he's white or black. But I personally think this particular nigra must of been one of those wise ones that are moving into the county from the North; I think he must of started shooting off his mouth: otherwise nothing like this would of happened, and you know it. They're good people here, but they won't put up with a smart-ass nigra. I can't blame them for that. Can you, Tom?"

"No, I can't blame them for that," Tom said and started out the door.

"Get some sleep," the sheriff called. "And don't worry. They got it all out of their system tonight!"

Got *what* out of their system? Tom thought.

The night air was moist and hot and windless, and the dark streets were empty now. Tom McDaniel walked to his car, got in and lit a cigarette.

The people I've lived with most of my life would have murdered that Negro, he thought, if I hadn't called Parkhouse. That's certain.

What is it that the people have to get out of their system? What is it that stays so close to the surface that a few words from a Yankee stranger can send it flooding out?

Tonight, he thought, was the beginning.

A war is coming to my town; and I don't even know whose side I'm on.

11

He had been staring at the blank sheet of paper for over an hour. His mouth was full of the taste of coffee and cigarettes, his eyelids were heavy, and he could no longer focus his mind. It kept blurring. Little wild thoughts kept running through it.

The telephone rang and he answered it and took down the copy for the McMahan ad, impaling it on the ad spindle, but he could not control the thoughts.

He pushed his chair back and listened for a while to the rhythmic sound of the presses. Then he got up from the chair and walked into the back room, where the heavy black presses were. They were working now; working hard.

Jack Allardyce ambled over slowly. "You want me?" he said.

"No." Tom watched Lulu. The thrust of her gleaming rollers hypnotized him momentarily, and he was forced to look away. "No, just stretching my legs."

"You got the copy?"

"Not yet."

"We ought to have it pretty soon," the old man said.

"I know." Tom picked a cigarette out of Allardyce's shirt pocket. "Jack," he said, almost to himself, "tell me something. Have you ever thought about newspapers?"

"What's that?"

"Oh, nothing. Nothing. I was just thinking—you remember what Will Rogers said? He said, 'I only believe what I read in the newspapers.' A lot of people, most people, feel exactly that way. Why do you suppose that is, Jack?"

"I'm not sure I know what you mean, Tom."

"Neither am I, really. But what I'm getting at, I think, is this: words by themselves don't carry much weight. I could tell you that the world was flat, and you'd call me a liar. Wouldn't you?"

The old man laughed. "No, I'd just say you'd had a couple too many, is all."

"But it's the same thing: you wouldn't believe me, that's the point. Neither would anybody. But if every newspaper in the world came out and said that the world was flat, there's quite a few people who wouldn't doubt it, for a second."

"I don't know about that," Allardyce said, rubbing his chin.

"I do. The minute a sentence gets set up in type and put on a piece of paper, suddenly it's important. It's permanent, it's chiseled in rock; it will last forever."

The old man cocked his head. "Tom," he said, "it ain't none of my business, but you don't look so good. Why don't you lay down and I'll get Freddy to do the editorial this time."

The presses roared in Tom McDaniel's ears.

"*Running a newspaper is not a job,*" Professor Cahier had said. "*It's a responsibility. Some books may have told you that newspapers reflect public opinion. They are wrong. Newspapers mold public opinion. They are more powerful than all the bombs in the world, more influential than all the politicians put together ...*" Tom's mind traveled back to that little room, to the earnest young faces in the room; and he heard the words of a dead man ringing loud and clear. Professor Cahier.

"*Newspapers comprise the greatest single force in the world today. They can hurt, heal, kill, crucify, resurrect; at will. They can start wars, and have, and will continue to do so; as easily, they can stop them. They can make gods of humble men, and cause the world to worship these gods. Or, if it is their desire, they can destroy the gods and create new ones. Nothing is beyond the median effect of newspapers, gentlemen. They are the true teachers, priests, judges and executioners of this age. They tell us whom to hate and whom to love, they tell us how to dress, how to eat, how to sleep, and, most important, how to think. They speak and their voices are heard. And they are obeyed.*

"*And, yet, a newspaper is an abstract thing. Newspapers do not, in fact, exist. What exists is a relatively small group of human beings—newspapermen. A few thousand of them, at most. And how many of these, I wonder, realize the power they represent? How many understand the extent of their responsibility?*

"*You were all attracted to journalism, my friends, because it seemed a bright, shiny and marvelously romantic subject. It is romantic, but I hope that I have shown that it is also the hardest and perhaps the most important work in the world.*

"*To become journalists, you must automatically—if you are honest men—give up the individual prejudices and biases that we equate with personal freedom. You must see that subjectivity has no place in the newspaper business, that it must be submerged and dissolved, always. Which is to say, you must tell the truth.*

"*Before you settle on this career, gentlemen, examine the question: Are you willing, are you able, to tell the truth? Is it within your*

*power to make the intellectual and physical and spiritual sacri-
fices that are necessary to do that seemingly simple thing, and do
it consistently? Can you tell the plain, unadorned, unslanted truth,
regardless of the consequences real or imagined?*

*"If the answer is yes, then you should not hesitate to give your
lives to journalism, for you will become forces for incalculable good
in the world.*

*"If the answer is no, then I beg you to take up other pursuits—
any other pursuits. For a weak journalist can bring darkness to the
earth more quickly than the mightiest king . . ."*

Tom shook the words away. They had seemed painfully
pompous when he'd first heard them, almost twenty-five years
ago, and now he was embarrassed at remembering them with
such accuracy. Cahier had been, after all, a teacher, not a newspaperman. It did the old boy's ego good to think he was preparing
the future rulers of the world.

But Tom watched old Lulu, pumping and throbbing, her
metal arms lifting out the printed sheets, and he thought of the
many things he'd caused her to say.

"Tom!"

"It's okay, Jack. Just a little sleepy, is all. Rough night."

The old man seemed alarmed. He had known Tom McDaniel
as a calm person of clockwork routine. "It's about that thing, that
speech, ain't it?" he asked.

"I guess."

"Well, you let me call Freddy and—"

"No," Tom said, pulling himself back to Caxton, back to the
Messenger building, to 1957. "I'll have the copy to you in a half
hour."

He went to his office, ripped the empty sheet of paper out of
the typewriter, inserted a fresh one.

Pompous, perhaps, he thought. But Cahier had been mostly
right. I can shout at the people in the crowd and they won't listen,
but when I put those words down in cold, hard print—the same
words—they'll pay attention.

That's what Cahier was talking about.

LEADING SCIENTISTS DISCOVER WORLD IS FLAT he typed,
in capitals. "The Oakville Research Center today released the

news that, contrary to previous belief, the earth is not round. According to Albert Einstein, Jr., 'A spectro-inductive photograph, taken from a height of three hundred miles, shows that the so-called curvature of the Earth is due wholly to a warp in the ionosphere. It is now absolutely certain that our Earth is as flat as a flapjack ...'"

Tom looked at the paragraph, smiled faintly and dropped it into the wastebasket.

He typed THE WAY WE LOOK AT IT and paused. "As everyone knows, the *Messenger*, along with school officials, the county court, the Mayor of Caxton, and most Caxton citizens, was opposed to the move toward integration of the races," he wrote, and felt his heart inside his chest. "We fought the issue from its inception to the final decision of the Supreme Court of the United States, employing every legal means. However, we believe that the government of the United States is a government of law and not of man, and that the Supreme Court is the final arbiter in deciding what is law. Therefore, once the Supreme Court has spoken and until the decision of that Court is changed by an amendment to the Constitution by a vote of the people, we have no choice except to obey the law.

"Last night, the law was broken. A young Northerner named Adam Cramer delivered an inflammatory speech on the steps of the county courthouse, in which he indirectly exhorted the citizens of Caxton to become renegades.

"This speech resulted in an unprovoked attack upon an out-of-county Negro family who happened to be passing through Caxton.

"It was considered by some unthinking officials to be a minor incident. But it was not a minor incident. In just this way—"

"Mr. McDaniel?"

Tom looked up from his typewriter. Standing in the office, smiling pleasantly, was Adam Cramer.

"How are you this morning, sir?"

Tom stared at him, but did not accept the hand. "What do you want?" he asked.

Adam Cramer continued smiling. "Not much," he said. "I just want to give you a little business."

"Yes?"

"You do run ads, don't you?"

"If they meet certain standards."

Adam Cramer withdrew a folded paper from his breast pocket, read it once, and dropped it on the desk. "I just heard about what happened last night," he said. "It was a shame."

"You must be proud."

Jack Allardyce knocked on the open door. "We're waiting on the copy," the old man said.

"You'll keep on waiting until I finish it," Tom snapped. "Now don't bother me."

The old man left, shocked.

Adam Cramer seated himself in the cane-bottomed chair and crossed his legs. "I'm not sure exactly what you meant by that remark," he said, "but I can tell you, Mr. McDaniel, I was very upset."

"Really?"

"Yes. If you managed to catch my speech, you'll recall that I emphasized the legal aspects of fighting integration. Just as you've been doing in your paper. I certainly had no idea that—"

"That's a lie!" Tom said, feeling the hot redness creep into his face. "You knew exactly what would happen. Cramer, I'm glad you're here because I have some things to say to you, and I'd advise you to listen."

"I'll be happy to," Adam Cramer said.

"First, I think you're a fraud. I don't know that for sure, but I think it. Whether you are or not is incidental right now. What is certain is that you're a rabble-rouser, and I don't like rabble-rousers. If you'd come to the officials of the town and presented the plans you think you have, everyone would have co-operated —because we are in trouble, and we could use help—maybe. But you didn't do that. You weren't about to do it."

"Go on," Adam Cramer said.

"Instead you got the people worked up. You played on their fears and on their hates. Then, before the fireworks went off, you sneaked away. You might as well know that I did my level best to have you thrown in jail for what you did."

Adam Cramer was silent.

"We don't want your type here," Tom said, realizing suddenly that he was becoming altogether too angry. "You understand?"

"Who is 'we,' sir?"

"The responsible citizens of this town."

"I'm sorry, Mr. McDaniel, but I'm afraid I'll have to disagree. I feel that my 'type' is not only wanted, but also, needed. That was made pretty clear last night."

Tom rose. "Get out of Caxton, Cramer," he said. "Get out today."

"Are you telling me?"

"I'm advising you."

Adam Cramer smiled again. "I honestly don't understand your attitude, Mr. McDaniel—and I don't think I want to, either. But it doesn't matter. It so happens that I plan to stay here until my job is finished. I'd hoped we could work together; I still do, in fact, but if we can't, then that's the way it is."

"I'll fight you," Tom said. "Every inch of the way."

"That's your right."

They stared at one another for a moment, and Tom knew precisely what his visitor was thinking. "There is one thing I *can* tell you," he said. "Stay away from my daughter."

"I should think that would be her decision," Cramer said.

"It isn't. If you go near her, you'll be sorry."

Adam Cramer smiled. "That," he said, "would be taking the law into your own hands, wouldn't it, Mr. McDaniel?" He paused. "I'd like to talk more with you, but I'm afraid I have work to do. You want to set up the ad?"

Tom picked up the sheet of paper, read it quickly. IF YOU ARE INTERESTED IN KEEPING CAXTON HIGH SCHOOL WHITE, DON'T FAIL TO ATTEND THE FIRST GENERAL MEETING OF SNAP—*The Society for National American Patriots. Saturday, 7:30, Joan's Cafe.*

"The ad," he said, "isn't suitable. We can't run it." He folded it and tossed it back across the desk.

Adam Cramer did not move. "I think you'll change your mind," he said. Then, carefully, he took out another piece of paper and handed it to Tom.

It read: *Tom, put this in a box, with heavy border, on page one. V. S.*

"A quarter column ought to be all right," Cramer said. "The typeface isn't too important—so long as it's big."

Tom threw both sheets of paper into the wastebasket. "The ad is not suitable," he repeated. "Please close the door after you."

Adam Cramer walked to the door; turned. "You hate me, Mr. McDaniel," he said. "I don't know why, but you do. However, I regard my work here as something vitally important to the country. There's no room in it for personal quarrels. After all, we're both trying to achieve the same goal. Aren't we?"

Tom did not answer.

"We're like soldiers on a battlefield," Adam Cramer said, "fighting a common enemy. If we can't get along together, let's at least not weaken our own offensive by engaging in private wars. I've read your editorials, sir. They were thoughtful and brave. You fought damned hard, and I think maybe now you're a little tired of fighting. Well, I'm a fresh recruit, don't you understand? I simply want to carry on where—"

"Get out," Tom said firmly.

The door closed.

He flexed his fingers and wrote, "—in just this way are insurrections begun. The majority of citizens will always resist the hate mongers and their methods, but there is a constant minority who are taken in. And a strong, loud minority is more powerful than a silent majority, always. Therefore—"

He looked at the first paragraphs, restating his anti-integration policy; and Adam Cramer's words stung his mind.

"After all, we're trying to achieve the same goal." And other words: *". . . the plain, unadorned truth . . ."*

He picked up the telephone, dialed, waited. Mrs. Mennen answered. "Is Verne in?" he asked.

"Who is this?"

"Tom McDaniel."

"Oh, hello, Tom. Yes, Mr. Shipman is out with the dogs. Do you want me to call him in?"

"No, just tell him that I'm on my way over there to see him. It'll take about fifteen minutes."

He hung up and walked into the back room. "Jack," he said, "call Freddy. I can't get the damn thing going."

"Okay."

"Have him play down the speech, just mention it and say it was unsuccessful. For the rest, use my notes on the fluoride business in Farragut."

He put on his hat and walked into the brassy sunlight.

"Tom, by God, it's good to see you. Why don't we ever get together any more?"

Verne Shipman looked fat and red and healthy. Years seemed to have dropped away from his face.

"I'll come directly to the point, Verne," Tom said. "A young punk from the North blew in yesterday. He's been raising seven kinds of hell ever since, and this morning he as much as told me that he had you on his side. I told him he was a liar. Was I right?"

Shipman dropped his smile. "Are you talking about Adam Cramer?"

"That's the name he uses."

Verne Shipman opened his mouth and closed it. He walked over to the bar by the window.

"You're still a gin man, aren't you?"

"This isn't a social call, Verne."

The big man proceeded to fix the drinks, deliberately.

"Okay," he said, handing a gin and tonic to Tom, "what kind of a visit is it?"

"I'd like an explanation of that note."

"What note?"

"The one about the ad."

"I thought," Shipman said, "that it was clear enough."

Impulsively, Tom took a swallow of the drink. "Verne," he said, "I can't believe that that kid has taken you in, too."

Shipman shook his head. "He hasn't 'taken me in,'" he said. "I know what you're thinking. When he came by here, I thought the same thing. Another hustler. Another guy out for the buck. But that isn't true, Tom. He may be young and an outsider and all that, but he's on the right track. Did you hear his speech last night?"

"Yes."

"Well, you can't argue with that kind of facts. Let me tell you something. When he started blowing off, when he was here, about this 'snap' thing of his, I thought, oh-o, here comes the bite. But he didn't ask for one solitary cent. He said that he would get a certain amount of money from the people and only then, when he could prove that he got it, would he accept any from me. And then, you could of knocked me over with a feather—he said he would put all the cash in my hands. Which is pretty good proof that he isn't any faker, wouldn't you say? Of course, I didn't believe any of that at first. But he said, 'Just come to the meeting, that's all I ask.' So I did. And I mean to tell you, he has the people behind him. I never saw anything like it!"

"Neither did I," Tom said. He asked if Shipman had heard about what had happened afterwards.

"No, I hadn't heard about it. But it don't prove anything, that I can see. Probably the nigra was uppity, or something."

"He wasn't uppity or something," Tom said, angrily. "He was just passing through. They stopped his car."

"Well, so they stopped his car. So what? I mean, you can't blame that on Cramer: he was with me. He didn't have a thing to do with it."

"He had everything to do with it, damn it. He inflamed the people."

Shipman laughed. "Oh, come on, now, Tom. You're just mad because it took somebody from out of town to show us that we've been falling down on the job. I was mad, too. In the beginning. But there's no two ways about it, this thing has got to be stopped and it's got to be stopped now."

"How?" Tom said. "By attacking Negroes in the street?"

Shipman walked over to the bar and refilled his glass. He seemed to be enjoying himself. "If that's what it's going to take, yes."

"Verne, for Christ's sake! Do you know what you're saying?"

"Yes; but I don't think you do. I'm saying that we fought fair and above board and it didn't get us nowhere. Now it's time to fight their way."

"Whose way?"

"The politicians'. I've talked the thing over with Adam, and you listen—there's plenty we can do. And it's all perfectly, absolutely legal." The big man lit his pipe, puffed vigorously.

"Then why didn't he go to the officials?" Tom said. "If he's got such big plans, why didn't he take them to—"

"Because he wouldn't have got to first base. Be realistic for a minute. Satterly is a namby-pamby fool, and the lawyers we got just aren't smart enough. Worse than that, they're not gutty enough. And that's what we've got to have now, Tom. Guts."

"I didn't know you had such an interest in politics, Verne," Tom said disgustedly. Shipman still looked boneless and soft in the hard light, like an overfed baby. All of a sudden Tom wanted to say, *After a life of doing nothing, you're concerned about Caxton. You never gave this place a thought before Cramer arrived. You didn't care whether we integrated or not. Now you're talking about guts.*

"That's a little harsh," Shipman said, controlling his voice. "But, it's true, and I'm man enough to admit it. Tom, you've known me for a long, long time, so I can't fool you. I've been remiss in my duties."

Remiss! Tom thought. *You haven't even been aware that you had any duties.*

"But a person can always wake up, and that's what's happened to me," Shipman went on. "I've waked up. And now I'm ready to fight to save my town." He warmed rapidly to his subject, began pacing the room. "If we all pitch in now," he said, "we can have this licked inside of a month. Maybe less. And those knotheads in the Supreme Court, they'll see that their little plan wouldn't work—and that'll be the end of it. By God, it makes my blood boil to think that right now, at this minute, there's niggers sitting next to white girls in our school!"

Shipman took Tom's glass, sloshed a quantity of gin into it. "It's going to be a hell of a battle," he said.

"Almost as much fun as hunting!" He hadn't meant to say it. But it was too late to stop now. "That's it, isn't it, Verne? You've been bored of everything for years, now there's some excitement and you're raring to go."

"No," Shipman said slowly, "that isn't it at all, as a matter of fact."

"I'm sorry. It was a stupid thing to say."

"Yes." Shipman relit his pipe and walked to the desk. "Whatever you think, Tom, it happens that I'm convinced. Maybe you don't like the boy. That's all right. But he's opened my eyes, wide; and he's shown me that he's a leader. People listen to him." He rummaged in the top drawer. "Have you seen this?"

Tom took the photograph of the Negro kissing the white girl. He glanced at it and tossed it back. "I saw it ten years ago," he said. "That thing's been floating around since 1946. It was taken in Paris. The Negro is a G.I."

Shipman flushed. "Well, that doesn't make any difference. The same sort of thing is going on in America, right now. It could just as easy go on in Caxton."

"I'm not so sure of that," Tom said. "What makes you so damn certain that the minute we have integration all the Negroes are going to start sleeping with the white women? Do you think these women are standing around, waiting for it to happen?"

"That isn't the point," Shipman said.

"Well, I don't care what the point is. I just know this. We've done everything that can be done to keep integration out of Caxton, but the law says we've got to have it, and I believe in obeying the law. Cramer apparently doesn't. I don't like him; I don't trust him and I am certainly not going to run his stinking ad. You can tell him that." Tom got his hat and opened the door. "He seems to have forgotten that I'm the editor of the *Messenger*."

"You seem to have forgotten something along the way, too," Shipman said.

"What's that, Verne?"

"I own the controlling stock in the *Messenger*. You're working for me."

"Well?"

"I want the newspaper to support Adam Cramer and SNAP. All the way."

Tom looked at Shipman for several seconds. Then he said, "Before I took over as editor, the *Messenger* had a circulation of two thousand. It was coming out three times a month and losing money. Six months later the circulation was twelve thousand. Now it's over twenty. We're in the black. And we've won three prizes for outstanding journalism. In all that time, you never set foot in the office or even bothered to write me a letter. Are you going to tell me how to run a newspaper now?"

Shipman wavered between uncertain anger and conciliation. "It isn't that, Tom," he said. "You've done a fine job, and I wouldn't deny it. I'm not telling you how to run the newspaper . . ."

"Then what *are* you telling me?"

"It's a matter of basic policy, that's all. Plant a few ads, build up Cramer a little—hell, that can't hurt."

"What if I refuse to run the ad? What if I tell you right now that I plan to do everything in my power to get rid of Cramer and his organization?"

Shipman drew himself up unsteadily. "We've been friends for a good long time, Tom," he said. "But if you told me that, I'd have to ask for your resignation."

"That's the way it is?"

"That's the way it is." Shipman hesitated. "Well?" he asked. "What are you going to do?"

Tom thought of the job that was waiting for him in New York, then of Ruth and Ella, of his home, of the years that he had spent growing to love this town, this country.

"I don't seem to have much choice," he said, and hated himself for saying it. He hated the weakness that had come over his legs. All the way to Shipman's house he had told himself that he would lay it on the line. Things would be run his way, and if Shipman didn't like it, he could get himself another boy.

But then it had gone wrong.

"All I ask, Tom," Verne Shipman said, smiling, "is just a few little plugs. You're still the editor!"

The big man saw him to the front door, a thick arm resting on his shoulder.

"We'll have this rotten business cleaned up fast. You wait and see. Caxton is a town the world won't soon forget!"

Tom walked down the gravel path to his car, feeling as he had often felt years ago when he was young, struggling with a mind full of questions and no one in the world to answer the questions.

On the way back to town, he thought again of Professor

Cahier, and remembered, suddenly, a bushy-haired, nervous fellow named Lubin. The part of his mind that had pulled out the memory of those days before, apparently without purpose, kept forcing him back.

Herman Lubin, laughing and untoughened then; a balding, staccato-voiced desk chief now. Lubin, the ambitious ...

"Thomas, you're nuts. You'll sit in that crummy little village all your life and maybe once or twice you'll publish an editorial and they'll shoot you an award—'To the fighting editor of the Mouse Breath Bugle!'—and you'll frame it and die happy. Stinko, Thomas. Small time. You're too good a newspaperman for that."

Tom's hands began to perspire against the glossy dark plastic steering wheel, as he realized now why he had been remembering.

He mashed the accelerator pedal to the floor and kept it there for most of the length of the straight road. A few minutes later, in his office, he picked up the telephone and dialed long distance, noticing, with some annoyance, that his fingers had begun to tremble slightly.

Fifteen minutes later, after a series of crackling pauses, poor connections, and transfers, he was talking to the man he'd corresponded with often but had not actually seen in over twenty years.

Lubin's greeting was loud. In the background, Tom could hear typewriters and other machines, and he had a quick, painful vision of the immense city room. "Chrissakes, man! You still got that houn-dawg accent? Jesus, I can't believe it. Doesn't anything change down there?"

Tom smiled, without mirth, without real bitterness, with admission, only, that he was talking to *newspaper* and that he wasn't *newspaper*. "Well," he said, "we did get a new door for the privy."

The voice, distorted by distance, roared good-naturedly. "So," Lubin said, "how the hell are you, anyway?"

"Okay, Herman."

"Hard to tell, y'know. You Southroners all sound alike. Constipated. Ooop, hang on a second, Thomas—"

While Lubin made some improbably enormous and important decision, Tom wiped his forehead and looked around his shabby, cluttered little office. He looked at the framed awards on the wall. The mountain of ads on the desk. The gritty, unmopped, unswept board floor.

"Thomas?"

"Yes, here, Herman."

"Sorry. Where were we? I know—you were about to tell me you're fed up with all this country stuff and you want a job with me. Right?"

Tom half-lowered the receiver, feeling the sharp, childish chill, the accelerated tempo of his heartbeat; then, quickly, he said: "I don't know, Herman; I don't know how I'd work out as a copy boy."

Again the roar. "Copy boy! Hell, man, I'm talking about something big. Really big. Night janitor! Right? *Big.* How's the wife and kids?"

"Fine. Herman—listen, before this phone bill goes so damn high I'll have to up my sub rates—"

"Country, typical country. Scared of telephones. Terrified of long distance."

"I have something serious to talk over with you."

"Should have known," Lubin said. "You're such a serious bastard. Always were. But insecure. . . . Go ahead."

"We've got a thing brewing here," Tom said. "It could mean a little trouble or a lot, I can't say yet. But it's trouble."

"Don't tell me. Mrs. Murgatroyd's husband is cheating."

"Herman, goddamnit, shut up and listen, will you!"

"Okay. Go on."

Tom cocked his head and locked the receiver between his neck and shoulder and lit a cigarette. As quickly as he could, he told Lubin about Adam Cramer, about the speech, about the situation.

When he'd finished, he realized how wild the story must sound to someone in New York. "It's just starting," he said, almost apologetically, "and maybe it'll go nowhere, but I have a feeling. I have a feeling—"

"What do you want me to do?" asked Lubin crisply, the humor gone from his voice.

Tom wiped his palm against his trousers nervously. What *did* he want Lubin to do? "The kid says he comes from Los Angeles."

"Yeah?"

"You've got a man there, haven't you?"

"We've got a dozen men in L. A. But I don't get—"

"Is one of them available?"

A bit impatiently, Lubin said, "Sure, of course."

"Good?"

"Oh, come on now. What the hell is it you're getting at?"

"News," Tom said. "A story. The kind your boss goes for. I want you to have a man run down some facts on this Cramer kid—"

"K or C? Real name?"

"C. I think so. I have a hunch something interesting might turn up."

"Like what?"

Tom hesitated. "I don't know, Herman," he said. "It may all be a waste of time; but you can afford to waste a little time, can't you?"

"I guess so," Lubin said casually. "Got a man named Driscoll, goes in for this kind of thing. Good boy: took a Pulitzer a few years back on the Nuremberg Trials—not for us. How about this? I'll give him a ring and tell him to shoot a couple of days, just in case. Okay?"

"No. Let me have until tomorrow. I'll call you then with something more definite."

"Do that," the voice said. "Maybe it's something." A pause, and: "Thomas, you're sure you won't change your mind about the job? Got a desk all warm for you."

"Keep it that way," Tom said. "Before this is over, I may *have* to change my mind."

He replaced the telephone slowly. Perspiration coated his body in a thin, dripping film. The call had been a ridiculous impulse, and he seldom yielded to impulse these days. In a way, he was ashamed.

Ashamed? he thought. Why?

He sat quietly for a while; then, as if he had been holding his breath, he sighed and got up and went outside.

He walked for almost an hour.

12

They marched across the glass-smooth clover in cowboy boots and ragged sneakers and shoes with little holes for ventilation. Eighteen men; five women; a dozen teen-age children, some with the look of acres and forests about their faces, some of a sharp and city cast. The men and women were frowning. They all carried lightweight sticks stripped from orange crates, and the sticks pierced squares of light cardboard.

PATON YOU ARE A WEAKLING, read the signs. SEPARATE BUT EQUAL! WE DON'T WANT NIGRAS HERE! KEEP OUR SCHOOL WHITE!

Bart Carey, walking in long, deliberate strides, headed the group. He was a large man with a Buddha belly and flabby, clay-brown arms. The spectacles he wore contrasted sharply with the rough and craglike features of his face; it was the spectacles you saw first. His shirt was transparent and sleeveless, wrinkled and stained with sweat. Somehow Carey gave the impression of having lived for years alone in some forgotten forest, of subsisting for this time on snakes and berries, of being rescued and returned to civilization, quickly shaved and bathed and dressed, and set before a hundred whirring cameras.

Next to the dark young man in the trim suit who walked beside him, Carey seemed almost savage.

Phil Dongen, who had left his assistant in charge of the store, jogged along fast enough to keep slightly ahead of Rev. Lorenzo Niesen.

No one spoke.

They marched across the lawn. When they reached the entrance to the high school, they stopped.

"You want me to call him out?" Carey asked.

Adam Cramer glanced at his wrist watch. "No," he said, "wait a few minutes. It isn't noon yet. We want everyone to hear this."

They waited quietly, holding their signs.

*

Harley Paton stared at the large black 8-ball that had been given to him recently by a friend, and decided that it was the most appropriate gift he had ever received. He reached out and lifted the heavy object, rotated it, and read the fortune that appeared in a tiny slot at the bottom.

Patience, it said, *is a virtue.*

He set the ball down again and tried to concentrate on the papers, but this was impossible. He could think only of the telephone call that had wrested him from his bed at two A.M., and of the strained voice that told him he had betrayed the people of Caxton.

Things had gone more smoothly than he'd expected. So far there had been no riots, no gangs, no fights. But there was something hanging heavy in the air. You could smell it. You could almost touch it.

"Mr. Paton, are you busy?"

He looked up. Agnes Angoff was standing in the doorway. "No," he said. "Come in."

The English teacher closed the door angrily. "Have you looked outside your window?" she asked.

Paton turned his chair, looked briefly, turned back again. "That's the Cramer fellow, I suppose," he said.

"Yes."

"I heard about his speech last night. Tommy Finch told me. I think, Miss Angoff, that we are going to have some problems . . ."

"I know we are. That's why we ought to do something now. Things can work out—they can, I see that; don't you? If we're let alone. The new students are doing fine."

"That isn't quite the report I get from Mrs. Gargan," Harley Paton said, smiling.

"That—" Agnes Angoff swallowed. "Mrs. Gargan gives me a swift pain. I've watched the children, and if they get the smallest chance, they'll make it. We've *got* to do something!"

The principal nodded. "I share your sentiments," he said, "but there are those who say we've done too much already. What do you suggest?"

"I don't know." Agnes Angoff sank into a chair. "I just don't know. But if those … people … outside get what they're after, we'll be set back fifty years. That mustn't happen."

She tried to control herself, but she had been controlling herself too long.

Harley Paton felt suddenly embarrassed. He wanted to comfort the woman, tell her somehow that he understood; but he could only watch.

"I was threatened last night," she said. "If they'll go that far—I know they must have called you too. Did they?"

"Yes," Harley Paton said, soberly. He recalled the droning words: *"If you don't want nothing to happen to your family, mister, you better get rid of them coons …"*

Agnes Angoff said: "Shouldn't we—" Then the twelve o'clock bell began to shriek, and the halls filled up with noise.

There was a knock at the door. Harley Paton opened it and faced a young boy in levis. It was John Christiansen, a freshman. His parents had called on Monday and said that they did not intend to allow their son to go to school with Negroes.

"There's a committee of citizens outside," the boy said rhetorically. "They want you to meet them."

The principal looked at Miss Angoff. "All right, John," he said. "Tell Mr. Cramer that I'll be out shortly."

"Okay."

"John—"

The boy stopped. "Yes, sir?"

"Come here for a second. As I remember, John, we spent some time together last semester; it had something to do with failing grades. Do you recall?"

"Yes, sir."

"I got to know you a little, then, and I thought you were a pretty good boy. I was honest about that. Will you be honest with me?"

The boy looked frightened and embarrassed. "Sure," he said hesitantly.

Harley Paton said, "Fine. Now would you please tell me why you didn't come to school yesterday."

John Christiansen squirmed. "Well, sir," he said, "my pa didn't want me to. On account of the nigras, you know. He didn't want me to go to school with them."

"Was it your idea? That is, did you ask your father to call me?"

"No, I didn't do anything like that. He just called."

"In other words, it was his idea?"

"Yeah. But—"

Harley Paton smiled warmly. "And you didn't mind getting out of a little school, either, did you?"

"I gotta get back outside," the boy said.

"Just one more question. If your father hadn't brought it up —I mean, if he hadn't told you to stay home—would you have come?"

"I guess so," the boy said.

Harley Paton looked at Miss Angoff meaningfully.

"You better not say anything about my pa," the boy said, "because he's outside right now and he's plenty sore."

"I'm not saying anything about him, John. You may leave now."

The boy turned and ran out the door.

After a few moments, Harley Paton said, "Well, we might as well get this over with," and he started down the hall.

When he walked onto the stone steps, he looked suddenly very small and frail to Miss Angoff. Watching from her open window, watching the gathering crowd of children and the band of adults, and then turning her eyes to Harley Paton, she grew fearful.

Paton was thin almost to the point of emaciation. His tonsured head seemed too heavy for the stemmed neck, and his clothes hung loosely from his light and bony frame. It was the expression on his face that saved him from looking either comical or pathetic. And the warmth of his smile intensified this grace.

Now, however, he was not smiling. At his appearance, the children on their lunch period had quieted; and now they waited.

In precise, nearly accentless tones, Harley Paton said, "You wanted to speak with me?"

Adam Cramer stepped forward. "Yes. The people of Caxton want to know why you have allowed Negroes to mingle with their children in this school. We want an explanation."

Bart Carey jerked his head around. "That's right," he said loudly.

"What about it?" others called.

Harley Paton waited for them to be still. He addressed himself to the young man. "Apparently you haven't heard about the Supreme Court decision," he said.

Rev. Lorenzo Niesen spat a stream of tobacco onto the grass. "Don't hand us that stuff now," he yelled.

"We're quite aware of the decision," Adam Cramer said.

"In that case, the question does not make sense and requires no answer."

"The people think otherwise," Adam Cramer said. "Why didn't you refuse to open the school?"

"Because I chose to obey the law."

The group of adults moved closer to the steps. "That's a crock, Paton," someone shouted. "You could'a shut down."

"I don't have control over such decisions," Harley Paton said quietly. "An appeal of this sort was made to the school board, and it was refused. There was no choice in the matter."

"In other words," Adam Cramer said, "you would have been fired. In other words, you let the Negroes come in because you were too scared of losing your job to do anything about it!"

Harley Paton's hands bunched into fists. He put them behind his back. "I don't know who you are, young man," he said, "but I think you know perfectly well that you're talking nonsense."

"Mr. Paton, the people of Caxton demand that you turn the Negro students out of this school at once," Cramer said. "And if you haven't got the courage to do that, then the people demand that you resign your post."

"That'd show how you feel about it," a woman said, from the back.

"That's right!"

Phil Dongen stepped up. "Paton, let's get one thing straight here and now. Are you for or against this integration?"

The principal looked over the lawn, at all the children, at the people in the group; he looked up and saw Miss Angoff, standing at the window, waiting, along with the others, for his answer.

"I am against integration of the races," he said firmly, "but —I am for law and order. For that reason, I have no intention of either sending the new students home or shutting down the school. As for resigning my post—I don't believe, Mr. Cramer, that you represent the people of Caxton. However, if you can prove to me at any time that fifty-one per cent of the people no longer want me, I will leave. Until then, I am in charge, and there will be no change in the routine."

"That's the man who's taking care of your children!" Phil Dongen shouted.

"Fifty-one per cent," Harley Paton repeated.

"You might just as well start packing, Harley! It'll be more like one hundred per cent."

"That remains to be seen."

"Don't worry; just don't worry!"

Harley Paton met the eyes of the group, stared levelly for a moment, then turned and went inside. He closed the door. He felt his heart rapping deep in his chest.

He walked to his office and watched the people on the lawn, the familiar people, the people he had seen a thousand times and, perhaps, had never seen at all, watched them form into a loose parade and march with placards high into the quiet street.

He barely heard the door. "Yes?"

It was Miss Angoff. She walked to his desk and stood there.

"Yes, what is it?"

She looked at him and he found that he could not decipher her expression. Unaccountably, however, he glanced away, down from her gaze.

"Why did you say that?" she asked.

He focused on the 8-ball. "Say what?"

"You were strong and you faced them, but you lied. Why?"

"I don't know what you're talking about. It's almost one, Miss Angoff, and—"

"I don't care about that. Mr. Paton, I've been with the school for four years. That isn't very long, I suppose, but even so, I feel a part of Caxton High. It means a great deal to me."

Harley Paton nodded, realizing that he would have to say it now.

"You mean a great deal to me too," Miss Angoff said, then added quickly: "in the sense that I've always respected you, I've always felt that—well, that we thought alike. Even when you decided to go along with the Board; even then. But when you went down there just now—"

"Yes?"

The English teacher trembled slightly. "Mr. Paton, are you really against integration?"

Harley Paton picked up the 8-ball and turned it upside-down.

"I realize I'm overstepping myself," she said, "but I've got to know. Because if you don't believe, you can't fight with me. And I can't fight alone."

The slender man turned in his chair and faced the window for a time; then he turned back.

"You won't be fighting alone," he said.

"Then why—"

"Miss Angoff, I'm going to tell you something now. I've never told anyone else, except my wife, and if you repeat it to a living soul I'll deny it. I'll say you misquoted me. Is that understood?"

Miss Angoff nodded.

"All right. I am in favor of integration. It has, in fact, been a dream of mine ever since I can remember. I not only want it to happen, I know that it *must* happen. And that is why I lied to them a few minutes ago and why I shall go on lying. If I took a radical stand now; if I proclaimed myself an antisegregationist, I would lose my power to help. The people would no longer trust me. And they have to trust me, that is vitally important." He looked at Miss Angoff. "Do you understand?"

She hesitated, then said: "I think so."

"But you're not sure. I know. It took me a long time to get it clear. I thought, Whom will you offend by telling the truth? Only the bigots, the fools—but that isn't true. If it were only the bigots and the fools we had to contend with, we'd have no problem. No; it's the ordinary people, Miss Angoff. It's our own friends. Mrs. Gargan and Mr. Spivak and Mrs. Seifried, schoolteachers, businessmen, politicians ... Intelligent, honest, kind people. They're the ones we're contending with."

Miss Angoff shook her head.

"That's the most important thing to understand about the problem," Paton said. "It's a war in which you must defeat your own side." He smiled bitterly. "Which almost makes us espionage agents. That's right. I'm a saboteur, Miss Angoff. And saboteurs have always been more effective than assassins."

"I'm sorry," the English teacher said.

"Don't be, there's no reason for it. Direct action is wholesome. It's honest. There is, please believe me, nothing I would rather do than go out and shake some sense into these people. I have arguments, just as you do, that are completely unassailable. Dialectically you and I could tear down the whole wormy edifice of segregation. We could call the children into the assembly hall this afternoon and lecture to them. But if we did that, we'd strike the most telling blow of all against the thing we want. I know that to be true." He slammed the 8-ball down on the desk. Suddenly he looked angry. "This young demagogue, Cramer—he can do a lot of harm. But it's nothing compared to the harm we can do, simply by telling the truth."

"I'm ashamed of myself," Miss Angoff said.

"So am I! I'm ashamed every time I sit at that table and listen to Harkins and Peterson talk about their law and order—as though this were the issue! I'm ashamed every time I tell that whole PTA crowd that integration is very bad, of course, but we must be good citizens and obey the law, though we may quarrel with it. Every time I hear an unthinking remark, or see one of those illiterate orange posters, or think of Simon's Hill—I'm ashamed."

Somewhere, far from Paton's consciousness, a bell rang shrilly. He folded his hands and spoke in a soft voice. "Not so ashamed, though," he said, "as I would be if I were to weaken now, when we're so close."

The door opened and a blonde girl came in. "Jimmy Foster wants to see you, Mr. Paton," she said.

The principal glanced up. "All right, Leona. Tell Jimmy to come in." Then to Miss Angoff: "Remember, I'll deny it."

"You won't have to."

As she walked down the teeming hall, Agnes Angoff thought about Harley Paton, and about the many faces of courage.

Hers was burning red.

13

The torero pants were tight; they reminded Ella of her body and of her years and of her excitement. She knew that Adam Cramer was going to kiss her tonight. But she did not know whether he planned to touch her. No one ever had, at least not as Lucy had described it, and she hoped, without realizing that she hoped, that it would happen. There wasn't anything wrong about letting someone touch you, after all. Not really wrong. A lot of girls, some of them younger than Ella, just took it for granted. And with her own eyes she'd seen Alfred Clancy put his whole hand over Dorothy Watkins' right breast and keep it there—on the outside, of course.

She drained the soda glass noisily and looked at the clock. It was seven-ten. In five minutes, she thought, he'll pick me up. It didn't even occur to her that Adam Cramer would be late. He wasn't that sort.

She took thirty cents out of her wallet, went around the counter and put the money into the cash register. Mr. Higgins jumped at the sound.

"I'd forgotten you were here," he said. Then, "Why *are* you here, anyway, all by yourself?"

"I'm meeting somebody," Ella said.

"Oh. I beg your pardon."

She went outside and waited and presently the Chevrolet pulled up. Adam Cramer got out and opened the door for her.

"I really appreciate this," he said.

Ella got in and waited until they were headed down the street before she said, "I told Mother I was meeting Lucy."

"My God, is she against me too?"

"No, but she doesn't like the idea of me going out on a school night, you know. What's this about, anyway?"

"Well," Adam Cramer said, "it's mostly about you."

Ella shivered slightly; it was the same feeling she'd had before, alone with Adam Cramer. She tried to think of an answer, or a question.

"Mostly I wanted to see you again, that's all. But for some reason your father plain doesn't care for me. He told me I wasn't ever to see you again. And that, milady, was a bitter, bitter pill."

"But you said you had some important business or something."

"Isn't being with you important business?" Adam Cramer patted the space next to him on the seat. "Come on over here. I hate to shout."

Ella moved a few inches toward him.

"I do have a little business you can help me with, as a matter of fact," he said, "but it won't take long. I want to speak to some of the kids at Rusty's."

"How can I help?"

"Just by being with me. That way I'm not a total stranger to them. See?"

"I guess so."

"Afterwards we can take a drive. You still have a lot to show me."

Ella saw the way his eyes traveled over her sweater, and suddenly she felt quite sure that he would touch her. And she would let him do it. On the outside.

She could think of very little else.

"Has he spoken to you?" Adam Cramer asked.

"Who?"

"Your father. Has he said anything about me?"

"Well, he hasn't talked an awful lot. He—I don't know. He doesn't like you."

"But why?"

"He says you're a rabble-rouser."

"I am, in a way. But is that bad?"

Ella shrugged. "I don't know. Daddy seems to think so."

"He must. My God, you'd think I'd poisoned his favorite dog or something, the way he acts. I mean, I'm working for the same thing he is, just in a different way, that's all. You can see that, can't you, Ella?"

"Sure, I guess."

They were silent for a time. "Are you worried about being out with me?"

"Not exactly," Ella said. "But I've got to get home early. And —well, I don't like to tell lies. We better not do it again, not like this, anyway."

"If you were worried, why did you agree to meet me?"

"I don't know." Ella bit her lip. Everything I say around him, she thought, comes out so dumb. I sound like an idiot.

Adam Cramer drove over the bridge, turned into the gravel path and parked the car beneath a large tree. He left the engine running. "Maybe if you put in a good word for me I could talk with Tom, with your father, and maybe then he'd see I'm not such a bad guy."

"He's pretty set in his ways."

"I know. He tried to get me arrested—had you heard?"

"No!"

"It's true. He claimed that I goaded the people into attacking those Negroes in the car—you must have been told about that. Or maybe you were there?"

"I heard some of the speech."

"Then you know that I wasn't even around when the incident happened. But your father blames *me*! He blames me for the whole thing. Ella, listen to me, listen now. If I'd been there, I would personally have called the sheriff, even before your dad did. That's the truth. I don't like to see people get hurt."

Ella looked into his eyes, and she believed him. Most of the speech had been boring to her, because it didn't seem that he had said anything other than what everyone else was saying, and it was all political stuff anyway, but she'd noticed how all the people had listened to him. All the grownups, listening to this young man. And a portion of her had begun to regard him as a celebrity—almost like a movie star. That was part of it. She was being courted by a celebrity.

"I wouldn't get too upset about tonight, in any case," he said. "I'm working very closely with Mr. Shipman, the man who employs your father. I think that when the two of them get together for a talk, Tom will be a little friendlier."

Ella felt his hand cup her chin, gently. She relaxed and allowed his lips to press against hers, allowed them to linger. Then Adam Cramer pulled away. "You're a lovely girl, Ella," he said. "Let's get the dull stuff over with and then I can tell you more about it."

They drove to Rusty's and went inside.

The juke box was blaring a popular song, but few of the teen-agers seemed to be listening. Some clapped listlessly; others huddled in tight groups, talking loudly above the music. Ella slipped her arm inside Adam's and smiled faintly, as they cut their way to a free booth.

"I've never seen it so crowded on a school night," she said.

"Well," he said, "I guess I'm slightly responsible. I had Danny Humboldt spread the word."

Danny and George walked over, followed by Lucy and a girl whose name Ella had forgotten.

"Good deal, Danny," Adam Cramer said.

"No sweat," the young man said casually. "But I don't know about talking. You got to see Joe Mantz about that. He's the big guy over there behind the bar."

"I've discussed it with Mr. Mantz."

Danny Humboldt grinned. "You wheel and deal, man," he said.

Adam Cramer laughed, and Ella saw that his teeth were white and straight. She was glad he did not show his gums. "You want to squeeze in?" she said.

Lucy winked. "Huh-uh." Then she said, "Hank's here. Over by the juke."

Ella turned her head quickly, and back.

"He doesn't look so happy."

"No. Boy!"

Hank Kitchen, dressed in regulation open-collar white shirt and dark trousers, was not happy at all: Ella knew. Sitting there, he appeared to be brooding—and this was nice. Let him brood.

Ella moved a bit closer to Cramer and pretended to be ab-sorbed in the conversation.

". . . and you really shook up old Paton, *man*! I thought he was gonna blow away!"

"He's a weak person, Danny. We can't allow weak persons to lead us . . ."

Ella wished that they would get it over with in a hurry. She was anxious to stride back out with the young stranger, anxious to be kissed.

Danny and Adam Cramer spoke for another three or four minutes, then Adam got up, excused himself, and walked over toward the bar.

"That," said George Humboldt, "is one hell of a guy. I mean it. You know?"

Danny nodded. "Yeah."

Ella felt proud and excited; the boredom of the years was swept away. They were talking about the man who was going to kiss her and touch her later on!

"What's he like?" Lucy said, sliding into the booth. "I mean, really?"

"Oh, I don't know. He's a gentleman," Ella said.

"He sure likes you, I can tell. The way he looked at you. I bet old Hank is just furious!"

"It serves him right."

Ella put her hand around the cold-beaded coke glass and pretended that she was Deborah Kerr and that Adam was Rossano Brazzi and Hank was Dan Dailey and they were in a real triangle.

She turned in the booth when, suddenly, the juke box fell silent. Within a few moments the talking quieted, also. Then Adam Cramer began to speak.

He repeated most of what he'd said in front of the courthouse, about taking action and stopping the Negroes from attending Caxton; but, somehow, his voice wasn't the same. It was more . . . boyish, and more cultivated.

". . . and we're going to need *your* help, kids," he was saying, "most of all! But I want to stress something right here and now. It's something most outsiders don't understand. We have nothing against the Negroes themselves. We don't hate them or wish them harm. But—and, see, this is the point—we do know that as a race they're inferior, they've always been inferior, they'll always be inferior. That isn't only an opinion. That's a recognized, accepted scientific anthropological fact! They have certain racial characteristics buried deep inside them which render them unfit for the responsibilities they would be forced to assume upon the acceptance of desegregation. Now that's pretty general, and you're all sharp, intelligent people. So I'll be specific. I'll go back and trace this thing, if you'll let me. Because some of you may feel very strongly that integration is bad but maybe you've been hoodwinked by the race-mixers, those left-wingers with the big thick glasses—maybe you've heard that it's impossible for an intelligent person to accept segregation, because we're all humans and all humans were created equal, and so forth. Maybe some of you have begun to wonder if it is only so-called 'tradition' that makes you curl away from the idea of mongrelizing the South. So let's look at the thing intelligently, with facts behind us. Let's see exactly *why* we're against it.

"In 1619 twenty African savages were bought from a Dutch man-of-war by the Virginia settlers. They were taken from a Godless, amoral culture, from the disease-infested jungle where they had lived like wild animals for centuries—for centuries!— and given homes in America. At that time they were put to work with indentured white servants, but it was soon seen that the Negroes were only half as capable, although the work required no particular intelligence. Later, with the accretion risen to many thousands, with most of these thousands having been born in the United States, the same fact was observed. The Negroes simply could not be counted on to work. They lacked an abstract quality shared by almost all white people, *personal* initiative; and, in view of their backgrounds, this was certainly not due to any decrease in their living standards. In Africa, they were slaves to the elements, to their own ignorance, to swift mortality; here they were slaves only to men. If anything, they have been rid of their shackles! It was a perfect climate for self-improvement. But they did not improve. They remained one step removed from the poor savages they or their parents had been.

"Everyone understood this particular racial characteristic in those days, including the Negroes themselves. We are told that they thirsted for freedom—a concept they could not possibly grasp—yet, throughout all the years of slavery, there were only three insurrections worthy of the name. And these three were abortive, they got nowhere. The Underground Railroad you hear about all the time was, of course, simply a clever business scheme on the part of certain whites. If these white renegades had not fomented unrest, I believe—and so do many sociologists—that there would have been scarcely a handful of voluntary escapes.

"Now what does this indicate? Clearly it indicates that the Negroes were eminently satisfied with their slave status, and that even if they weren't, they would have done nothing about it.

"It's common sense.

"But we had our fanatics then, just as we do now. We had white Yankees with hero complexes who rushed in, without ever bothering to get the true facts about Negroes, and started yelling 'Free the slaves! Give the Negroes equality!' It sounded like a fine sentiment and added inches of height to whoever expressed it. So, the slaves were freed. The Negroes didn't care, of course. They'd of been just as happy if the decision had gone the other way. But now they were 'free' and when a war is fought to get you something, you've got to do something with it. Right?

"When it was too late, people saw that freedom can be just a word. And in the case of the Negroes that's all it was. A fine-sounding word, meaning absolutely nothing.

"Most of them stayed on at the plantations, and there might not have been any change whatsoever, except that our white Holy Men got sore. 'Come on, on your feet!' they yelled. 'You're free, don't you understand? You can't just keep on doing the same thing! Go out and get free!' And they hammered away at the Negroes until they managed to convince a lot of them that they were equal. And that's when the trouble really started.

"They were like a bunch of baby gorillas in a toy shop, running loose. They spread out and started playing this thing for what it was worth . . . and in a way, I can't blame them. They didn't want it. It was forced onto them.

"You all know what they did to half of Chicago, New York, and all those places where segregation isn't officially in force. They ruined the neighborhoods, they reduced the level of education in all the mixed schools, they brought filth and disease with them!

"Now the Supreme Court is trying to force the final 'freedom' onto them. Despite the proven, incontrovertible facts which show how nothing but disaster can follow such a move; despite the warnings by prominent sociologists that laziness, lack of initiative, inability to experience strong emotions, lower brain capacity, utter lack of morals—the incapability of distinguishing right from wrong—that these are definitely pure racial characteristics shared by all Negroes since the beginning of time! People who have studied the subject know that integration can never work, for solid factual reasons having nothing to do with prejudice. But the men who sit in our Supreme Court have *not* studied the subject. They are all unqualified men, all politicians—and, they are determined to ruin the South.

"If we let it happen here in Caxton, we are opening the door for a true Dark Age, believe me!"

Adam Cramer looked over the silent, staring group of young men and women, held them another moment with his eyes, and stepped back.

The applause was a gigantic, spontaneous roar. It continued for almost two full minutes.

Then Cramer said, "Are there any questions?"

Ella, who had not listened very carefully, saw Hank Kitchen stand up. She had never seen him look so angry. His face was red.

"Yes?" Adam Cramer said.

"Mr. Cramer, that was a real clever speech. And you speak well, too. I don't. But I think you ought to know that you're not fooling all of us."

"I don't believe I follow you."

"Oh, you follow me, all right. I mean like the way you twisted all the facts just then." Hank Kitchen turned to face the other young people. "I been studying up a little on this thing, too. And for one thing, what he says about our being so nice to the savages and all and taking them away from the jungle and that stuff, that's all wrong. The Africans had a very advanced civilization, as a matter of fact—"

"Who told you that?"

"I read it in the same books you did, mister. And those insurrections—listen, there were plenty of them. They were going on all the time."

"Then why didn't they succeed?" Adam Cramer asked calmly.

"Because someone always betrayed them."

"Someone?" Cramer said. "Yes. To be exact, the Negro house servants. But I've already shown that they are untrustworthy."

There was raucous laughter.

"That's clever, too," Hank said. "You've managed to walk all round one thing, though. And that's where it says in the Constitution that all men are created equal..."

"That particular phrase does not happen to include Negroes," Cramer said. His expression was serene. "At least, that's what the Supreme Court—the body that can do no wrong—said regarding a certain Dred Scott. 'A Negro is assumed, prima facie, to be a slave.' Of course, the Supreme Court had qualified men in those days."

Hank Kitchen stood, groping for words. Adam Cramer continued:

"It's quite obvious what the phrase meant, because I personally cannot imagine an intelligent group of men making a statement that is biologically and sociologically ridiculous. Can you?"

"No. I'm not going to argue. I just want you to know that there are some of us who see right through you."

"And a good many more," Adam Cramer said loudly, "who know that I'm right and are willing to show a little American courage!"

Hank Kitchen sat down. A group gathered around Adam Cramer for a while, then he returned to the booth.

"They're good kids," he said. "You'll always get a couple like that one, though."

"That's Hank Kitchen," Danny Humboldt said. "He's president of the school."

Cramer frowned. "Didn't your grandfather say something about Hank Kitchen, Ella?"

"I guess he did. We used to go steady."

"Oh?"

"Let's go," Ella said. "I've got to get home. If you don't mind..."

Adam smiled. "Sure." He took her arm, said good-bye to Danny and George and Lucy, waved to the crowd, and stepped outside.

As they were about to get into the car, Ella heard Hank's voice. "Wait a second."

Cramer turned. "My favorite heckler," he said.

"Ella's my girl, mister. I'm going to take her home."

"Really? I think that ought to be up to the young lady, actually. Don't you?"

Hank Kitchen took Ella's arm. "Come on," he said.

Ella pulled away. "Just a minute," she said. She had an instantaneous vision of the two of them fighting over her and everybody watching.

"Come *on*. I don't want you hanging around this creep any longer."

"You take your hand off me right this minute!"

"I'd say," Adam Cramer said, "that Miss McDaniel isn't exactly enthusiastic about your plan. Why don't you go on back and have a beer, and—"

"Shut up!" The young man in the white shirt took a step. "I listened to your filthy speech at the courthouse," he said, "and I saw what happened afterwards. I don't know what you're after, but I know that you're nothing but trouble. It wasn't easy getting this thing going right. But a lot of us worked and it went okay, it was going okay—until you showed up. Now you want to ruin everything. Well, you're not going to do it."

Suddenly Ella saw Adam Cramer step back. She saw something else, something you couldn't pin down—a softening, a change, anyway, in his features. She knew there wouldn't be a nice fight. There would only be the rest of the evening spoiled. By Hank.

"I appreciate the sympathies of anyone who wants to obey the law," Adam Cramer said, "but you don't seem to understand—you and that principal, Paton, and some others—that there are ways to beat this and still stay inside the letter of the law. You're young, Mr. Kitchen. You're fiery. And that's good. But make sure of your enemy."

"I am sure. It's you."

"Oh, I'm sorry. I thought you were a Southerner."

"You thought right."

"And you're *for* letting the Negroes in the school?"

"I'm for it; that's right. All for it."

Adam Cramer shrugged. "You can go with him if you want

to, Ella," he said. "Maybe he's got some dark friends he'd like to introduce you to." He turned and started inside the car. Hank's hand darted out and caught his shoulder.

"Mister, you said you were for violence, if there wasn't any other way. I'd like to see how much you believe your own words."

Adam Cramer glanced at the hand that held him, then at the boy.

"You look a little scared," Hank said. "That's the way those Negroes in the car felt."

Ella watched transfixed for a moment; then she touched Hank's arm. "Come on," she said, "stop it, right now. You're acting silly."

"Move away, Ella."

"What are you so mad about?" she said.

Adam Cramer smiled. "Don't you know?" he said.

"No, I don't. Honestly! I just shouldn't have gone out at all tonight."

"That's right. That's why Hank here is mad. Isn't that so, Hank? I suppose you've told everyone that you're performing a civic duty. But the truth is that ideals and politics have nothing to do with it. You want to fight with me because I'm out with your girl."

"That's a lie," Hank Kitchen said.

"You're afraid of admitting it, so you pretend to oppose my politics. Let's be honest now, friend. Let's be honest. As far as the other goes, you've been beaten already, and you know it. You heard them in there, you heard them last night, too. The people want me."

"You're chicken," Hank Kitchen said.

Adam Cramer continued to smile.

"I say you're a lying fake and you're stirring things up to make a few quick bucks. You're taking advantage of a girl who's at least ten years younger than you and not very sharp and she's falling for it because she thinks you're a big man. But you aren't any big man. You're just a cheap Yankee punk!"

Adam Cramer did not move.

He did not breathe hard.

He stood there, smiling.

Hank Kitchen made a disgusted sound and turned toward Ella. "Let's go," he said.

Ella found that she was furious, in a way she'd never known. "You just—" she began, but her heart was beating so fast that she couldn't get the words out.

"Let's go, Ella! If you want to make me jealous or that stuff, okay, I'm jealous. Anything. Well?"

"I hate you!" Ella said. "I'm tired of listening to you and watching you act like a jerk around people and treating me like a— Just don't even try to talk to me or anything, ever."

She ran around to the other side of the car and got in. She slammed the door hard.

Hank Kitchen walked to Adam Cramer slowly. "You're lucky this time," he said. "But if I hear that anything has happened to Ella—and you know what I mean; don't pretend you don't, either —if anything like that goes on, I'll kill you."

Adam Cramer moved behind the wheel and turned on the ignition.

"Ella," Hank Kitchen shouted, "does your dad know you're out with this nut?"

Ella looked the other way and said nothing.

"I'll tell him. We'll see what he has to say about—"

Adam Cramer dropped the gearshift into low and accelerated swiftly.

"I'm so embarrassed," Ella said, "I mean it. I don't know what to say."

"Don't bother. He's just fond of you, that's all."

"Oh, he is not. I've known Hank for, just for years, and he isn't fond of me or any other girl. Not really, I mean. I mean, he's so square all of the time with the football games and the basketball games and being president . . . I haven't ever seen him like this."

It was true. Now that the anger was wearing off, the embarrassed fury, she realized that she *hadn't* ever seen Hank this way.

"I like him," Adam Cramer said.

"What?"

"I said, I like him."

Ella shook her head. "Then maybe you are a little nuts. There hasn't ever been anyone as rude and impolite and nasty as he was to you just then. He acted just like a . . . an animal, or something."

"Well, that's the way it is when you're in love."

"He isn't in love. For gosh sakes, can't you get that? He doesn't know what it is. He never even heard of it. *Hank!*" Ella felt frightened now that Adam would forget that she was desirable and pretty and, above all, a woman, that he would class her with Hank and those kids with the pimples in Rusty's.

Adam Cramer laughed softly. "Forget it, anyway," he said. "If I can, you ought to be able to."

"But the way he acted—"

"Forget it. Hank's an intelligent boy, and he's got a strong mind."

"I'll say. Strong as an ox or something. He's supposed to be the smartest boy in school—but he certainly didn't get very far when he tried to argue with you."

"You've got to remember, Ella," Adam Cramer said, "that Hank is—how old is he?"

"Seventeen."

"Seventeen. He's still a kid. And for a kid, he did very well."

"I suppose that means you think I'm a kid, too."

"Not at all," he said. He kept the car at an even fifty down the dark, narrow road. "Physically and mentally you're grown. I wasn't speaking of chronology. I know some thirty-year-old women who are still in their early teens."

He paused to remove a cigarette, punch the lighter, suck smoke slowly into his lungs.

Ella felt the early fear replaced by a better one, the one she had come to thrill at in the minutes before sleep each night. "Well, anyway, I want to apologize for him. Hank and I haven't been what you'd call close for a long time, he's not my boy friend and I'm not his girl friend, or anything—but even so, I apologize."

"Accepted. Now will you stop huddling over there in the corner? I don't bite or pinch."

Ella moved over and allowed his arm to slip around her shoulder. His fingers touched the flesh of her arm beneath the short-sleeved sweater.

"Can you drive?" he asked.

"Sure, a little."

"Then you shift for me."

Dutifully she shifted from third to first when they stopped at the highway that led over the bridge.

Then, with great deliberation, Adam Cramer turned left. Away from town. Away from town and toward the forests.

He drove for ten minutes, then pulled off onto one of the tiny paths and continued for a mile.

"When the world ends," he said, almost in a whisper, "it will sound something like this. Have you ever been alone in some quiet place and pretended everyone else was dead?"

Ella had, but it was one of her secret thoughts and she was surprised to hear it voiced. "Yes."

"Really? Try it now. Close your eyes and think, No one's left on the earth, no one but us. The cities are empty and the machines have all stopped and there's only the wind, singing through the buildings . . ."

Ella pretended.

"It's a funny feeling, isn't it?"

"Uh-huh."

Adam Cramer lit another cigarette. The smoke had a nice smell, and the little glowing tip of fire excited Ella for some reason. She slowly became all the movie stars she had ever envied from her seat in the dark theatre, and this moment was the fantasy world of her sighs. She could not think of her father and how peculiarly he had been behaving, or of her mother, or even of the strange and complicated things Adam Cramer had been saying. He wasn't real. He was only a means of showing her, briefly, what lay beyond this town of hers, beyond her years, beyond the tight little knot of her experience.

She thought none of these things, however, consciously.

When he turned in the seat and put his arms around her, she made her mind go white of any thoughts at all.

"Do you want me to kiss you?"

Ella closed her eyes.

Adam Cramer parted his lips and pressed them against hers, but not softly this time. She could feel the heat of his body, the moist heat of his mouth.

Then the kiss became something else.

His lips parted wider and she felt his tongue moving. Lucy

had told her, but still it made a sudden chill go across her flesh. His tongue touched hers and traveled deep. He pulled her closer, until her breasts were pressing against his chest, hard, and then his hands began to move also.

Ella trembled. She felt an odd pain, a hurting; and when Cramer's fingers traveled to her sweater, she became frightened.

"Do you want me to do this?"

She resisted for a moment, but she had only known Hank's chaste, scared little kisses before, and she did not know how to resist.

Adam Cramer's fingers burned across her breasts. But she could not stop him. And she found that she did not want to stop him, either. Something inside her said, It mustn't happen, and something else said, soothingly, If it does, it won't be your fault. You told him not to. But he didn't stop.

Everything blurred for Ella then. Her mind became a wash of fear and hunger and shame, all bright pain and new feelings she'd never dreamed; but mostly it was the hunger, the scared wanting for the ugliness to happen.

At the height of the pain, the night stopped. Adam Cramer pulled away and slumped back against the seat of the car. He was breathing heavily, and he was trembling, also.

"I'm sorry," he said, in a pinched voice. "Ella, I am."

Ella sat perfectly still, trying to shut out the thoughts.

"I didn't mean for it to go that far. Will you forgive me?"

She still felt the touch of his fingers against her naked flesh, the perspiration, the longing that squeezed her heart.

"It won't happen again," he said. "I promise."

Still she said nothing.

He started to touch her, then drew back. "I just wanted you to like me, Ella," he said, and she'd never heard that particular tone in his voice before. "That's all."

"Why did you stop?" she said suddenly. She hadn't meant to say it.

"I had to," he whispered.

"Why?"

She saw his fingers pull together and become fists; in the moonlight, his face appeared to harden.

Without speaking, he started the engine and drove back onto the highway.

14

It had been the identical pattern, the identical story, exactly, and he cursed himself for hoping it might be different. It was this sort of stupidity, he thought, that ruined the finest plans. Of course he felt the same overwhelming pain, the same fury at his body for betraying him; but he was also glad that it had happened. Now the girl would become infatuated with him, perhaps. Which would be a help.

He walked into the lobby of the Union Hotel. Mrs. Pearl Lambert sat alone in the big room, statue-still, eyes fastened to the flickering television screen.

"Is it a good one?" he asked cheerfully.

The old woman glanced up, startled; and grinned. "This couple moved into a haunted apartment because the man is a writer," she said. "He writes mystery novels. So they moved there to get atmosphere! Then the wife found a body in the bathroom, only it vanished. The husband won't believe her. He thinks she's just imagining things, y'see? But the killer knows the woman seen the body and— Sit down."

"To tell you the truth, Mrs. Lambert, I'm kind of tired. I thought I might get to sleep early."

"You been working hard?"

"Pretty hard, yes."

The old woman looked at him. "I heard about your speech. It kicked up quite a little ruckus. I suppose you know that."

"Well, I'm not exactly sure what the word 'ruckus' means?"

Mrs. Pearl Lambert laughed. "I guess I ain't, either. Anyway, lots of people heard it. Mr. Polling told me—he's the owner of the car place—and he said he was very impressed. Mr. Polling's a smart man. Of course he's sort of mad at us lately. On account of what Sam did."

"What was that?"

"Oh, you know Sam. He's a fast talker, and he got Mr. Polling to agree to come down almost five hundred dollars on a new car. Just like that!"

He laughed, but as he laughed, he remembered something—something he'd been asked to do. "Is Sam here now?"

"Huh? No, he's over at Farragut. He'll be back tomorrow though, I guess. Sam comes and goes, all the time. He's so nice, him and his wife. Don't you think so?"

He started for the stairs. "Yes," he said, "I liked them a lot."

"She's sort of funny, in a way—stand-offish, you might say. Just the opposite of Sam. I mean, you wouldn't think they'd exactly fit together, if you know what I mean. But he just worships her."

"Yes, you can see that."

"I like Vy, too, don't misunderstand me. But she's a Northerner, you know, and—well, different. Like she belonged in a big city and didn't know what to do with herself in a little-bitty place like Caxton. She never comes down to talk with any of us, or look at TV, or anything. It's odd."

"How do you mean, odd?"

"Well now, it's none of my business. But knowing Sam the way I think I do, you get what I mean, and how he never talks about where they met or anything, I kind of get the feeling there's a lot to that story."

He smiled. "Maybe she's a murderess," he said.

Mrs. Pearl Lambert clapped her hands. "Wouldn't it be wonderful!"

"Good night," he said. "Let me know how the mystery turns out."

"I will. Good night!"

He walked up the dark stairway, onto the buckling linoleum floor. Yellow light poured out from the transom of room 22. He walked by the doorway briskly, and entered his own room.

He lay down on the bed.

The heat was still inside him, and the aching between his legs was almost unbearable. As he lay there, he thought of the girl, Ella, and of all the other Ellas in his life. The first had been a Jewish girl named Jeaness. She was fourteen years old, and he'd sat beside her every day for a whole semester, watching the sun on her legs. They were beautiful legs, with a coating of tan gold on them. He used to think that one could scrape the gold away with a knife. And the Jewish girl, unlike the others, obviously had breasts. They were small but pointed and high, and she always wore a locket which fell between them and accentuated them. He'd been afraid, then, to speak to her, because he knew how ugly he was, how repellent all the pimples and blackheads that covered his face were. But then had come the evening of the big dance, and he'd been more afraid to stay at home, alone, thinking of it; so he'd put powder on his face, and ointments, and he'd gone. And when he'd worked up the courage to ask for a dance, Jeaness had said (and the words rang clear in his mind): "Who let you in?"

Later, when the pimples had disappeared magically, and he'd found ways of gaining popularity, he met the little French girl, Steffie. She was beautiful and desired by all the boys, but now he was adept at campaigns—all sorts of campaigns—and he won an evening with her. It went perfectly, he recalled: perfectly. The dinner at Chapeau Rouge, the drive down Sunset to the beach, along the beach to Malibu, up into the lonely and deserted hills. And after he'd kissed her and felt her breasts and put his hand upon her, she'd told him that she wanted him.

He stubbed the cigarette out in the glass ashtray and tried not to think of these forgotten things.

He tried not to remember how, suddenly, he'd been unable to take Steffie, how she'd wept and begged him, and how he could only say, "I can't, I can't..."

Or how he'd taken her home and then driven all the way to Tijuana, three hundred miles distant, and paid the first pimp and stayed with a scrawny, stupid Mexican girl all night.

It had always been that way.

And now, again, because he'd wanted to, he'd been unable; and the pain of it filled him.

He got off the bed quietly and walked with great care out into the hallway.

He stopped at number 22, and knocked softly.

"Yes?"

He did not answer, but knocked again.

"Who is it?"

"Adam Cramer," he said. "Your neighbor."

There was a long pause; then: "What do you want?"

"A cup of coffee, a little conversation."

After almost a full minute, the door opened. Vy Griffin was dressed in a pleated pink robe. Her hair was down, and she wore no make-up.

"Sam asked me to drop in on you," he said, smiling.

"Did he?"

"Yes. He said he was going to spend the night in Farragut and maybe you could use a little company. If not, I'll go on back to my room."

"That would be a good idea," she said, staring at him.

He did not take his eyes away. "Is it what you want me to do?"

She pulled the robe closer about her. "Yes," she said.

"Why?"

"I'm—tired. I want to go to bed."

He took a step into the room. "At ten-fifteen? I thought you never felt sleepy until one or two."

"Please, I—"

"Sam would be very put out with you if he heard that you weren't hospitable to a friend."

"You're not a friend."

"Unkind. Definitely unkind. I only want a little cup of coffee." He took another step and closed the door. "They usually don't allow hot-plates in boardinghouses. You must be a special case."

Vy Griffin was breathing heavily now. She walked angrily across the room, put the coffeepot under a faucet, snapped on the miniature stove.

He glanced at the unmade bed. "Why did you say that?"

"Say what?"

"That I wasn't your friend."

"I don't know. I'm tired, that's all."

"You behave as if you were afraid of me. Afraid of something, anyway. Are you?"

She said "No!" quickly.

"Well, don't bite my head off!" He sat down on the chair next to the bed. It was an old bed with a large, soft mattress. The center was indented. The sheets smelled of cheap perfume.

He turned to gaze at Vy Griffin, and he could tell that beneath the robe she was small and firm and hot. She would have a fine body. "Mrs. Lambert was telling me how Sam jewed-down Mr. Polling," he said. "Five hundred dollars is a lot to shave off the price of a car. He must be a pretty good pitchman."

"He is."

"You know, that's sort of a paradox to me," Adam went on. "I just can't connect it with the other side of Sam's personality. He seems too honest and—simple."

Vy Griffin fumbled in a bureau drawer, extracted a cigarette. Adam leapt up and struck a match. The woman met his eyes for a moment, then accepted the light. He did not move away.

"How do you stand it, anyway?" he asked softly.

"I don't know what you're talking about."

"Oh, this town, you know—I should think you'd get awfully lonesome. Especially with Sam leaving you half the time."

"I stand it just fine, Mr. Cramer."

"I'm sorry, I'm sorry, I'm sorry. I can't seem to say a thing that doesn't upset you!"

He walked back to the chair and sat down with exaggerated resignation.

"If you don't like my personality, you don't have to subject yourself to it," Mrs. Griffin said. "What are you after, anyway?"

"At the moment, a cup of coffee."

They were quiet for several minutes, then Vy Griffin said: "I listened to your speech. You had them all buffaloed."

"But not you?"

"No; and not you, either. I know a pitch when I hear one, Mr. Cramer. You're a good salesman, but I don't like what you're selling."

"What do you think I'm selling?"

"I'm not sure. But I don't like it, whatever it is. And I don't like you, either. Why don't you leave right now?" She put the cigarette out and turned toward the window.

"I apologize, Mrs. Griffin. I was trying to be friendly. Whatever I've done or said to make you angry, I'm sorry. Good night."

He started for the door.

"Wait." The woman turned around slowly. "The—coffee's ready. There's no sense in wasting it."

She took two cups from the medicine cabinet in the bathroom. "Do you want anything in it?"

He shook his head. "Black is all right. I go both ways."

She handed the coffee to him, and he saw that her hand was trembling. Very slightly.

"I didn't mean to be rude to you," she said.

"I'll still leave if that's what you want."

"No, there isn't any reason for you to. No reason at all."

"You're not sleepy any more?"

"No. Just tired. There's a difference." Vy Griffin sat down at the foot of the bed, drew her legs beneath her and adjusted the robe. "Well," she said, "what would you like to talk about?" Her voice was strangely hard and brittle.

He sipped the coffee. "Since I'm not very interesting," he said, "let's talk about you."

"What makes you think I'm interesting?"

"I know you are. The second I laid eyes on you, I said to myself, Now here's a fascinating woman. Attractive, sexy, smart, sharp. What's she doing in a place like this? I wondered. Then I found the answer."

Mrs. Griffin stared at him. The black hair was lustrous against her white city flesh, and Adam pondered whether or not she was wearing a brassière. If not, then she was built even better than he'd hoped.

"The way I figure it," he said, smiling widely, accentuating his boyishness, "you're an East Indian princess. You were born of a tragic union between an errant Lascar and an island Queen. Sam adopted you at the age of six, then discovered, suddenly, one day, that you were no longer his little girl but instead a ripe, full-blown woman! Am I warm?"

Mrs. Griffin was making an effort to remain formal, but a faint smile curled her lips. He looked at her over the coffee cup. His eyes were large and he used them.

Her smile began to fade.

"That gives us a great deal in common," he said quickly. "Actually, you see, I was the first experiment in artificial insemi-

nation. My mother was brought up very strictly. When Dad
tried to make love to her, she would scream and call the police.
Every time. It was one of those little quirks that people have
sometimes, you know. Anyway, Dad wanted a child in the worst
way, so he talked Mums into going with him to see a doctor, Dr.
Schleckinger. 'We want to have a baby,' Dad said. 'What can we
do?' The doctor dropped his stethoscope. 'Are you serious?' he
demanded. 'Absolutely,' said Dad. 'Well, they have got a new
thing called sex—' And you know what? The minute he said the
word, Mums slapped him and took a taxi home. Can you imagine that?"

Vy Griffin put the empty coffee cup on the floor.

"But wait. You may not believe this, but they did the whole
thing in secret. When Mums got pregnant, she went to a gym
to take off weight. Really! No, I'm deadly serious. After it was all
over, she was so ashamed she never ventured outside the door.
As for me, I developed an overpowering affection for test tubes
which lingers to this day. Whence I actually sprang, I didn't discover until I was seventeen. And who do you suppose it was?"

Mrs. Griffin shrugged.

"Doctor Schleckinger!" He laughed. "All that trouble just because of a basic misunderstanding of a pleasant, simple human
pursuit. Now there's a subject for us! Sex. Are you fer it or agin
it?"

Mrs. Griffin stopped smiling.

"Strike the question. It's irrelevant!" Adam wiped his forehead. "If you don't mind, I'm going to take off my coat. I'm getting
rather hot. Aren't you?" He removed the jacket and walked across
the room to the metal closet. On the bureau was a small antique
lamp with a shade of tinted shell. "You know, I hope, that that
hundred-watt bulb is giving off a lot of heat. Look at the difference." He walked quickly to the center of the room and pulled the
tiny chain connected to the overhead bulb. The room was immediately thrust into blackness. He turned on the shell lamp. It put
out a soft, violet glow. "See?" he said.

Mrs. Griffin did not answer. Her breathing was quick and
loud.

"Zip, we're down five degrees, I'll bet!" Adam walked to the bed and sat down on the edge, then he reached up and touched Mrs. Griffin's forehead. "You're not very comfortable, are you?" he said softly, removing his hand.

The woman's voice was a whisper. "Please," she said.

"Please what?"

She was quiet.

"You want me to leave?"

She made no sound.

"Vy, it does get lonely for you, doesn't it? I know it does. I feel that way myself, a lot of the time. I do." He put his hands on her shoulders. "I find myself alone in some little town and I almost go crazy because there isn't anyone who feels things the way I do. And I think how wonderful it would be to meet a person like that and be with that person for a little while. Not for long. Just for a little while." He could feel the heat of her body through the robe, he could feel the pulsing of her heart through his palm.

Very firmly he drew her close and kissed her. Her lips were full and soft, but they resisted him, as her body resisted him, and he found that this added to his excitement.

"You want it," he said. "I knew that when we met. You may not like me, but you want me, and there's no point lying."

Vy Griffin tore his hand away from her breast. "I love Sam," she said.

"Of course," he said. "But that doesn't make any difference. We're not hurting Sam. You won't tell him, and I certainly don't intend to. So relax. It isn't the first time, is it?"

Her hand stung sharply across his face. He grasped her wrist and forced her across the bed. Without speaking, he untied the cord that held the robe, and remained motionless.

"Tell me you're not excited," he said. "Tell me you don't want to sleep with me now." He pulled the robe apart. She was naked beneath it. Her body was white and glistening in the violet light. Adam knelt and kissed her breast and felt the nipple harden against his tongue. He placed his hand, almost casually, between her legs. "Go on," he said, "tell me you don't want me. If you do, I'll leave right now."

But Vy Griffin could not speak. In that moment she seemed to relax, to stop fighting and thinking and being afraid. Her arms reached up and pulled Adam down tight upon her. Her mouth parted and covered his, hungrily.

He took off his clothes and lay down next to her again and lay there waiting for the pain to grow, smelling the cheap perfume and the heat and the night.

It was a sickness, someone had once told her. Just like other sicknesses. You went to a doctor and he cured you. So she'd gone to a doctor, and he'd talked with a lot of big words, but what he'd ended up saying was what she'd known all along: there was no cure. You can take the needle away from an addict and you can lock him up, but you cannot take away his hunger and his need.

For five years she had fought the need, ever since Sam had come into her life. But she knew it was there, like a cancer in her blood; and she knew, also, that it would consume her one day. And that would be the end of everything.

Now, with this strange young man touching her, lighting fires inside her, she remembered the five years as though they had been moments—the only happy moments in her life . . .

She had been working a cocktail bar called The Cat's Pajamas in New York, in company with three other professionals. What were their names? Sally, the big girl with the light tan skin and slanting eyes who palmed herself off as Spanish and got away with it. Jewel, an old Negress, very dark and very stupid, but acclaimed because of her special abilities. And Irene. And it was getting late that night, and business had been slow.

The memory came into sharp focus; she lived it more clearly than she was living these moments now. And she could hear the voices of the Negro women more clearly than Adam Cramer's . . .

"I don't know," Jewel said, "but it's probably the weather. I dropped into Hardy's and you know how it is there all the time, but there was only the regulars. And they were watching TV."

"You shouldn't ought to go there," Irene said. The brown fur matched her skin perfectly. "It's bad for all of us."

Jewel laughed. She was the independent one, the smart one. A few bottles of blonde hair dye and some make-up had lifted her from the eight-dollar class to the twenty-five-dollar class, but she had little pride. Hardy's had been her hang-out for six years.

It was a rough Harlem joint, but, as she put it, there were a lot of nice men came there. It almost seemed that she missed the free-wheeling, above-board atmosphere there, where a prostitute was a prostitute and everyone knew it and there was no monkey business, like at the Cat, of pretending you were something else.

Sally giggled. Despite her flashy modern dress, she had an air of the 'twenties about her, a fragile, little-girl appearance. This, combined with the sultry Latin quality, made her the most popular of the four. All men were "Daddy" to Sally, all tricks "nice times," and she always lowered her eyes when she mentioned money. "We could go to a movie and come back," she said.

"We've been to a movie," Irene said.

"Well, I'm getting tired. Aren't you, Vy?"

Vy nodded. She didn't actually like any of these women, but working alone was unbearable. It gave you too much time to think. For a while, after the last job fell through, she had been able to persuade herself that she was nothing more than an up-to-date, twentieth-century person, living and loving free. But when the money ran out and she began accepting "gifts," she faced it squarely. If you're going to take money, then you're a professional, and you might as well work like one. It's all you know how to do, anyway. You can't type or take dictation, and you're not pretty enough—in the light—to get by without it.

So she worked with Jewel and Sally and Irene, because that gave the customers a choice. A white girl was good for business.

Especially a peroxide blonde who knew how to wear furs and had smooth, clean skin.

But she had nothing in common with them. They were stupid and vulgar and hard. Sex was their line of work and that was how they regarded it.

When she'd been younger, Vy had read novels about sloppy old whores with hearts of pure gold, basically lovable creatures, and this had comforted her at first. But she had never met anyone in the profession who fitted that description. The whores she knew were frequently sloppy and sometimes old, but their hearts were shriveled and they were far from lovable. It was not so much that they were evil, merely that they were stupid. That, Vy soon found out, was the characteristic of the real professional.

With the hundred-to-five-hundred-a-night girls, and the Holly-wood crowd she'd heard about, maybe it was a little different. She doubted it. In the years she'd worked she'd come into con-tact with a great many prostitutes, and they were all pretty much the same. They worked a few hours at night, slept most of the day, died poor. And she was no different. That was the important thing to remember. Despite the way she felt, her reasons, despite everything, she was no different.

"Well, it's hot in this fucking place and I'm tired," said Jewel. "I'm going to—"

"Don't use that word, don't use that word," Sally said.

"Why not?"

"It isn't ladylike."

They sat over their glasses of Scotch and crushed ice and waited, and then three men came in and Vy could tell that they were marks. They laughed too loudly, and when they sat down, they looked around the place too hard, and they were not New Yorkers.

"See, now?" Jewel whispered. She smiled faintly in the direc-tion of the men and returned to her drink.

A few minutes passed, then one of the marks got up from his seat and walked over. He was blushing fiercely, and Vy could tell that he was drunk. Not too drunk, maybe. But drunk.

"Hi," he said.

Sally giggled.

"I'm, uh—well, what I want to know is, I wonder if we could buy you girls a drink."

He was looking at Sally. In the dim bar light, she was sexy, and she made the most of her breasts. She'd had the muscles tied in one of those operations, and they stuck out, erect and hard. "Well, I just don't know," she said. "You know anybody here?"

"Know anybody?" the man said. He craned his neck to look at his friends. "Oh. Well, see, we're just sort of visiting here in town. We're just visiting, on a trip. We thought we, uh, might could have a little fun."

Vy took her eyes away. He was ugly and close to middle years, and the other two didn't look much better. But that didn't count, she told herself as always. If you're a professional, you're a professional. Weed out the wild ones and the disgusting ones, but take anything else. You can't afford to pick and choose the way amateurs do.

"We're not allowed to unless you know somebody," Sally said, giggling. "I'm sorry."

It was almost like prohibition. Since the lid had been put on, you had to be careful. The cops were real bastards now.

"Well," the man said, "maybe I do know somebody at that. Let me just check a little, and I'll be back. You wait, now."

He went over to the booth, and Vy saw one of the men, a heavy, red-faced fellow, grin and shake his head. He looked like a pleasant sort, and it was obvious that he was new at this sort of thing.

The first man pointed to Vy and the red-faced man looked over at her. He stared for a long while. Then he turned away.

"I think it's gonna be okay," Irene said.

Sally said, "I hope so. I'm tired."

The first man went to the bar and got Ewald aside. From the corner of her eye, Vy could see the bill pass hands. Then Ewald walked over and said, "Girls, this is an old buddy of mine, Howard De Vries. He and his friends would like to buy you some drinks. Do you mind?"

Sally giggled again. "Not a little bit of it," she said.

The man called De Vries winked at Ewald and went to collect his friends. Soon they were all seated in the large, semicircular booth.

"This is Billy Diamond," De Vries said, gesturing at a thin, scared man with sandy hair; then, looking at the fellow with the red face, "and this is Pete Jones."

Vy smiled at Jones and knew, instantly, that he would choose her.

"How about it?" De Vries asked, much more at ease now. "What you want to drink, girls?"

Jewel said, "Scotch."

Ewald nodded and went away.

"I thought we was going to be out of luck," De Vries said to Sally. "Things have changed."

"Not too much," Sally said, fluttering her eyes.

"No, guess not too much!"

Ewald returned with the drinks. The man called Diamond dropped a ten-dollar bill onto the plastic tray and said, "Keep the rest."

Vy could feel Jones's eyes on her. They were kind eyes, she could feel that, too. He would be all right.

After the introductions, it was clear that Jewel would be left out. She threw down her drink and said to De Vries, "You aim to go out afterwards?"

"Sure."

"I know a way you can have twice as much fun."

"Well," De Vries said, "I don't know, I don't think so."

"You ain't heard about Jewel?"

"Well, we're sort of low on money tonight. And—"

"Okay," she laughed, "forget it." She rose from the table. "Night's still young." She looked much older than her thirty-eight years, standing there. The blonde hair was grotesque in the blue light. "Have fun, kids."

"Don't you go to Hardy's," Sally said. "We don't want no cut-rate anything's goin' on, now. Hear?"

Jewel grinned and walked away.

Pete Jones took a swallow of his drink and said, "You think you could go with me this evening, miss?"

Vy kept the professional tone in her voice. Maybe it was the hot waiting and the liquor, or the time she'd had to think, she didn't know; but she felt something near shame, now, the feeling she'd had to fight down the first two years. "I don't see why not, Mr. Jones."

"I'd like that." He bent his head to look at her. "You know, miss, I think you're about the prettiest girl I've seen in New York."

She smiled professionally. "That's nice, Mr. Jones."

He turned a little redder then, and took another swallow. She could hear the other voices, Sally's fantastic giggle, Irene's husky tones. They seemed to contrast sharply with this man's soft, Southern accent.

"My name isn't really Jones," he said. "The boys decided we ought to make up names. But I'd slip, I just know I would. So I might as well tell you the truth—it won't hurt, anyway. I got nobody."

"You don't have to."

"I know, but I'd as soon. My name is Sam Griffin. I'm a pitchman, I sell things. But I'm not having much luck here. This is an awful cold town."

Vy sipped at the Scotch. She heard Irene say, "You don't have to worry about nothing, honey."

Diamond had begun to whisper. "Do you do—everything?" he asked, and seemed startled at his courage in asking it.

"I haven't had no complaints from my customers," Irene said, smiling.

"Call me Sam. Not many people do. I travel around so much of the time, I don't get a chance to make friends. These other fellas are pitchmen too; I run into them last night, over at the department store. Ed's got a line of wind-proof cigarette lighters, Harry's pushing a fabric cleaner. Pretty good line, too, but the people are so cold in New York. They just stare at you. I mean, it's the biggest city in America, but I never did feel so alone." He paused. "I suppose that sounds kind of sappy to you."

"No," Vy said. "It doesn't."

Sam Griffin beamed. "But I don't see how you could ever feel alone—" He blushed. "What I mean to say—well, that's me, putting my big foot in my mouth all the time! What I meant was, a pretty girl like you, there must be fellas . . ."

"Relax, Mr. Griffin. I know what you mean."

He looked at her. "I think you do, you know? Nobody else does. These guys, Ed and Harry, they're happy as pigs all the time. Got everything they need. No matter where they light, it's home to them—and most pitchmen are that way."

Vy straightened in the seat. They're not men, she told herself, they're customers. And it's getting late.

"You want to go with me tonight?" she said suddenly, in a different tone.

Sam Griffin smiled. "I sure do."

"It's twenty-five dollars, hour limit," Vy said.

A hurt look came into Sam Griffin's eyes, as though she had disappointed him; but he did not stop smiling. "You want it now?" he said.

"No. Afterwards."

"Anything you say, Vy."

"Are you ready, or do you want to drink some more? If you do, I'll have to charge."

"I'm ready now," he said. "Gosh, you got pretty hair. I don't think I ever saw such pretty hair."

"Go to the James Hotel," Vy said, avoiding his eyes, shutting out his voice. "Register as Mr. and Mrs. Taylor. You know where the James Hotel is?"

"No."

She gave him the address. "Remember, register as Mr. and Mrs. Taylor. They'll take you to room 7. Lock the door and wait for me there."

"Yes, ma'am."

"Get a cab now. I'll stay here fifteen minutes and come over."

"Is it real?"

"What?"

"Your hair."

"No. Dye."

"Well, it's pretty, anyway. It smells good." Sam Griffin started out. Then he turned. "You'll come, you promise?"

"Sure."

The man who called himself Diamond stopped Sam Griffin and whispered loudly, "Griffin, listen, you ought to try the dark stuff. I'm not kiddin'. They really know how, things you never even thought of."

"I'm okay," Sam Griffin said. "I'm fine."

"Yeah, but you could come over to the joint with us afterwards. You ever had any dark stuff?"

"No, but—"

"I'm tellin' you, Sammy. They're a hundred million times as good. Skillful, what I mean. And you don't need to worry, let me tell you. Clean."

Vy pretended not to listen, for she knew instinctively that Sam Griffin would be terribly embarrassed.

"You hear what mine just said? I asked her, you know, 'Are you okay?'—and she said, 'Honey, you may love me but I love me more!' These are twenty-five-dollar whores, Sammy—they douche before and after, they go to the doctors for check-ups. I never heard of anyone getting anything offa them."

"Keep your voice down, Ed."

"What?"

"Shut up, shut up, keep your goddamn voice down."

"Why, what's the matter with you, anyway?"

"Nothing."

"Then why you looking that way?"

"No way, Ed."

"I'm just trying to give you a good time. You never tried the dark stuff. I'm just telling you it's great, that's all."

"Okay, you told me. Now forget it. I'll see you tomorrow."

"Okay! But you're screwing yourself, that's who you're screwing, believe me. The white dames, all they do is a job; I know. They ain't got their heart in it. And for anything extra, man, you go through all kinds of crap. Now you don't want to throw your money down the drain, do you?"

Vy heard Sam Griffin walking away, and she was glad when he was gone.

"Am I right?" Diamond said to Sally.

Sally giggled, and Vy wished, suddenly, that she'd not decided to work tonight.

What was the matter with her, anyway?

The voices and the bar-sounds faded, and she found herself thinking of Hammond, of August and the rich yellow hay smells, and Bo. It was almost corny, the way it happened that first time. Bo—she'd never learned his full name—had been a trouble shooter for the telephone company. And he'd come by when Mother was visiting Maudie for the weekend. There wasn't anything wrong with the telephone, but he had to check, that was his job. His sleeves were rolled up, and the cords stood out beneath the rippling tanned flesh, and she had the feeling, the same as she'd had so many times before. Only, Bo hadn't looked at her as if she were a child. He'd laughed a lot and poured himself some water and told her she was pretty. And when he'd asked if she was alone, she'd told him the truth.

He had been the first.

She'd felt miserable afterwards, when he'd gone, and she knew how wrong it had all been; but that night she'd dreamed of his hands and of the sight of his big tanned body in the bedroom, of his rough, harsh, unmusical voice.

Bo came back the next day, and she gave herself to him again, and on the next day, and on every day until her mother returned.

She could remember the second man, but the others all seemed to blur into one faceless male entity. The mathematics teacher, Mr. Loge, the shy little boy who'd been so surprised when she'd not pushed him away, the sailors and soldiers, all giving her what she wanted and did not want, desperately did not want, but had to have.

Of course, no one understood, because she didn't understand, either. When her mother found out about it, she called her a filthy tramp, and Vy supposed that that was right. So she quit high school and came to New York. In New York she could start fresh, get a job, meet someone nice. But it was only a continuation of the same. In every office there would be at least one man who could recognize her, see this thing that burned inside of her. How? How could they know? She looked no different from the other girls, she dressed well, she was proper and ladylike. Still they knew. And they would tell, afterwards. And that would be the end of the job.

Now it was too late to go back, even if there were anything or any place to go back to. She still had this hungry thing that could not be cut out of her, and it still needed to be fed.

Forget that you ever wanted a normal life, she told herself. You're not sick or neurotic or tragic. You don't long for love or tender words. You're just a beat doll who can't get along without a good time. It doesn't matter who does it, just so there's some variety!

Irene patted her hand. "We're goin' now, Vy," she said. "It's about time for you, isn't it?"

"I guess so."

"See you back here in about an hour?"

"Maybe."

She got up and walked down the narrow aisle. The mirror threw back the reflection of an overdressed blonde. Vy looked away: all she needed was a scarlet letter sewn to her dress or a sign reading WHORE. Of course, that was good. People had to be able to pick you out from the crowds of normal women. . . .

The cold February wind knifed into her. As she walked toward the taxi stand, she thought, I've got ten years left, maybe less. Then I'll have to lower my rates. A year or two of that, and I won't be able to give it away. No one will want Vy then. Look at Jewel. Poor old Jewel, she's just about finished.

What do you do when you're finished and no one wants you?

"James Hotel, please."

The cabbie nodded and they traveled, too fast, as always, too fast, through the frozen night. "A buck," he said, and then he roared away and Vy stood facing the familiar hotel. It looked like a perfectly ordinary hotel, and there were hundreds of guests who thought it was, but the seventh floor was reserved. A dozen prostitutes kept permanent rooms there. The rent, plus a regular cut to the manager and the night clerks, came to fifty dollars a week. Then there were the doctor's expenses, the bites taken by the bars, certain taxi drivers, "life insurance." It was a hard way to live, at best. One slow week and you had to work overtime to break even.

Maybe I should go to Cuba, she thought, as she walked inside the gray lobby, or Mexico—they say white girls make out all right there.

"Is Mr. Taylor in?" she asked.

The clerk was a thin, bored man named Alex. He smelled of perspiration and cigar smoke. "Heavy guy, blue suit, freckles?"

"That's right."

"Upstairs." Alex returned to his paperback book.

Vy straightened her clothes and entered the rickety, ancient cage-elevator. When the door closed, she thought of Sam Griffin. Just a customer, she told herself. Remember that. Be professional, be casual, be hard.

She rapped on the door lightly. It was opened immediately by Sam, who looked even more cheerful than before. Perhaps a little frightened, but mostly cheerful. "Hi," he said. "I was beginning to think maybe you'd forgotten about me."

He helped Vy with her coat and stepped back. "It was awful nice of you to come," he said.

She looked at the solid, honest bulk of him, at the trusting eyes that had the light of youth in them but also a certain deep sorrow behind the light, and she knew instantly.

"This is your first time, isn't it?" she said.

Sam Griffin blushed. "How'd you guess that?"

"You're still dressed."

"Ma'am?"

"With most of them, by the time I get here they're lying on the bed naked. All ready."

"They are?" His eyes grew with wonder, and the blush deepened. He took a few steps toward her. "My God, you're pretty, Miss Vy. I like that dress."

His voice was gentle and soft. Sometimes the young kids were that way, because they were scared, but this was different. Sam Griffin didn't seem to be scared. He didn't seem to be accusing her, either, but she felt the shame again. She felt the shabbiness of the room, the dirt in the carpet, the cheap lamp that hid these things and hid the things that showed in her face.

"That's nice, honey," she said, and her voice sounded brittle. "You want to get started?"

"Whatever you say."

"Not whatever I say, honey. It's your money." She turned away so that she would not have to see the hurt look that kept jumping into his eyes. "You pay in advance, by the way."

He put two tens and five ones on the bureau. She counted them and stuffed them into her purse.

"Now it's your show," she said.

Sam Griffin stepped closer to her and put his large hands on her face. "Wouldn't you just like to talk a while?" he said. "I haven't had anyone to talk to since I got to New York."

"It doesn't matter to me. But remember, you only got an hour."

"Miss Vy, listen. I think I'm a pretty good judge of people. I deal with 'em all the time in my work. I can spot the hard ones and the dishonest ones and the sharp ones right off the bat; I can spot the good ones, too. When I seen you tonight, when I seen your eyes, I mean, I knew you were a good one. I got the idea that maybe you were a little bit like me—now, don't laugh. I mean it. See, I sell things, too, and I work alone most of the time, like you, and I guess I'm pretty good at my job—but there's something missing. I don't notice it except when I'm all through for the day. But then I get to thinking about it, wondering what it is. Do you —know what I mean?"

Vy said "No" very distinctly. "But you tell me all about it, if you want to. I'll listen. I got nothing to do."

Sam paused a moment. Then he said, "What's the matter? Don't you like me to talk to you this way?"

"What gives you that idea?"

"You're fighting me. Like customers do when they know they want to buy something from me but they're afraid to part with the money. I'm only trying to be friendly. I thought we had something in common—"

"Well, we don't. We don't have anything in common. And forget trying to be friendly!"

"You don't want me to talk nice to you?" Sam seemed to be honestly amazed.

"No! Please, I—"

Then he kissed her, and the sweet strength of him covered her and made her warm. She pulled away. "And don't do that, either! Don't do that!"

"Why? Don't you like me?"

"That hasn't got anything to do with it. You just don't kiss prostitutes, it isn't being done."

"I don't like that word, Miss Vy."

"Well, that's what I am, and don't forget it. You're just a little drunk, mister, and you're lonesome and feeling sloppy. If you want to get laid, okay—but if you're going to carry on like this, let's forget the whole thing. You can have your money back."

The big man searched her eyes for a long time, then went to the bed and sat down. "I apologize," he said. "Like you say, I was feeling sloppy."

"So what do you want to do?"

"I—" He looked over at her. "I want to be close to you."

"You want to get laid? I do a good job. Ask anybody."

He did not answer.

"You want to watch me undress? Sometimes they do."

He sat still; then, slowly, he turned, and the expression on his face was new. Vy winked at him and took off her clothes, slowly. Her body was good, the breasts firm and erect, the hips large. "You like it?" she said, keeping the professional tone in her voice.

Sam Griffin said nothing. He only stared. But not, she knew, at her body alone. He was staring at *her*.

"Strip down, honey," she said.

"Why?"

"Because it's the rule. Some customers have guns in their pockets. You get some queer ones."

"I don't have a gun."

"I know. But strip down anyway. You'll be more comfortable. You want me to help?"

She began unfastening his shirt. His hands did not move toward her body. "Why are you acting this way?" he asked suddenly. "This isn't you."

"It's me, all right," she said. "Come on, you want to feel the titty? Come on." She placed his hand around her breast and felt the nipple swell against his palm. "You like that?" She started to pull at his trousers when Sam put his arms around her, tightly, and held her.

"Don't do that, mister. Come on. I want to get screwed. I want—"

"Shut up!" He pulled away and shook her and said, "Shut up! That isn't you talking. Didn't I tell you, I know people. I know you. You're afraid of being yourself. I don't know why yet, but you are. Well, listen to me—I'm going to find out, I swear by God."

Vy tried, then, but she was tired of fighting now and the strength of Sam Griffin overwhelmed her. The tears came and she did not try to halt them. They trailed down her face like acid, the burning sorrow and loneliness of all the years of her life.

She put her head against Sam Griffin's chest and wished that she could die there.

After a long time, he said to her, "I'm going to see you tomorrow, Miss Vy. And the day after that. I'm going to keep on seeing you, and we're going to get to know each other."

And he'd walked with her to her apartment that night, and she'd dreamed of the big, honest man. . . .

*

Vy heard the door close, and she listened until the footsteps had disappeared and the room was still.

She thought of Sam, and was, oddly, relieved. It was over now. She had been given five happy years, and she was grateful.

Dear Sam, she thought. You didn't really think it would happen, did you? She's cured, you thought. My love cured her.

But I knew. For five years I stayed beside you or in my room, alone, because I knew that sometime, somewhere, an Adam Cramer would show up, and that it would all end then.

I've betrayed you. And I know that I could never make you understand that while it was happening, I loved you more than ever, and wanted you, and needed you. How could you understand that?

But oh, Sam, I do love you! But it's happened now and maybe it will happen again, and I could never bear to look at you and see the pain in your eyes.

This way you won't know.

Forgive me. Please, God. Sam—forgive me!

15

Dear Max:

I said I'd keep you posted, and so I shall. I am, as you know, a man of my word—when it's convenient.

As explained in previous letters, the phone calls worked very well indeed—and Mr. Shipman turned out to be a prize catch! We have more than enough for the work at hand, for I'd forgotten the "crackers" and "red-necks" who didn't have telephones, also the outside fringe element, all of whom have joined up—

But don't let me get ahead of myself!

The plan is still fairly vague, but it's beginning to take on form; and pretty unique form, at that. One thing is certain, I have submerged the Adam Cramer you and I knew and loved (!)—Requiescat in Pace! A charming lad he was, full of wit and intelligence, but he don't go so good here. His replacement would nauseate you: a gentle, courteous, polite young feller that talks the people's talk, yes sir. Now I am like a bar mirror, in a way. The folks look at me and see themselves (and all their prejudices) in a soft, flattering light. I'm their idea of a smart, civilized, educated man. Since I think exactly the same way they do, they regain respect for themselves. And they love me for it!

I know this isn't entirely original. The *Trattato di Sociologia Generale* proved useful, oddly, if only in what I rejected from it; and Sorel's syndicalism provides a nice little first-attack theme—you know what I mean. (Syndicalism in the old sense is far from what I have taking shape, but ideas exist from which one can select. There is "peace" here, but I discovered a San-Andreas-fault of violence lying below. Recently a "scab" coal miner from a nearby town was buried alive when he refused to kowtow; and there have been other incidents. They take their groups seriously.)

Anyway, belief is important: that, I think, is my first job—to believe deeply everything I say. At all costs, I must avoid intellectuality; except of the kind we discussed. I will not think of my "system"; later on, when it's successful, I can, like Benito, order a philosophy to be delivered within two weeks, or else.

Do you recall when we used to discuss the importance of public-speaking abilities? Well, we were wrong. I never excelled particularly at this sort of thing, yet my speeches have been enormously successful. You would not believe it. The first one whipped the crowd into a wonderful fury, and afterwards they shuffled about like Pavlovian dogs who have heard the dinner bell. A good many were roughnecks and hooligans and there were, of course, several impressionable children; but several of Caxton's so-called "good people" were there, too, and their reactions were exceedingly gratifying. All were frustrated. Their blood was hot, and they wanted to do something—right now. When a car full of Negroes passed—I heard about this later: I was with my "sponsor," Shipman, at the time —they stopped it, and the local sheriff had to be called!

There are a few moderately intelligent foes with whom I shall have to contend, but by and large, Max, the town is with me. SNAP is flourishing, and it will not be long before

we can ease into some action. It will be necessary to show the
bad influence of the Negroes in the school (a simple matter,
now, with SNAP treasury funds available for pay-offs) and
then, rather than have the whites withdraw (my first thought)
which would seem a bit defeatist, we will—

He stopped writing; the heat began to press in upon him, and
now that the pain was gone, he found that he was tired.

He removed his clothes and fell, naked, upon the bed; almost
immediately he dreamed of the girl in the stateroom who rotted
at his touch, but now she looked like Ella, and the laughing people
were Jeaness and the French girl and his father and, peculiarly,
Max Blake. They hung on the hooks and laughed hysterically.

Then the dream shifted, and he fell into a twilight state, conscious enough to realize that he was dreaming but unable to do
anything about it, anything whatever, except watch.

He saw the times that were lost, which he loved and missed
because they were lost. Himself at six, squeezing his thin body
between the sink and the wall and watching, with awe and with
a deep warm pleasure, the ritual of his father shaving, asking
"Will I ever be able to do that?" And his father, in one of those
foolish, unfunctional, armless undershirts, looking so odd and
different that way but still carrying the dignity of his light gray
suit-and-vest, somehow, even with the gigantic moles and warts,
like mushrooms, dangling from his pale skin, saying, "Of course,
of course, now go away!"

Himself at seven, in the evenings just before bedtime, when
he would lie down on the floor, the upper half of him beneath
the brown radio which sat high on carved stilts, and listen in this
single world wholly his own. Never real, he thought, dreaming.
I've made them up. I didn't have a childhood. There was no brick
house, no serpentine river, no Danny and Marty and me shooting at the used prophylactics that we called balloons because we
thought they were balloons, what else could they be? And no
dark sewer that went beneath the ground for a thousand miles, so
far that you could lose sight of the opening; certainly no baseball
in the streets before the fall of night, or rides on scarlet horses, or
beds for sleeping . . .

No, his life had begun at the age of twelve, when the sickness came like a thief and stole away the man who might have been and put a wrinkled mummy in his place.

16

The cars moved slowly, quietly, down the street and into the uphill gravel path. Seventy models, many bright and new and shining, many old and streaked with filth. A multicolored centipede, an endless creature inching forward, its hundred and forty eyes unblinking in the summer night.

Within the cars were ghosts. All silent, sheeted white and capped with peaks of white, riding stiffly, sitting straight.

The car in front, a Buick, slowed. A hooded figure turned the wheel, and next to him, a young man nodded, smiling slightly.

"We won't have to stop," he said, "just keep it steady."

Up the grade, past all the lighted houses, across the dark fields, then to Simon's Hill; the cars rolled on, their engines humming softly.

Past the rotted wooden shack where Negroes sat on stools, drinking coffee, cola; eating pie;

Past the first apartment;

Past the tailor shop, the barbershop;

—"Just keep it steady."—

Past the open windows, slowly, winding, tire treads snapping pebbles, deep internal springs in dry squeaks making rhythm.

And the ghosts sat straight.

"Hey, lookit," said Stuart Porterfield. He'd finished his work and watched TV, and then he'd gotten kind of restless, kind of hungry: at The Huddle there were always friends. He poked Andrew McGivern's shoulder.

"What's that?"

"Out the window, there."

The small, dark man who had been talking of family life in a high-pitched voice put down his fork and squinted.

"That's the Klan," said Porterfield.

"You guess?"

"Hell, yes. Look at the sheets, and all. That there's the Klan."

The other customers had paused in their talk and all were staring now. The owner, French Rosier, a big, scarred man, wiped the palms of his hands on his spotted apron quietly.

"What they gonna do?" asked Andrew McGivern.

"I don't know." Stuart Porterfield shredded a paper napkin from an aluminum dispenser, touched his mouth and swiveled on the stool. "Christ, I don't know what they gonna do."

"I tell you this," said a husky young man, to no one, "if they on the Hill for trouble, I see to it they ain't disappointed."

"You shut up, Glad Owens, now, you just shut up with all that," said French Rosier. "Ain't a damn thing happened yet."

"Maybe they're kids," a man on the last stool said, "having a little fun, you know."

"No," the young man said. "They ain't kids."

"How do you know? Where you get this inside information?"

No one moved. They sat with their heads turned slightly, watching.

"... twenty-seven, twenty-eight, twenty-nine," said Stuart Porterfield.

"There sure a lot."

"Yeah." Porterfield was rigid on the stool, the stained and yellowed cigarette close to his flesh, the clinging ash about to fall. Above the café's grill a plastic radio made hissing sounds: the radio was cracked from all the times it had been dropped, and the cracks had spread, unhealed, the Scotch-tape bandages now curled and blistered, dropping. On the wall a cheap alarm clock ticked. A tinted photograph of a smiling man in uniform hung crooked: *To my Dad, This is the life, Sandy.*

Stuart Porterfield felt the bite of the fiery tip, but he did not look down. Slowly his fingers pulled the paper from the tobacco, crushed the wrinkled flakes, transformed the glowing end to black ash.

"Fifty-seven!" said the husky young man. "Bullshit they ain't planning somethin'. Listen, why we sitting here like dummies with our women home alone?"

"Don't move," said French, "I'm tellin' you."

"Don't move! Like hell!"

"Glad, I seen all this before in other places," French Rosier said, wiping his hands. "You got no call to be afraid."

The boy got up and glared and walked across the floor and stood there.

"Listen," French went on, "all those fellas want to do is scare us. They just like a bunch of kids on Halloween. You remember when you was a little boy, on Halloween?"

Glad Owens did not answer.

"What I bet is, you got yourself one of your mama's sheets and went outside at night. Now ain't that true? Why, sure, it is. You made believe you was a spook and hid behind a bush and when somebody passed, you jumped out. 'Boo!' We all did that. But think back, Glad. You was with a lot of other spooks, I bet, you wasn't by yourself."

"Oh, shut up, French, you talking crazy!"

"No, I ain't. I'm saying that those fellas out there ain't no different from the kids at Halloween. They got to be bunched together and they got to hide behind bedsheets because every one of them is scared to death. In the daylight you'd laugh at them; they'd laugh at themselves."

"I don't know about all that, French. It might could be: I never said they wasn't chicken-shit. But they *ain't* alone. They together. All it takes is one to say 'Let's do it' and the whole damn bunch'll do it."

Stuart Porterfield said, "That's a fact, French, that's a fact."

"They only trying to scare us! Take it easy. There ain't nothing going to happen tonight; it ain't the way they work. This here is just a warning, like; a chance to strut a little. Come on, now, forget about them. Finish up your coffee!"

Stuart Porterfield took out a handkerchief from his back pocket and wiped his forehead slowly, and as all the others did, stared out.

They say they pay a whole lot better in New York, he thought; *a plasterer can make himself a pile there, easy. . . .*

Up the gravel path the cars rolled, headlights reaching out

beyond the farthest rise, the men in sheets inside the cars all straight and silent.

The license plates were varied: some were from Farragut County, some from nearby towns, and several from other Southern states.

But no one looked at the licenses.

"I didn't know they still had such a membership," said Elbert Peters, looking down upon the seemingly endless parade.

"I didn't either," Charley Hughes said. The cards lay on the table, the half-drunk bottles of beer, the can of peanuts, all untouched since John Holbert's call, his breathless "Go look out the window!"

Helene Peters, Elbert's wife, sat in a chair. Her eyes were wide.

"You know, in a way, though," Charley Hughes said, "I'm kind of glad to see them. When I was in Georgia, oh, it must be twenty years ago, they had all sorts of demonstrations—but I always missed the fun. It got so I didn't really believe there was a Ku Klux Klan." He smiled good-naturedly, glanced at his friends, and picked up a bottle of beer.

"Who's the Dragon in Caxton?" he asked.

"I don't know. It might be that fella, you know, Carey, that's been ranting and raving. Or the Jumpin' Preacher."

"Niesen?"

"Yeah, it could be him—except the people who would follow him I don't think could afford those cars."

They leaned on the windowsill, watching. Suddenly Charley Hughes laughed.

"What is it?"

"Oh, I just thought, now, wouldn't it be funny if one of them had a flat tire along about now!"

"Man, you have a peculiar sense of humor, that's all I can say." Elbert Peters got his bottle of beer and took a swallow, and grinned.

"It would be something, though, wouldn't it, El? You're riding along and looking fierce and ugly and then, boom!—a flat. Right in the middle of the parade. You have to get out and change the tire, but look—do you take off the sheet? If you don't, it'll get all soiled; and if you do, then everybody sees that you're the little bookkeeper over at the Mill who's afraid of his boss. And think about all the others, sitting in back of you, waiting. They can't even blow their horns—by God, I got me half a notion ..." He took another swallow of beer and turned toward Helene Peters. "Honey, you got a box of carpet tacks around this place? Elbert and I're going to wipe out the Ku Klux Klan!"

Eternities were gone before the last car disappeared and the street was empty again and night was night. Above, and creeping toward the Height, a hundred and forty red and angry little eyes grew smaller. Then, at last, they closed.

Joey let the curtain fall.

Albert walked over, chewing a piece of salami.

"What you think of all that down there?" Joey said.

"It's a pistol," Albert said.

Charlotte Green was seated in the chair. She was reading, or pretending to read.

"Did you think there really were things like that?" Joey asked.

"Sure. What wrong with you?"

"Were you scared? Are you scared now?"

Albert pulled Joey's head down. "Listen, I tell you: they try anything, there's plenty guys around like Glad Owens that they've got a whole arsenal, just waiting. I seen some of his stuff, he showed me once. He got a .38 and his brother that's in Louisville, Arnie, he's gonna get a machine gun to him. He says. I don't know if he can do it in time, but that's what he says."

Joey looked at his mother and tried to guess what lay beneath the calm, untroubled surface. It was as if she weren't at all surprised, or worried, or disturbed; as if a line of cars with hooded men inside were the most natural thing in the world.

Charlotte Green did not lift her eyes from the book.

You'll send me off to school tomorrow, Joey thought, and if I come home with my throat cut, you'll be sorry but you won't let up, you won't stop fighting. Nothing changes, Ma, he tried to say, and couldn't. There's a big white wall between you and what you want, always has been, always will be. You can beat your head against it, but that wall won't crack.

"Would you get me a glass of milk?" Charlotte Green asked.

Joey rose and poured the milk and watched his mother drink it. She looked very small and frail to him, not like the leader of an army.

He lay down on the couch by the window again. Uncle Rowan, he remembered, had gone into the bathroom when the cars appeared. The door was locked, the old man still inside. Joey could picture him, sitting on the toilet, hands folded, certain that this night would be his last.

Well, let it come; that's all I wish now, let it come and be over with! he prayed.

The automobiles were silent, neatly parked along the side of the road, hand brakes firmly on. The hooded men were walking up the hill, but no one spoke: there was a quiet, priestly slowness to their movements, as if each was thinking, It's too bad we've got to do this, but it must be done. It must be done, and no one else has got the strength or courage: we are forced to show our steel! They walked along the rutted path.

The hill grew steeper, brush and rocks appeared.

The path became invisible.

Inside his chest, the heart of David Parkinson beat quickly. Climbing, and the sharp excitements that had pierced him from the time he'd first picked up the telephone and organized the meeting, drained his strength: but none could see this. He had not walked so straight and sure for years.

When, finally, they reached the small plateau atop the hill, he could not breathe! The pains were fists about his throat. But he was glad of them, and fiercely proud.

He raised his hand.

Six men came forward, lifted up the heavy wooden cross and set it down with care.

It had been made by the Reverend Lorenzo Niesen. He'd gone to the McGraw Lumber Company and purchased, with the money given to him by the young man, Adam Cramer, six long planks. A buzz saw had cut them to the proper size. He'd worked on them with nails and braces then until they were quite solid. Then he'd gone to the back of the department store and found the paper-wrapped excelsior that is used in shipping to protect furniture, and wired this material to all sides of the cross.

It was the finest, best-constructed cross, the men admitted, that anyone had seen for years.

"A real professional job," David Parkinson said, and Lorenzo Niesen was happy that he'd worked so hard.

"Let it burn bright!" called a man when the gasoline had soaked into the wrappings. "Let it burn so they can see!"

Another man produced a box of matches, struck one, shielded the tiny flame from the nonexistent wind.

Again David Parkinson raised his hand.

A leaf of fire grew from the bottom of the cross. Then suddenly it spread, enveloping the structure wholly, carving blackness, filling all the dark and silent night around the hill with brilliance.

Adam Cramer smiled.

He stood beneath the flaming cross and stared down at the feeble lights. At Caxton, at the houses where the people now were looking out their windows, dumb, unmoving, fearful. And the fire was hot upon his face ...

Silent moments later, the hooded men went back to their cars and drove away.

In time, the hill was dark again.

17

It was a typical Southern California apartment, five years old and falling to decay. The white plaster was streaked with rust from the screens, cracked and crumbling at the foundations, ready, it seemed, to burst at any time like an eggshell. Other, identical apartments, some painted green, some pink, some yellow, lined the block like abandoned crates. There were no trees, no hedges, nowhere any growing things to block the steady, grinning sun.

Ed Driscoll and Peter Link got out of the rental Ford and made their way across the pockmarked lawn. At 11550½ they paused, and Driscoll knocked. The door was opened by a middle-aged woman in a light green dress.

"Yes?"

"Mrs. Cramer?"

"That's right."

"I'm Ed Driscoll. I phoned you this morning about an inter-view."

The woman smiled. "Yes," she said. "Come in, please."

The men stepped inside the apartment, and Ed Driscoll made a swift mental note. Ordinary. Perfectly ordinary. Two bedrooms, dime-store pictures, television. Cluttered with fake antiques. No trace of a child's presence, or evidence there had ever been a child. No—there.

He stared for a moment at the framed photograph of a two- or three-year-old boy that sat on the mahogany secretary.

"Good-looking kid," Link said, adjusting his camera. "Mind if I take a shot?"

"I'd rather you didn't."

"Why is that, Mrs. Cramer?"

"I'd just rather. He was my boy then, you see. The best and the nicest you could find."

The men looked at one another briefly.

"He isn't my boy any more," Mrs. Cramer said. She sat down on the dark couch and began to fan herself with a Chinese ivory fan. "I suppose that sounds dreadful, but it's the truth. I don't even know this fellow you're writing about. He's a stranger."

Driscoll took out a small writing pad and a pencil. "Go on, Mrs. Cramer," he said; but the woman merely fanned herself slowly.

"I'd like to get a few facts, if you don't mind. Is Mr. Cramer, your husband, around?"

"No. Adam died four years ago, of a coronary they said. They said a coronary. But that isn't true. He died of a broken heart!" The woman's expression did not change. As she spoke, her voice grew softer, lower, became a whisper. "Adam was the best man in the world, Mr. Driscoll, and certainly the best husband. He was a marvelous provider."

Driscoll nodded. "I thought—"

"We met in Chicago, when I was a young girl. Do you know how old I was then?" She smiled. "I was seventeen. I'd been mar-ried before, of course. My first was a charming person, and it all happened very fast; I'm ashamed to say how fast. But we were married, and it seemed to be just fine. Then he started to gamble. With cards. Henry always seemed to lose, he lost all the time, but it didn't cure him. I'd plead with him and beg him, and he'd say 'Laura, don't you worry, I'm finished with that life!' but it would go on happening. You have never seen such a handsome man. I'll show you his picture, and you'll see."

She rose before Driscoll could stop her, and went into the bedroom. She returned within moments, holding a thick, square photograph album. The pages were an eighth of an inch thick, and the sides were dusted with gold. She turned three pages and gave the book to Driscoll.

"Have you ever seen such a handsome man?"

Driscoll looked at a foxed, stained photograph that could not have been taken any later than 1910. The man was certainly handsome, though the youthful features seemed spoiled by the traditional mustache. He passed it to Link, then said, "Very handsome, Mrs. Cramer. May I ask his name?"

"Henry. He sang, Mr. Driscoll, and his voice was as sweet as the wind in a meadow. But perhaps all Irish people have that ability, I don't know. Do they?"

Driscoll shrugged.

"He would sing at night, in bed. I'd say, 'Henry, that's bad luck!' and he would kiss me and say that whenever he was next to me he just couldn't help it, he had to sing. That was the kind of man he was. But, he gambled." She began to fan herself more quickly. "And then he started to drink, Mr. Driscoll. My mother and my sisters told me then that I had better divorce him because it could only mean trouble, but I didn't have the heart to, or the strength. He didn't get drunk the way some people do, you see. Alcohol affected Henry in a different way. It made him gentle and kind. He'd come back from some tavern and tell me that he had never seen such a beautiful place as our home. Our home!" Mrs. Cramer shook her head. "It was a terrible little hotel room, and we owed three months' rent on it because of his gambling, and Mrs. Gottlieb would not speak to me. We had no furniture, no lovely things. But to Henry it was beautiful!

"He'd ask me to drink with him, too, Mr. Driscoll, and that

was the shocking thing. 'Come on, Laura,' he would say, 'join me. You'll see things straight, for the first time. The ugliness will all go away! You watch, a few snorts, and we won't have any problems. The bills will vanish! Mrs. Gottlieb won't exist! And the whole world will be a wonderful place!' He talked that way. Of course, I never touched a drop, and I have my mother to thank for that."

"About Adam," Driscoll said, glancing again at Peter Link. "If you would—"

"Henry," said Mrs. Cramer, "got so that he was drunk almost every night of the week. Nothing bothered him, nothing at all! I'd ask him for money to pay the grocers and he'd cry and plead for my forgiveness, because, of course, he wouldn't have a penny left. And that is the way it went for months. I couldn't begin to count the times he promised he would straighten up and get a job and stick to it, but finally I told him I did not believe him any more, and that is when he stopped crying and making promises. Mother told me to leave him at once. She told me to come home where I belonged—we lived in Washington, my mother and sisters, and I'd gone to Chicago for a lark. I thought it would be fun to work as a secretary, so I went to a school. But I could never seem to learn much. That is when I met Henry."

Ed Driscoll folded his pad resignedly and replaced his pencil. "Yes, Mrs. Cramer," he said. "Please go on."

"Would you gentlemen like some tea?"

"No, thank you."

"Tea is very nice on hot days. Henry hated it, though. He would never drink it. I loved him." The woman straightened her green dress and stared through Driscoll. Her voice was a distant echo. "I thought I loved him," she said. "But what does a sixteen-year-old girl know about such things? Do you know what I mean?"

"Yes, certainly," Driscoll said.

"And, oh, he was wild over me. You might not guess it, but I was a very beautiful woman some years ago. The men said so. Henry worshiped me, he said; he called me his little girl. Isn't that odd?"

"No."

"Of course, the truth was, he was the child in the family. Ten years older than I was and yet he had no sense of responsibility. I had to take care of everything! And what if I hadn't? What if I'd gone along with him and lived his kind of life? We would have starved." She rubbed her hands together and knotted her fingers tightly. "Well, it finally got so I was losing weight from the worry, and I told Henry I would have to leave him. He got on his knees and begged me not to. I said, 'If you love me, why do you act this way?' And he said, 'Laura, this is my honest, bounden word. So help me God, I'll give you no more heartache!' He swore on it, and reminded me that at least, for all his carousing and crazy ways, he had never looked at another woman—which was the truth. So I gave him another chance, I told him I wouldn't leave him if he'd do the right thing.

"He got a job next day, at a barbershop, I think. And for a while, I thought he had truly reformed, because he always came home on time and without any liquor on his breath, and he did not gamble any at all that I know about. Then on a Thursday night it was, on a Thursday, the first, he was late. I waited three hours, and supper got cold. Then I knew it was all over, and I started packing. I had packed two suitcases when the doorbell rang. It was Henry. I could hear him singing. And I thought, No, I won't answer. But I have never been strong, the way some women are. So I went to the door and opened it and there he was, drunk, with his hands behind his back. 'Hello, my little girl!' he said, and bent down to kiss me. I went crazy then, I think, because I slapped him. It was the first time I had ever slapped anyone in my entire life. It made my palm sting. He stepped back and put out his hands. Do you know what he had in them?"

Driscoll shook his head.

"Flowers! The biggest bouquet of orchids I have ever seen. With us months late in the rent and owing everybody and Mrs. Gottlieb not talking to me, he had gone and spent his entire pay check on a bouquet of orchids!" She lowered her head slightly, then looked up, and her eyes snapped angrily. "I took them and put them in a vase, Mr. Driscoll, and then I finished packing and I left Henry." She breathed heavily. "What else could I do? He was insane! Of course, I missed his sweet singing for a while, and the sound of his voice when he laughed, but Mother knocked all of that out of me soon enough. She said good riddance, and she was right. I don't doubt that for a moment."

Mrs. Cramer rose. "Henry went to Alaska," she said softly, "and drank himself to death. He died of cirrhosis of the liver. It's funny, but I heard about it only a week after I met Adam. Wouldn't you please have some tea?"

"Thank you. We'd be glad to have some."

"It won't take a minute. You can look over the photographs."

Peter Link walked over and squatted by the chair. When Mrs. Cramer disappeared and the door closed, he snapped the shutter of his camera four times, quickly.

"Nothing is ordinary," Driscoll said.

"What?"

"Never mind. I was just thinking." He studied the photographs, which looked oddly out of place in the heavy family album. At a small snapshot of a child in a striped sunsuit seated by a washpan, fishing pole in hand, he stopped. "Doesn't look much like a firebrand there, does he?" Driscoll said.

"That's all right. Hitler was a baby, once."

"Yeah."

"Ed, it's not my job, I only take pictures, but I think you ought to turn her off."

"Why?"

"Why? Because Lubin wants a story on this guy Cramer—not on Lady Macbeth."

"I know." Driscoll nodded. "But Lubin doesn't tell me what methods to use. I use my own. And they vary. Right now I think I'll use the listening method."

The younger man lowered his voice. "I understand about all that," he said irritably, "only she isn't talking about *him*, for Chris-sake!"

"Isn't she?"

Link grunted softly and made a gesture of hopeless, resigned confusion with his hands. Grinning, Driscoll closed the album.

Several minutes passed, then Mrs. Cramer swept back into the room.

"These are potted-ham sandwiches," she said, "and I've iced the tea. Do you gentlemen like potted-ham sandwiches?"

She sat down on the couch and took up the fan. Her skin was as white and delicate as the ivory, almost translucent in the louvered sunlight.

"Mrs. Cramer," Driscoll said, "we'd like to hear the rest of your story, if you don't mind."

"I don't mind at all," the woman said. "But, you know, you sounded almost like Adam then. He was always talking about facts and substantial things like that. Good, Mr. Driscoll, that's what he was. A good man."

"Your second husband."

"Yes. Oh, yes."

"Tell us about him."

"A rock," Mrs. Cramer said. "A beacon. I'd gone to Tish's to stay —Tish was a nickname for Mrs. Violet Miller; she ran a boardinghouse in Chicago. Of course, Mother had wanted me to come home. But I was stubborn: I couldn't come home. Mama was very disgusted. You never knew her, Mr. Driscoll. She and Papa went to Washington to live and for a long time, after he died, there was the bunch of us in that big house that had been a sort of hotel. Five sisters, a brother, and Mama. Wonderfully happy days!"

Peter Link rubbed his temples and seemed about to speak; then he settled back in the chair with a look of defeat.

"That was why Mama wanted me back, so it would be like the old days, don't you see? But I was upset, which is certainly normal, considering. I looked for a job, but I couldn't find one, and my money was running out—then Adam came to Tish's to stay. You have never in your life seen a finer-looking gentleman. That's him, over there, on the piano."

Driscoll looked at the picture. A stern man with a full mustache looked back at him. It was a very old photograph.

"Tish introduced us properly," Mrs. Cramer continued, "although he had noticed me almost at once. I was pretty then. And young. Still, he was a perfect gentleman. After we were introduced, he waited two weeks before asking me out. We went to a little place called Kitty Kelley's, which is on the North Side of Chicago, and they have a dog there, it sits at the entrance. The tablecloths are green check. We had steaks, I remember, and baked potatoes. Adam called me Miss Laura. Wasn't that nice?"

"It *cer*tainly was," Link said, glancing defiantly at Driscoll.

"Yes, and I called him Mr. Cramer. There was no funny business, either, you know. Once he touched my hand and he went beet-red. Beet-red! He was twenty-six years older than I, you see, and probably that had something to do with it. He'd lived with his mother until she died, at the age of eighty-three, and I can't think of anything finer or nobler than that. He wouldn't get married or even go out with girls as long as his mother was alive!" Mrs. Cramer sighed and dabbed at her eyes with a small, diaphanous handkerchief. "Adam was everything that Henry wasn't. He worked for the railroad and had already made a considerable name for himself in that line. People respected him, which was the thing. Everyone respected him. When he asked me to marry him, he told me how he had figured it all out and decided that we would be happy." Mrs. Cramer laughed, "I hardly had a thing to say about it! Mama came to Chicago to meet him, and she told me this was the sort of man I ought to have. Tish said it, too. So we were married.

"Adam did not laugh much, and he never sang at all, and of course with me only seventeen and him forty-three, there were certain little difficulties, times when I would lie awake and think —But I soon realized how fortunate I was to have a substantial man like Adam. On our honeymoon we went around the country—by train. He had a pass, you know. You couldn't believe the places we visited, and in only two weeks! He had planned it very carefully a long time in advance, with timetables and maps. I was so scatterbrained, too. I'd say to him, 'Adam, let's stay another day in Yellowstone!' and he'd smile and say, 'Of course, my dear, if that's what you want. But if we do, we'll miss seeing Seattle and Tacoma.' And we wouldn't stay. More tea?"

Driscoll shook his head. "Mrs. Cramer, when did you have Adam Junior?"

The woman did not seem to hear. "He treated me like a doll, like a pet, Mr. Driscoll. No one could have been more thoughtful and considerate. When we came back from our honeymoon to Chicago, I was surprised with a beautiful red brick house— built especially for us. Can you imagine? Then Adam gave me a check for five thousand dollars and said, 'Laura, now I want you to go down to the Loop this afternoon and spend this money on furniture and whatever else you might like. It's your house.' I loved antiques so I went to antique stores and—this is what's left. It looks sort of pitiful, doesn't it?" She gestured about the room. "This is all that's left," she repeated.

Driscoll waited patiently.

"Life was so fine then," she said. "Adam hired a colored girl to do the work, and gave me enough money to buy anything I might want. He never bothered me with details—I never saw where he worked or knew how much he had in the bank or anything like that. 'That's business,' he'd say, 'that's business. My job is to bring home the bacon, Laura. Your job is to stay pretty and happy. That's all you ever have to do for me. It's payment enough.' Oh, the lovely things, the friends I had . . ." She tossed her head.

"Then I found out that I was going to have a baby. I had been healthy and there wasn't anything wrong, the doctors said, but I got sick. Very sick. The baby was born in seven months. Little Adam, young Adam. He lived less than a month."

Driscoll took out a cigarette and lit it. Link continued to rub his temples.

"A year later I had twins," Mrs. Cramer went on. "They were born dead. Doctor Abrahams told me that I could never have a child, ever. It would kill me, he said. Adam wanted a child, though. He wanted a son. So we tried again, and Adam Junior came.

"It turned out that Dr. Abrahams was right, or almost right, because I nearly did die. I went down to eighty-nine pounds, and had to stay in bed for six months.

"I gave up my health for both of them, Mr. Driscoll. Nothing could ever be the same for me. I couldn't go downtown to shop, or go to the opera clubs and socials with Edna, or even to a movie. Everything taxed me terribly. My blood pressure went sky-high at the least little excitement, and—well, never mind that. I'm not one to wish my troubles off onto another person."

"Tell us about Adam," Peter Link said, in an almost desperate tone. "Junior."

"He was a good child at first, but frail, so frail, and sensitive. A beautiful child, as you've both seen. Adam loved him

... sometimes I think perhaps more than he loved me. Lots of things changed then." She went to the window and adjusted the shade carefully. "Adam Junior," she said, "was what you might call normal for a little while. Then, I think it was when he was seven, he suffered a burst appendix; and that was the beginning of his illness. At nine we had to operate on his tonsils, and they were rotted and he was confined to bed for eight weeks. We grew closer then, you see, while he and his father drifted farther apart. I can't explain that, exactly. Adam never did understand illness too well, I suppose that's most of it. He was seldom sick, himself. Hadn't ever missed a day at the job! He just didn't ... *grasp* the idea of not being healthy, if you see what I mean. He felt that his son was letting him down, I think, by being ill so much of the time. Betraying him.

"Well, though he'd stolen my best years away, I gave the boy all the love anyone could ask. I tended to him day and night until, you can see for yourself, I was a physical wreck. Doctor Abrahams couldn't understand how I managed to go on. But, if I hadn't—that child would never have lived, I can say that to you right here and now! Ask anyone!

"When he was twelve, he had spinal meningitis, and we were sure he was finished. No one had any hope, in particular Doctor Abrahams and the specialist he called in from I don't know where. But I sat up, in the same room, holding Adam's hand, and he lived through it, Mr. Driscoll. Thanks to me.

"But—everything seemed to change then. Adam Junior became a different boy, a different person. He didn't get along at school; sat in the house reading most of the time, reading, reading; and talking smart to his mother. To me! Why? The God above, I was the best friend he ever had; the only friend, really; and I *tried* to make him see this. 'I've given up my life for you,' I told him, 'and you're all I have. You're my own baby.' But it got worse and worse. Until it got so we had a stranger in the house, Mr. Driscoll; someone we didn't understand at all and didn't understand us.

"Then Adam had his first coronary. It struck him down and he never recovered. It was the boy did it to him, though, that boy! And he'll kill me, too. You wait!"

She was weeping now, her face red and wrinkled.

"I came here," she said, "just to be near him, hoping he'd come back to me, hoping I would have my child, Mr. Driscoll. But except to get some money once, he never even bothered to visit me."

The room was still for a long time. Then Driscoll set his glass of watered tea down upon the carved coffee table. "Do you want us to print that, Mrs. Cramer?" he said.

"Yes," the woman said firmly. "I certainly do. Mothers all over the world ought to be warned that this can happen to them. They should know that you can work your heart out and give your child everything and then have him turn on you like a serpent. Perhaps if they know, it won't be such a terrible shock."

Peter Link stood up. "Would you mind, Mrs. Cramer, if I took a picture of you?"

"Not at all." She struck a pose. The camera flashed four times. Before the fifth shot, Mrs. Cramer picked up the photograph of the boy and held it to her breast. "I'm sorry I couldn't be of more help to you," she said, blinking.

"You've been more help than you know," Driscoll said. "Before we wind it up, however, I'd like to ask if you can tell us anything about his current activities. That is, why do you feel he has made segregation such a personal cause?"

"I don't have any idea, Mr. Driscoll."

"Will you answer a rather touchy question?"

"I'll try."

"What, Mrs. Cramer, are your own views on desegregation in the South?"

The woman shrugged her shoulders. "I really couldn't say. I don't read the papers much, you know. You mean mixing them up, don't you?"

"Yes, that's what I mean."

"Well, of course that might mean the whites marrying the Negroes and I'm certainly not for that. But ... well, I haven't thought much about it. And we never discussed it, or anything, before."

"Then you never taught your son to be prejudiced?"

"Absolutely not! We had two lovely colored maids, in the old days, and they—in particular, Rachel—just adored little Adam. Prejudice is something I can't have any use for."

"I see." Driscoll rose. "One last question, Mrs. Cramer. When he was young, in the, you might say, formative years—did you ever encourage him in any of his ambitions? Or his father, did he? You know what I mean: give the boy a feeling of self-confidence?"

"That," said Mrs. Cramer, "would have been wrong. Don't you understand—he was frail, and sick. We knew that he'd never be fit for any kind of job. But my husband had saved a good deal of money, enough to last us a long time, so there wasn't—he'd invested it in stocks, too—any need for Adam Junior to worry." She looked at the men. "Why, if I'd encouraged him, the way you say, he'd have gone out in the world and failed! I wanted to shield him from that. Any decent mother would have done the same." She folded her hands tightly. "Can you blame me for wanting to protect my only child?"

"No, Mrs. Cramer," Driscoll said. "I don't blame you. I don't blame anyone for anything."

"I did what I thought was best."

"Of course." Driscoll walked to the door and motioned to Link. "Thank you very much for your time," he said. "We'll send you a copy of the story."

Mrs. Cramer sat quietly on the couch. "If you see him," she said, "tell him he can still come back. If he wants to."

Driscoll nodded and closed the door.

He and Peter Link got into the car and did not speak until they had pulled out into the flow of traffic.

Then Driscoll looked over at his friend and smiled. "Well?" he said.

"Well what?"

"What do you think of our little dictator now?"

Link loosened his collar. "Christ, I don't know," he said. "With a dame like that for a mother . . . At the moment, I'm confused."

Driscoll laughed. "That's the trouble with this goddamn job, Linker," he said. "It muddles your thinking. A couple of hours ago we hated the guy's guts. He was a pure son of a bitch, that's all. Everything was nice and clear and tidy. Right? Well, nothing has changed. He's still raising hell in the South and he's still a pure son of a bitch. But—it isn't so nice and clear and tidy any more, is it?"

Link was silent. He fingered his camera.

"You know something?" Driscoll said, keeping his eyes on the road. "I was in Nuremberg during the trials. It was a great assignment. All of the monsters: Schacht, Speer, Streicher, Göring, all of them; going to get the works. You're not too young to remember those trials, are you?"

Link shook his head. "I read about them," he said.

"Well, see, I'd visited some very pleasant resort spots in '45 —Belsen and Dachau, to name two. And I was around even earlier, when the Nazi organizations—the Gestapo, the SS, the Reich Cabinet, the OKW—were great big things. I saw what they could do. And I got to really hating them. Everybody did. And it was such a strong hate, see, that maybe it was this that kept the people going. As long as we could despise those symbols, with their black uniforms and swastikas and shiny boots, we could go on fighting them. As long as we could believe that they were inhuman, soulless creatures of absolute evil, we could hope for victory. Actually, we didn't see much more of the Gestapo or the Storm Troopers than the kids at home did in the movies. But the German propaganda boys were doing a great job, a great job. They kept telling us that they *weren't* human: they were super-human. They were the Master Race.

"So it didn't even occur to me, or anyone else, that these guys were real people who got hungry and lonely sometimes, who got colds in their noses and farted at parties. No muddled thinking there, boy. No confusion. Just a nice, steady hatred building up. And, of course, the same thing—even more so—was happening with the Japanese. God knew *they* weren't real people!

"Anyway, I went to the trials feeling the way you do in the last reel of a Western, where the villain is going to get his guts shot out by the hero. I wanted to watch those bastards crawl and whine and cry..."

Driscoll turned left and pointed the car down the long, crowded Los Angeles freeway.

"I wanted to see them get it, too. But something went wrong, Linker. I arrived at the courthouse, and I couldn't find a single goddamn monster. Not one. All I could find was a bunch of tired, scared, neurotic old men. Ribbentrop was getting roasted by a smart-ass lawyer, and I thought that was swell, because Ribbentrop deserved it if anyone did; but the more I watched him, the more human he got. Even Göring, the most hated of them all, the one we used to dream of boiling in hot blood—he wasn't a monster, either. Shifty, shrewd, unctuous; yes. But mostly just nuts. Just crazy.

"A couple of weeks went by and suddenly the trials began to lose their meaning. The people, all the outraged people whose families had been broken up, even they started to get bored. They started feeling almost sorry for these poor misguided bastards. Poor Ribbentrop, you know, he's way too old to sit there and get pounded by that lawyer. Somebody ought to get him a drink of water, or something!

"See, now, if they'd shot these guys right away, it would have been okay. But no, they let the damn thing drag on; they let the monsters talk and let the people listen and look at them in the morning.

"When we finally got around to hanging them, Linker, nobody really gave a rat's ass. Nobody who'd attended the trials, anyway. It was a dull circus, and we were all relieved to see it end. That was the only thing we felt deeply. Relief."

Driscoll honked his horn loudly and angrily at a car that had cut in front of him from the next lane. "That's what I mean about this job," he said, grinning. "It muddles your thinking. You have to talk to people and then you start understanding them. Once that happens, there's just nobody around to hate. And I ask you —without hate, where the hell would the world be now?"

18

"You all saw what happened last night," the tall man said, "and you all know what it means. Now, I'm for law and order, always have been; and so is Georgia, my wife; and no matter what we might have thought personally to ourselves about the ruling, we tried to abide by it. 'Most everybody in Caxton did. But it seems pretty clear that it isn't going to work. Attendance at the school is down from eight hundred to four hundred and twenty—*four hundred and twenty!* It's going to keep dropping, too. Every day."

Tom looked at the man who had been his friend for eight years and tried, as Dave Masters continued to speak, to remember the times they had shivered in duck blinds together, slept in fields and talked all night. He could remember the times well, but somehow, he could not connect them with this thin, stuttering, apologetic person. Dave wasn't a coward, not the Dave he'd known! Where'd this guy come from, anyway?

He glanced at Ruth. She was listening, as she had been listening all evening, intently.

So were the others: tense in their chairs, silent, hanging onto the words. Randolph Underwood and Mrs. Underwood; the Moodys; the Perkinses.

Listening.

"Well," Masters went on, "what I'm saying is, I feel that we're on the brink of something pretty terrible here. And it scares me. Not for my sake, though; for my daughter's sake. Judy. She tells me that with everything upset the way it is, I mean right now, she isn't learning anything at all! They go through the motions, but since the opening of school, she says she just might as well have stayed home and listened to records. Okay. I thought, like everybody, Well, you have to expect that kind of thing at first. It's bound to happen. But, listen: school's been open for quite a little while now, and instead of conditions getting better, they're getting worse. Okay. So let's look at the long view. My wife and I talked about it, and I believe it's something every parent here ought to talk about, too. I mean to say, about the long view: *Where do we go from here? What's going to happen? Where are we headed?*"

The tall man took a handkerchief from his pocket and wiped his palms. He met Tom McDaniel's gaze briefly, and there was, or seemed to be, a flicker of guilt. It came out as anger.

"Let's be realistic for a minute here," he said. "Judging from what we've seen so far, I think we can say there are only a few possibilities. One, of course, is that everything quiets down suddenly and the kids go back to school and everything is fine. It's a possibility, but I'll tell you the truth, I don't think it's a very good one."

There was a slight murmuring.

"Second thing is: Attendance drops even more, and we get into real gang fighting. You all know that there's been three incidents already. Just today, they expelled a nigra named Archibald Vaughan for pulling a knife."

"Just a second now, Dave," Tom said, trying to control his voice. "That's the way it'll read in the Northern papers, but the facts are a little different. We know that the Vaughan kid was attacked by three white boys in the bathroom. Jake Nolan's son saw the whole thing. Archie Vaughan was only trying to protect himself."

"I know, Tom, I know. But—"

"*And* in addition, we have information that Adam Cramer and Bart Carey have both offered twenty-five dollars to any white kid who can prove he hit a Negro. Fifty dollars if the Negro hits back."

"I know! But that doesn't change what I'm saying, Tom. Violence is violence. I'm only trying to put across that it exists now in Caxton High and might get worse. Whether anybody's paid or not, or whatever, doesn't alter the fact that there have been three incidents and there might be more and kids might get hurt."

Tom closed his mouth and tried to hold the fury down. It was white-hot inside him.

"Okay," Masters said, "the next possibility is that we go on exactly like we have been. No worse, no better. Then maybe two months from now, when everybody sees it isn't working and can't work—but those people in Washington won't cancel the ruling—maybe the Governor steps in and closes the school. Or the other way: if there is a flare-up in fighting, or what have you, he sends state troops. So then we got the town full of soldiers. Or even this, and don't think it isn't possible, because it is. Plenty stranger things have happened. These boys with the citizens' councils might just decide to tear up the school for good.

"Well, I'll go back to what I said at the beginning. I'm for law and order. Right or wrong—and it's wrong; we all know that—we've been given a ruling and it's our duty to try to carry it out. Okay. But it isn't a black and white problem, and I don't mean that as a joke. It isn't cut and dried. Because we have got to think now not only about how we feel, but about our children's education and maybe even their lives!"

Dave Masters paused, and glared at Tom.

"You see," he went on, "even if there was a chance this business of forcing integration down our throats like a big horse pill could work, it would still mean that our kids would suffer. The government has got the right to try an experiment to see whether it's going to fail, and in theory I'm for that. I really am. In practice, though, since we know the thing's bound to fizzle out and end worse than it ever was, I wonder if it's right for us to sit and watch and do nothing.

"If our children don't get killed, they'll be wasting their time at school, and I don't think much of either way. I figure, let somebody else pay for the mistake: not my Judy.

"That's why I'm withdrawing her from school, and that's why we're moving away. If enough of us do that, maybe they'll get the point. If not," Masters cleared his throat, "we may be headed for a second Civil War."

There was applause and the people gathered around the speaker, and Tom wanted very much to grab his friend's lapels and scream the truth at him; but his anger had become something else, something that did not spread anxious strength through him but instead drained this strength and left him with a feeling of sadness.

He took his wife's hand and left the hall.

When they had driven for three blocks, Ruth said: "You know, Tom, there's a lot in what Dave said. Maybe we ought to withdraw Ella, too."

In a sense he'd been waiting for it, and was not surprised; in another, he was no less surprised and shocked than if his right hand had suddenly risen of its own accord and slapped him. It was horrible enough to hear your friends talking hateful nonsense, but—

"Tom?"

"I'm sorry. A little heartburn."

"Probably it was the fried onions. You know you should never eat fried onions."

"Go on with what you were saying."

"I was only thinking that maybe it would be best to take Ella out of school for a while. Just for a while. Until we see how this thing is going to go."

He pulled over to the side of the road, cut the engine, pulled on the brake. "Do you mean that?" he asked.

"Why yes," Ruth said. "After all, it's pretty obvious, isn't it, that Dave's right?"

She waited.

"Tom, what *is* the matter with you?"

Something inside exploded, and he could not check the force of it. "Forget it," he said. "Ella goes to school and that's that. Do you understand?" He reached for the ignition key.

"No," Ruth said, slowly, "I *don't* understand." She paused. "Would you like to talk about it?"

"There's nothing to talk about. Ella stays at school. Period."

She touched his arm. "Darling," she said, "please. You've been so upset the past week that we've hardly exchanged a word. It seems to me that this is important enough to discuss. I mean —Tom, don't you think you're being a little unfair? You've had problems before, all sorts of problems, and you always told me about them. And we've had differences of opinion, too—but we talked them over, together. We're not together any more," she said, and he could see the tears gathering in her eyes. "I don't know you any more. I used to think I did, but—"

Still he could not find words, and he could not bring himself to comfort Ruth, to put his arm about her, pull her head to his shoulder.

"This is the biggest thing that's ever come into our lives," she said. "I didn't realize that at first, but I do now. We have a decision to make. I don't want to make it alone. But you're forcing me to. I asked to discuss it a thousand times, but every time you've turned me down. You wouldn't talk with me, and you won't talk now. I decided what I thought we'd both consider best, and now you're angry. Why?" Her voice was rising. "There isn't anything illegal about removing a child from school, and you know it. That doesn't break the precious law! *Does it?*"

"No," he said.

"Well, then, what are you so mad about? Why are you looking at me as if you hated me?"

"I don't hate you," Tom said.

"Then talk to me! Tell me what I've done that's wrong. Tell me why you've shut yourself away from me and all our friends. Tom —I love you, and I want to do what's right. But I can't do it by myself. I need your help."

Peculiarly, Tom McDaniel found himself remembering, as his wife spoke, a time when he was nineteen years old and how, although he'd long since given up belief in God and Heaven, he could not keep from crossing himself whenever he passed a church. He knew that it was merely an extension of the childish habit of stepping on cracks in the sidewalk, for magic reassurance, for luck, still he could not stop, for to do so would be to admit, irrevocably, that he was an atheist. Eventually, however, Paul Strauss caught him and asked what he was doing and then asked, point-blank, whether or not he was a Christian. And he had to answer, voicing it for the first time: "No."

"All right," he said, looking at his wife. He saw the urgency and love in her eyes and knew, as he had known with Paul, that there could be no more hiding, no more fence-walking, no more comforting self-deception. "I haven't talked with you," he said, "because I've been afraid. Afraid of what I'd say and of what I'd hear. I don't think it's something new, either, because"—the thoughts formed as he spoke—"we've never really talked about this."

Ruth nodded. "I know," she said.

"We didn't have to, before. It wasn't necessary, nothing depended on it. But now all that is changed. It's come too fast, I guess; or we went too long avoiding it, or something. You say it's important. It's more than that. Maybe I'm afraid we won't be able to stand up under it. And maybe we won't. After tonight, we may be so far apart, Ruth, that we'll never get back together again. Do you want to risk that?"

She nodded her head slowly. "Yes."

He loosened his tie and watched a car roll past and disappear into the darkness.

"Tell me first," he said, "what you think about the question. I mean the whole question." His heart was beating fast; his palms were perspiring.

"I'm not sure what you mean."

"About integration," Tom said. "And—be honest."

Ruth appeared to be confused, nervous; but, he sensed, also somewhat relieved. "Well, I—I think it's a terrible thing," she said.

And it was said, and there was no turning back now.

"Why?" Tom asked.

"Why?" She stared at him wonderingly. "Because it isn't right, that's all."

"Do you feel that you're prejudiced?"

"Against the Negroes?"

"Yes."

"No, certainly not. You know that. Tom, that isn't what you think, is it?"

"But you believe it's wrong for them to go to our schools."

"Of course! So do you!"

He could not blame her for saying it: all she knew of his feeling on the matter was what she read in his editorials. And his editorials were and had always been pro-law and pro-segregation. "What do you think should have been done?" he asked.

"Instead of this?"

"That's right. I mean, you don't think things were very fair before, do you?"

"No. But—well, they should have raised the money to improve the schools." She paused. "And the homes, and jobs."

"Then it would be fair?"

"Tom, I don't see what you're getting at, really I don't. This is just what everybody thinks, isn't it?"

He forced the words out. "You still haven't said why you believe it's wrong for the Negroes and whites to go to the same school together. You've said it's a terrible thing, but I still haven't heard why."

Ruth was silent.

"You're not prejudiced, but you don't want them in the same school with Ella. Do you have a reason?"

"Of course I have a reason!"

"Honey, please; I'm not arguing. We've simply got to get

these things out, or talking won't mean much. Now—what *is* the reason?"

"I—" She fumbled with a handkerchief. "For heaven's sake, Tom, you know as well as I do. There'll be intermixing for one thing..."

"And you object to that."

"Intermixing? Why—"

He hoped she wouldn't ask how he'd like his daughter to marry a Negro.

"Are you being serious? Are you really asking me if I object to it?"

"Yes."

"I certainly do," she said in a firm voice. Then she said: "I think you'd better talk now."

The wound of hearing what, in fact, he'd known, hurt badly; but he feared the moments that were coming. *I'm a coward!* It was something he'd only suspected before, and had been able to bury beneath a routine of work and diversion....

"Tom, are *you* in favor of integration?"

The question stunned him, silenced him for moments. Then he heard his voice say: "Yes."

He began to tell her, then, in the slow, hesitant tones of a confession, everything. How he had been raised the way most people in the South had been, had taken segregation for granted in the way that you take the elements or mother love for granted, how in high school he had met Paul Strauss and, through this friend, had begun to think about the question.

"Paul was a Jew," he said. "From Milwaukee. He knew about persecution, and hated it. 'We've got the easy kind,' he used to say. 'But sometimes the easy kind is the worst. You go along thinking you're free and everybody's equal, then suddenly a hotel clerk tells you there aren't any rooms when you know there are, and you remember that you've just been dreaming. You aren't free.' We didn't talk a lot about it, or anything, but it did start me wondering. I'd always thought, you know, the Negroes have got it fine. All of a sudden I wasn't so sure. You never met Paul, did you?"

Ruth shook her head.

"He was killed in the war. Someone dropped a grenade in

front of him in—I forget, some Italian town they were occupying. Blew his stomach apart. Anyway—"

Paul! Were two friends ever closer? Tom thought instantly of all the night-long sessions, the electric talk, the plans they'd had for working together on the same paper; and the big, friendly horse-face of Paul Strauss lived for a moment in his mind.

"In Caxton, it was easy to forget these things. The Negroes stayed on the Hill, no one ever saw them. We did an occasional obit, once in a while a robbery or a fight; otherwise, they might not even have existed. There were no complaints. And I was so busy with the paper that I guess I never allowed myself to think too much about what was happening in other places. When the Supreme Court decision came, I was like everyone else. I didn't believe anything would come of it."

Ruth said, "But you wrote that you thought it was a bad idea. I remember your editorials. You said—"

"—what you've just said. I know." Tom tapped his pocket, took out an empty cigarette package and crumpled it. "The same as everyone, I thought it was a mistake."

"I didn't believe him," Ruth said suddenly.

"What?"

"Jim. I went over to see Mary, and he was there and told me. But I didn't believe him. I said he must have misunderstood. He said . . ."

Tom knew what he'd said; he remembered vividly the conversation he and Jim Wolfe had had the previous evening. He'd gone over—why? To get away from Ruth, to get away from the responsibility of picking Gramp out of the saloon—let the old bastard take a taxi!—and they'd listened to an old recording of "Beale Street Blues"; and then, incredibly, Tom had said: "You'll collect their records, but you wouldn't let any of them stay overnight at your house, would you?"

And Jim had frowned and said carefully, "No. Would you?"

And so the discussion had begun.

". . . in the first place, those fellows on the Supreme Court are a motley crew, Tom. All you have to do is study their records. One of them was even a member of the Klan. Politicians, that's all; not a damn one of them qualified to serve. You take this—"

"Hold on, now, damn it. Just because you're a lawyer and you say they're not qualified doesn't mean they're not. And what's the difference, anyway? If a cop stops a thief and brings him in, does it matter how many years he's been on the force, or what his record was, or what he eats for breakfast? He brought in the thief —that's all that counts, isn't it?"

Jim Wolfe had stared.

"Tom, are you saying you think the decision was a good one? Are you saying that?"

"For the sake of the argument, maybe."

"Well, it's a pretty fast switch, that's all I can say. Hell, anyone with an ounce of sense can see that it's the worst thing that's happened since Roosevelt! Understand: *I'm* not in the least prejudiced. When I said I wouldn't have, well, Louie Armstrong over for the evening, I was taking a lot of factors into consideration. What I mean is, well, like: maybe I've got nothing personal against spiders, you understand? I might even like them and realize that they're man's friend, eaters of insects, harmless, docile, see? But I certainly would think twice before I decided to bring one of them home as a pet ... at least I would until Mary, and Beth, and—well, you and Ruth—and all my neighbors got over their fear. There might not be any basis for it at all, but it's a plain fact that most people are scared to death of spiders. They hate 'em. All right—let me pursue this a little further. It's an interesting parallel. Since there's no real reason why people should hate spiders, the Supreme Court decides that spiders are being persecuted, and this persecution has got to stop. Instead of setting examples, instead of sending scientists all over to talk to the people, to let them understand that their prejudices are wrong and giving them time to adjust, instead of this, the Court all of a sudden drops a nest of the hairy bastards down every chimney! Step on just one, they say, and we put you in jail!"

"We're not dealing with insects, we're dealing with human beings!"

"The spider doesn't happen to be an insect. It's an arachnid. But, all right. What I'm saying—and you've been saying it, too! —is, it's naïve, man, naïve to suppose that generations of tradition can be dissolved simply because somebody gives an order to that effect! But that isn't the only trouble. No matter whether we're responsible for it or not, it remains that the Negroes as they are today are definitely inferior to whites. Not potentially, no; but in actuality. In ratio, they've got more crime, more incest, more divorce, more disease, less morals and less intelligence. Period. Is this condition going to change automatically with the inception of integration? Is it?"

Tom had remained silent.

"Answer: No. Instead, since they can't be expected to jump up to our standards all of a sudden, the standards will have to be lowered. Look at what happened in Washington, if you doubt it. Of course, that's taking the happiest view. That's assuming the most probable result won't occur—I mean an outbreak of violence; the worst kind of violence we've known in the South since 1860!"

Wolfe had sucked on his pipe, looking both serious and intelligent. *He is intelligent,* Tom had thought.

And he had known, suddenly, that this was the face of the Enemy.

"I hesitate even to mention the significance of all this in terms of international relations," Wolfe had continued. "The Communists have already made Jim Crow as well known as Uncle Sam. Better known, by God. Just with the situation we've had. But you just watch what happens when the fighting starts! They'll have a damned field day! Ten to one that kid from the Hill, that Vaughan kid they had to expel—I'll bet his name gets more publicity than Marilyn Monroe, all over the world. I'm telling you, Tom, American prestige is going straight to hell with this business. Every minor skirmish, every little incident . . . it'll be the next best thing to another War Between the States. Every day another Emmet Till will bite the dust— And when the whole miserable thing explodes in our face, it'll be heard in every corner of the earth! This is common sense. And you tell me—even for the sake of argument—that 'maybe' the decision was a good idea!"

Wolfe had removed his pipe and stared at Tom.

"Well," he'd said, "do you care to challenge any of these points?"

And Tom, given no choice, had been forced to answer: "Yes."

"By all means then," his friend had said, stiffly courteous. "I'd be delighted to listen."

"I'm—not going to tear your argument down piece-by-piece, or even try. It's basically true. But all you've said, in essence, is: A wrong that has stood so long that it can't be corrected without a lot of trouble ought to be allowed to stand."

"Absolutely not! No, that isn't right. When I say that I disapprove of this legislation, I mean I disapprove of it as a means of correcting the wrong. It'll only compound it, because of the sure result; don't you see? Look, Tom—you know as well as I do that an idealist without a plan is a dangerous person. Any half-baked neurotic can look at something he doesn't like, even if it's four thousand miles away, even though he knows nothing whatsoever about the factors involved, and say: 'That's wrong! Change it by three o'clock tomorrow!'

"Now I personally didn't much care for the way California treated its Japanese citizens right after Pearl Harbor. You remember? But I at least had sense enough to know that maybe there were things I didn't understand. Maybe they had reasons of their own that would have justified tossing everyone of Japanese descent into what amounts to concentration camps. Who knows? But these same California people aren't hesitating to throw rocks at *us*!"

"A wrong," Tom had said, knowing how feeble it sounded, "is a wrong, whether it's justified or not. All crimes have got their reasons. You could carry that to ridiculous lengths and show that every murderer and every petty thief and every dictator in the world does what he does for very damn good personal reasons. Hitler probably could have given you a pretty logical explanation why he burned millions of Jews, why it was necessary to the economy and the moral health of Germany. A man who has just raped my wife could produce great psychological excuses, I'm sure. And maybe I couldn't judge him—but I sure as hell could stop him from doing it again!"

"Aren't you reaching a bit, old man?"

"I don't think so. There are reasons why we brought the Negroes over here as slaves in the beginning, and there are reasons for the situation that exists now. But it's morally wrong, nonetheless.

And whatever is morally wrong must be redressed at once, regardless of the consequences."

"This 'at once' business," Wolfe had said, "is the whole difficulty. Some things, by the very nature of them, simply can't be changed 'at once.' What we have now didn't just pop up, for God's sake; it was over a hundred years in the making! It's easy to stop a man from *raping* your wife. But what if you had to stop him from *hating* her? What would you do then? Besides, you're still talking all around the point. Which is: the wrong can be corrected, it is being corrected, it will be corrected ... if only they will let us alone! Things are better now than they were five years ago. They'll be better in another five, or would have been, anyway. The strain of prejudice is getting weaker with every generation, Tom. We don't laugh at midgets in a circus any more. Why? Because we're more sophisticated than our fathers were; we know that midgets are caused by a general endocrine deficiency. The same thing holds true here. We used to have a fundamental, economy-based need for segregation and prejudice; now we don't. Since prejudice is an unnatural thing, it follows—"

"Do you believe that?" Tom had asked.

"Believe what?"

"That prejudice is unnatural?"

Jim had risen, then, and walked toward the cabinet that held the hi-fi components. "Why, anyone of intelligence—" he'd begun.

"What about the Jews? Around here, the Catholics? The Chinese? The Mexicans? The Poles? In some places, even the Irish? No; it isn't unnatural. This 'progress' of yours is a nice little argument, only it doesn't happen to be true. I believed it, until this business started; then I realized I was mistaken. Because if it *was* true, the decision wouldn't have kicked up much trouble. The fact that it did kick up trouble—and that there might be more: how'd you say? 'the worst kind of violence the South has known since 1860'—proves—can't you see that, Jim?—that there hasn't been any *real* progress, that it's just an illusion we've hung onto to justify our failure to do anything about the matter. Your failure and mine. It's us, the nice people, the intelligent, sophisticated people—*we're* the ones to blame for this, not the ignorant hillbillies and the cheap neurotics! They have no power to act; we have, and always have had. But we didn't act. The guilt is ours, and we've got to keep this thing alive because if we don't, then we'll know the guilt is ours and that wouldn't be pleasant, would it! Not a damn bit pleasant."

His voice had been tense, while Jim's had remained for the most part calm and relaxed; now they both knew, with certainty, that the friendship that had been theirs was gone, forever and irretrievably gone.

Jim had not even tried: "I'm sorry," he'd said, "that this has happened. At the moment the most important reason is that I'm forced to take sides. And I'm not on yours, Tom."

Now Tom McDaniel wondered how many people there were, not only in the South, but all over, who had to 'take sides' and found themselves for a faceless legion of strangers and against those whom they loved: against their friends and wives and the selves that they had been.

He talked with Ruth for an hour, and she listened quietly, and he told her the same things he had told Jim Wolfe; but robbed of their righteous anger, the words sounded false, and he was almost ashamed. Still, they had to be said. All of them.

When he finished, Ruth sat perfectly still. She breathed softly.

Then she said: "What are you going to do?"

He shrugged. "I don't know. I'm not sure." And it was true. In every other matter, he had been ruthlessly honest; the *Messenger* had won prizes for its liberal, forthright views; his blistering, knowledgeable editorials had achieved a measure of renown. In this matter, however, he had not been honest. Far from stating his belief that accepting the decision was a moral duty, he had not even stated that it was also a legal duty—not recently, anyway.

He was a pimp now, peddling diseased goods.

Why?

He started the engine, switched on the lights and pulled back onto the road.

If I have so little regard for a small town newspaper, if these people are my enemies, why don't I move away? I could accept Lubin's offer. In New York. On a pro-integration paper.

Is it because, he asked himself, you like Caxton, and you like these people—even if they are enemies—and editing the *Messenger* is exactly what you want to do?

"Shipman won't let me tell the truth," he said to Ruth, to himself. "If I do, I'll be fired." He looked down at his wife. "Well, what do you think of me now? What do you think of a man who's a nigger-lover and doesn't have the guts to say it out loud?"

Ruth was silent.

"Go on! I know what you're thinking. Why don't you say it!"

"I'm—confused," she said, pressing her hand to her forehead. "If you'd told me any of this before, or even hinted—if you'd tried to make me understand—"

Tom nodded. "Instead of 'jamming it down your throat' ... I know." He felt angry and disgusted. "It's all ruined now, I suppose," he said.

Ruth did not answer. He could see the tears that had fallen, unchecked, down her face.

"I'm sorry," he said. "Please believe that. I'm sorry."

They drove home, then. They went into the darkened house and did not speak or look at one another; neither knew what to say, what to do: *We're strangers,* Tom kept thinking; *strangers.*

"Dad!"

He turned and saw Ella standing in the bedroom doorway. She was in her pajamas, but she had not been sleeping.

"Dad, call Mr. Allardyce right away. He's been trying to get you for an hour."

"All right, thank you, kitten. You go on to sleep now; it's late." Tom picked up the phone. "He didn't say what it was, did he?"

"Huh-uh. But he said it was real important. You two been warring?"

Ruth wiped her face with a handkerchief and smiled. "No. Come on, now, off to bed."

Ella shrugged. "Okay," she said dubiously, and closed the door.

"Tom?" Jack Allardyce's voice was loud with excitement.

"Yes. Ella says you were—"

"Tom, you better get over to Simon's Hill right away."

"Why?"

"You ain't heard about it?"

"Heard about what?"

The old man almost shouted the words.

Tom said, "All right," and put down the phone slowly.

"What is it?" Ruth asked.

"The Baptist church on Simon's Hill has been dynamited," he said. "The preacher was inside."

19

They drove slowly past the cemetery into the section known as Death Row. It was like any other section of Los Angeles—old, gray, quiet—except that the streets were lined with funeral parlors. They began as rather ornate establishments, mostly in the colonial style, but as you proceeded toward the Civic Center they grew smaller, less fancy and more to the point.

From the third block onward, they dropped their disguises entirely. The barbered lawns and Southern mansions gave way to bleak little structures of plaster and wood, and there was no attempt made at a cheerful atmosphere.

Peter Link said, "If you ever plan to die, Driscoll, this would be the neighborhood to do it in."

Ed Driscoll nodded. He had instinctively cut his speed down to twenty-five miles per hour, and he noticed that the other cars were moving slowly also. There were few pedestrians to be seen. Few signs of life.

He drove another hundred yards, then parked in front of an old frame house with a sign in front of it which read: HALLER BROS.—MORTUARY.

"You want a shot of it?" Link asked.

"Might as well."

Link got out of the car and took a number of pictures of the establishment; then he and Driscoll walked to the front door.

A balding Negro in a black suit answered. His voice was soft. "Yes?" he said. "Can I help you, gentlemen?"

"In a way," Driscoll said. "We're looking for a fellow named Preston Haller."

"That's my son," the man said. "He's in the back, working. You want me to call him?"

"We'd appreciate it."

"Certainly. Come in, gentlemen."

Driscoll and Link stepped into a dimly lit living room. It was neat and heavy with the sweet smell of flowers. They sat down on a couch and waited quietly. Then a young, handsome man in his middle twenties came in.

"I'm Preston Haller," he said. "Dad says you wanted to see me."

Driscoll proffered his hand. "We're reporters, Mr. Haller," he said. "We're doing a story on Adam Cramer. Maybe you'll help us."

The young man's expression grew suddenly hard.

"He's a friend of yours, isn't he?" Driscoll asked.

"Who told you that?"

"It's true, isn't it?"

Preston Haller walked over to the window and stood there for a time. "It used to be true," he said finally.

"Then I suppose you've read about his activities."

"Yes, I've read about them."

There was a silence. "Mr. Haller, Adam Cramer is a pretty big news item these days. We're trying to do a story on him, but we're not going to be able to unless you give us a hand. You can see why, can't you?"

"I think so. Because I'm colored."

"Because you're colored and because you were close to him. If the two of you are friends and he's out to stop integration, well —there are quite a few questions to be answered."

Preston Haller smiled, but without amusement. "I'm afraid I can't be of much assistance to you. I don't know the answers to those questions."

"But you do know Cramer well?"

"No. I thought I did, once; but I was wrong. So were a lot of other people."

"Will you tell us about it?"

"About what? I could only tell you what he was, mister, or what I, anyway, thought he was. That fellow in the South—he doesn't know me and I don't know him."

Driscoll shrugged. "Frankly, Mr. Haller," he said, "I don't be-lieve you. I think you're telling us this because you know what we can do with your story, and you don't want to see that done to your friend—no matter how he's behaved. Of course, I may be wrong. We can't force you to talk, in any case. But I'd like to submit something to you. May I?"

Preston Haller said nothing.

"If you tell us your story—and it's a long one; we picked that much up from the kids at the university; some of them remembered—Adam Cramer will get hurt. It may not stop him, but it'll slow him up. If, on the other hand, you decide to respect the friendship that you had with him and refuse to tell the story, a *lot* of people are going to get hurt. More than you can imagine, maybe. The choice is yours."

Preston Haller rubbed his forehead, walked to the large couch and sat down.

The scent of flowers became heavier on the air.

A clock ticked loudly.

"Well?"

"All right." Preston Haller sighed, and it was, clearly, a sigh of immense relief. He rose. "But let's go somewhere to talk. Wait here and I'll tell Dad."

He returned in a while and they walked down the street to a small, dark bar called Ada's and ordered beer.

Preston Haller said, "He's got to be stopped?" It was almost a question.

"He's got to be stopped," Driscoll said.

"Yeah." The young man took a large swallow of beer and licked his lips slowly. Then he said: "I met him in Switzerland. We were both attending the University of Zurich. Adam—"

"Never mind about Adam for a while," Driscoll interrupted. "Tell us about you first. It's important."

"Well, I was there on a scholarship. I'd been majoring in philosophy at the university here and, I don't know, they had a lot of lectures lined up, a lot of important people. The truth is, I went there to get away from death."

Driscoll waited.

"My father's a mortician, you know that. So's my uncle. They wanted me to take over the business—only, I didn't care for the idea. On the other hand, I wasn't able to come up with anything better. I mean, if I'd said to them, 'I can't cut it because I want to be a doctor'—or a trumpet player, or something—anything—Dad would have understood. But it wasn't that simple. All I knew was what I *didn't* want to do; and that wasn't enough. I thought that if I went away, maybe I could figure it out." He paused. "You want to hear about all this?"

"Yes," Driscoll said. "You keep talking, Mr. Haller. When I think you're off the track, I'll let you know. Okay?"

Preston Haller said "Okay," dubiously, and went on: "Anyway, it didn't work too well. I played with the idea of becoming a professor, but professors are supposed to know things; and the more I went to school, the more I realized I didn't know anything at all.

"Living in a mortuary, growing up with death all around me, you understand, I *wanted* to believe. I wanted to believe in God and Heaven and Eternal rewards—or Eternal damnations, it didn't matter. Anything would do. Anything to persuade me that a shabby old house in L. A. wasn't the end of the line.... But it seemed the harder I tried to be like Dad, or my mother—maybe you've wondered about morticians, how they keep from being morbid. They keep from it because they don't believe in death. It's their business, but they don't believe in it. Corpses are objects, that's all: empty containers, shells. I've never met, I'm telling you the truth, an atheistic mortician!—Well, the more like them I tried to be, the further away I got. I studied all the great religions thoroughly, I mean it; and sometimes, like with Roman Catholicism, or Zen, I'd think I'd found it, finally. But you can't kid yourself long on the big things. The little things, yes. Not the big things." He took a long swallow of beer. *"Quo vadimus,* man?" he said, smiling suddenly.

"Nowhere, for a while. I hope," said Driscoll. He ordered more beer. "Go on."

"Yeah. I was living with a family named Schöngarth, in Zurich. It was February, and the roofs had snow on them. I'd never seen snow before and I remember this gave the Schöngarths a laugh. They thought students had seen everything.... Well, this wasn't too long after the war. Our particular age-group, we were feeling sorry for ourselves because we'd been cheated anyway. Emancipation, Fornication, Dissipation: those were the watchwords. Why not? It'd only be for a year, in spite of all the threats of staying on and dying in a *pissoir.* Only for a year. Then home, to reality.

"But I was getting damn lonely because it was too cold to go walking, or whatever the reason was; and I took to dropping by Jackie's. That's an American bar. I met Adam there.

"I remember I was having a glass of beer, sitting in a corner near the fireplace. It was around midnight. Jonas Brady was trying to get me to go with him to a girl's house. A *'complaisant* Swiss,' he said, 'amply upholstered,' who'd seen me around and told Jonas—it was probably a lie!—that 'she thought it would be fun to sleep with a Negro.' A real typical gesture: Jonas was a guy who was filled with Sartre and Celine, and Huysmans; tiny perversions were all that interested him any more. He existed on Pernod, which he got by playing ragtime tunes on Jackie's piano. Open-toe, broken-toenail set. You know? He liked me for only one reason: he didn't dare not to. Lot of people that way, afraid to dislike any one Negro because then they'd be accused of prejudice. It's prejudice-in-reverse, you might call it. Anyway, there was Jonas, babbling away, and me pretending to listen, when this dark-haired kid walked up and asked to bum a cigarette.

"Jonas introduced me and said for the guy to join us. He did, and for a while I was afraid that he was just another carbon copy of Jonas. *'Reprieve* Carriers' we called them. But I was wrong. Adam Cramer turned out to be very bright and very friendly, and he was the only one who managed to persuade me that my color didn't signify.

"He was taking a criminal medicine course at the time, but he knew philosophy, and we used to walk outside of the town, across the fields, freezing our asses and arguing, I don't know, Kant, or whoever. He became my only friend in Zurich, and later, when we returned to America to finish up at the University here, we stayed friends.

"I was still groping, still not quite sure; and upset at finding nothing solid to hang onto. I went along with Adam conversationally, but inside it was different. Maybe it was with him too.

"We made quite a pair. But while I was looking for a meaning to life, he was working on finding the way to—well, it's hard to put. With Adam, you see, this was a personal thing. He didn't care why other people were around; he wanted to know why *he* was around. But that was okay. One, I figured, would answer the other.

"It's for certain that he was looking, though. Every bit as hard as I was."

Preston Haller shifted his position on the bench and drank the rest of his beer.

"What about Blake?" Driscoll said. "I hear there's a connection."

"Max Blake teaches political theory at the U. We'd heard about him, Adam and I, and liked what we'd heard. So we enrolled. It was a disappointment at first. Whatever we'd expected, we didn't get it. Professor Blake taught a slightly liberal but pretty orthodox course, and neither of us could dig the secret reputation he'd built up. For real leftist kicks, there were a dozen better classes. For brilliant remarks, great oratory, sly humor, almost every other full professor had him whipped. Blake was a washout. So pretty soon Adam decided to plant the needle, mostly out of boredom. He was a hell of a debater, following Schopenhauer's bit to a T, and I'd never heard anyone get the best of him. He sounded off three days in a row, pulverizing certain theories that Blake was in the process of making—but it wasn't a fight. 'Very interesting point, Mr. Cramer,' the old man would say and that would be it. We got fairly contemptuous of him finally. Then one day Blake mentioned that he was having an informal discussion at his home that night and that perhaps we'd be interested in attending. Adam didn't want to, but we didn't have anything else to do, so we dropped by. And that was the bomb.

"The daytime Blake was a masquerade, we saw: a masterful pose. The real Blake was a completely different person. These 'informal discussions' were his actual classes, and he reserved them for a handful of the sharpest students.

"It was here that he showed his wit, his thing with sarcasm —Adam tried to joust only once, but he was cut down; here that Blake came out as one of the most *electric* minds either of us had known. He threw off ideas like sparks. Finally they caught fire in Adam."

"What sort of ideas?"

"Difficult to explain," Haller said. "At first I was as knocked out as anyone else, but when I began to understand what it was he was saying, I took off. Blake was (and I haven't heard that he's changed) essentially a Fascist, in the way that he follows the theory that the Masses are incompetent to rule—you know. However, he's a 'leftist' Fascist: he believes that the 'small governing body of men'—expressed in fascist doctrine—is by nature a chimerical ideal. I'm quoting him now, I think. That's one of his expressions: chimerical ideal. It comes simply to a rule of one man, and, according to Blake, even if that man is a tyrant, it's better than any so-called democratic form of government. Hitler almost made it work, but Hitler—I *am* quoting now—was both ignorant and mad. Mussolini had brains, but he was pompous. They both had too much regard for humanity."

"So that was the trouble," Link said, grinning mirthlessly.

"According to Blake, yeah. He used to refer to his after-hours class as a 'nursery for dictators'—because that was what he was proposing. He even outlined a general plan for success. Let me remember: 'A man could succeed by seizing upon an area of unrest—'"

Preston Haller hesitated and looked at Driscoll, who nodded and said, "Don't stop now."

" 'By taking over as a *negative* force, spouting a communist-inspired line—to gain the support of the sheep who would not yet consciously understand the concept of single authority—then, by instituting small pogroms and purges, destroying all but the single power, keeping the minor counselors in a state of nameless and faceless flux, he could switch carefully to a semi-fascist line, and become a dictator before the people's eyes without anyone's seeing it happen.' Unquote. His dicta were 'Play on their ignorance; underline and reflect their prejudices; make them afraid.' But, of course, this is a pocket edition of several months' discussions, before I quit—it was all vague and diffuse.

" 'Be ruthless!' he told us, though. 'Be ruthless! If you're to be a dictator, employ every low trick there is. Deceive, cheat, lie, steal, murder. Show no mercy whatever. In that fashion, perhaps you will succeed. The Great Unwashed'—no; he said, 'The Great

Unwashable'—live on fear and hate alone; their prejudices keep them afloat—it is the only strength they have. Your success, *ipso facto*, will demonstrate the gift of man; it will raise your estate a bit higher than that of the animals ... for what animal ever led more than a small pack?'

"That's the gist of what Max Blake had to say. I said it was complicated because fascism itself isn't acceptable to him. Some of the literate Fascists, like Alfredo Rocco, or even Ernest Renan, talked of the glorification of man; but the point that was important to Blake was the glorification of *men*, at the expense of others. That was his big bit. One great man, devil or saint, he said, is quite adequate. 'History is not Man, but men—and very few of them, at that.'

"Well, Adam begged me to keep going to the classes, but I couldn't see it. Fun was fun, and it was okay for a man to exercise his mind but this was too thick. With Adam, no. He told me that Max Blake had helped him find the thing he had been looking for, had acted as a catalyst to his thoughts.

"But you've got to understand, because I can see what you're both thinking, that there was a kind of a sense of make-believe to the whole thing. Most of the time we were together, Adam and I were never all-the-way serious—it's a fine point, hard to put across. In a way, it was like the Jonas Bradys in Switzerland: we were in school, school was unreality, and we could afford to let our minds fall into dissipation. We could go on intellectual benders and know, at the same time, that it wasn't of any account. Do you understand that?"

"Sure," Driscoll said. "You might not believe this, Mr. Haller, but I went to college once myself. For all I know, so did Link."

"I'm sorry, I didn't mean anything. It's just that it's a little confusing to me, and *I've* gone through it ... What I'm trying to say is that it was, in a *sense*, no more than a game. Go over to the University right now, and you'll find hundreds of avowed Communists, you know? Some of them might even know what communism means. But it doesn't signify, except the taking advantage of a nice situation. The newspapers and magazines certainly don't understand this. They're always attacking the 'college Commies' and urging all sorts of ridiculous measures. Which is stupid—

the truth is that it's healthy to be able to dabble in these things in a state of harmlessness. For that reason, what the hell, I never objected to Max Blake's courses, any more than I would object to fraternity orgies. Because the few students whose thinking is actually shaped by university life are always able to bring these things into their proper focus.

"Adam and I stayed friends, even though I was no longer attending Blake's courses. We occasionally went out on double-dates together, or, sometimes, for a drive down Sunset to the beach, alone, to talk. It wasn't strained.

"But I began to sense a change in him. He wouldn't allow any disrespectful remarks to be made about Blake, and even went so far, once, as to suggest that the reason I withdrew was because I was afraid. Again, it was part of the game; and I went along with it. Maybe so, I said. Maybe I don't want to be a dictator. And he'd laugh then, and everything would be okay.

"But he was changing. He seemed troubled, not in the way we'd been, but in a deeper way. Once he said, 'What does a guy do, Pres, when he's been told all his life that he can't do anything? When he's been trained through the years for failure?'

" 'Succeed,' I told him.

"He said that was right.

"Then—it wasn't too long ago—he came to my room and woke me up one night and said he was going away. Quitting, with only a few months to go for his graduation. I thought he was kidding at first. But Adam never kept a gag going long, so I tried to talk him out of it. He wouldn't listen, and he wouldn't give me any hint where he was going, or why. All he said was that he'd found what he could do, and that whatever I heard, I should believe it. 'Because it will be true, Pres,' he said. And then he asked to borrow my gun. I gave it to him and showed him how to work it, because even then I wasn't absolutely sure he was serious.

"He left that night.

"I haven't heard from him since, except for what I've read in the newspapers."

Preston Haller folded and unfolded his hands, and for a time the three men sat quietly, listening to the deep hum of the air-conditioning unit.

Driscoll was the first to speak.

"You still like him, don't you?"

Preston Haller said: "Yes, but he's got to be stopped. Use whatever you want . . ."

"Maybe we're too late to bomb him out of there completely," Driscoll said, "but we can go a long way in that direction. That isn't supposed to be my interest: I'm not crusading, only writing about a guy. But the piece is going to have quite an effect on his plans. Mr. Haller, I'd like you to answer a few direct questions. One: Did Adam Cramer ever, to your knowledge, go out with any Negro girls?"

Preston Haller said, "Yes. Several times."

"Are the girls around? Can you give me their names?"

"I think so."

"Question number two: In all the time you knew Cramer, did he ever express to you any anti-Negro or anti-integration views?"

"Never."

"So it can be said, can't it, that he's doing this for, you might say, intellectual reasons; he isn't really against integration; that the whole thing is an effort to put the theories of an off-horse college professor into actual practice."

"Nothing is as simple as all that," Preston Haller said. "He has other motivations, I'm sure."

Driscoll said, "Yes; we've spoken to one of them already."

He removed a five-dollar bill from his wallet and picked up the check. Then they walked out of the darkened bar, out into the hot, white sun.

20

Past rows of shacks and broken toys, past garbage heaped in careless mounds and scattered by the dogs that roamed these streets, gray wood, frayed clothing hung on rusted wires, past fat and scarred-up men who stood on corners laughing in the vomit-heavy air, he walked; and thought that hours had gone by, although, of course, that couldn't be.

I ought to go on back, he thought.

I got no business here.

But somehow, the quiet of the hospital, the slow-moving nurses, all the eyes, had grown unbearable, and he had rushed out, suddenly, and wandered to this part of Farragut, where rats were known to eat dead children, where the women sold their evil-smelling bodies for a buck, where men carried ritual scars and believed in voodoo.

I got no business here!

But Joey knew that it wasn't wholly so. For standing in the little room, the dark face there about to vanish, he had heard a voice: *Go take a walk, boy. Go to Jeremiah Street. See all the sights. See your people. Your people. Then come back. There's time!*

"Hey, Jim, you got a cigarette?"

He turned and faced an old Negro in a double-breasted blue suit, wide tie, sweat-soaked gray hat. The man was drunk, and dirty.

"You got a cigarette for Sonny?"

Joey reached into his pocket and withdrew a package of Pall Malls. The man took one of the cigarettes and tried to light it. In the darkness, Joey saw that he bore scars and bruised marks on his flesh.

"You want some fun?" the man said.

Joey shook his head and started away. A clawlike hand tightened on his shoulder.

"Wait, I ask you, you want some fun? Listen. Come on, you ain't in no big fucking hurry. Come on. Listen."

"Get your hand off me."

"Bullshit," the man said. "What kind nigger are you, anyway? You a fairy-boy? Maybe you think I kidding you. Listen, I don't kid nobody. I got my little girl staying with me, and I mean, she something. She really something. All this other ginch around here ain't worth poking a finger in. But Harriet—let me tell you something, Jim. She been a year in New York. She ain't really working, now, I mean, she just paying her daddy a visit, see. But she do anything I tell her. Five dollars and she go down, you do anything you want. She—"

Joey grasped the wrist firmly and pushed it away. He began to walk quickly. The man danced along behind him, shrieking:

"You no fucking man, you a fucking queer. Hey, queer! Hey, fairy-boy!" Then the man stumbled, and Joey glanced back; but the man did not move.

Joey walked to the hospital, which was an old house like a boardinghouse, and went up the steps.

The waiting room was filled with people.

He passed the receptionist's desk, turned right, and climbed the flight of stairs. They were covered with dark linoleum which had worn through in the center and was edged with misshapen aluminum stripping.

He entered the silent, sharp-smelling hall. His fingers drew into fists. A large woman in the well-lit alcove where the nurses made their reports and took their calls looked up.

"Is he any better?" Joey asked quietly.

"Just a moment," the nurse said. She got up and walked down the hall to room twenty-two. She returned with a large, well-built man.

"Is he any better?"

The doctor shook his head. In a professional whisper, he said, "Mr. Green, do you want me to tell you the truth?"

Joey thought, *No!*

"Yes," he said.

"Dr. Henderson and I spent quite a while trying to restore what we call basic somatic balances. And we managed it. But there is no way of telling whether or not he will have the strength to overcome the shock, because he's still in a very deep coma. There has been nothing to indicate that he will come out of it."

"He can't die," Joey said.

"I'm afraid he can," the doctor said, staring levelly. "We don't know exactly the degree of the injury to the brain, but it's very severe. You say his head struck the edge of a desk?"

"It looked that way." Joey had blotted out the memory; now it returned, in a quick wave.

He'd been lying on the couch, trying to sleep, when he heard the explosion. For some reason, he knew what had happened. Within moments his trousers were on, and he was rushing down the gravel path, heart hammering, toward the church.

It had caught fire, and was burning, a deep orange against the night sky. Joey leaned against the radio tower, got his breath back, and saw that both the damage and the fire were relatively slight.

There was a jagged hole on the left side of the church.

He rushed to the door. It was locked. He screamed: "Reverend Mead! Reverend Mead!" and waited; then he kicked the ancient lock, broke it, and went inside.

The smoke was bad. He put a handkerchief to his mouth and walked to Reverend Mead's study.

The old man was lying on the floor, silent and unmoving. A bright wash of blood covered his face.

Joey lifted him into his arms and walked back outside. By this time, people were gathering.

"Call an ambulance," Joey said and waited eternities for the ambulance to come, while buckets quenched the small flames.

No one said much. Joey did not think of who had done this, or why: he thought only of getting the preacher to a hospital and curing him. He tried to stanch the wound, but was unsuccessful. Blood continued to flow. So he put his handkerchief against the gaping hole and pressed softly, and hoped he was doing the right thing.

Within an hour, the heavy doors of St. Vincent's were pushed open (and they had to go to St. Vincent's, there was no choice) and the preacher, under woolen blankets, was wheeled into the emergency room. There was no expression on his face.

Joey waited.

Later, they wheeled the preacher out and past the waiting room, and in a while they said that Joey could see him.

He lay breathing hard. A blood transfusion was being made. Bandages covered his skull.

"We can't tell you anything yet," one of the doctors said, and he stayed a long time, looking down at the dark, expressionless face; then he heard the voice that was not a voice and went out and walked through Jeremiah Street. . . .

"I wish I could offer some hope," Doctor Grant said, "but—it's a strange thing about head injuries, Mr. Green. There are only two kinds: bad and very bad. The human head is like an egg. You can't 'almost' crack it, or crack it halfway. Your friend is an old man. He has sustained compound fractures, and the shock to the brain—"

Joey nodded. "Can I go in?"

"It won't do any harm. But if you want my opinion, you're putting yourself through a lot of unnecessary discomfort."

"You mean he won't wake up?"

"Very probably not. He might, but the chances are slim."

"I can't leave him alone."

"He isn't alone. The nurses—"

Joey turned and walked down the hall and carefully opened the door.

There was no change in Reverend Finley Mead. He lay in exactly the same position, still as a discarded doll. No longer did he seem tall and brave and strong. No longer the man who had told Joey about the Tiger.

Doctor Grant appeared in the doorway, nodded at the nurse; she walked out.

Joey heard: "Tracheotomy may be needed; Dr. Henderson—"

And: "I've talked to Dr. Henderson. There doesn't seem much point to it."

The old man's breathing was ragged.

Between breaths, there would come a silence deeper than any other silence, for Joey would hold his breath also, automatically, waiting.

He sat and stared at the preacher.

Now was the time to think. The others had been turned away; a night would pass before the relatives' arrival; time to think.

But he could not. Only the despair he'd felt before was in him; the futility; and the red words trailing through his mind: I'll find them and I'll kill them for this.

The vigil lengthened and still the old man did not move. From time to time the doctor came in and checked him and went out again.

I'll kill them, said the words.

Then, so much later, after he had waited for that breath and it had, incredibly, finally come, Joey tore himself away from the bed and glared down at the preacher.

"Well, die, for Christ's sake! Die!" he cried. "And don't blame anybody, you stupid old fool—don't blame anybody but yourself! You wouldn't see the way things are. I tried to tell you, but you wouldn't see. So they blew up your church! Where was your blessed God when they were doing that, preacher? Where was He then?" Joey's arm raised; the finger of his hand stiffened and pointed at the old man. "Where will your dear Lord be when those same guys come and plant dynamite under the other homes, when they blow up Simon's Hill and everybody on it?"

The preacher stirred.

"Right now, right now, Reverend—maybe my own mother and father are dead. Maybe their guts are all over the floor! Is it worth it, all them words? Freedom!"

He rushed to the bed and shook his arm away from the nurse's grip, and screamed at the still figure: "Tell me about our rights now, you old son of a bitch! Oh, Christ, tell me about them now!"

"Doctor!"

"Leave me alone. He did it himself. He killed all of us. My mother's dead, they blew her up—"

Strong hands pulled him away. He felt the hot tears on his cheeks and he began to fight, when suddenly the doctor froze.

There was the ghost of a sound from the bed.

"Joey," the sound said.

They waited.

Again: "Joey Green."

He tried to pull away, but the hands held him firmly.

"He's calling me!"

"You're in no condition to—"

"I'm all right now, I am, I'm okay. He's calling—"

"He won't recognize you, Mr. Green."

Joey pushed the doctor aside angrily and knelt by the bed.

The old man's eyes flickered, opened; there was a light behind them, but it was a dim light.

"Joey . . . must not blame them all. A few . . ."

He strained to hear.

"A few. Tell Irma, tell her I don't mind. Are you here, Joey?"

"I'm here."

The doctor and the nurse stood very still, watching.

"Joey, you remember . . . you remember once I told you everybody got a test . . . for him alone?"

"I remember, Reverend."

"This is your test."

The voice stopped; there was a long pause; then some hidden strength inside the preacher pulled more air into his lungs.

"Promise me," he said, so softly only Joey Green could hear. "Promise me you see the job gets done."

Joey's teeth were clamped together tightly; he was holding off the scream that was a solid thing within his throat.

"You're the only one . . . can do it now. Joey? Promise?"

He tasted the salt and thought of all the Jeremiah Streets and felt the shudder then that chilled along his arms. He put his head against the white sheet, heard his own voice say:

"I promise."

21

He sat on the bunk in the cell and absorbed the experience, relishing, in order, the faraway sounds of conversation (muffled, as though coming from midgets and dwarfs), the metal smells and dirt smells and the stale, leftover, unidentifiable smells; the gray door and green walls and actual real-life bars; relishing the role of the revolutionary jailed for his patriotic fervor. Thus it had been (exactly!) with De Valera and Paine and, yes, Dostoevski and Seneca . . .

They also had sat in tiny cryptlike rooms, trapped by the unjust many, punished for their courage and their wisdom.

Yes!

Of course, it hadn't been difficult to read the poor sheriff. Any one of a dozen possible approaches would have sufficed, probably the best being a shocked reaction followed by a nicely humble statement of his whereabouts at the time of the blast ("I was watching a mystery on television, sir. Mrs. Pearl Lambert and I do that quite a lot. She was with me. You can ask her, if you'd like. But—gosh, I just can't believe what you say!") and a sincere expression of faith in the sheriff's ability to round up the culprit.

Instead, he'd called him a strutting martinet with a power complex and warned him that if he didn't get out of the room in a hurry, he'd have a lot to answer for.

The alibi stuck, but Rudy Parkhouse had had his pride wounded; so he'd booked Cramer on the charge of inciting to riot.

Which was fine.

Adam dropped the cigarette and squashed it with his heel. He prepared to lie down on the bunk when the heavy steel door opened.

"All right, Rudy. You can leave us alone."

"Ten minutes," the sheriff said. "That's the limit."

"All right, Rudy."

Verne Shipman waited until the door was locked again; then he walked over and sat down on the bunk.

Adam smiled. "How are you, Verne?" he said, putting out his hand.

Shipman avoided it. "I might as well tell you right off the bat," he said, "that I don't cotton to any of this. I figured you were smart. I strung along with you because that's what I figured. Now I'm beginning to wonder."

"Oh?"

Shipman gestured about the cell. "Smart people don't end up here," he said.

Adam got up from the bunk and walked to a corner of the cell. He looked outside and smiled even more broadly. "But I'm not 'ending up' here, Verne. This is only a little visit."

"Don't be too sure of that. The way you smarted off to Rudy, I wouldn't be surprised at anything. He told me what you said. With an alibi like that Lambert woman, you could have kept out of here easy!"

"I know that."

Shipman stared.

"Look, Verne," Adam said, "it's a little difficult to explain, but this is actually a vital part of the operation. It's a big step forward."

"Getting tossed in jail is a step forward?"

"Uh-huh." Adam chuckled. "I don't know whether you've ever studied political history, but it so happens that an occasional jail sentence can do more good for the leader of a cause than a dozen speeches. The theory has been proved out time and again. See: the people, Verne, the *people* have always hated cops. Cops are supposed to be our protectors, keepers of the peace, enforcers of the law—and that's what they are in theory, you see what I mean. But the truth is, folks think of 'em only as enemies. *Enemies.* They get respect born of hate; and the hate is grounded in fear."

Adam saw that the big man was not following him. "Try looking at it this way," he said. "Everybody in America is afraid of being thrown into jail. Right? It's something they have night-mares about. Okay, so when a person they know is held unjustly, when it's perfectly clear he's innocent, they empathize—put themselves in his shoes."

Shipman continued to stare.

"The whole thing will help turn them against the authority they're afraid of. It'll break down their resistance to our organiza-tion—and quite a few have resisted, you know. Just because of the fear-respect of this so-called 'law' . . ."

"I don't know. That's a lot of fancy talk."

"It's true, nonetheless. The value of jail shouldn't be underesti-mated by anyone who wants to get ahead in this country."

Shipman took a handkerchief from his pocket and blew his nose. "Well," he said, "I still don't know. Bail is ten thousand dol-lars. What if I don't put it up? What if I decide to—"

"Forget it, Verne. I don't want your money."

There was a stunned silence.

"You have ten thousand dollars?" the large, baby-faced man asked.

"No!" Adam laughed. Then, quickly, he sobered.

"You know, I'm a little disappointed in you, Verne," he said. "I'd expected a certain amount of faith by this time. Haven't things gone as I told you they would?"

"Well, yes, I suppose so."

"Haven't I kept my word straight down the line?"

"Sure. But—"

"Then—if you're still interested in being a part of this—I would suggest that you show a bit more trust. I didn't call you here, remember. You came on your own accord." Adam grinned suddenly and clapped Shipman on the shoulder. "But cheer up now," he said. "And save your money: there'll be a need for it—and for you—later on. This is only the beginning." He held out his hand for the second time.

Shipman accepted it hesitantly; then he rose, and walked halfway across the cell.

"Where are you going to get the bail?" he asked.

Adam shrugged and gestured toward the window.

Below, on the sidewalk in front of the jail, was a crowd of men and women and children. Many of them held placards.

The placards read: FREE ADAM CRAMER! JUSTICE FOR CRAMER! CRAMER INNOCENT!

They were moving slowly, circling, like pickets.

Shipman stared out the window until the steel door opened.

"Time," said Rudy Parkhouse impatiently.

Shipman looked back one time, then he went out of the cell.

Three hours later, Adam was informed that Bart Carey, Al Holliman and Phillip Dongen had deposited the ten thousand dollars in bail money.

Twenty minutes after that, he walked out of the jail and drank in the sweet music which the crowd made for him. They roared and yelled and hit him on the back; and even though there weren't more than twenty of them, they seemed an army.

Adam walked with Bart Carey to Joan's Cafe.

The back room was filled to capacity.

The Rev. Lorenzo Niesen shouted a greeting, and stepped away from the central table.

Adam raised his hands.

"I want to thank Mr. Carey and Mr. Dongen and Mr. Holliman," he said, "for what they done for me. Our friend Verne Shipman offered to get me out, but I told him no, I told him, 'Looky here, the people will see to it!' Now, listen, he's a good man; but he didn't believe me. And now I want you to know, I'm mighty glad to show him I was right. He knows for sure the folks in Caxton won't stand still for no injustice!"

"Yah!" called someone.

"Yah! It's so!"

Adam's hands lifted again.

"What the sheriff thought," he said, "was that I was responsible for that dynamiting up on Simon's Hill. I couldn't hardly believe he was serious! Said to him, 'Sheriff, whoever planted that bomb, it wasn't anybody in SNAP, I can tell you that right here and now!' 'Who *was* responsible?' he wanted to know. Said, 'I wouldn't want to say for sure. But it's my notion it was one of them nigger-lovin' integrationists!'"

He looked about the suddenly quiet room.

Rev. Lorenzo Niesen was beginning to fidget. Adam saw him throw a glance at another man.

"Well, sir, the sheriff didn't understand at first. He was so dumb he asked me why an integrationist would want to kill a nigger! Honest! I told him. 'Sheriff,' I said, 'it's simple. We all are *fighting* integration. Good God Almighty, we got sense enough to know that killing a nigger preacher and blowing up a church can't do us nothing but harm!' But he still didn't catch on. 'How you figure that?' he asked.

"I didn't hardly know what to say, it was so clear—clear as the nose on his stupid face. 'Sheriff, instead of jawing with me, why don't you take a run down to the N-double-A-C-P,' I said, 'and see what alibis *they* can give you! This is their style. They know that the best way to hurt the cause of segregation is to use the martyr system. Like with Emmet Till, when they killed him and tried to pin it on a Southern white man. I wouldn't be a bit surprised if they engineered this bombing, too. Because now that old nigger preacher will be a martyr, see what I mean? People will feel sorry for him. He'll be mourned, like an assassinated hero! So you can see, I hope, Sheriff,' I said, 'that nobody in my organization and nobody with any brains had a thing to do with it.' He got the point then, but I guess it was so obvious that he was sore at me for havin' to spell it out for him."

The silence deepened, as Adam gazed at the men.

"Well," he said, "that was what I thought, anyway. But while I was in jail, I got to studying. And it occurred to me that maybe I was wrong. I began to wonder: could it be—now, just for an instance; *could it be*—that somebody in SNAP actually *did* have something to do with this? Somebody who acted, you might say, on impulse, and didn't consider the consequences? It didn't seem possible, of course. But I knew that people sometimes do crazy things and think they're absolutely right, even though what they do is bound to go against 'em, in the long run. So, even though I

don't believe it, I'm gonna pretend that somewhere here in this
room is the man who bought that dynamite and hauled it over to
the church and lit it. It's him I'm gonna talk to, and you-all please
just bear with it. I don't mean it for those of you with common
sense."

Rev. Lorenzo Niesen shifted his position, fingered a sprig
of Beech Nut Chewing Tobacco from a crumpled package and
began to chew quickly. His eyes seemed filled half with amusement, half with anger.

Adam knew, without any doubt, that it was this poor rooster
of a man who had been responsible. He could see Niesen crawling up to the church, carrying his bundle of death; and all in the
name of Jesus, sweet dirty-nailed leather-fleshed unwashed Jesus
of Nazareth, Who spat streams of tobacco accurately into the eye
of falseness and caused the fig tree to wither because it would not
yield fruit.

But, he wondered, was it Niesen alone?

Of course it was. The others were his good soldiers, were they
not?

He tried to read the expressions on Bart Carey's face, on
Dongen's, Holliman's, Richey's, Humboldt's.

"Throwing a scare into the nigras is good," he said. "But we got
to be very, very careful. Because, always remember, we're trying
to do more than just keep integration out of Caxton; we're trying
to kill it for good and all. I've outlined some of the ways. There's
lots of others. But every one is calculated, planned so that it's
them—the *nigras*—who dig their own graves. We hand 'em the
noose, see? That's fine. But *they* do the lynching. *They* hang their
selves!"

The faces in the room were impassive, inattentive. There was
soft whispering.

A voice called: "How do we know that's gonna work?"

A stranger to Adam. A broad-faced, hairy man. "Sir, you
take my word for it. And you look at the record. Demoraliza-
tion has been proved a thousand times more effective than any
bomb ever was. Can't you see that making someone surrender
is better than conquering him? It's just a different type of war. A
smarter type. Okay, now you might think, Sure, that's okay for

here, where we outnumber the nigras, but what about where it's reversed?—Well, there are answers to that, too. If we were like certain towns in Mississippi, we'd use different means. We'd use what is called 'economic pressure.' It would be put on all niggers and whites who didn't support segregation. No loans to any of them; the supply houses and wholesalers just all of a sudden no longer provide customary credit; and so on. It's another way of 'opposing the law by every lawful means.' No one gets murdered or blown up, no nigger gets to be a martyr, but they get beat just as sure as if we'd strafed 'em with machine guns." Adam Cramer held up a finger. "So listen: I'm not condemning anybody. Who-ever blew up the church, if he's here, was doing what he thought was right; but he was wrong. I hope you all see that now, and will go on acting according to the orders of SNAP."

There was a short silence. Then Rev. Lorenzo Niesen said, "I don't know about any of that, son, but I know one thing. There ain't one solitary nigger'll have the guts to step into our school tomorrow. It's all over!"

A cheer swelled the room.

Adam looked at Carey and Dongen, who were smiling quietly.

"All over," Niesen cried to the others. "Caxton's a white town again, and that's for sure!"

Joan, the owner of the Cafe, limped inside the room and ap-proached Carey.

"Ollie Underwood's coming," she said.

"So what?" Carey said pleasantly. "We're just having us a little old meeting. Tell Ollie he's too late, though: we just about all cleaned up. Ain't we?"

Adam nodded.

Joan limped back into the main dining room. The people began milling about, some left, others turned to their bottles of Dr. Pepper.

"Don't feel bad," Dongen said, putting his hand around Adam's neck. "The dynamite just speeded things up a speck."

"I don't—"

"Not that I approve, good God, no. But the thing is, whoever done it just saved us some work."

"We got to thank you," Carey said, and Adam thought he saw

the man wink at Dongen. "You put the strength in our arms, boy."
He turned and yelled, "Three cheers for Adam Cramer! Three
cheers for the man who showed us the light and rid our town of
the pestilence!"

There was applause, and laughter.

Someone muttered, *"Hope they want to fight . . ."*

Another answered: *"They too scared. But if they do, I guess
we're ready, don't you guess?"*

Adam nodded to Carey and said, "The next meeting will be
announced in the paper."

"Okay, but just see you stick around." The man grinned.
"We got to have you here in case they might be more trouble.
And there's that little business of ten thousand dollars setting in
Rudy's desk, too, don't forget that!"

Adam shook hands and walked outside.

Something had gone wrong, something was wrong. What?

He walked up the slight hill slowly, wondering why he was
disturbed. It was foolish. He had succeeded beyond his most op-
timistic dreams, had he not? He came to Caxton to stamp out
integration and now it was stamped out.

And, after all, they did put up the money for his bail, didn't
they?

He entered the hotel.

It was the same as it had been a century ago when the town
was quiet and no one thought much about the Negroes; when, in
the afternoon, he had walked into the lives of all these soft people.

The three ladies sat in ivory silence on the bright red couch,
and the television set was shrilling: *". . . cuts your cleaning time in
half, and saves you double . . ."*

Mrs. Pearl Lambert looked up from the book she was reading, which was a Dorothy Sayers mystery, and then looked down
again.

Billy Matthews dozed, motionless in the railroad chair.

There could be a war outside, Adam thought, fighting in the
streets, bombs falling, and nothing would change here.

"Good evening, ladies," he said.

No one answered.

He moved across the floor and up the flight of stairs. And in the darkness, walking, suddenly he thought of all the empty sea-shelled men he'd ever seen, the old and trembling ones in whom the light was gone, the fire extinguished—and how close, how near he'd come to being them.

He paused.

Now what, he thought, and shook away the black disturbances, in all the world could be so sweet as this: cursed, prayed to, hated, loved, a leader?

"You put the strength in our arms, boy!"

I've got to write to Max, he thought, and walked across the buckling floor.

He turned the knob and went into his room.

It was cave-black, but Adam knew, before he flipped the switch, that someone else was there.

He turned and faced his visitor.

"Hello, Sam," he said. "When'd you get back?"

22

—Afterwards, she had lain on the bed, unmoving, cold as she had never been before. There were no tears left. Deep inside her chest a pain was throbbing, in her head it throbbed, because she could not stop her crying—but the tears were gone.

She did not move.

The bed was rumpled, sodden with the oils that had come rushing from her body, joining his, her sweat, his sweat, together; in the center was a stain, still fresh.

She forced herself to touch it.

She forced herself to bring the smells into her nostrils, breathing deeply, locking them inside forever.

He was here, on top of me, she told herself. He was a stranger, I didn't like him, he didn't like me, but when he came on top of me I spread my legs apart and let him do it.

I didn't have to.

I could have screamed. You say it was terrible, you didn't like it, but you know that isn't true. He didn't rape you. All you had to do was scream.

But you didn't.

Instead, when he held off, you moved up and down, and you wanted to beg him to come, now, now!

So you're not cured.

And you can't blame him, because there was bound to be an Adam Cramer, somewhere, some time. It was bound to happen.

Vy Griffin ran her fingers along her body, which was still moist with perspiration. She clutched her breasts. The nipples were tender. She touched her lips and remembered how she had pressed them against his and locked that memory also.

Don't forget any of it, she thought.

Not ever.

She moved suddenly, firmly, and switched on the light, and looked at the bed. Then at the robe that lay where it had been thrown, next to the bed.

Then she moved to the mirror.

She stared at the reflection of her naked self.

No; don't look away, she thought. *It's you, Mrs. Griffin.*

It's what you really are.

She stared for almost a full minute, then turned and went into the bathroom. She ran the water until it was hot, took a bath, dressed in her green dress and packed one medium-sized suitcase, filling it mainly with clothes and items of utility.

When this was finished, she soaked a washrag in cold water and scrubbed the stains from the bed, and made the bed.

Satisfied that she had been thorough, she took a business letter from an envelope and turned it over to the blank side.

She hesitated a long moment.

Then she wrote a note quickly, and inserted it in the crack between the frame and the mirror.

She looked once at the room, turned and walked out into the quiet hall.

Mrs. Pearl Lambert was not in the lobby.

The ladies on the couch did not notice her.

She walked very fast until she reached the highway; then she began walking slowly.

Within twenty minutes a gray Plymouth sedan pulled up.

"Want a lift?" the man in the car said.

Vy Griffin said "No"; then, before the door closed again, she said
"Yes."

"Going far?"

"Yes," she said, and got in—

"How are things, Sam?"

The big man was perspiring. His face was red, and there were still the laughter lines about the mouth; but he looked different.

"All right," he said.

"Good!"

Adam tried to be casual, but his mind worked quickly. Probably, he thought, she's told him about it. Probably that's it. It wouldn't be in character for him to break into my room otherwise.

But, don't second-guess him. Hang on.

"How'd you do in Farragut? Sell many—what is it?—pens?"

Sam Griffin moved his head up and down, slowly.

"Well now, I'm glad to hear it. Uh ... did you want to see me about something? To tell you the truth, I'm kind of pooped. I—"

The big man rose suddenly; his fists were clenched. "Adam," he said, "I know this isn't any of your business, and I got no right to be bothering you with it—but I got to talk to somebody! I just got to. I'll go crazy if I don't!"

Adam hesitated; then he moved toward Griffin. "Sam," he said, "what's the matter? Is something wrong?"

The big man nodded. "It's *my* business, though," he said. "I don't know why I come busting in here. Mrs. Pearl Lambert give me the key. You've got your own problems, I guess—everybody does." He started for the door. "I'm sorry."

"Wait a minute. Hold on, now," Adam said. "I thought we were friends."

Griffin stood still, breathing heavily. He seemed lost, afraid, like some gigantic animal.

"Aren't we friends, Sam?"

"Sure, I guess. Sure. But you're tired—"

"Not any more." Adam took the man's arm. "Sit down over there, Sam. Right now. And tell me what's on your mind. Maybe I can help."

"No. You can't help."

"I can listen, anyway. Come on."

Griffin paused. Then, still breathing heavily, he turned and walked to the bed and sat down. Several times he opened his mouth, and closed it.

Then he got up and walked to the wall. He turned away and his thick red fist smashed against the plaster, hard.

"She's gone," he said.

"Who is?"

"Vy," he said. "She's gone. Left me. Ran out."

He began to pound the wall, but Adam said, "Sam!" and he stopped. "Sam, pull yourself together. Listen, I'm no stranger— we settled that the first day we met. I like you one hell of a lot. And I'm happy you came to me. Really. Now take it easy, and tell me everything. From the beginning."

Griffin did not turn. His voice was like a sob.

"I—come home from Farragut," he said, "about two o'clock. I had a lot of presents, little things I picked up for her. I knew she'd like them. Costume jewelry, pretty good stuff. Vy loves jewelry."

"Uh-huh."

"I come upstairs and I opened the door, the door to our room. It was empty. She wasn't there. I thought that was kind of funny, but maybe I missed her in the lobby. You know, maybe she was watching TV with Mrs. Pearl Lambert and just didn't see me when I come in. So I went back downstairs. But she wasn't there, either. That's when I started to get a little scared. I went back to the room and hollered for her, then I found the note."

He reached in his pocket and took out a piece of paper and read it.

"May I see the note?" Adam said.

Griffin handed it to him and turned again, facing the window this time.

Adam read:

Dear Sam:

I know this is going to hurt you terribly but I can't go on lying to you anymore. The marriage isn't working. I thought it would I really did, and you gave me some wonderful years,

Sam, but—I'm no good for you. It's all over and I'm leaving you. Don't try to look for me, it's finished. Believe me I'm no good for you. You're a wonderful person and maybe you'll find a nice woman it cant be me. I loved you, really. Forgive me.

VY

He put the note on the dresser, walked over to Griffin and touched his shoulder.

"I'm really very, very sorry."

Griffin nodded. "We was planning a little farm," he said, "and maybe some kids. That's what I was working for. Now I don't have nothing to work for. The one thing that meant something to me, the one thing that was good and fine in my life—is gone."

Adam pressed the man's shoulder again and walked back across the room. "Do you have any idea," he said, "why she'd do a thing like this? I mean, it was pretty obvious that you were better to her than most husbands are to their wives. And, like I say, she seemed to be happy. I mean, everything seemed to be fine!"

Griffin was silent. "I think—" he said.

"Yes?"

"I think I can maybe guess part of the reason."

"Oh? What is it you think?"

"Well," Griffin said, "I've never told anyone this, but I'm going to tell you, Adam. You—understand things. I seen that right away. So I'm going to tell you this secret. When I first met Vy in New York, she was—well, I'll be honest. She was what they call a professional woman. But not like the others. No. It's hard to put, but—Vy was a good person. Except, she had this itch, and there wasn't nothing she could do about it. Doctors got a name for it, maybe you heard. They can't cure it alone no more than they can cure every kind of headache, see, because it isn't like with a broken leg or a case of diphtheria or something. No; they got to have help, from the patient. But Vy couldn't believe in all that talk, she didn't think she was really sick. She thought—well, that God was punishing her for something, and that it was His curse. And with an attitude like that, there wasn't nothing a body could do for her. Before, I mean. Before I met her."

"Go on," Adam said.

"I never told anybody this."

"I know that, Sam, and I appreciate your faith in me. It goes without saying that I'll respect the confidence."

The big man still did not move. His back was to Adam. "Well, we met, like I said, and I fell in love with her. Underneath all the city hardness, I saw there was a fine woman. It's my business to know these things about people. And I knew. It took a long time to convince her, but finally I did, and we got married. She told me she was happy and wouldn't cheat on me. And she never, either. For five years we was just as happy as two pigs in the sunshine."

There was a silence.

"Well, it certainly beats me," Adam said. "You say you've got a theory?"

"I think so," Griffin said. "The way I figure it, she must of got into some trouble."

"What sort of trouble?"

"Man trouble," Griffin said. "Some fella or other must of caught her at a weak moment. And she just, like they say, reverted back. What do you think, Adam? You think that might be it?"

"Well, it's possible, I suppose," Adam said. "But, somehow, I can't bring myself to believe it of Mrs. Griffin. She doesn't seem to be that type at all, you know? Sam—judging from what you say, couldn't it be equally possible that maybe she just got bored here in Caxton? Maybe she just got bored and, you know, restless. Was it her period? Some women get that way during their period, I hear. It affects their minds."

"No," Griffin said, "I'm sure it didn't happen that way. It was a man."

"But who? Who would do a thing like that?"

Sam Griffin turned.

"You," he said. In his right hand was the gun Preston Haller had given Adam. It looked very small, and unreal.

The expression on Griffin's face was unlike anything Adam had seen there, or suspected could ever be there; an expression of emotions a man like this could not possibly feel. The eyes were very clear. And there was a new, thin smile, not at all like Sam Griffin's usual smile.

"You don't need to bother thinking up a lot of talk," he said.

"I know what happened. This is an old hotel. The walls are thin. The floors are thin. Mrs. Carstairs told me all about it."

Adam stared at the gun, fascinated. "Sam," he said softly, "I wasn't going to deny it. The reason I didn't tell you before was just that I didn't want to hurt you more than you've been hurt already. Really. Honest, that's the truth." He felt the perspiration gather and trail down his sides, and he felt the fast, trip-hammer beat of his heart high in his throat. "Blame me, if you want to. But before you—Sam, listen, I'm going to level with you. It was a lot my fault now, sure, I won't pretend it wasn't. But you asked me to cheer her up—you remember, you asked me that?—and I went into her room for that reason, you understand? We were talking, just, you know, talking, when—I don't know, everything started to go wrong. This is going to hurt you. She had on a robe, that flowered one. And she kind of let it slip apart. I tried not to look, but Jesus Christ, Sam, you know people—that's your business— and you know how much a man can stand. After all, your wife is a very attractive woman." He stopped and tried to swallow. "Well, I'll agree all the way with you, that's when I should have left. But I didn't. I couldn't. It happened so fast—can't you understand?"

"I understand," Griffin said, holding the gun steady.

"I hoped you would. Excuse the way I'm talking: put yourself in my shoes, for a minute. I mean, I'm not too comfortable!"

Griffin said nothing.

"So I slept with her. Okay. I admit it. But you've got to know this. However much you blame me and hate me and want to shoot me, it wasn't all my fault. And there's something else. I shouldn't tell you, because you'll probably be so sore you'll pull that trigger without thinking. But I've got to. She told me . . . oh, never mind. Let it go."

Griffin did not move or speak.

"No," Adam said, "no, it wouldn't be right for me to keep it from you. Sam, so help me God, this is the truth. Mrs. Griffin told me that I wasn't the first—I mean, since you've been married. She's slept with plenty others, and she said she knew it didn't matter because you'd never catch on. I'm forcing myself to say this to you, Sam. It's the truth."

Sam Griffin transferred the gun to his left hand, took four

steps forward and slammed the back of his right hand against Adam Cramer's cheek.

Adam felt a sharp pain, then a spreading hot numbness. He was terribly afraid now. But when he looked up, he saw that Sam Griffin was smiling.

"Sit down," the big man said, and suddenly all the warm good nature and pleasantness returned. He laughed. "You know, you missed your calling, boy. You would have made a fine pitchman. Where you learned it, I don't know, but you know just the right way to work on folks' weak spots, the way a piano player goes through a piece—soft and loud, soft and loud, gentle and hard. But you forgot the first rule. Never try to con another conman!"

"Sam, listen to me for a minute, listen: I'm not lying to you."

Griffin laughed even more heartily.

"It's the truth!"

"I ought to kill you," the big man said. "As a matter of fact, I'll tell you something—that's the reason I come to your room. I was gonna beat you to death, and I could do it, I think. I got pretty strong arms. But then I started getting kind of bored, so I went through some of your things. It was very interesting stuff!" His eyes twinkled. "I found the gun and I thought, Well, why not just shoot him instead? Blow his brains out."

"Sam—"

" 'Why not?' I said, so I aimed to do that. But you didn't show up, and I didn't have anything to do but sit around and wait. And think. You know? Just sit around and think. First time I done it since I was in school!" The big man shook his head. The air had gone from the room, and there was only a thick mold of heat, prickling Adam's flesh, and the seeping sweat.

Griffin looked at the gun, twirled it on his finger, tossed it onto the pillow.

"Really fooled you, didn't I!" he said.

Adam opened his mouth.

"No, I mean, you really thought you was in for it when you seen me here. Then it turned out old Sam was even stupider than you imagined! Right? 'Poor sap, he still hasn't caught on!' Right? But, boy—you should of seen your face when I turned around with that pistol!" Griffin laughed. "That was a study. Right now, you just don't know what to think, do you?"

The sound of the courthouse bell rode the silence, briefly.

"Well, it should be a lesson," Griffin continued. "One of the first things a pitchman's got to learn is never to underestimate anybody. I remember once I conned a wall-eyed farmer into buying fifty dollars' worth of automobile gimmicks. He was a real yokel, you know what I mean? Freckles and a straw hat and over-alls all covered with dirt. Told me, 'Let me take 'em home to the wife so she can see; then I'll bring you back your money.' I said sure, because I figured anybody this dumb would simply *have* to be honest. Only, I was wrong. He never come back at all. And the name he had give me, nobody ever heard of. So I was out fifty dollars. But I figure it was money well spent, because it taught me something I won't ever forget. You know what it was?"

Adam was silent.

"This," Griffin said. "When you act like a clown, everybody trusts you. They take it for granted you're straight. And that makes things *so* much easier! People get to laughing so hard with you, why, hell, they don't even feel it when you dip into their pockets!" He guffawed loudly. "But anyway," he said, "I was gonna kill you. Only I had this time to think. And I realized, see, I'd been playing this part so long I was fooling *myself*! That's a danger. I realized that when I asked you to take good care of my little girl, and all, all I was doing was planning this whole thing. Of course, I didn't know it up here." He tapped his forehead. "Sometimes you get so clever and secrety, you're afraid even to let *yourself* in on it! But that's the way it was. The minute I seen you, I started working things so you'd think I was just a big, stupid loudmouth, under-stand. Because I caught all that went on between you and Vy's eyes. I caught every bit of it.

"So, you might say, I set everything up. But how come? Why would I do a thing like that?" Griffin wiped his face with a hand-kerchief, and puffed.

"I think it's because we always been afraid of this. Afraid be-cause we never knew if we'd be able to take it. So we shut our eyes, you might say, and pretended it really wasn't ever gonna happen, not really. But at the same time, both of us *knew* it would. And the longer we waited, the harder it got. After a while, it was like a black cloud hanging over us ..." Griffin wiped his face again. "Now," he said, "it's all over. And Vy's proved she loves me. If she didn't, she wouldn't of ran away. She'd of kept it to herself. But it's right out in the open now and we can fight it together."

Griffin got up.

"She's gone," he said, "but you know what? I'll find her. I know I will because I know *her*, everything about her, the way she feels, the way she thinks. It's a funny thing: people got the whole world to hide in, but they can't get away from somebody who knows them and really wants to find them. 'Course, it may take a while. But I'll keep looking and when I do get her, we'll be closer than ever. So I think I'm going to say thanks. You done us a great favor!"

He moved very close to Adam.

"Truth is, though," he said, "the best way to return the favor'd be to put a bullet through your head right now. It'd be a whole sight easier on you, take old Sam's word on that. A *whole* sight. See: we're both in the same line, you and me, Adam—only I been at it longer, and I can see where you're making mistakes. They're beginning to pile up on you now. In a little while, they'll smother you."

"Get out of here," Adam said.

Griffin did not make a move. "I been studying your pitch," he said, "and I admire it. You got technique, fine technique. But you know what's wrong? You're missing another one of the basic rules! That's right. You can sell people something they don't need, but you can't sell them something they don't want, leastways, you can't keep on selling it to 'em. And the people—most of them, anyway—don't want what you're selling. Maybe they think they do, right now, but they'll get over that. Then, just watch out."

Griffin went to the sink, poured a glass of water, drank it.

"Right now, I bet you think you're right on top of the heap, don't you?" he said. "Everything going smooth, clicking right along. Uh? Well, let me tell you something. You're wrong. You're on the way down, boy, and it's going to be a real long trip."

"I don't know what you're talking about," Adam said angrily, wondering why he was angry. He ought to feel relieved.

"Come on now, you're a smart boy, you went to college. They taught you how to read, didn't they? Well, *read*. The handwriting's on the wall, big as life. You ain't the boss any more, and you won't be, either. These fellas, Carey and, what's his name, Dongen —and the Jumpin' Preacher—they're all just dumb tools to you. They sprung you out of jail—"

"How did you know that?"

Griffin continued smiling. "I said, I been studying you. Besides, Mrs. Pearl Lambert knows a few things. She's got a little telegraph system inside her head: nothing happens she don't hear about it a few minutes afterwards. Nothing."

Adam remembered that Mrs. Pearl Lambert had not greeted him when he came in.

"So, okay, Carey and Dongen and that other fella get you sprung, and this means you're still the big cheese. Don't it?"

"It happens that they mortgaged their homes, and—"

Griffin laughed. "Sure," he said. "Sure. Those ignorant little old tools! They're just gonna hop every time you say hop, aren't they, and before we know it, you'll have Shipman in the Governor's chair and then—why, hell, maybe we'll even make him President! *You* will, that is. Mr. Adam Cramer will."

Adam leaped from the chair, ran to the bed, picked up the gun and pointed it at Sam Griffin's belly. "I'm sick of listening to you rave," he said. "Now get the hell out of here before I pull this trigger."

Griffin laughed even louder. "People," he said, "are wonderful. Adam, you couldn't pull that trigger if your life depended on it. Because when you get right down to it, you're gutless—and you know you're gutless, too. That's why you're doing all this: to prove you ain't."

"I'll give you five," Adam said. "If you're not out of here by then, I'll shoot. One. Two. Three—"

Sam Griffin scratched his arm.

"Four—"

Sam Griffin began to walk toward Adam. "Five," he said, and plucked the gun away. "See what I mean? Of course, you never want to be too sure of anything, either—" He reached into his shirt pocket and took out five bullets.

"Fuck you," Adam said.

"Now I sure wish I'd of gone to college and learned useful words like that. I sure do," Griffin said. "Once when Vy and me were traveling through Georgia, we run into an evangelist by the name of Stevens, and he listened to us pitching a special fuel filter and come over afterwards and told me I'd made a total of seventy-nine errors in English. He knew because he'd counted 'em! But then he said that if I ever got an education, I'd stop selling filters. Maybe that's part of your trouble. You think? Maybe when you get educated your head's so full of knowledge there ain't any room for intelligence. Because if you was intelligent, you'd be able to see that it isn't Carey and Dongen who's the suckers—it's you. They're using you and your name and this Snap thing, and the whole kaboodle for themselves. What I mean, like with the King of England—you're nothing but a figurehead, Adam."

"That's a lie!"

"Did you order 'em to blow up the church?"

"No. But—"

"Well, that's just the beginning. Plenty more'll happen without you having any say. Only when the troops come in—guess who'll get the blame. Except there won't be nobody around to spring you then. These boys don't give a hoot for all this fancy line you been feeding out. I mean the real bosses don't. All they want is a good fight, a chance to kill some nigras, right here in Caxton. When they get it, just where do you think young Mr. Cramer's gonna be?"

Sam Griffin laughed one more time; then he walked across the room and opened the door.

"In a way," Adam said coldly, "it's a shame you've got to go looking for your wife. I'd love to have you stick around for the show. You might be surprised."

Griffin's laughter hardly diminished, but a strange, hard look came into his eyes. "Now, you ought to know me better than that, Adam," he said.

"Which is supposed to mean?"

"Well, like I said with the gun: You never want to be too sure of anything. Rule of the trade, boy. I never told you I was going after Vy right *away*, did I?"

Adam looked at the heavy sweating man with the red face.

"No, boy. I'll find her just as easy a day from now—or a week from now. In the meantime, just in case old Sam is wrong, in case you got a little high card stashed away somewheres, I believe I *will* stick around. You won't see me, likely, but I'll be here." He winked and started down the hall; then he turned. "Always did like fireworks," he said; and Adam could hear his laughter long after the door had slammed.

23

It was when he paused to rest, to wait for his breathing to return to normal, that he was first aware of the silence. And suddenly this was all he could think of. Up ahead, submerged in the gray dawn, sat the village; and nowhere could he find a sign of life, a sign that anyone was truly here. The gravel street was empty. Dogs should have been frisking in the littered yards, but there were no dogs, and there were no chickens, either. Just the houses, with their eyes closed, and the store fronts, and the street, and, high above, the telephone wires still as harpstrings.

Tom held his breath a moment, listened, then walked to the third apartment, went up the steps and knocked on the door.

It opened slowly.

A middle-aged Negro man stood tall in the gray light. "Yes?"

"Are you Mr. Green?" Tom said.

"That's right." The door did not open farther.

"My name is McDaniel. I think we met once. I'm editor of the *Messenger*."

The man frowned. "What do you want?"

"To talk with your son Joey. If I may."

"What for?"

Tom looked downward, wondering how he could answer the question. It took all of last night, lying awake, thinking, sorting things out and putting them in orderly piles and examining them, to reach a decision; and even then, he was afraid it was not the thinking that had done it. He only knew that when the first cool wash of sun had spread across the sky, he'd thought of the frightened children and realized that there was only one thing for him to do. So, in a sense, it wasn't a decision after all. And it wasn't an act of bravery, either, for he knew equally well that if he did not do this thing he would never be able to face himself.

So quietly he'd dressed and started out. And when Ruth had awakened and asked him the question, he'd answered it truthfully. And she had stared at him, saying nothing, her eyes searching and full of fear.

"What do you want with my son, Mr. McDaniel?"

"I want to accompany him down to school," Tom said.

The man shook his head. "He ain't going to school."

A young boy appeared at the door. "I'm going," he said.

"I said no!" Abel Green clenched his hands, looked at his son for a moment, then back at Tom. "You come here to gloat?" he said. "Well, get on back to town, hear? Get on back. You all done your job. Put it in the paper—us niggers give up. You don't have to kill any more of us, we—"

"Pop!"

"Mr. Green," Tom said, "I know that you don't have any reason to trust me. I don't have any right to expect you to, either. Like a lot of people, I've been pretty mixed up by this thing. But I'm not mixed up any more. I'm on your side—"

The man laughed harshly.

"Please! Please believe me," Tom said. "I don't know who planted that dynamite. But neither do you. It isn't fair for you to blame me—"

"You talking about fair, mister?"

"Yes."

"Maybe you think it was a colored man killed the reverend and blown up his church, huh?"

"No, no, no. It was a white man, I'm sure of that. But—it was just one man, or one small group. It wasn't the people of Caxton. They're not that way. I mean—if one of the men here on the Hill came into town and shot the sheriff, would *you* feel responsible? Would it be right to blame everyone here for it who happened to be the same color? There's a bunch of bad apples in town, Mr. Green—you'll find them in *every* town. They're hateful and mean and vicious. But you mustn't judge the town by them! The *people* of Caxton are good."

"Sure. Down deep, what they want more'n anything is to see our kids go to their schools, don't they?"

"No. I've heard that you're an intelligent man, Green. You have sense enough to know that it's going to take time for this thing to start working smoothly. Most of the people *don't* want this form of integration. But most of them are law-abiding citizens, and if the Supreme Court gives an order, they'll obey it."

"Except for blowing up a few churches and riding the Klan through town, you mean."

"Pop!" Joey Green stepped forward. "Give the man a chance. Maybe he's telling the truth."

"I am," Tom said. "If you give up now, Mr. Green, you'll lose everything you've been fighting for all these years. It won't be the town that beat you, though. It'll be a little bunch of ignorant fanatics who think they're strong enough to defy the United States government. Are you going to help them do this? Are you going to give them the power they think they have?"

"That's a lot of nice talk," Abel Green said. "I been hearing it from my wife for twenty years. But ain't all the talk in the world going to bring Finley Mead back to life! Whether it was a little group like you say, or every white man in Caxton, that church was dynamited and that preacher was killed. Them are facts. And if whoever done it decides to do it again, that's what'll happen. Maybe we'll be next. What'll you do then?"

Tom tried, desperately, to find the words. "I understand your feelings," he said. "I know it's hard. And I can't promise you that no one else will get hurt—maybe they will, I don't know. But you *mustn't give up*. Your boy and all the other children here have *got* to go to school this morning. It means everything!"

"Easy for you to say," Abel Green said. "Even if you do mean it, and I ain't sure you do. For all I know, you got a gang waiting down below. But if you talking what you believe, I say it's easy! What have you got to lose, white man?"

Tom looked at him. "My job," he said. "My home. And," he paused, "maybe my family. Is that enough?"

Joey Green went back into the living room and returned with three books.

"Joey—"

"Don't try to stop me, Pop. You know he's right and so do I. We can't give up now." He turned to Tom and said, "We better hurry. I got a feeling it's going to take a lot more talking to get the rest to come along."

Tom nodded and the two of them went down the stairs.

They called on the Simmonses first. Roger Simmons was at work, but his wife, Angie, was home. She said she didn't think Joanne should go, but eventually she agreed to it. Joanne herself was willing, so long as she knew Joey would be along.

They stopped at the Dupuys next.

Then they woke up William Hubbs and called on the Andersons and the Frondels and the Joneses and the Treiberts.

Wallace Treibert was the only one who absolutely refused, but Joey told Tom that was all right, because he never cared much for Wallace anyway.

At seven minutes to eight, they gathered in front of The Huddle.

From his window, Glad Owens watched them. He had oiled his guns and cleaned them, but he'd been unable to recruit an army; and he had decided to rest a while before going to war.

He watched.

"Everybody okay?" Joey asked.

The kids nodded. Some seemed nervous; others smiled, happy with excitement.

Tom said, "Let's go."

They walked down the gravel path quietly, Tom in the lead; down the path and across the street of old houses and black cars and into the main section of Caxton.

Heads turned slowly.

People walking along the sidewalk stopped walking.

Mabel Dodge very nearly dropped her bag of groceries. She squinted, saw Tom, and opened her mouth.

"Thomas McDaniel!" she said, in soft amazement.

Down the street, Mr. Higgins stepped out of his drugstore and smiled broadly. "Hi, Tom!" he yelled. "What'cha got there?"

Tom waved.

The tiny parade continued.

Crowds were gathering now. Lucy Egan said something to

Ella, but Ella did not answer. She watched her father and tried to understand, and could not.

"That's your father, Ell!"

Tom stopped by a cleaner's window and ripped loose a poorly pasted rectangle of paper.

The paper read:

James Wolfe is a nigger lover. He is a Devil's Disciple and liar.

These are Caxton nigger-lovers:
Frank Grover: Grover's Dairy
Rolfe Higgins; Higgins drugstore
James Wolfe: lawyer
Mac Considine: Considine-Millers
Horace MacDonald: New York Cleaners
Polecat Nelson: lawyer
Sidney Arthur: lawyer
Anthony Ferman; Jew policeman

Jigs Leave Our Caxton High School, You Stink!

KEEP OUR SCHOOLS WHITE

The Caxton High underground is watching you . . .

Abel Green is the N.A.A.C.P. nigger in Farragut County

COONS GO HOME!
HARLEY PATON GET OUT!
WHITE NIGGER TEACHERS
RESIGN . . .

Attorney Wolfe is a nigger lover.

COONS GO BACK TO LINCOLN HIGH.

The courthouse Click is:
Crook Lawyer James Wolfe
Attempted murderer, Crook-lawyer Polecat Nelson Moron, Sidney Arthur, Crook-lawyer Fred Unser, City Judge Maxwell, Crook-lawyer Ollie Dodds

The school Click is:
Agnes Angoff, former whore, sleeping with Jew-Principal Harley Paton Behind His Wife's back;
Drunkard David Segrist's Wife
Crook-lawyer Fred Unser's Wife
Jew-Principal Paton and his Jew-Wife
All nigger lovers

The Skool-board Click is: Vicious Thief Carl Curtis
Crook Frank Leroy
Home-Wrecker Joel Nearing, Jr.
Nigger-lover Harley Paton

Preacher Samuel Ginther is a nigger-lover, a communist stooge, half Jew.
He was caught by the river 5 years ago, with another man's wife. Said, he was holding a "Prayer meeting."

> Je'ge Silvuh!
>   He our boss,
>   Yessuib, he loves
>   us nigguhs.

Tom methodically tore the orange paper into several pieces and dropped the pieces onto the sidewalk.

He continued walking.

They crossed another street and proceeded through the crowd of young people on the wide school lawn. The children there were standing about in loose groups, watching.

Some whispered or spoke softly.

"I'll be goddamned. It's old man McDaniel."

"Yeah."

"Never thought we'd see them again!"

"Me neither."

"Boy."

A half-block from the school, the Rev. Lorenzo Niesen and Bart Carey stepped out of the Sunshine Cafeteria, which fronted George Street.

They stood on the sidewalk and watched, chewing their scrambled eggs slowly.

Neither spoke.

"I guess this is good enough," Joey Green said when they had crossed the length of the lawn and reached the schoolhouse steps.

"Okay," Tom said.

Joey nodded to Clarence Jones and the young Negroes went into the building.

"Thanks," Joey said, but he did not put out his hand. "I don't think I could of swung it all by myself."

Tom took a cigarette from his shirt pocket, lit it and walked away. He knew that all eyes were on him, but it was over now and he felt fine. He had to be careful not to feel too fine, however. You're no hero, he thought. A short walk down a hill with a bunch of scared kids doesn't make you a hero.

Still, the eyes followed him.

He got halfway across the lawn when a group of boys walked up. Hank Kitchen was among them.

"Hi, Mr. McDaniel," Hank said.

"Hello, Hank."

Suddenly a boy cried "Yay!" and others cried "Yay!" and soon a large group of children were shouting this word, and smiling.

Tom gestured and did not, this once, try to fight the good feeling that had been coming upon him.

He blushed and walked quickly away from the lawn, never looking back, into the streets, far from the crowds.

And now what? he thought. Where do you go now?

He cut diagonally across the street, walking vaguely in the direction of his automobile, which he had parked because there would not have been room inside for all the kids.

He felt the weariness of hours spent awake last night, and thought—I'll sleep a while; no, first I'll call Jack; then I'll sleep a while. Then, afterwards, I'll phone up Verne and give him my resignation; then I'll get in touch with Lubin. Lubin wants me, and probably I'll do just fine with a paper like his; and—

"McDaniel!"

Tom blinked away the heavy, tired thoughts, and turned to face the stunted, shirt-sleeved, red and trembling figure of Lorenzo Niesen. Next to the Jumpin' Preacher was Bart Carey.

"Yes?" Tom said.

"You got anythin' to say?" Lorenzo Niesen glanced at Carey and cocked his head.

"About what?"

"You know what."

Tom flicked his cigarette away and started past the little man.

Carey moved to block him.

"We seen you, McDaniel," he said. "And we want an explanation."

Tom's throat went dry: his heart began to throb. From the corners of his eyes, he could see other figures approaching. Mabel Dodge; he recognized her. Dongen. Simpson. Holliman. The bullnecked one in the grocery store, Manners, Manning—Ted Manning.

"We're a-waiting," Carey said. He seemed to tower there beside Niesen. A giant of a man, with silly little spectacles perched on his nose, and a sweat-soaked nylon shirt.

"Please get out of my way," Tom said, ashamed at the sudden weakness that had come upon him.

More people were closing in, he saw; moving slowly, tentatively, about him.

Carey stepped aside. Tom walked past him and reached the car. He was about to open the door when a hand closed on his shoulder and pulled him around.

"You just hold on."

Tom looked at the man, then at the fifteen others who had circled the area. Men, mostly, but also a few women. To the right was a pretty girl of twenty-five or so, someone he could not remember having seen before.

Their eyes were filled with hatred. Perhaps it was this (he hoped it was!) that terrified him so: this concentrated hatred, turned directly onto him.

"Look," he said, "what is it you want, Carey?"

"An explanation," the large man said.

Niesen's shrill voice added: "Yes! Tell us, Mr. McDaniel, how come you walked that bunch of black niggers to our white school."

"I don't see that what I do is any of your business," Tom said.

"Oh, you don't!"

"No, I don't." He reached again for the door handle, thinking, *If I can just get inside, God, let me just get inside and get the thing started—*

Again, Carey's huge hand stopped him.

"We didn't think you was a nigger-lover," he said. "We figured you was against all this."

The people moved in closer. Tom could feel their breath, and he could feel the heat that came from their bodies.

"When we seen you taking them jigs to school, we got kind of a surprise, see. That's why we think you ought to do some talking."

Tom was horrified to hear himself say: "I'll talk to you tomorrow. Right now, I've got to get home."

Carey smiled. "You wasn't in such a hurry you couldn't spend time with the jigs, Mr. McDaniel. Now surely you can give us white folks a couple of minutes. I'd hate to think we wasn't good enough for you."

Tom was afraid. Afraid in a way he had not been since he was a child and (all the nightmare parts of life which are erased from memory!) would walk whole blocks out of his way to miss a fight. In these long, silent seconds he found himself, incredibly, observing such things as the split bone button on Phillip Dongen's shirt; the deathly, powdered whiteness of Mrs. Mabel Dodge's face, and the way her one good eye seemed to be shrieking; the crazy web of lines and wrinkles on Lorenzo Niesen's flesh; the fact that almost all the shoes were brown; and he thought also, as the people moved in closer, that the whole thing was a dream, because he was in America, in his own town, Caxton.

Then he remembered the Negroes in the car, and the faces he had seen on Simon's Hill.

They know this fear, he thought.

They know it all the time. And they are fighting it.

And suddenly he was not afraid. He looked at the hulking figure of Carey and felt, in addition to dislike, a touch of pity.

"Well, mister," somebody said, "you got anything to say for yourself?"

Tom looked at Carey, then allowed his eyes to travel over all the faces. Some stared back; some glanced away.

"Which one of them niggers paid you off?" Lorenzo Niesen asked.

Bart Carey drew his fist back, drove it hard into Tom's stomach. Tom wasn't wholly unprepared, he'd tensed his muscles, but the pain was great. He stumbled back across the fender of his car and tried to keep from vomiting.

"It ain't polite not to answer a civil question," Carey said. "The reverend here wants to know who paid you to betray your people."

Tom tried to speak, but could not.

"Go on, teach him a lesson!" someone cried.

He dragged air into his lungs, straightened, leaned against the fender. Perspiration gathered on his forehead. He fought the dizziness and the awful nausea. "Why don't you get another fifteen or twenty people, Carey?" he said, in a choked voice. "Then you'd *really* be safe."

"Shut your mouth, nigger-lover."

"Oh, you're tough!" Tom said. "With a mob to back you up, you're tough as nails!"

"I told you, shut your mouth!"

"Teach him, Bart!"

Tom stepped up to the big man. His blood was hot now, and the ache in his stomach had eased some. "You're so full of questions," he said, "let's see how you are on answers. Where were you when that preacher was killed, Carey?"

"You keep quiet," a voice said, "or you'll get the same thing!"

"Where were you?"

Bart Carey made a sound in his throat; then he lunged forward. Tom's fist lashed out and caught the big man in the face. There was a tinkling sound as Carey's glasses dropped to the pavement and shattered.

"Get the nigger-lover!"

Tom tried to open the door but he was not quick enough. Carey had grabbed his legs and was trying to throw him off balance. He attempted to pull free and so did not notice the man who had walked over.

Phil Dongen's knee came up. It crashed into Tom's testicles and Tom screamed; but before he could fall, he felt another searing pain, in his jaw, and heard the dull interior crunch.

Then he fell and lay there retching, and was only vaguely aware that Lorenzo Niesen had begun methodically to kick his head, his ribs, his stomach.

Just before he fainted, he heard the people screaming—"Kill the nigger-lover! Kill him!"—and caught a glimpse of their excited faces.

Then something sharp went into his right eye and Tom McDaniel twitched and lay still in the cold brightness of his blood.

24

In his dream, the girl's flesh had just begun to fall when the knocking suddenly woke him. It was not Mrs. Lambert. He could tell that. Her knock would be short and solicitous. This sound was full of urgency.

"Yes?"

"Adam?"

His head ached dully; as always, his throat was dry and he was not sure that he was not still asleep and dreaming.

"Adam, let me in."

He got up and put on his trousers, then looked at the clock. It read: 9:16.

"Just a minute."

He went to the sink and splashed cold water onto his face and drank some of the water also. He took a glass from the cabinet, poured a white cascade of Bromo-Seltzer into it, put it under the faucet.

"Adam."

"All right." He drank the foaming solution, which tasted sharp and cool, set the glass back down and walked to the door.

"Who is it?"

"Open the door!"

The voice was familiar: he knew it well; and yet he could not place it. It wasn't Shipman, it wasn't Parkhouse. McDaniel? No.

Wake up!

He shook his head and walked to the door.

He unlocked it.

A short, stubby man was standing in the hall, neither frowning nor smiling. He might have been sixty; he looked sixty, except for the hair, which was black and long and curly. He wore horn-rimmed glasses.

Adam grinned in real surprise. "*For Christ sake!*" he said.

"You keep poor hours," Max Blake said. "May I come in?"

"What? Well, of course. Of course! I'm sorry. I didn't—well, I just can't believe it, that's all! What in the name of God are you doing here, anyway?"

The stubby man walked inside. He was dressed in a sports coat and gray flannel slacks. His black shoes were highly polished. "On my way to New York," he said, looking at Adam.

"Sabbatical?"

"No. Hookey."

Adam shook his head again and laughed. Much of the old nervousness was returning swiftly, and a certain embarrassment which he couldn't understand at first, and then understood perfectly: it was that he'd never seen Max Blake except in the classroom or at his home, and he was finding it difficult to take the man out of context, to extricate him from those surroundings.

"You're kind of out of your way though, aren't you?" he asked, stuffing his shirt into his trousers. "I wish I could offer you a drink—"

Blake did not answer; it was a familiar characteristic. He glared about the room disdainfully, then again back at Adam.

"You're looking bad," he said.

"Well, I've been working hard."

"Yes."

"Did you get my letters?"

Blake's eyes flicked across the empty gun that lay on the dresser. As was habitual with him, he muttered soft incoherences deep in his throat, and with his right thumb moved the large ruby ring he wore on the fourth finger of his right hand, up and down, up and down. He looked at the bed, then walked to the window and raised the shade and looked outside.

It was the way the evenings in the past had always begun. A few meaningless remarks, then Blake gathering his thoughts, and Adam waiting for them to be stated. Instantly he was back in the large living room in Westwood, with its immense drapes closed, its thousand-volume bookcases, the books with all their jackets off, their titles rubbed two-thirds away ("There's nothing so degrading to a library than books in 'mint condition'; one can't, after all, consume a turkey without damaging its feathers!"), and those mad cats, Aleister and Crowley, crawling over you and dropping hairs; and Max in the big leather chair that sat a little higher than the other chairs and had a thronelike quality so strong that once, when Max had gone to the bathroom, Adam had stolen quickly to it and sat down and felt as daring as Zorro; Max, making his usual inscrutable and surfacely fatuous statement ("It occurs to me that the principal trouble with the world today is that there's entirely too much love in it!"), then developing the statement with enormous skill and zest, forcing you to argue, and demolishing you with a solitary sentence; and, too, the smells—the coffee perking in the silver pot, the exotically

seasoned meats for nine o'clock sandwiches, the special lotion
Max wore constantly, a bit like shaving lotion, but not masculine; yet Adam did not really think, as Preston did, that Blake was
homosexual—if it were true, he'd certainly have known, for they
had been alone together often. Still, it was a little strange, that
lotion-smell, the cats, and Blake's misogynous ("No, that isn't
quite correct; you mean misogamous!") attitude, which came out
strongly in the classroom when some girl would dare a question.
"Oh, the hell it's strange," Pres said; "the guy's a fruit, that's all! I
just can't take him any more. I was impressed at first, like you,
and I won't argue that he's smart—the word is brilliant, maybe
—but here's the thing: a lot of guys are brilliant. It isn't such a rare
commodity. Look, if he's such a hot-dog nihilist, how come he
isn't rich, you know what I mean? Just why the hell is he hanging
around this lousy university, teaching a course in political theory
to future ad-men? Why isn't he out showing the King of Sardinia
how to take over the world? He's phony, that's why. And he's got
you snookered, good. And that's the whole thing. You don't look
a bit upset." "I'm not upset, Pres," he had said. "I'm just a little sad,
that's all. The way I look at it, I haven't lost a friend; I've gained an
acquaintance."—Instantly, in that quiet hesitation, Adam lived
the time again.

Then he shut out Preston Haller from his mind and said, "You
fly?"

Max Blake looked away from the window. "Yes," he said.
There was something in his face, but Adam could not read it. It
was new. "I'm launching a rather large project," he said. "A book.
It will require extensive research, and the most elaborate sort of
organization. It will also, by reason of this, require a collaborator.
I've decided you're as good as anyone else for the job."

Adam stopped combing his hair.

"Well," Blake said gruffly, "are you interested, or aren't you?"

"Interested? Of course," Adam said. "I mean, my God, it's a
hell of an honor, and I certainly appreciate—"

"Then pack your bag." Blake pulled up his sleeve and studied
his wrist watch. "I should like us to be on our way within a half
hour. There's a plane from Farragut at 12:40."

"Hey, hold on, Max! Wait a second."

"I have no time for waiting," Blake said, "particularly in such dismal surroundings. Either you wish to collaborate with me on a book, or you do not. If you do, then you will stop sputtering and mooning about in front of that mirror, pack at once and accompany me to New York. If the prospect of sharing a name credit with Max Blake doesn't interest you, on the other hand, then—"

"Max, didn't you get my letters?"

"I did."

"Well, I mean—you read them, didn't you?"

The stubby man kept pushing at his ring. "Yes, yes," he said.

"Then you ought to know, you ought to understand—I *can't* go with you to New York. I can't go anywhere, not right now."

"Nonsense!" Blake's voice was loud and angry. "I took you for an adult, Cramer. Surely you don't suppose that what you are doing here has the remotest importance!"

Adam stepped back, recoiled as though physically struck. "You're joking, aren't you, Max?" he said slowly.

Blake stared for a moment, then, in a somewhat altered tone, said: "Well, perhaps a bit. I have an obsession with rudeness, as you know. Polite people always seem to wind up in unholy ground." For the first time, he smiled. "Anyway, I thought you'd become adjusted to my manners."

Adam relaxed slightly. "I'm sorry," he said. "It's just been a while, I guess. And I have been working like a bastard."

"I know," Blake said, and the smile vanished.

"But, it's been going beautifully. They've accepted me here, and integration has been stopped; at least for the time being." Adam adjusted his coat. "Max," he said finally, because the question had been burning inside him, "aren't you going to congratulate me?"

Blake glanced away.

"I mean, it's—the whole thing's perfect, really. Exactly as we discussed it. I think I've been doing an excellent job." He paused, waited, waited hungrily for the crooked grin and the gruff words.

"I am not in the habit of asking people to do things," Blake said. "But I'm going to ask you to reconsider your decision. After all, you've proved your point, haven't you? Not that it needed proving: I told you long ago that people were sheep. Your work is finished. Why go on?"

"Finished?" Adam grinned. "My work is just beginning! I've made contacts in half a dozen other states. The organization is building all the time; it's building, growing stronger. Fellow in Alabama called me long distance yesterday, wanting to start a chapter in Mobile. He can get a state charter. Hell, Max—there's no telling how far this thing can go! Did I write you about the university?"

Blake shook his head slowly.

"White Citizens College!" Adam said. "No kidding. I've got a promise of funds from this guy Shipman I told you about, and we'll be ready to lay the foundation in a few weeks. Also, I've found another way to corral the herd, and it's working: the fluoride gimmick. You know: 'They're poisoning our water and charging us for it!'" He laughed softly. "Half of Farragut will shift over to our side when I bring this out."

He went to the bureau and withdrew a newspaper.

"I'll pick up five thousand of these this afternoon from the Orange press. Guy in the Council, Holliman, runs it. Take a look —and don't laugh, because this is the kind of thing that's dragging them in. I spent two hours with the PTA—with quite a few of them, anyway—and all I talked about was Frobenius! And you know what? They *loved* it!"

Blake glanced at the newspaper and tossed it aside. He removed his glasses and pinched the bridge of his nose and then replaced the glasses. "Very—impressive," he said.

"Well, it wasn't all me. You helped an awful lot."

"Don't say that!" Blake began to breathe heavily. "I am going to be frank with you now," he said. "I want you to stop what you are doing here. I want you to stop and leave the South immediately."

Adam froze.

"Why?" he said.

"Because you *must*!" Blake's shirt front was stained dark with perspiration now. The muscles in his throat were moving. "Do you have any idea of the notoriety this nonsense has attracted? It's on the front of every newspaper in California!"

"Well?"

"Is that what you're after? Notoriety?"

Adam looked at his former teacher, and tried desperately not to believe the thoughts that were crowding upon his mind.

"I can answer that best," he said, "by quoting a guy who lives in Westwood and teaches political theory: 'Today's notoriety is tomorrow's fame.'"

Blake frowned. "That doesn't matter," he said, "never mind all that. The fact is that you're making a perfect ass of yourself. This whole, this whole thing—is ridiculous!"

Adam knew that his own face was growing hot and red, and he had the same angry, hopeless, terrified feeling he'd had so often in the past when his father had snatched books from his hands and exasperatedly commanded him to be a boy, a boy, to be a regular boy ("Why don't you get outside, for the love of God, and stop this slouching around! You *want* to be sick, is that it? You *want* to stay sick the rest of your life?"), and he found that he wanted to cry.

"Max," he said, and tried to steady his voice, "what's wrong?" And in his mind, the words that were not words rushed: *Professor Blake, don't look at me that way, please don't. Can't you see, I did it just as much for you as for myself. I wanted you to be proud. I wanted that, so much, because no one has ever been proud of me before, not ever. But you helped me. You gave me faith in myself. You believed in Adam Cramer, Max, and I loved you for it and I was grateful. Please don't look at me that way! I haven't failed. I haven't failed! Don't say I have and take away the single thing I've loved—I love you! Love me back, please. Max!*

"Everything," Blake said.

"How?" Adam could not control the tension. "It's gone exactly as we planned it; every—"

"*We* planned nothing!" Blake said, in a voice too loud, too nervous. "*You* planned! I have no part in this, no part whatever, and I forbid you to mention my name again! Is that clear?"

Adam did not move. He could not.

"You have caused me acute embarrassment," Blake said. "As a result of that newspaper article my position at the University has actually become precarious."

"What newspaper article?"

"Letters!" Blake said. "I have received dozens of them! Phone

calls, telegrams. Even the privacy of my home has been invaded
—all because of this. All because you chose to take some innocent theorizing literally. This," he stammered, "this is a mistake."
He was breathing more heavily than before. "A great mistake!"

Suddenly the man who had sat in the leather throne and ruled
the air was gone; that man existed now, along with Marty, in the
shadow-world of the empty lot and the river and the streets at
dusk where the guys played ball and tried to hold the night away;
the world that never really was; and in his place was a sweaty little
man with glasses, scared of his job, scared—

—*of me*, Adam thought.

"Why is it a mistake, Max?" he said, looking at the man's reflection in the mirror.

"Because it won't work."

"But it is working. You said so yourself, earlier. Or don't you
remember? No; I guess you don't. The conversation has been a
little diffuse. Anyway, if it *does* work, then is it a mistake?"

Blake's mouth opened and closed. The perspiration glistened
on his face like a fine coating of oil, and now he seemed *physically*
a different person from the one who'd walked in and arrogantly
surveyed the room a few minutes ago.

"Well?"

"Of course, of course it is. It's wrong—"

"Wrong?" Adam threw back his head and laughed. "Wrong!
Oh, Max. Really."

"Listen to me!"

"Quote," Adam said. "'The only actual wrong in the world
is our belief in the concept of wrong.' Unquote. Whoever said
that, Max? Or this. Quote: 'The words good and evil are techni-
cal terms and have no business in the general vocabulary; a law
should be passed by which only professional pragmatists are allowed to use them.' Unquote. You see. I did listen to you. In fact,
I memorized everything you ever said, every priceless little epi-
gram."

"Adam, please. This is a serious matter."

"No! Max, I almost get the feeling that you're concerned!
But that couldn't be, because you *never* get concerned. Quote.
'I regard the world as a cheap burlesque in which the girls are

all knock-kneed and the comics have but one routine; and I am
doomed to watch this repetitious show because I can't be sure
that things aren't worse outside.' Unquote. I got a million of 'em!"

Blake had begun to pale visibly, and this shocked Adam.

"Go out and conquer the world, Max. If anything is worth
doing, it's that. You said it. I'm doing it. Following your own blue-
print, too. And you want me to stop! Because I'm failing, because
you're fond of me and don't want to see me get my feelings hurt?
Is that it?"

"It's part of it, yes," Blake mumbled.

Adam stared at him coldly. "As they say in these parts, Professor Blake, that's a plain crock of shit. Let me straighten you out.
You came in here with a problem. You thought that you'd managed to convince me that you were an intellectual giant: a bored,
cynical, knife-brilliant guy who'd seen everything and didn't give
a damn for any of it. The Dark Socrates! I'll admit you played
the role to perfection. And you were right: I *was* convinced. Pres
caught on early and told me you were a phony—you remember
Preston Haller—but I argued. For one thing, I didn't believe him;
for another, it would have been pretty hard to admit that I'd been
fooled so easy.

"So I went on believing. And you knew it, too. In the Blake-ite
sect, Adam Cramer was Apostle Number One!

"It was all you really needed, wasn't it? As long as you had me
—or somebody like me—sitting at your feet, things were dandy.
That way you could pretend you were something special—you
could pretend you really were Max Blake, Genius First Class.
Sure. I've heard that actors sometimes fall into the parts they
happen to be playing. Why not? Acting, writing, painting—they
all come from incipient schizophrenia, don't they? By God, you
know, the more I think about it, the more I'm sure you *did* believe
in the legend—just as strongly as I did! And that's probably why
you were so convincing."

"I will not listen to this!" Blake exclaimed furiously.

"It was a perfect setup, I'll say that," Adam went on. "It justified the life you were leading, and filled in almost all of the holes.
With your little band of idolators, you never had to think much
about the truth—which was that you were a two-bit professor

without the creative talent to do, or the guts to undo, anything worth while. Or, like Pres said, a phony."

Max Blake tensed, then suddenly relaxed. His face remained pale. He seemed to be drained of emotion. Seated on the bed, he looked very small, and very weak, to Adam.

"Of course, down-deep you knew that it was all in fun. When a man professes to believe in nothing, as you did, he's considered either a fool or a genius. You were obviously not a fool. So it wasn't too difficult persuading people you were a genius. But you never dreamed anyone would take you seriously—actually think of putting your lack of principles into practice! Good God, everyone knows that this is just talk! Everyone knows that the really important things are money and jobs and the rent paid up and three good suits and insurance—

"So you were troubled when I took off. You were shocked and worried at my letters, although you probably didn't believe them. Then you realized that it was true. Somebody had taken your routine seriously and was actually carrying it out! Worst of all, this somebody was going around mentioning your name. The newspapers were picking up on it.

"It would never do. You knew you'd have to leave your ivory outhouse and stop this crazy hooligan before he got you into trouble with the faculty.

"The problem was—how to swing it? After all, the disciple was only doing what the Master had told him to do.

"But it wasn't really a problem. It was a choice. In order to keep the illusion of the Great Amoralist, you'd have to stay home and applaud; any other course would screw it up. So it came to a question of values. Who was more important to you—Blake the god or Blake the man? Because one of them had to go.

"You made your choice. Of course, you tried to hang onto both when you swept in here with the big book proposition, but it was a lost cause, and you knew it would be."

Outside, the late morning heat pressed up against the windows and made invisible snakes swim over the streets. An occasional auto horn moaned, but there was otherwise no sound.

"Now I suppose you're not talking because you think I'm sorry for you. You're wondering if I'm sorry enough—and disillusioned enough—to call everything off and maybe go shoot myself, or something. Right? I mean, it'd be pretty horrible, wouldn't it, degrading yourself like this in front of a mere boy and all for nothing? God, then you wouldn't have *anything* left! No idolators, no pride, no job. No nothin'."

Blake sat tensely; his eyes were moist and wild behind the heavy glasses.

Adam grinned and walked close to the bed. He lit a cigarette, dropped the match into a glass ashtray, and said: "What would you do, Professor? Where would you go?"

"Stop it!" Blake cried. "Stop it, Adam, please. I don't care what you think. Perhaps some of it is true. That doesn't matter now. I'm asking you as a friend—"

"Quote. 'A friend is one who, after he has stabbed you in the back, will be moved to select a tasteful tombstone.' Unquote. Try asking me as an enemy, instead. Only remember, 'One is judged by the quality as well as the quantity of his enemies.' Or look: why not go right to the bottom and beg me. Be pitiful. Be pathetic, even a little comical. Maybe I'll be so disgusted I'll give up. Well, aren't you going to beg?"

Slowly Blake said, "Very well. I beg you."

"I don't know, I don't think you have your heart in it. I tell you what, though. Try it on your knees. That might help."

Blake's eyes flashed. His right hand clutched the edge of the mattress, and Adam could see that the little flexible bones across his knuckles were white.

"Okay, forget it. I thought this meant something to you. Apparently it doesn't, though."

"I'll pay you," Blake said. "I'll give you whatever you ask, within reason."

"A bribe? Gee, I don't know. There's something so cold and businesslike about it. Besides, it wouldn't really solve the situation. For you, that is. I mean, let's say I took your money and promised I'd be a good boy. What assurance could you have that I'd keep the promise? A crazy guy like me, I might do anything! You'd worry day and night, lose all kinds of weight, ruin your health—no. I've decided that I can't swing it, Professor Blake. I am sorry for you but I think that if I just sort of keep on with

260CHARLES BEAUMONT

this thing, it'll be good for you. In the long run. Without a job, you'll be free, and maybe that'll force you into doing the things you want to do . . . Of course, it'll be tough at first. But—"

"*Please!*"

Adam thought of going further, but he looked again at Max Blake and knew that it would be pointless. The man *would*, literally, do anything, just as he'd promised.

"May I ask what you intend to do?" Blake said.

"You'll find out, Max. Just keep reading the newspapers. And watch for your name, because I'm going to spread it around like manure on a lawn. You're going to be famous—just like Frankenstein. I can see the headlines now! 'PROFESSOR BLAKE'S MONSTER GOES WILD AGAIN!' Or: '*Cramer reports, All I know I learned from my teacher, Max V. Blake. He's the man who deserves the credit.*' Think of it: all your wonderful epigrams, your philosophy, everything, in print all over the world! Think of it, Professor, and remember that whatever happens, *you* helped make it happen. Now get out of here before I throw up."

Adam pulled the door open. He grasped Max Blake's arm and pushed him into the hall; then he slammed the door.

Joan limped toward him with the cup of coffee, managing, as always, not to spill any. The coffee was too strong and too bitter for Adam's taste, but it was hot and it helped.

"You ask me," the toothless man named Harold said, "it served him right."

"What's that?" Adam said.

". . . wouldn't of dared to come down to school. It was him started the whole thing off again! Him and that Green kid. I say that was plain asking for it."

"It's sure funny," Joan said. "Mr. McDaniel looked to me like a right sensible man. Why'd he want to go and do a thing like that, I couldn't even begin to guess. I thought—"

"A thing like what?"

"Don't you know?"

Adam saw the look of amazement and said quickly, "I was up pretty late last night, working on some papers."

"You mean you ain't heard about it?"

Harold had put down his newspaper, the Farragut *Express,* and was also staring. "The nigras is back in school," he said. "Right now. All but a couple."

Joan took a bite from her chocolate doughnut.

"Mr. McDaniel, over to the *Messenger,* gone up to Simon's Hill," she said, "and walked 'em all down, right through the streets this morning. Then he got into a fight with"—she hesitated—"with some folks, and he's in the hospital. Hurt pretty bad, I hear. Some busted ribs and a lot of what they call internal injuries. What'd Viola tell you, Harold, about what else?"

"Well, I guess he might lose one of his eyes."

"Such a smart man!"

"Sure would hate to be that smart," Harold said. "Look where you land!"

"Who was it?" Adam asked suddenly. "I mean, that he got into the fight with?"

"Can't say for sure," Joan said, winking. "Old Ollie managed to arrest three—Ted Manning and two others, I forget. He claimed there was at least fifteen, but they got away. Ted and them said they never touched Mr. McDaniel and they can't remember who did, either, or even who else was there."

"What about McDaniel, though? He should remember."

"Yeah, but he ain't conscious yet," Harold said. "What they did was, they put him under dope right away. But he ought to be coming out of it any time, that's what Viola said." The toothless man chuckled. "I expect there's a few people kind of worried along about now. You suppose that might be right, young fella?"

Adam put down a fifty-cent piece and started for the door.

It opened before he could reach it.

Bart Carey, Phil Dongen and Lorenzo Niesen came inside.

"There he is," Niesen said, in a high-angry voice. "Right there."

"Keep your mouth shut," Carey said and walked up to Adam.

He held out the newspaper he had been carrying. "I guess you seen this," he said. "There was a shipment sent to Higgins' Drugstore and some others."

Adam said nothing, but took the paper. It was, he saw, one of the sensational New York dailies.

The large type on page one read: FIREBRAND IN THE

CHARLES BEAUMONT

SOUTH. And underneath, in smaller print: SEE PAGE 16 FOR SHOCKING STORY OF ADAM CRAMER, YOUNG TERRORIST WHO SEEKS TO DEFY U.S. GOV'T.

He looked up at the unsmiling faces and turned to page sixteen of the paper.

A quarter of the page was filled by a poor photograph of Adam on the courthouse steps, surrounded by a large crowd. It had been taken during his first speech.

Beneath the photograph was the title again, with the by-line: Edward Driscoll.

He turned the page and was confronted with a second photograph, showing him and Preston Haller together. He remembered when they'd had it made—on Venice Pier, in one of those silly snapshot booths, almost two years ago; they'd been drunk.

There was also a picture of Adam's mother, with the notation: *Photo by Peter Link.*

"You got anything to say for yourself?" Lorenzo Niesen demanded angrily.

"When I've read the article, I'll answer you."

He sat down at one of the tables, spread the paper on the checkered oilcloth and read carefully. It was mostly about his life in Los Angeles, although there were some quotes from Caxton residents.

When he came to the section which recounted his dates with the colored girl, Alice, he tightened; but he did not change his expression.

"What about it?" Carey said.

Adam closed the newspaper. "I'm impressed," he said, smiling.

"What's that supposed to mean?"

"Just what I said. I'm impressed with the lengths they're willing to go to stop us. Apparently we're a lot more important than we thought!"

"Skip all that," Niesen said. "Just tell us what this means about you and the nigger girl."

Adam stared scornfully at the little man, and gave no hint of the wild thoughts that were exploding inside his mind, no hint of the cold terror he was feeling; the immediate, ineluctable sense of urgency.

"Well?"

"Relax, Mr. Niesen," Adam said. "I'll be happy to explain the whole thing."

25

Although he had been conscious for several minutes, fully aware of Ruth's presence and of Ella's, Tom did not move or speak until he was certain that he was truly himself.

Then, in a quiet but clear voice, he asked: "Am I going to lose the eye?"

This startled Ruth. Her head came up quickly, and she glanced at Ella.

"No," Tom said. "Don't call them, yet."

Ella stopped at the door.

He looked at Ruth. "I'd like to know," he said. "I'm pretty sure the rest of me will live."

She took his hand, and said, "It's badly damaged. But I spoke to Doctor Hill and he said—"

"Tell the truth."

"He said that there's a chance—" Ruth bit her lower lip and kept from crying in that way.

"What odds?" Tom asked. He was becoming aware of the pain now. It seemed dull and slight, but he knew that this was because of the drugs. It would get worse every minute. Probably it would be more than he could take. He wasn't used to pain.

"What odds, honey? Ninety-ten? Sixty-forty?"

"Doctor Hill doesn't know," Ruth said.

"But he thinks I'll lose it? Straight, now. Be honest."

"He doesn't know."

"Okay." Tom felt a tongue of fire lick suddenly across his head. He reached up and touched the bandages, then touched the other bandages on his face. "They did a thorough job, didn't they?" he said. "How many stitches?"

Ruth was about to answer, but Ella cried "Dad!" and ran to the bed and pressed her face against the sheets. She said "Dad" over and over into the sheets, and continued to sob. Tom had not felt such closeness with his daughter for many years. It warmed him. He lifted his hand and patted Ella's head gently and said, "It's all right, kitten. I'm all right. It's all right."

He held onto the closeness a few seconds longer, then motioned to Ruth.

Ruth took Ella's arm and walked with her to the door. "Go home, now," she said. "It's late, and we mustn't upset your father. He's going to be fine. I'll be along in a while." She unsnapped her purse and removed a five-dollar bill and gave this to Ella. "Take a taxi, dear," she said.

Then, when Ella had gone from the room, Ruth clutched Tom's hand and wept, also. The pains were becoming more frequent now and soon, he knew, they would have to call the nurse for some morphine, or whatever they were using; but for a while he could think clearly and sharply and be all aware, and this was precious time. He would hang on as long as possible and not show the pain.

He lifted his wife's face, and saw in her eyes—and knew he saw, because he was not hallucinatory or detached, as he had been at first—a new sort of light; and even though her next words might show that he had been right when he'd told Abel Green that perhaps he was losing his family, he had to hear the words.

"Pretty stupid of me, wasn't it?" he said.

She took from her purse one of those small, thin, useless handkerchiefs that women carry, and wiped her eyes.

She looked at her husband with this new light and said: "Yes, it was. You might have been killed. Or crippled for life."

"I know. I'm sorry."

"No," Ruth said. "Don't be sorry. Because I'm not."

He pressed his teeth together tightly until the hot lightning-streak had run its course.

"I'm not in the least sorry," Ruth said. She looked at her husband straight, and spoke the words distinctly. "It was the best thing you've ever done," she said, "and I'm proud of you. I never understood how you felt before. Before, it was a lot of words. I should call the doctor now; I should tell them to come; but I want to say this to you first. Can you understand me?"

Tom said, "Yes."

"I wish I could tell you that I know why you did what you did, or why you think the way you do; but I can't lie to you, Tom. We can't ever do that to each other, ever again. I *don't* know. Not in my heart. All my life I've taken certain things for granted, and I've never questioned them. You accept these things when you're young and you don't think about them afterwards. They're too deep, too much a part of *you.* . . ."

She sat quietly for a moment, then continued: "I don't believe in integration, Tom. The idea of Ella going to school with Negroes is repulsive to me. It would take all the strength I have to shake hands with one of them on equal terms. When I heard of what had happened to you, do you know who I blamed? Them. And I wished that they would all die for what they'd done to you." She paused again and chose her words carefully. "But I do believe in you," she said. "And if this means so much that you're willing to risk everything, even your own life, for it, then I know it must be right. I can't doubt that now. It's right because you believe it's right. So I'm going to try to understand. I'm going to try very hard, darling. I only ask you to give me a little time. Please. Please give me a little time—"

Tom McDaniel stroked his wife's face for a long moment, feeling the hot moisture of her tears and feeling a happiness so profound and so real that it smothered the pain. He could bear the pain now. He could bear anything.

"I love you," he said softly.

"Tell me it isn't too late."

"It isn't," he said. "It never is."

"I'll try. So will Ella. She's young; maybe it won't be so hard for her. We'll send Dad away—he was in that Klan parade. I've got to tell you the truth!"

"I knew about it."

"It was a circus for him. But I don't think he would hurt anyone, not even— We'll get him a room at the Union. Mrs. Lambert will look after him. I don't care what he says. It will be just us, darling, just us together. . . ."

Tom nodded; then a pain worse than any of the others came, and he tried not to make any noise but it was no use. He clenched his hands and moaned.

Ruth got up quickly and walked toward the door. "I'll call Doctor Hill now," she said.

Tom said, "All right."

He waited for the pain to go, then he lay back and thought many things.

Ella paid the taxi driver and went into the house. The television set was on, loud, and she could see the gray-thatched top of Gramp's head in the easy chair.

"Well, how is he?" the old man said, not bothering to turn.

Ella had stopped crying in the taxi, but for some reason Gramp's voice started the tears again, and she could not answer. She stood in the center of the living room, by the couch, her head bowed and her hands at her sides.

"Goddamnit, you gone deaf? I asked a question."

She tried again to answer, but could only succeed in making a choking sound.

Gramp twisted his head around, stared for a moment, then snapped the television set off and got up. "You look beautiful," he said. "Your face all red and snot running down your nose, you look beautiful. Ain't you got a handkerchief?"

Ella took a handkerchief from her purse and blew her nose. She saw Gramp and the furniture and the house, but all this time she also saw her father in the hospital bed, and the corridors of the hospital, and the fat, efficient nurse.

Gramp came closer. "What'd she do," he demanded, "tell you not to talk to me?"

Ella shook her head.

"Well, then, for Christ Almighty's sake, answer my question. Is he alive?"

"Yes."

"Well, go on, go on!"

"He had four broken ribs and—and—"

"Shit! You're just like your mother, you want to keep everything to yourself. Well, I happen to live here too, young lady. I got a right to know what the hell's going on. Four broke ribs and what else?"

"Internal injuries. And they hurt his eye. Doctor Hill says—"

"Yes?"

"Daddy might lose his eye."

"Anything else?" David Parkinson waited; then he made a snorting sound and shuffled into the bathroom. He opened a small box and took three red pills out of it. He swallowed the pills. "Well," he said, "he was goddamn lucky."

"Lucky?"

"That's right! In my day they'd of strung a man up for doing what he done. And I'd of helped with the rope, too! What's the matter with him, anyway? Has he gone cuckoo? Shit, I knew he was spineless and I always guessed he was a lot fonder of them niggers than he let on, but I never thought he'd go and disgrace us like this. How'm I gonna face my friends now? Huh? I ain't never been so embarrassed in my whole life!"

Ella could not believe the things she was hearing. Even from Gramp, it seemed impossible.

"Dad's hurt," she said, stunned.

"Hurt, my back end," the old man said. He sank onto the couch and put a hand to his chest. "That's the way it is, though," he said. "Your mother will probably simper around him all day, where they got doctors, and leave me here alone. She knows I could get an attact any minute! But does she care? *Hurt!*" He snorted again. "Listen, I had every bone in my body broke and you never heard any complaints. Nobody did. I bore it like a man. But Tom McDaniel ain't a man, and he never was, and he proved it today."

"You shut your filthy stinking mouth!" Ella screamed.

Gramp recoiled. Trembling, he said, "Why, you little no-good bitch! Don't you *ever* raise your voice to me or I'll turn your ass red, and don't think I can't do it! What I'm telling you is the truth. It's facts. That father of yours is a nigger-loving coward and when he gets out of that hospital he's gonna be ran out of Caxton on a rail, you mark my words!"

"You're a liar! You're a rotten liar!"

"You mean it was somebody else went up the Hill and brought them niggers down to school, it wasn't Mr. Thomas McDaniel? Who was it, then? His twin brother? I didn't know he had a twin brother."

Ella stood there, unable to move, unable to think above her fury.

"Oh, it was him, all right. But I wasn't surprised. If you hadn't of been sitting around all the time with your finger up your hole, and nothing on your brain but boys—and listen, I seen you plenty of times at night, when you was supposed to be asleep, reading them movie star magazines! And I know what you was thinking about! I know!—if you had even the sense you was born with, you could of seen this coming. Anybody could." David Parkinson removed a handkerchief and spat into it. "Well, you just wait," he said. "It'll only be a matter of time before he brings home a big buck nigger to spend the night. Of course, now, we're kinda shy on room, so like as not you'll have to share your bed with him. But you won't mind that, will you, because this here's a guest. And we got to be polite to guests!"

Ella tried to answer, but her mind was so full of thoughts, and her throat was so tight and painful, that instead she turned and ran to her room. She slammed the door and threw herself onto the bed.

No, she thought, no, that couldn't happen.

Then another thought came. It was very unclear, and she was not fully aware of it; but it came.

What is a Negro, anyway?

Are they what Gramp is talking about, what he's talked about for years: black brainless stinking creatures prowling the bushes of the night, glittering razors in dark hands, ready to kill and rob any white man or rape any white girl passing?

Is that what they are? And if it is, why would Dad want to help them?

That tall young fellow in the clean white shirt named Joey Green who is just as smart as anyone in English, and in math, and who would look so handsome if he—

Is *that* what a Negro is?

Or are there both kinds, like with us?

He's not brainless. I don't think he smells.

He's—

Ella felt a chill and curled up in the bed; she came so close to sleep, she scarcely heard the telephone.

It rang three times.

On the fourth ring, she got up and walked into the hallway. Gramp was sitting in the chair in front of the television set, but the set was not switched on.

Ella lifted the receiver and said, "Hello," mechanically.

The voice shocked her. "Ella, this is Adam. Don't hang up."

She had managed, somehow, to put him out of her mind, to forget (actually, to forget!) that she ever had anything to do with the person who was causing all this trouble.

"Ella!"

She pulled the phone away from her ear and heard the tiny voice calling her name insistently. Only now, at this instant, did she realize that it was true; that the handsome young man who had come to the town a stranger a few days ago was responsible for everything.

And realizing this, she was afraid.

"Ella, listen to me. It's important."

She put the phone back to her ear. She said, "What do you want?"

His voice was different now. All the humor was gone, all the grown-up, crazy fun. "Is your mother there?"

"No."

"All right, then; listen. You and I have got to talk. I'll pick you up in ten minutes."

"No. I don't want to talk to you. I don't want to see you."

"Ella, I know what you're thinking, but you're wrong. I can explain it."

"No," Ella said.

There was a pause. "If you're interested in saving your father's life," the voice said, "you'd better be ready in ten minutes."

The connection broke. The telephone whined.

Ella put it down slowly. Her hand was trembling, and she felt cold again—colder than she'd ever felt before. She wanted to go into the bedroom and lock the door and never leave, but she couldn't do that. She couldn't do anything.

In a short time, an automobile horn sounded outside.

She went to the door, hesitated a moment, then walked to the waiting Chevrolet.

Adam Cramer did not greet her; he simply pulled away, and they drove in the direction of the highway, toward the forest, and did not speak at all.

Then the car stopped under a quilt of green sunlight.

Adam Cramer shifted in his seat. "You said you didn't want to talk to me," he said, "so I won't ask you to. I will ask you to listen, however. And listen carefully." He lit a cigarette, and Ella could see that he was nervous also, for his movements were short and jerky and his eyes would not stay still.

"First I want to tell you that I'm sorry about what happened to your father. I don't know what made him do such a foolish thing, and it might even be said that he was asking for trouble, but—now understand this, Ella—I had nothing to do with it. Nothing whatsoever, in any way. Whoever it was, they acted completely on their own. In fact, at the time it happened, I was in my room at the hotel. You can verify that if you want to. Also, I had no part in the church dynamiting. And that can be verified too. Are you listening?"

Ella nodded. She was listening, but she heard with only half of her mind.

"All right. Now I'm going to have to say some things to you that I don't want to say. You'll end up hating me, if you don't already. And that makes me very unhappy, because for a while I thought we were pretty close. I thought there were wonderful things in store for us, and I was looking forward to them. So were you. But I've got to give all of that up now, because something far more important is at stake.

"I don't know how well you understand the situation. Maybe you do, more than I suspect; maybe you don't at all. Anyway, I have to explain a little of it before . . ."

Ella saw the fire in his eyes and knew that these eyes were not seeing her, were not traveling over her, but were full of an unseeing hot fire that frightened her.

"My organization," Adam Cramer said, "was going well and we were taking big steps forward in licking this integration law, until some people—their names aren't important—started to get ideas. They weren't willing to go along with SNAP. They got impatient. They made some mistakes, and it was enough to weaken the whole movement. We've begun to lose the support of the people. They're getting scared. Scared enough to pull out and just let things sit. But we can't let that happen, because the niggers are still in school. You see?

"Now maybe I can't expect you to know what all this is about, but you've got to understand that we're in a position where we've got to do something. Something that will win the people back. I talked to one of the men in the council, and we thought about it, and finally we figured out a way. And this is where you come in."

Ella kept looking at the fire in Adam Cramer's eyes.

"As a matter of fact," he continued, "the whole thing depends on you, Ella. Not only the organization and all, but your father's life as well. The men who beat him up this morning are desperate. You saw what they did. If we don't do something, I can promise you this: They'll kill Tom. I know it because they told me so. They'll go right into the hospital and blow his head off, and there'll be so many of them that the sheriff won't know what to do. Believe me, Ella. It's true."

Adam Cramer knocked the ash from his cigarette and looked at the glowing tip somberly for a number of seconds.

Then he said, "Apart from your father, there's one person holding the nigger children together now. His name is Joey Green. Have you heard of him?"

Ella nodded.

"All right. Then listen carefully, and I'll tell you what you must do. But remember that I don't like it any more than you will; and remember, too, that it's the only way we're going to be able to save your father's life."

He spoke slowly, in slow, measured, tones; but the fire in his eyes did not go out.

26

It had been easier this morning. The kids were afraid, but they did not argue; and their parents did not argue, although they were also afraid. A man who believed in them and had given them strength when they needed it, who stood to gain nothing by this and to lose much, lay in the hospital, wounded. And they knew they could not betray this man. So when Joey called, they came, and they went down the hill together, looking neither to the left nor to the right, and they went into the school; and Joey knew that they must win now.

As he walked along the corridor to Miss Angoff's classroom, he thought about Tom McDaniel and felt both ashamed of his earlier despair and happy that he could feel this shame. Because it meant that now he did not despair. Now he was not keeping promises to a dead man.

He stopped at his locker, calmly removed his handkerchief, wetted it, and wiped away the words that had been scrawled in chalk upon the green-painted metal:

JIGS GET OUT

He then opened the locker, placed two books on the top shelf and took out two more. As he was closing the locker again, he heard a voice behind him.

"Excuse me."

He turned to face a pretty white girl dressed in the regulation uniform. She looked nervous and frightened, and he decided that it would be best to close the locker and continue to the class-room and not stand here with a white girl so close.

"Are you Joey Green?"

He paused. The corridor was fairly empty; most of the other students were already in their rooms. That's right.

"Well, I'm Ella McDaniel. Tom McDaniel's daughter."

"Oh." Joey took a step. "I heard about what happened yester-day. I hope he's better. Is he?"

"Yes," the girl said. "He's a lot better."

"I wish you'd thank him for us, miss," Joey said. "He did a real fine thing. He's a fine man."

"I know."

Joey noticed that the girl did not look at his eyes, and that she seemed to be getting more nervous. He snapped the combina-tion lock together and twirled the knob. "Better get going," he said, and smiled. "That bell's about to ring."

The girl nodded.

He started off down the hall.

"Wait a second."

He turned. Four or five students were loitering in the hall now, reading the bulletin board, fooling with their lockers. One of them looked familiar.

"I wonder," the girl said, "if you'd do me a favor."

"Sure," Joey said. "If I can."

"It isn't much. I'm—well, see, I'm working in the supply room, and I have to get some things. I could use a little help."

"After class, you mean?"

"No. Right now."

"Well, I'll have to ask Miss Angoff. Wait right here and I'll—"

"I spoke to her," the girl said quickly. "She doesn't mind. It'll only take a few minutes. I just want you to kind of help me with some things."

Joey shrugged. "Okay," he said.

Ella McDaniel swung around and started walking down the hall. Joey followed. They went to the last stairway, down the long flight of steps, and into the lower floor, which was used for storage.

It was a black and silent place, all hot and heavy with the smells of paper, iron and coal dust; like a factory at night. The single wire-webbed light bulb high above put out a feeble glow, and Joey's eyes were slow to penetrate the dusk.

"Come on," the girl said.

Joey said, "All right," and blinked. About were cartons stacked in massive rows; between them, slim and shadowed passageways. "I can't see too good," he said.

"Just follow me."

He walked between the cardboard cliffs slowly, tracing lines along the dusty sides of the boxes with his fingers. Ahead, the girl walked briskly.

"Wait here a second," she said, when they had reached the end of the passageway, "until I get the other light on."

Joey waited; then the girl's voice said, "All right," and he walked into the small supply room.

Ella McDaniel stood by the door. "Up there," she said, turning and pointing, "on the top shelf. You see the box marked Pads?"

"Where? Oh, yeah. Under the two big ones."

"Yes, that's right."

"You want it down?"

"Yes."

"Okay. Is there a ladder around here anywhere?"

"I think so. Right there; it's folded up, I think."

Joey reached down and pulled out the small ladder. He set it on its legs and tested it. Then he looked at the girl and said, "You mind if I ask you a question, Miss McDaniel?"

She said nothing.

"How come you got me to help you?"

"I don't know," she said. "You looked strong."

"Well, I'm glad to help. But I don't think—I mean, maybe this isn't such a good idea. For you, I mean. You know?"

"I didn't think of it," she said.

Joey smiled. "That's a nice thing to say," he said, and started up the ladder. It was just tall enough. He braced himself and moved the top box, laying it on its side. Then he moved the second box, which was a more difficult operation.

The one marked Pads was heavy, but he got a firm and professional grip on it, made sure of his balance, and walked backwards down the ladder.

He set the box on the concrete floor and looked up.

The girl was gone.

He felt a small prickling sense of fear, but brushed it away. "You want the whole thing?" he said.

There was no answer.

He walked to the open door and peered out into the cellar-darkness, and saw only the mountains of boxes.

"Miss!"

He was about to return to the room when he heard the girl's scream.

It was high-pitched and hysterical, and instantly he knew what had happened. He knew what had happened and what was going to happen.

He stood listening to the screams; to the silence; then to the sounds of shoes slapping hard against cement, running, running down the stairs and across the floor, toward him; and he could only stand and wait.

27

They sat at the tables quietly, no one speaking, no one moving. The fat paddles of the dust-caked fan above revolved in lazy circles, but the air was not disturbed—it hung as still as mold in the café. Harold, dressed in white, sat dozing at the end of the counter; Joan was at the other end, reading a paperback book. The central table accommodated Bart Carey, Phil Dongen, and Abner West. They were playing gin rummy. Lorenzo Niesen watched them, but without interest. Several times he opened his mouth, but he did not speak.

At the corner table by the window, Adam Cramer sat with his hands folded.

Someone said, "It's ten of."

Niesen muttered "Sweet Lord" under his breath, removed a handkerchief and knotted it about his neck.

Five minutes passed.

Then the door of the café opened, and Danny Humboldt came in.

His face was red, and he was gasping for breath.

"Happened," he said.

Adam Cramer glanced at him sharply, frowned secretly, and said: "Go easy, Danny. We don't know what you're talking about. What has happened?"

Danny Humboldt grinned.

"Go easy."

Of the other men, only Carey showed any interest in the boy. He exchanged a glance with Adam and moved his chair around.

"Nigger at school tried to rape a girl!" Danny Humboldt said excitedly.

"What?" The Rev. Lorenzo Niesen came instantly out of his lethargy. Again, his features were hawk-sharp.

"Nigger. You know, one called Joe Green."

Adam Cramer walked over to the boy and put a hand on his shoulder. "Are you joking?" he said.

"Hell, no. Happened twenty minutes ago. Ella McDaniel, you know her, the fella who's in the hospital's daughter."

"Yeah?" Phil Dongen came over.

"Well, everybody heard this hollering, this screaming, you know? And she come running into Mr. Crandall's room, and her shirt was ripped and she was crying. What it was, she was getting some supplies for—"

"I knew it'd happen!" Joan said, in a tone of finality. "Harold, you hear that? Nigger tried to rape a white girl over to the school!"

"Where is he?" Dongen asked.

"Principal's office," Danny Humboldt said. "They got him locked up there."

"Well," Adam Cramer said, "this is precisely what we've been afraid of, isn't it?" He shot Carey a glance. Carey nodded. The exchange went unnoticed by the others. "Are we going to do something about it?" he demanded suddenly.

Niesen slammed his hand palm-downward on the table. "God damn!" he said.

Adam Cramer pointed at the little man. "All right," he said, "go and get every member of SNAP you can find—you, too, Phil. Right now. Tell 'em what come up. Tell 'em to meet here as quick as they can; right away."

"Lot of them won't," Dongen said. "People been reading that newspaper. People been quitting, on account of—"

"Don't any of that matter now," Adam Cramer said. "You just tell 'em what happened at the school, and they'll come. They'll come. Danny, you go on back. Round up as many kids as you can. Buck a head. Guarantee."

Danny Humboldt winked and ran outside.

Bart Carey wiped his forehead with a paper napkin and rolled the napkin into a ball. "It better work," he said, when the others had gone.

"It will," Adam Cramer said. He stared at the big man for a moment, then added, "If you keep your mouth shut. If you don't start trying to think on your own any more."

Carey said, "There's gonna be trouble!"

"Of course. But that shouldn't matter to you, Bart; because you're in trouble already, right up to your behind. And the jigs are still in school. Now if you want them out, you'll play along with me."

The big man ran his tongue along his lower lip nervously. "Jesus, that son of a bitch McDaniel's gonna talk, I know it!" he said.

"Probably so." Adam Cramer reached into his pocket and found a dime. "But maybe Mr. Shipman and I will be able to find a lawyer. *If* we're sure of you. You understand?"

Carey said that he understood.

"Now get out of here and round up some people. Fast." Adam Cramer walked toward the back room.

He put the dime into the coin slot of the telephone and dialed Verne Shipman's number.

28

The room was divided into a reception area, with a counter and four desks behind the counter, and the principal's private office. All doors were locked. Joey Green sat in the reception area, flanked by Mr. Crandall and Mr. Spivak. Inside the principal's office was Ella McDaniel.

She sat facing Harley Paton, although she did not look at him. She looked at the floor.

"Calmly, Ella," the principal said, "tell us once again exactly what happened. I know it's hard for you to talk, but this is a very serious charge you've made and we've got to get our facts straight. You understand that, don't you?"

Ella kept her fist at her mouth and continued to stare at the floor.

"Please," the principal said.

"I told you," Ella said. "I went down to get some pads for Miss Seifried and when I started back, I saw him standing there. That's all. He must have seen me go downstairs, or something. I don't know."

"Did he say anything?"

"Yes. He said—he talked about having a ball."

"That was the expression he used?"

"Yes. I didn't know what he meant. But I was scared, so I asked him to move so I could get back upstairs, only he wouldn't. When I tried to run, he grabbed me—"

"He grabbed you?"

Ella spoke in a mechanical, lifeless voice. "He ripped my blouse."

"Is that the truth?" Miss Angoff asked levelly.

"Yes," Ella said.

The English teacher turned to Miss Seifried, who looked terribly frightened, and said, "Did you ask Ella to get you the pads?"

"Yes. That is, she said she was going to, and I said that would be fine."

Harley Paton glanced at her. "But you didn't ask her specifically?"

"Not exactly," Miss Seifried said.

"Ella, why did you want to get those pads at that particular time?"

"Because we were out."

"Yes, I understand; but why didn't you have Miss Seifried ask one of the boys to do it?"

"I don't know."

Harley Paton tapped the desk with his finger. "The pads, I'm told, were in a very heavy box. Did you lift that box?"

Miss Seifried made a sobbing sound in her throat. "For heaven's sake, Mr. Paton!" she exclaimed. "Can't you see the poor girl is in a state of shock? Why are you torturing her like this? Do you doubt her word?"

"That isn't the point," the principal said coldly. "You know as well as I do what this means. I am simply trying to get the facts absolutely straight."

The little woman walked hurriedly to the door. "Well, I would like to be excused, if you don't mind."

Harley Paton sighed. "Very well, Miss Seifried. You're excused. But wait a moment . . ." He stared at Ella. "There is nothing more you care to tell us?"

Ella shook her head.

"All right, you can go. I called your house, but your mother isn't there. Do you want me to call her at the hospital?"

Ella said no.

"In that case, perhaps Miss Seifried will drive you home."

The little woman said, "I'll be glad to."

"One word of caution," the principal said. "We will have to talk with you again, when you're feeling better. So please stay within reach."

Ella nodded, got up and went out the door with Miss Seifried.

Miss Angoff turned the lock and returned to the desk. "I don't believe it," she said firmly. "I don't believe any part of it. Do you?"

"I—don't know what to think," Harley Paton admitted, picking up his 8-ball ornament. "If it had been any other girl, I'd have said she was lying. But Tom McDaniel's daughter—"

"I don't care whose daughter! The whole thing is rotten, from beginning to end. In the first place, nobody told her to go downstairs. Nobody asked her to get those pads. And I saw the boxes, Mr. Paton—there were two on top, and they were full of bottles of ink. I couldn't even move them, they were so heavy. But we're supposed to believe that that child lifted two fifty-pound boxes, then carried a third one weighing even more down a ladder— No. It just doesn't make sense."

The English teacher's eyes were flashing angrily. "Moreover, even if she did do all that—which I'm positive she didn't! —we both know that Joey Green is too smart to think of trying anything so stupid. He's been the backbone of all the Negro children...."

The principal and Miss Angoff looked at one another in a mutual exchange of understanding, pure understanding which could not be voiced.

"Yes," Harley Paton said, "I know. Without him, they'll stop coming. They'll give up." He slammed the ornament down on the desk and sat back in the chair. "Ella's a good girl," he said. "She's not especially bright—just about average, I'd say. Like most of the others, I doubt if she's even thought about this problem seriously. If she were going to jump one way or the other, it would certainly not be this way—not with her own father in the hospital. That's what makes it so damned hard to understand!"

"But you do know she's lying, don't you?"

The principal said, "Yes. I know that. However confusing it is,

I know that the Green boy is innocent of this charge. But it doesn't really matter now. It's her story, and she has enough evidence to convince any jury. The Humboldt boy says he saw Green sneak down after her . . . I'm afraid we're beaten."

He was about to call Joey into the office, when he saw Miss Angoff's face. She was staring out the window.

"What is it?"

The English teacher said nothing. Harley Paton rose from the chair and followed her gaze.

Outside, a river had begun to flow across the smooth lawn—a fast-moving, bright river of people.

"How could they have found out so soon?" Miss Angoff cried. "How could a crowd—"

"I don't know. But this proves it." Harley Paton lifted his phone and dialed the city jail. "Give me the sheriff," he said, "right away. Important." He waited impatiently, and the voices of the people began to grow audible.

When Parkhouse answered, he said, "This is Principal Paton. Get as many men together as you can and get over to the school right away. You hear? There's been some trouble with one of the students, and—yes, yes!—one of the colored students, and we've got a mob outside. Hurry."

Paton went into the reception area and found both Crandall and Spivak staring out the window. Joey Green sat quietly in the chair, clenching and unclenching his hands.

"Mr. Spivak, are the doors locked?"

"What?"

"The doors!"

"These are. Not downstairs though, I don't think."

Paton motioned to Joey. "Come into my office," he said. "And don't be frightened. I've called the sheriff; he'll be here in a minute. There's nothing to worry about."

Joey went into the small office and sat down. "I didn't do it, Mr. Paton," he said.

"I know you didn't," the principal said.

"I had to tell you."

"That's all right. We'll get it straightened out somehow."

"*Paton!*"

"Give us the nigger, Paton!"

The voices were loud now. Harley Paton pressed Joey's shoulder and carefully locked the inner door. Then he closed the window, and sat down. He noticed that Miss Angoff had left.

"How would you explain it?" he asked, struggling to remain calm.

"That Cramer fellow," Joey said. "I think he must have put her up to it, to get rid of me. This way he thinks he'll get rid of the others."

"But why would she go along with such a thing?"

"I couldn't tell you that, Mr. Paton. I don't know. She seemed to me to be a nice girl."

"She is a nice girl."

"Show your face, nigger-lover!"

"Cigarette?"

Joey's hands trembled badly, but he accepted the cigarette. It tasted good, it helped.

"It's a bad situation," Harley Paton said. "Even though she asked you to help, you should have had better sense."

"I know it. But I thought being Mr. McDaniel's daughter, and Mr. McDaniel doing what he did for us—"

The crowd was suddenly quiet.

A single clear voice rang out: *"Paton, you better show your face!"*

Harley Paton said, "Excuse me," and walked to the window and raised it.

He looked down on the crowd, and saw that Adam Cramer was at its head.

"What do you want?"

"You know what we want. We want the nigger that raped a white girl in your school."

"I would advise you people—"

"We're not interested in your advice, Paton! We're only interested in one thing—justice! You have exactly five minutes. If that nigger isn't out here by then, we're coming in to get him!" Adam Cramer turned his head toward the crowd and shouted, "Is that right?"

The answer came in an explosion of voices.

"Five minutes, Paton!"

The principal closed the window again and went to the reception area. Spivak and Crandall were gone. The door was unlocked. He locked it again and returned to his office.

"The sheriff will stop them," he said.

Joey nodded. His white shirt was stained with perspiration. "Yes, sir," he said.

Paton glanced out the window again, but there were no police visible.

"Of course," he said, almost under his breath, "Cramer found himself in the spot all self-styled dictators find themselves in sooner or later. He started the thing, but it got away from him. He couldn't hold it. And when it began to go wrong, he got panicky. Did you see the article on him?"

"No, but I heard about it."

"Interesting stuff, Joey. We must talk about it sometime. Interesting. He surely knew that his past life would have to catch up with him someday. But knowing this, why would he start such a project?" Paton kept talking, quickly, but he also kept glancing at the window.

Outside, the people stood quietly, like an army at rest.

"*Four minutes, Paton!*"

Joey looked at his hands; then he wiped them on his trousers and stood up, feeling the sick dizziness of fear but knowing that it couldn't count now.

"You're on our side, aren't you?" he said.

Harley Paton said, "Yes, Joey, I am."

"I kind of figured that. Only you think we're whipped now."

The principal looked at the window again. He tried to answer, but he was tired of lying and posing, and he could not be false in these moments.

"I thought so at first, too," Joey said. "Right from the beginning I didn't believe it would work. But then I changed my mind. Because, you know why? I saw people like you and Finley Mead and Mr. McDaniel and Miss Angoff and the kids in the school here and all over town, and I saw all of you believing in us and in what was right, and willing to help—I wish I could say this. I wish I knew how."

"*Three minutes.*"

"Maybe it's this," Joey said, moving toward the door. "I used to think *they* were the white people"—he gestured toward the window—"but, I found out that wasn't true. How many are there outside now? Thirty? Forty? Forty people, in a town of sixteen thousand. You see what I mean? I was prejudiced, Mr. Paton, because I judged the whole white race by *them*—a sick little bunch of hateful people. I said, They'll never change; and I was right about that, anyway. They won't. We'll always have them around. We always have—and not just here, but everywhere. There's a couple on the Hill. All the time, they got to be against something or against somebody, or they aren't happy. I don't know why. But I know this: they're not the people, Mr. Paton. The rest of the folks who don't want us, with them it's different. Just like me, they been thinking a certain way all their lives, and it isn't easy for them to switch around; but they will. Just give them a little time. They will."

"*Two minutes!*"

"Never mind the phone, Mr. Paton. I think the sheriff's going to be a little late."

"Joey—" Harley Paton's throat was dry. "Joey, I'm afraid you've embarrassed me. *I'm* the one who should have been telling *you* these things."

"It doesn't matter, sir. We both know they're true, and that's what's important." Joey unlocked the door.

The principal walked over hurriedly. "Come with me," he said. "My car is in the back. I'll drive you to Farragut, and we can at least give you protection until this—"

"No," Joey said. "That's what that Adam Cramer hopes we'll do. He's in trouble and this whole thing has got to go right for him or he's through in Caxton."

"What are you going to do?"

"Spoil things for him a little."

"Don't be foolish. If that stupid Parkhouse doesn't come, I can get Harmer in Farragut. They wouldn't dare to break into the school!"

"Those people have got their blood up, Mr. Paton. They'd dare just about anything. If we gave them a chance. We can't run now, and we can't hide."

The principal grasped Joey's arm. "I'm not going to let you go out there."

"It'll be all right. If Cramer is still in control, I don't think he'll let them hurt me too bad. It wouldn't be good for business."

"But *is* he in control?"

Joey shrugged. "We'll find out." He pulled Harley Paton's hand away and went out into the hall, which was still and empty. "I remember something a general once wrote down," he said. "He wrote, 'You can lose a lot of battles and still win the war.' What happens now isn't too important, Mr. Paton. We're going to win."

Joey smiled at the thin man, turned, and walked quickly down the hall, toward the door.

Adam Cramer looked at the fifty men and women behind him and at the hundreds of children pressed against the windows of the school, peering, then he glanced down at his watch and called, "One minute, Paton!"

The Reverend Lorenzo Niesen nodded. His hands were on his hips, and his eyes were glittering under their narrow leather slits, blackly.

Bart Carey stood with his feet planted wide apart on the lawn. He held his new glasses in one hand and wiped them rhythmically with the tail of his shirt.

Abner West and Phil Dongen had stationed themselves directly behind Verne Shipman, who stood proud and full of proud fury, his face composed into an expression of quiet determination.

Adam Cramer studied the eyes of these people around him and said, "Remember, there must be no violence. We gave the sheriff our promise to bring him to jail. We aren't a mob. We're a citizens' committee. All we want to do is make sure this nigger doesn't slip away. Understood?"

No one answered.

"Tell them, Carey," he whispered.

Bart Carey continued to wipe his glasses.

"No violence. That is strictly out," Adam Cramer said.

The murmur of the crowd began to swell as the seconds passed.

"Don't worry," Verne Shipman said. "They'll see what they caused. And they'll see how we take care of it. Don't worry."

Niesen slapped his hands together suddenly. "Come on," he yelled. "Let's get the nigger!"

The crowd broke; the people began to move toward the wide concrete steps.

Then the main door opened, and Joey Green stepped out.

He was alone.

Lorenzo Niesen stopped, and the others stopped also, and stood frozen.

Very slowly, Joey Green walked down the steps.

"Did you people want to talk to me?" he said, looking at Adam Cramer.

For a long while, there was no reply.

Then Verne Shipman stepped forward and said, "Are you Joseph Green?"

"That's right."

"You admit that you tried to rape one of our white girls today?"

"No."

"What do you mean, no?"

"I mean I didn't try to rape anyone." Joey looked up and scanned the windows carefully and saw the faces of Clarence Jones and Joseph Dupuy and Laura Lee Cook.

"That's a lie, nigger!" Lorenzo Niesen yelled.

Shipman jerked his head around sternly. "You be still," he commanded. "We're going to listen to what this boy has to say for himself."

Niesen's eyes snapped angrily, but he said no more.

"Now," Shipman said, turning again to face Joey. "You claim you're innocent, is that it?"

"That's right."

"Didn't anyone ever teach you to address a white person as sir?"

Joey shook his head.

Shipman drew back his hand and brought it across Joey's right cheek. The sound was sharp, and could be heard for a considerable distance.

"Let that be the first lesson," he said.

Joey did not reply. A trail of blood ran glistening from his mouth. Shipman took a handkerchief from his rear pocket and held it out. "You've gotten blood on your mouth," he said. "Wipe it off." Joey wiped the blood away and crumpled the handkerchief in his fist.

"What do you say?"

"Thank you."

"Thank you what?"

"Thank you, sir."

Shipman nodded. "Boy," he said, "I'm going to ask you again. But I want you to think before you answer this time. Think real hard. If you tell the truth, then you got nothing to be afraid of. But if you try to lie to us here, then, boy, you're in more trouble than you ever dreamed of."

Shipman cleared his throat and swept a glance across the crowd. "You understand?" he said.

Joey said, "Yes, sir."

"All right. Now, did you or did you not try to rape a white girl by the name of Ella McDaniel in the basement of the school today?"

"Oh, hell," Lorenzo Niesen began. "All this talk ain't—"

"Be quiet!" Adam Cramer said sharply. "Mr. Shipman and I are handling this."

"That's right," Shipman said. "Well, boy?"

"No, sir," Joey said.

The large, soft-featured man raised his hand, as though to hold back the crowd.

"Then you claim Ella McDaniel is lying?"

Joey was silent.

"Why would she want to do that?"

"I don't know."

"You don't know?"

"No, sir."

"Then you wasn't in the basement at all, is that it?" Shipman leveled his finger at Joey. "You wasn't anywhere around?"

"I was in the basement."

"With a white girl?"

"Yes, sir."

There was an ominous rumble from the crowd. Adam Cramer whispered to Shipman, "Verne, I think we'd better take him to the jail."

Shipman ignored the comment. He kept his finger straight. "You was alone with a white girl in the basement of this school but you didn't try to do anything. Is that what you're telling us? Is that what you expect us to believe, nigger? Speak up!" He leaned forward and slapped Joey, harder than before.

"It couldn't just be that you was taking a little advantage of the fact she was her daddy's child, now, could it? And it couldn't be you figured she wouldn't say anything because of what Tom Mc-Daniel done? I don't guess that had anything to do with it!"

Joey stood straight and tried not to flinch at the next blow, but Shipman's hand was fat and the man was stronger than he looked.

"Don't you know we got proof, nigger? It isn't just your word against hers: you was *seen* sneaking down those stairs. And how you think she got her dress ripped? On a nail? Listen. We're gonna give you one last chance to tell the truth. And you better tell it good and loud so everybody can hear plain."

Joey was prepared to be struck again, when suddenly the door opened a second time, and Harley Paton came outside. The frail, balding principal moved certainly and without hesitation down the stairs.

"Here comes the nigger-lover!"

Lorenzo Niesen spat a dark brown stream of tobacco onto the lawn. "There's the Palestine Indian," he said. "God!"

"Get inside, schoolteacher; go on!"

Harley Paton continued to walk. He walked to the end of the stairs; then, when he had reached the spot where Verne Shipman was standing, he said in a clear voice: "Only a coward would hit a defenseless boy."

Shipman's fingers knotted. "Is that what you're calling me, Paton?" he said.

The principal's face moved very close. "Yes," he said. "Exactly. You're a miserable, yellow coward, Shipman, just like every cheap bully in the world. Do I make myself perfectly clear?"

There was a pause.

Shipman's face was tense, and he stood there, frozen, his fists large and the tendons in his hands taut; then he laughed contemptuously and turned away.

Harley Paton went to Joey and took his arm, and started back up the stairs.

As though waking suddenly from sleep, Bart Carey leaped forward. "Where you think you're going with that nigger?" he demanded.

"He will remain in my office until the Farragut police arrive. If you want to avoid a jail sentence, I'd advise all of you to leave at once."

"Like hell!"

Abner West grasped the principal's shoulders and pushed him aside. "No, sir!" he said. "This coon ain't gonna get away with what he done and lying about it!"

Three men rushed up. Their faces were red and moist, their clothes glued darkly to their bodies. Two of them pinned Joey's arms behind him.

"You admit it?" Shipman said sternly.

Joey shook his head.

"That's too bad. You give us no choice."

Harley Paton tried to move, but was restrained by the bulk of Abner West. "Where are you taking that boy?"

Adam Cramer said, "To the jail, Paton. We—"

"Later on, maybe, to jail," Shipman said.

Adam Cramer faced the big man. "What do you mean?"

"I mean we're taking a little trip to the river first. Going to jail won't mean much unless this boy's sorry for what he did. But he isn't sorry. He don't even admit he's guilty." Shipman smiled at Harley Paton. "You know the old story, Paton: 'Spare the rod and spoil the child.'"

Al Holliman reached out and ripped Joey's shirt off. He tore it into three sections and used the sections to tie the boy's hands behind his back.

"You're going to regret this," the principal said. "Every one of you!"

"Maybe you'd like to come along, you so worried about the jig!" West said.

Niesen said, "Yes, yes. Why don't you do that, Mr. Paton, just join our little party and make sure nobody hurts nobody!"

Paton slumped weakly. His eyes burned deep into the eyes of the young man in the neat dark suit. Miss Angoff, who had come out, stood watching helplessly.

The hour rang out from the clock in the courthouse then, and someone shouted "Let's go!" and the crowd rushed in a tide.

They were halfway across the lawn, halfway to the street, when a single voice, louder than the angry murmuring, louder, it seemed, than the courthouse bell, cried: "Wait a minute!"

Joey Green looked up, saw two figures walking toward him. One, he recognized instantly: the girl. The other, a red-faced, fat-bellied man, he'd never seen before. The man was breathing hard. He held the girl in a firm grasp and pulled her along, like a cotton doll, and breathed hard.

When he reached the crowd, the man removed his hand from the girl's wrist and raised it in an odd salute to Adam Cramer. "Like I told you," he said, smiling, "you never want to be too sure of anything."

Shipman snapped "Who are you?" in an angry voice.

"Nobody too important. The name is Griffin. Sam Griffin."

"Well, what do you want?"

Sam stared at Adam for a long moment, then said: "Nothing, now."

"Then move aside. We've got important business to attend to."

"What kind of business, Mr. Shipman?"

Shipman glanced at Ella McDaniel, at Joey. A muscle in his cheek began to twitch.

"You fellas aim to do anything to this nigger-boy?" Sam asked quietly.

"Griffin, I don't know who you think you are, and I don't know why you've brought this girl—"

"Because," Sam went on, "if you do, I think maybe there's something you ought to hear. It just might affect that business you're on." He turned to Ella. "Tell them, Miss McDaniel," he said. "Tell them what you told me."

She was crying, her eyes were red and puffed, and her face was streaked; but when Ella looked at Joey, she caught her breath and said: "It was a lie."

There was, at first, no reaction whatever to the words. Then Shipman's hands curled slowly into fists. "What's that?" he said. "What are you talking about?"

"It was a lie," Ella repeated. "Everything. Everything I said about"—she pointed—"him. All of it."

Still Shipman did not seem to understand. He took a step. "What the devil you mean?"

"She means," said Adam Cramer quickly, "that her father told her to cover up for the nigger; and that's what she's doing." He gestured at Sam Griffin, who continued to smile. "That man, I happen to know, is in the pay of the NAACP. He's a pro-integrationist. Don't believe a word he says to you!"

The Reverend Lorenzo Niesen called, "What's all this talk? If we're gonna do something, let's do it and be about our business!"

"Right!" said Adam. "Verne, listen: If McDaniel was willing to go to the hospital for this thing, you know and I know goddamn well he isn't going to mind letting his daughter get raped!"

The crowd stirred, moved forward slightly. Bart Carey said, "Hell yes, that's it."

"We're wasting time," shouted another.

But Shipman did not move. His face was pale now. To Ella he said, "Girl, listen here to me. Why'd you ever want to go and tell a story like that in the first place, if it wasn't true?"

Sam Griffin chuckled. "That's what I asked myself," he said. "And that's why I went to visit Miss McDaniel—"

"What's your interest in this, anyway?" interrupted Shipman.

"Personal," Sam replied, winking at Adam. "But, y'see, it didn't smell right to me, just like all of a sudden it don't smell right to you, Mr. Shipman. That was the thing: *Why would she tell such a story if it wasn't true?*"

"Well?"

"Well, hold on, now. She wouldn't talk at first, and her grand-daddy give me a pretty rough time. But, see, I deal with people; have for years. It's my job. So I give her plenty of line and reeled in slow, so she wouldn't notice. I told her I been looking around, sort of studying this whole thing, and I had a theory. My theory was that young Mr. Cramer here had *made* her tell that lie—"

"Verne, look! This guy's a nut. I—"

Shipman glared at Adam. "Shut up," he said; then: "Go on, Griffin. We're listening."

"Well, that's about it," Sam said. "Old Adam, he's a pretty clever bird. What he done was, he told Miss McDaniel that her father would be killed if she didn't play along; that's all. After what happened to Tom McDaniel already, who could blame her for believing him? She just got scared. Like anyone else would of. Anyone here."

Shipman turned to Ella. "Is that right?" he said.

She nodded. "He promised me there wouldn't be any trouble. I mean, nothing would happen, he said, except that the boy would be expelled from school. I'm sorry." She looked at Joey. "Sorry; I didn't . . ."

"Go on back to the car," Sam said. "I'll be along directly."

Ella glanced once at Adam, then ran.

"Don't make sense," Shipman was saying, to no one in particular.

Sam shook his head. "You're right, it don't, when you get down to it. But you got to understand, Mr. Shipman, that your boy here was desperate. I mean, he was teetering on the verge of losing every single thing he built up. And the truth of it is, you was desperate, too—because you hooked up with him. The both of you were—"

"Verne!"

"—in bad trouble, Mr. Shipman. I ain't saying you knew anything about *this* little play: maybe you did, but I don't think so. I think it takes a real special kind of brain for something this dirty. . . ." Sam faced Adam. "It don't matter, though," he said, "really. Even if I hadn't got Miss McDaniel to tell the truth. Because the people never was with you, boy. And they'd of turned *against* you in time, just like they always do when somebody tries to sell them something they don't want. Remember? It would of turned out just the same whether I stuck my nose in it or not. Except there'd be an innocent boy dead and some stupid people with blood on their hands. . . ."

The crowd was silent.

It was frozen.

Adam Cramer looked at them standing there, like unfinished

statues in the sunlight, and screamed, "Lies!" suddenly, without meaning to. "Lies! I swear to Christ this man is lying to you!"

No one answered.

"Are you all crazy?" He rushed over to Sam Griffin and took the fat man's shirt in his fist. "Tell them the truth," he said. "Come on, you son of a bitch! Tell them about your Jew wife, maybe they'd like to hear about that!"

Sam Griffin remained motionless.

"Tell them about the nigger women you kissed on the mouth! You did, I've got proof. Proof, you hear me, you understand what I'm saying?" Adam stepped back. His breathing had become quick and heavy and his eyes were wild. "Oh, you don't think for a *minute* you're fooling these people, do you, Griffin? Because if you do, you're wrong. They're too smart for you and your filth. Believe me. I *know* them. I *know* they're too smart. They laugh at you, Griffin. Understand? Because you are *nothing* on this earth; nothing, *nothing*." His voice had risen to a high pitch now, and the people stared. "Folks!" he cried. "They think they've got us scared. But they haven't. We're not about to give up, not now nor ever, no sir! Hear that, Griffin? Paton, you hear what I'm saying?"

Harley Paton and Agnes Angoff walked over to Joey Green and untied his hands and led him away, back toward the school.

"Go on, you miserable cowards. Run!" Adam clutched Verne Shipman's sleeve. "You talk to them," he said. "Tell them, listen, Verne—tonight! a meeting, at Joan's; seven-thirty! We're —Paton! You and your nigger better listen to this! We're gonna show you you can't stop justice and right, no matter what you do. This is only the beginning! We—"

Suddenly Shipman drew back his hand and slapped Adam's face. The sound was sharp. He slapped him again, harder.

Then, slowly, he turned and began to walk across the lawn toward town, the way men walk in their sleep.

Bart Carey opened his mouth, but he said nothing. He and the Reverend Lorenzo Niesen squinted at the others and followed Shipman.

The crowd broke, dispersed, the men and women walking off singly, by themselves, in all directions.

In a while they were gone.

"Boy?"

Adam Cramer opened his eyes. Sam Griffin was standing over him, reaching down his hand and smiling in the old way, without the hardness.

"Boy, you're gonna get grass stains all over those trousers if you don't get up."

Adam felt himself being lifted, gently. He did not resist.

"I figure our work in this town is just about cleaned up," Griffin said. "If you pack in a hurry, you can grab a bus to Farragut. They got trains to Los Angeles there." He paused. "If you're a little light on ticket money, I'd be proud to—"

Adam pulled his arm away.

"Right certain now?" Sam Griffin waited; then he sighed and reached into his pocket. "Here."

His hand unfolded. In the center was a gleaming copper fire.

"I wouldn't want to steal from you," he said, and tipped his palm. The bullets spilled out, one by one, and fell in their bright skins without a sound.

"They're yours, boy."

Adam watched until the man had gone. But even then he did not move, or think except of all the scarlet horses he would never ride.

Lightning Source UK Ltd.
Milton Keynes UK
UKHW040626080822
406994UK00001B/52